THE BEST OF
DARK TERRORS

PRAISE FOR THE *DARK TERRORS* SERIES

THE BEST OF
DARK TERRORS

Edited by
Stephen Jones and David A. Sutton

Subterranean Press 2021

First Edition

ISBN
978-1-64524-007-5

Subterranean Press
PO Box 190106
Burton, MI 48519

subterraneanpress.com

Manufactured in the United States of America

Originally published in different, abbreviated form in the UK
as *Darker Terrors* by Spectral Press in 2015.

For Jo Fletcher,
the best editor two editors could ever have.

ACKNOWLEDGEMENTS

Special thanks to
Bill Schafer,
Geralyn Lance,
Simon Marshall-Jones,
Bob Eggleton,
Peter Coleborn,
James R. Wagner,
Susan Ellison,
John Kaiine,
Frances Moira Cooper
and, of course,
the incomparable Jo Fletcher.

TABLE OF CONTENTS

Acknowledgements —— *7*

Introduction —— *13*
JO FLETCHER

Foreword —— *15*
STEPHEN JONES

More Tomorrow —— *19*
MICHAEL MARSHALL SMITH

I've Come to Talk to You Again —— *53*
KARL EDWARD WAGNER

A Really Game Boy —— *61*
BRIAN LUMLEY

(Melodrama) —— *75*
DAVID J. SCHOW

To This Water —— *95*
(Johnstown, Pennsylvania 1889)
CAITLÍN R. KIERNAN

The Museum on Cyclops Avenue —— *117*
HARLAN ELLISON®

Free Dirt —— *133*
RAY BRADBURY

Self-Made Man —— *143*
POPPY Z. BRITE

The Wedding Present —— *165*
NEIL GAIMAN

Family History —— *179*
STEPHEN BAXTER

Inside the Cackle Factory —— *193*
DENNIS ETCHISON

My Pathology —— *217*
LISA TUTTLE

At Home in the Pubs of Old London —— *245*
CHRISTOPHER FOWLER

Barking Sands —— *259*
RICHARD CHRISTIAN MATHESON

The Abortionist's Horse —— *265*
(Johnstown, Pennsylvania 1889)
TANITH LEE

Destroyer of Worlds —— *281*
GWYNETH JONES

Pelican Cay —— *297*
DAVID CASE

The Retrospective —— *413*
RAMSEY CAMPBELL

The Two Sams —— *427*
GLEN HIRSHBERG

The Prospect Cards —— *447*
DON TUMASONIS

Afterword —— *471*
DAVID A. SUTTON

Index to
Dark Terrors: The Gollancz Book of Horror —— *475*
Volumes #1 – 6 (1995 – 2002)

About the Editors —— *487*

INTRODUCTION

Jo Fletcher

WE TRAVELLED A lot when I was a child, moving first from one part of London to another, and then from one end of Canada to the other, before finally, in my teens, finally settling for a while in the seaside town of Whitstable, in Kent.

Because of our perambulations, we didn't have many possessions—so thank heavens for public libraries! It was in the libraries of Britain and Canada that I, like so many others, was made. However, many of the places we lived in—usually for a year or so—were small, which meant that within a few months I'd worked my way through the children's section and, armed with my parents' library tickets, was let loose amongst the adult shelves. (My parents never saw the need to distinguish between 'suitable for a child' and 'not', and most of the librarians—in my life, at least—agreed with them, for which I remain profoundly grateful.)

What's this got to do with *Dark Terrors* you may ask? Well, everything, really; for it was in these libraries that I first discovered Herbert van Thal (1904–83) and *The Pan Book of Horror Stories*: a treasure-trove of short fiction guaranteed to keep any self-respecting person shivering under bedcovers long after they'd been told to put the lights out and *go to sleep!* I sometimes

wonder how many young eyes were ruined by the impossibility of such an order when you're halfway through a Joan Aiken or Nigel Kneale tale and you *just have to know what happens next…*

All of this goes to explain why, when I landed for a few years as an editor at Pan Books, continuing with *Dark Voices: The Pan Book of Horror Stories* seemed like an excellent idea: there was a whole new crop of amazing young writers of dark fiction coming along, not to mention those equally remarkable writers who'd been scaring us silly for decades, and Stephen Jones and David Sutton were the perfect editors to take the venerable horror series into a new decade.

As is the way of publishing, both my tenure at Pan and *Dark Voices* eventually went the way of all flesh and, after a pit-stop at Penguin's short-lived Signet imprint, I joined Victor Gollancz, then still a much-lauded independent publisher of hardcover fiction and non-fiction…and it felt like a good idea to keep the legacy of Mr. van Thal going, this time in the form of *Dark Terrors: The Gollancz Book of Horror*, once again ably edited by Steve and Dave.

It was unfortunate that the horror boom started in the mid-1970s by writers such as James Herbert in the UK and Stephen King in the US was coming to an end, because the editors were discovering some phenomenal new voices out there—as proven by the number of stories from *Dark Terrors* that appeared on awards shortlists and in annual 'Best of' anthologies.

The reviews were great, but sales were not—in truth, it's been hard for mainstream publishers to sell collections and anthologies, no matter how good the stories, for decades now—and eventually, we had to bow to financial good sense and bring the run of *Dark Terrors* volumes to a glorious end.

I still miss it, and so I am delighted to see this new volume, bringing some of those wonderful stories back into print after all these years. Let's hope it's the start of a whole new horror revival, and another page not only in Herbert van Thal's legacy, but also that of its esteemed editors…

—Jo Fletcher
Publisher, Jo Fletcher Books
London in lockdown, 2020

FOREWORD

Stephen Jones

I AM VERY proud of the six volumes of *Dark Terrors* that David Sutton and I produced between 1995 and 2002.

The series grew directly out of another anthology series that we had edited together for another publisher—*Dark Voices: The Pan Book of Horror*. Following on from my reboot 'Best of' anthology, Pan Books had offered us the opportunity to take over this British horror icon—albeit under a title we weren't happy with, along with a new numbering system. Despite that, between 1990 and 1994, we compiled five paperback volumes under the aegis of three different in-house editors before the title was unceremoniously dumped when the post-1980s horror boom began to cool.

However, by that time our middle—and longest-serving—editor at Pan, Jo Fletcher, had moved on to the prestigious Gollancz genre list, and she immediately decided to commission a series of original horror anthologies along similar lines, although this time to be initially published in hardcover. And thus, *Dark Terrors: The Gollancz Book of Horror* was born.

And the connections didn't end there. We carried over two series, by Kim Newman and C. Bruce Hunter, from the Pan volumes, along with several of what now can be regarded as our 'established' contributors. These 'regulars'

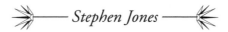

included Ramsey Campbell, Christopher Fowler, Graham Masterton, Kim Newman, Nicholas Royle, Michael Marshall Smith and Conrad Williams from the UK, and Dennis Etchison, Caitlín R. Kiernan, Richard Christian Matheson and David J. Schow from America.

We were also lucky enough to feature the occasional contribution from a Big Name Writer like Clive Barker, Ray Bradbury, Harlan Ellison', Neil Gaiman, Tanith Lee, Brian Lumley, Julian Rathbone, Peter Straub, Thomas Tessier, Karl Edward Wagner, Gahan Wilson and Hollywood director Mick Garris, and we also helped further the careers of such (at the time) relative newcomers as Gemma Files, Charles A. Gramlich, Glen Hirshberg, Brian Hodge, Jay Lake, Terry Lamsley, Tim Lebbon, Lisa Morton, Jeff VanderMeer and James Van Pelt, to name only a few.

In short, *Dark Terrors* did exactly what any non-themed horror anthology series should do—it balanced out its contents between providing a showcase for established writers and giving a professional market to newer names, while also striving to entertain a loyal readership.

The reviews were great, but the book never sold in the numbers it should have. After the first four volumes, the writing was on the wall. However, to Gollancz's credit, they did everything they could to keep it going.

This included the somewhat perplexing decision to turn the final two books into 'double' volumes. David and I agreed to go along with their plan in an attempt to save the series but, unfortunately, sales remained level. As Gollancz was essentially paying twice as much for what was, basically, the same book, it was obviously an unsustainable situation; and when we were forced to use one of the ugliest covers I've ever had on any book for the sixth volume, it came as no surprise to anyone when the series was cancelled.

In the end, *Dark Terrors* lasted exactly the same number of volumes that the earlier *Dark Voices* had. But it allowed us to present some terrific stories during the seven years it was published, and it provided a paying market during a period when times were tough—when aren't they?—for writers of short horror fiction on both sides of the Atlantic.

Which brings us to this present volume. To be honest, *The Best of Dark Terrors* is not really a 'Best of', but more a representative 'sampler' of the type

of stories we published over those six volumes. We worked with many remarkable writers while the series lasted—as illustrated in the Index at the end of this volume—and published more than our fair share of memorable stories.

So when it was suggested that we compile this present volume, David and I obviously had a wealth of material to draw upon. As much as we would have dearly loved to include certain authors or specific stories, we were obviously limited in our selection by the size of this book (which, thanks to our publisher, is extensive anyway). In the end we decided to balance out our choices of what we considered to be some of the finest stories we published between the different volumes, therefore giving the new reader a representative 'taste' of what the series was about.

In fact, it was a surprisingly simple process—after all, the two of us have been working together now for more than forty years—and although the table of contents might not be what either of us would have gone with had we been putting this book together on our own, it is certainly representative of how we work together as an editorial team. It is, however, by no means definitive, and there is no reason why we couldn't compile another 'Best of' sometime in the future. The material is certainly there for it.

So, if you were a reader of *Dark Terrors* back in the day, then we hope you will enjoy revisiting the twenty exemplary stories presented here once again for your entertainment; and if you are new to the series, then we trust you will be as equally blown away by them as we were back when we first read them.

And, if this retrospective volume is a success, then who knows where it may lead…?

—Stephen Jones
London, England

MORE TOMORROW

Michael Marshall Smith

I GOT A new job a couple of weeks ago. It's pretty much the same as my old job, but at a nicer company. What I do is trouble-shoot computers and their software—and yes, I know that sounds dull. People tell me so all the time. Not in words, exactly, but in their glassy smiles and their awkward 'let's be nice to the geek' demeanour.

It's a strange phenomenon, the whole 'computer people are losers' mentality. All round the world, at desks in every office and every building, people are using computers. Day in, day out. Every now and then, these machines go wrong. They're bound to: they're complex systems, like a human body, or society. When someone gets hurt, you call in a doctor. When a riot breaks out, it's the police that—for once—you want to see on your doorstep. It's their job to sort it out. Similarly, if your word processor starts dumping files or your hard disk goes non-linear, it's someone like me you need. Someone who actually *understands* the magic box which sits on your desk, and can make it all lovely again.

But do we get any thanks, any kudos for being the emergency services of the late twentieth century?

Do we fuck.

I can understand this to a degree. There are enough hard-line nerds and social zero geeks around to make it seem like a losing way of life. But there are plenty of pretty basic earthlings doing all the other jobs too, and no one expects them to turn up for work in a pin-wheel hat and a T-shirt saying PROGRAMMERS DO IT RECURSIVELY. For the record, I play reasonable blues guitar, I've been out with a girl and have worked undercover for the CIA. The last bit isn't true, of course, but you get the general idea.

Up until recently I worked for a computer company, which I'll admit *was* full of very perfunctory human beings. When people started passing around jokes which were written in C++, I decided it was time to move on. One of the advantages of knowing about computers is that unemployment isn't going to be a problem until the damn things start fixing themselves, and so I called a few contacts, posted a new CV up on my web site and within twenty-four hours had four opportunities to choose from. Most of them were other computer businesses, which I was kind of keen to avoid, and in the end I decided to have a crack at a company called the VCA. I put on my pin-wheel hat, rubbed pizza on my shirt, and strolled along for an interview.

The VCA, it transpired, was a non-profit organisation dedicated to promoting effective business communication. The suave but shifty chief executive who interviewed me seemed a little vague as to what this actually entailed, and in the end I let it go. The company was situated in tidy new offices right in the centre of town, and seemed to be doing good trade at whatever it was they did. The reason they needed someone like me was they wanted to upgrade their system—computers, software and all. It was a month's contract work, at a very decent rate, and I said yes without a second thought.

Morehead, the guy in charge, took me for a gloating tour round the office. It looked the same as they always do, only emptier, because everyone was out at lunch. Then I settled down with their spreadsheet-basher to go find out what kind of system they could afford. His name was Cremmer, and he wasn't out at lunch because he was clearly one of those people who see working nine-hour days as worthy of some form of admiration. Personally I view it as worthy of pity, at most. He seemed amiable enough, in a curly-haired, irritating sort of way, and within half an hour we'd thrashed out the

necessary. I made some calls, arranged to come back in a few days, and spent the rest of the afternoon helping build a hospital in Rwanda. Well actually I spent it listening to loud music and catching up on my Internet newsgroups, but I could have done the other had I been so inclined.

The Internet is one of those things that more and more people have heard of without having any real idea of what it means. It's actually very simple. A while back a group of universities and government organisations experimented with a way of linking up all their computers so they could share resources, send little messages and play *Star Trek* games with each other. There was also a military connection, and the servers linked in such a way that the system could take a hit somewhere and re-route information accordingly. After a time this network started to take on a momentum of its own, with everyone from Pentagon heavies to pin-wheeling wireheads taking it upon themselves to find new ways of connecting things up and making more information available. Just about every major computer on the planet is now connected, and if you've got a modem and a phone line, you can get on there too. I can tell you can hardly wait.

What you find when you're there almost qualifies as a parallel universe. There are thousands of pieces of software, probably billions of text files by now. You can check the records of the New York Public Library, send a message to someone in Japan which will arrive within minutes, download a picture of the far side of Jupiter, and monitor how many cans of Dr Pepper there are in a soda machines in the computer science labs of American universities. A lot of this stuff is fairly chaotically organised, but there are a few systems which span the Net as a whole. One of these is the World Wide Web, a hypertext-based graphic system. Another is the newsgroups.

There are about 40,000 of these groups now, covering anything from computers to fine art, science fiction to tastelessness, the books of Stephen King to quirky sexual preferences. If it's not outright illegal, out there on the Infobahn people will be yakking about it twenty-four hours a day, every day of the year. Either that or posting images of it: there are paintings and animals, NASA archives and abstract art, and in the alt.binaries.pictures.tasteless group you can find anything from close-up shots of road-kills to people with

acid burns on their face. Not very nice, but trust me, it's a minority interest. Now that I think of it, there is some illegal stuff (drugs, mainly)—there's a system by which you can send untraceable and anonymous messages, though I've never bothered to check it out.

Basically the newsgroups are the Internet for traditionalists—or people who want the news as it breaks. They're little discussion centres that stick to their own specific topic, rather than wasting time with graphics and Java applets which play weird tunes at you until you go insane. People read each other's messages and reply, or forward their own pronouncements or questions. Some groups are repositories of computer files, like software or pictures, others just have text messages. No one, however sad, could hope to keep abreast of all of them, and nor would you want to. I personally don't give a toss about recent developments in Multilevel Marketing Businesses or the Nature of Chinchilla Farming in America Today, and have no interest in reading megabytes of losing burblings about them. So I, like most people, stick to a subset of the groups that carry stuff I'm interested in—Mac computers, guitar music, cats and the like.

So now you know.

———

THE FOLLOWING TUESDAY I got up bright and early and made my way to the VCA for my first morning's work. England was doing its best to be Summery, which as always meant that it was humid without being hot, bright without being sunny, and every third commuter on the hellish tube journey was intermittently pebble-dashing nearby passengers with hay fever sneezes. I emerged moist and irritable from the station, more determined than ever to find a way of working that meant never having to leave my apartment. The walk from the station to VCA was better, passing through an attractive square and a selection of interesting side-streets with restaurants featuring unusual cuisines, and I was feeling chipper again by the time I got there.

My suppliers had done their work, and the main area of VCA's open-plan office was piled high with exciting boxes. When I walked in just about all the staff were standing around the pile, coffee mugs in hand, regarding it with

the wary enthusiasm of simple country folk confronted with a recently-landed UFO. There was a slightly toe-curling five minutes of introductions, embarrassing merely because I don't enjoy that kind of thing. Only one person, John, seemed to view me with the sniffy disdain of someone greeting an underling whose services are, unfortunately, in the ascendant. Everybody else seemed nice, some very much so.

Morehead eventually oiled out of his office and dispensed a few weak jokes which had the—possibly intentional—effect of scattering everyone back to their desks to get on with their work. I took off my jacket, rolled up my sleeves and got on with it.

I spent the morning cabling like a wild thing, placing the hardware of the network itself. As this involved a certain amount of disrupting everyone in turn by drilling, pulling up carpet and moving their desks, I was soon on apologetic grinning terms with most of them. I guess I could have done the wire-up over the weekend when nobody was there, but I like my weekends as they are. John gave me the invisibility routine that people once used on servants, but everyone else was fairly cool about it. One of the girls, Jeanette, actually engaged me in conversation while I worked nearby, and seemed genuinely interested in understanding what I was doing. When I broke it to her that it was actually pretty dull, she smiled.

The wiring took a little longer than I was expecting, and I stayed on after everybody else had gone. Everyone but Cremmer, that was, who stayed, probably to make sure that I didn't run off with their plants, or database, or spoons. Either that or to get some brownie points with whoever it is he thought cared about people putting in long hours. The invoicing supremo was in an expansive mood, and chuntered endlessly about his adventures in computing, which were, to be honest, of slender interest to me. In the end he got bored of my monosyllabic grunts from beneath desks, and left me with some keys instead.

The next day was pretty much the same, except I was setting up the computers themselves. This involved taking things out of boxes and installing interminable pieces of software on the server. This isn't quite such a sociable activity as disturbing people, and I spent most of the day in the affable but distant company of Sarah, their PR person. At the end of the day everyone gathered in the main room and then left together, apparently for a meal to celebrate someone's birthday. I thought I caught Jeanette casting a glance in my direction at one point, maybe embarrassed at the division between me and them. It didn't bother me much, so I just got my head down and got on with swapping floppy disks in and out of the machines.

Well, it did bother me a little, to be honest. It wasn't their fault—there was no reason why they should make the effort to include someone they didn't know, who wasn't really a part of their group. People seldom do. You have to be a little thick-skinned about that kind of thing if you work freelance. There are tribes, you know, everywhere you go. They owe their allegiance to shared time (if they're friends), or to an organisation (if they're colleagues): but they're still tribes, just as much as if they'd tilled the same patch of desert for centuries. As a freelancer, especially in the cyber-areas, you tend to spend a lot of time wandering between them; occasionally being granted access to their watering hole, but never being one of the real people. Sometimes it can get on your nerves. That's all.

I finished up, locked the building carefully—I'm a complete anal-retentive about such things—and went home. I used my mobile to call for a pizza while I was en route, and it arrived two minutes after I got out of the shower. A perfect piece of timing, which sadly no one was on hand to appreciate. My last experiment with living with someone did not end well, mainly because she was a touchy and irritable woman who needed her own space twenty-three-and-a-half hours a day. Well it was more complicated than that, of course, but that was the main impression I took away with me. I mulled over those times as I sat and munched my 'Everything on it, and then a few more things as well' pizza, vague-eyed in front of white noise television, and ended up feeling rather grim.

Food event over, I made a jug of coffee and settled down in front of the Mac. I tweaked my invoicing database for a while, exciting young man that I am, and then wrote a letter to my sister in Australia. She doesn't have access to Internet email, unfortunately, otherwise she'd hear from me a lot more often. Write letter, print letter, put it in envelope, get stamps, get it to a post

office. A chain of admin of that magnitude usually takes me about two weeks to get through, and it's a bit primitive, really, compared to 'Write letter, press button, there in five minutes'.

I called my friend Nick, who's a freelance sub-editor on a trendy magazine, but he was chasing a deadline and not disposed to chat. I tried the television, but it was still outputting someone else's idea of entertainment. By nine o'clock I was very bored, and so I logged on to the Net.

Probably because I was bored, and feeling a bit isolated, after I'd done my usual groups I found myself checking out alt.binaries.pictures.erotica. 'alt' means the group is an unofficial one; 'binaries' means it holds computer files rather than just messages; 'pictures' means those files are images. As for the last word, I'm prepared to be educational about this but you're going to have to work that one out for yourself.

The media has the impression that the minute you're in cyberspace countless pictures of this type come flooding at you down the phone, pouring like ravening hordes onto your hard disk and leaping out of the screen to take over your mind. This is not the case, and all of you worried about your little Timmy's soul can afford to relax a little. Even if you're only talking about the web, you need a computer, a modem, access to a phone line, and a credit card to pay for your Internet feed. With Usenet you need to find the right newsgroup, and download about three segments for each picture. You require several bits of software to piece them together, convert the result, and display it.

The naughty pictures don't come and get you, and if you see one, it ain't an accident. If your little Timmy has the kit, finance and inclination to go looking, then maybe it's you who needs the talking to. In fact, maybe you should be grounded.

The flipside of that, of course, is the implication that *I* have the inclination to go looking, which I guess I occasionally do. Not very often—honest—but I do. I don't know how defensive to feel about that fact. Men of all shapes and sizes, ages and creeds, and states of marital or relationship bliss enjoy, every now and then, the sight of a woman with no clothes on. It's just as well we do, you know, otherwise there'd be no new little earthlings, would there? If you want to call that oppression or sexism or the commodification of the female body then go right ahead, but don't expect me to talk to you at dinner parties. I prefer to call it sexual attraction, but then I'm a sad fuck who spends half his life in front of computer, so what the hell do I know?

Still, it's not something that people feel great about, and I'm not going to defend it too hard. Especially not to women, because that would be a waste of everyone's time. Women have a little bit of their brain missing which means they cannot understand the attraction of pornography. I'm not saying that's a *bad* thing, just that it's true. On the other hand they understand the attraction of babies, shoe shops and the detail of other people's lives, so I guess it's swings and roundabouts.

I've talked about it for too long now, and you're going to think I'm some Neanderthal with his tongue hanging to the ground who goes round looking up people's skirts. I'm not. Yes, there are rude pictures to be found on the net, and yes I sometimes find them. What can I say? I'm a bloke.

Anyway, I scouted round for a while, but in the end didn't even download anything. From the descriptions of the files they seemed to be the same endless permutations of badly-lit mad people, which is ultimately a bit tedious. Also, bullish talk notwithstanding, I don't feel great about looking at that kind of thing. I don't think it reflects very well upon one, and you only have to read a few other people's slaverings to make you decide it is too sad to be a part of.

So in the end I played the guitar for a while and went to bed.

THE NEXT FEW days at VCA passed pretty easily. I installed and configured, configured and installed. The birthday meal went pretty well, I gathered, and featured amongst other highlights the secretary Tanya literally sliding under the table through drunkenness. That was her story, at least. By the Monday of the following week everyone was calling me by name, and I was being included in the coffee-making rounds. England had called off its doomed attempt at summer, or at least imposed a time out, and had settled for a much more bearable cross between spring and autumn instead. All in all, things were going fairly well.

And as the week progressed, slightly better even than that. The reason for this was a person. Jeanette, to be precise.

I began, without even noticing at first, to find myself veering towards the computer nearest her when I needed to do some testing. I also found that I was slightly more likely to offer to go and make a round of coffees in the kitchen when she was already standing there, smoking one of her hourly cigarettes. Initially it was just because she was the politest and most approachable of the staff, and it was a couple of days before I realised that I was looking out for her return from lunch, trying to be less dull when she was around, and noticing what she wore.

It was almost as if I was beginning to fancy her, for heaven's sake.

By the beginning of the next week I passed a kind of watershed, and went from undirected, subconscious behaviour to actually facing the fact that I was attracted to her. I did this with a faint feeling of dread, coupled with occasional, mournful tinges of melancholy. It was like being back at school. It's awful, when you're grown-up, to be reminded of what it was like when a word from someone, a glance, even just their presence, can be like the sun coming out from behind a cloud. While it's nice, in a lyric, romantic novel sort of way, it also complicates things. Suddenly it matters if other people come into the kitchen when you're talking to her, and the way they interact with other people becomes more important. You start trying to engineer things, try to be near them, and it all just gets a bit weird.

Especially if the other person hasn't a clue what's going on in your head—and you've no intention of telling them. I'm no good at that, the telling part. Ten years ago I carried a letter round with me for two weeks, trying to pluck up the courage to give it to someone. It was a girl who was part of the same crowd at college, who I knew well as a friend, and who had just split up from someone else. The letter was a very carefully worded and tentative description of how I felt about her, ending with an invitation for a drink. Several times I was on the brink, I swear, but somehow I didn't give it to her. I just didn't have what it took.

The computer stuff was going okay, if you're interested. By the middle of the week the system was pretty much in place, and people were happily sending pop-up messages to each other. Cremmer, in particular, thought it was just fab that he could boss people around from the comfort of his own den. Even John was bucked up by seeing how the new system was going to ease the progress of whatever dull task it was he performed, and all in all my stock at the VCA was rising high.

It was time, finally, to get down to the nitty-gritty of developing their new databases. I tend to enjoy that part more than the wireheading, because it's more of a challenge, gives scope for design and creativity, and I don't have to keep getting up from my chair. When I settled down to it on Thursday morning, I realised that it was going to have an additional benefit. Jeanette was the VCA's Events Organiser, and most of the databases they needed concerned various aspects of her job. In other words, it was her I genuinely had to talk to about them, and at some length.

We sat side by side at her desk, me keeping a respectful distance, and I asked her the kind of questions I had to ask. She answered them concisely and quickly, didn't pipe up with a lot of damn fool questions, and came up with some reasonable requests. It was rather a nice day outside, and sunlight that was for once not hazy and obstructive angled through the window to pick out the lighter hues amongst her chestnut hair, which was long, and wavy, and as far as I could see entirely beautiful. Her hands played carelessly with a biro as we talked, the fingers long and purposeful, the forearms a pleasing shade of skin colour. I hate people who go sprinting out into parks at the first sign of summer, to spend their lunchtimes staked out with insectile brainlessness in the desperate quest for a tan. As far as I was concerned the fact that Jeanette clearly hadn't done so—in contrast to Tanya, for example, who already looked like a hazelnut (and probably thought with the same fluency as one)—was just another thing to like her for.

It was a nice morning. Relaxed, and pleasant. Over the last week we'd started to speak more and more, and were ready for a period of actually having to converse with each other at length. I enjoyed it, but didn't get over-excited. Despite my losing status as a technodrone, I am wise in the ways of relationships. Just being able to get on with her, and have her look as if she didn't mind being with me—that was more than enough for the time being. I wasn't going to try for anything more. Or so I thought.

Then, at twelve thirty, I did something entirely unexpected. We were in the middle of an in-depth and speculative wrangle on the projected nature of their hotel-booking database, when I realised that we were approaching the time at which Jeanette generally took her lunch. Smoothly, and with a nonchalance which I found frankly impressive, I lofted the idea that we go grab a sandwich somewhere and continue the discussion outside. As the sentences slipped from my mouth I experienced an out-of-body sensation, as if I was watching myself from about three feet away, cowering behind a chair. 'Not bad,' I found myself thinking, incredulously. 'Clearly she'll say no, but that was a good, businesslike way of putting it.'

Bizarrely, instead of shrieking with horror or poking my eye out with a ruler, she said yes. We rose together, I grabbed my jacket, and we left the office, me trying not to smirk like a businessman recently ennobled for doing a lot of work for charity. We took the lift down to the lobby and stepped outside, and I chattered inanely to avoid coming to terms with the fact that I was now standing with her *outside* work, beyond our usual frame of reference.

She knew a snack bar round the corner, and within ten minutes we found ourselves at a table outside, ploughing through sandwiches. She even ate attractively, holding the food fluently and wolfing it down, as if she was a genuine human taking on sustenance rather than someone appearing in amateur dramatics. I audibly mulled over the database for a while, to give myself time to settle down, and before long we'd pretty much done the subject.

Luckily, as we each smoked a cigarette she pointed out with distaste a couple of blokes walking down the street, both of whom had taken their shirts off, and whose paunches were hanging over their jeans.

'Summer,' she said, with a sigh, and I was away. There are few people with a larger internal stock of complaints to make about summer than me, and I let myself rip.

Why, I asked her, did everyone think it was so nice? What were supposed to be the benefits? One of the worst things about summer, I maintained hotly, as she smiled and ordered a coffee, was the constant pressure to enjoy oneself in ways which are considerably less fun than death.

Barbecues, for example. Now I don't mind barbies, especially, except that *my* friends never have them. It's just not their kind of thing. If I end up at a barbecue it's because I've been dragged there by my partner, to stand round in someone else's scraggy back garden as the sky threatens rain, watching drunken blokes teasing a nasty barking dog and girls I don't know standing in hunched clumps gossiping about people I've never heard of, while I try to eat badly cooked food that I could have bought for £2.50 in McDonald's *and* had somewhere to sit as well. That terrible weariness, a feeling of being washed out, exhausted and depressed, that comes from getting not quite drunk enough in the afternoon sun while standing up and either trying to make conversation with people I'll never see again, or putting up with them doing the same to me.

And going and sitting in parks. I hate it, as you may have gathered. Why? Because it's fucking *horrible*, that's why. Sitting on grass which is both papery and damp, surrounded by middle-class men with beards teaching their kids to unicycle, the air rent by the sound of some arsehole torturing a guitar to the delight of his fourteen-year-old hippy girlfriend. Drinking luke-warm soft drinks out of over-priced cans, and all the time being repetitively told how nice it all is, as if by some process of brain-washing you'll actually start to enjoy it.

Worst of all, the constant pressure to *go outside*. 'What are you doing inside on a day like this? You want to go outside, you do, get some fresh air. You want to go outside.' No. Wrong. I don't want to go outside. For a start, I like it inside. It's nice there. There are sofas, drinks, cigarettes, books. There is shade. Outside there's nothing but the sun, the mindless drudgery of suntan cultivation, and the perpetual sound of droning voices, yapping dogs and convention shouting at you to enjoy yourself. And always the constant refrain from everyone you meet, drumming on your mind like torrential rain on a tin roof: 'Isn't it a beautiful day?' 'Isn't it a beautiful day?' 'Isn't it a beautiful day?' 'Isn't it a beautiful day?'

No, say I. No, it fucking *isn't*.

There was all that, and some more, but I'm sure you get the drift. By halfway through Jeanette was laughing, partly at what I was saying, and

partly—I'm sure—at the fact that I was getting quite so worked up about it. But she was fundamentally on my side, and chipped in some valuable observations about the horrors of sitting outside dull country pubs surrounded by red-faced career girls and loud-mouthed estate agents in shorts, deafened by the sound of open-topped cars being revved by people who clearly had no right to live. We banged on happily for quite a while, had another cup of coffee, and then were both surprised to realise that we'd gone into overtime on lunch. I paid, telling her she could get the next one, and although that sounds like a terrible line, it came out pretty much perfect and she didn't stab me or anything. We strode quickly back to the office, still chatting, and the rest of the afternoon passed in a hazy blur of contentment.

I could have chosen to leave the office at the same time as her, and walked to whichever station she used, but I elected not to. I judged that enough had happened for one day, and I didn't want to push my luck. Instead I went home alone, hung out by myself, and went to sleep with, I suspect, a small smile upon my face.

NEXT DAY I sprang out of bed with an enthusiasm which is utterly unlike me, and as I struggled to balance the recalcitrant taps of my shower I was already plotting my next moves. Part of my mind was sitting back with folded arms and watching me with indulgent amusement, but in general I just felt really quite happy and excited.

For most of the morning I quizzed Jeanette further on her database needs. She was lunching with a friend, I knew, so I wasn't expecting anything there. Instead I wandered vaguely round a couple of bookshops, wondering if there was any book I could legitimately buy for Jeanette. It would have to be something very specific, relevant to a conversation we'd had—and sufficiently inexpensive that it looked like a throwaway gift. In the end I came away empty-handed, which was probably just as well. Buying her a present was a ridiculous idea, out of proportion to the current situation. As I walked back to the office I told myself to be careful. I was in danger of getting carried away and disturbing the careful equilibrium of my life and mind.

Then, in the afternoon, something happened. I was off the databases for a while, trying to work out why one of the servers was behaving like an arse. Tanya wandered up to ask Jeanette about something, and before she went reminded her that there'd been talk of everyone going out for a drink that evening. Jeanette hummed and ha-ed for a moment, and I bent further over the keyboard, giving them a chance to ignore me. Then, as from nowhere, Tanya said the magic words.

Why, she suggested, didn't I come too?

Careful to be nonchalant and cavalier, pausing as if sorting through my myriad of other options, I said yes, why the hell not. Jeanette then said yes, she could probably make it, and for a moment I saw all the locks and chains around my life fall away, as if a cage had collapsed around me leaving only the open road.

For a moment it was like that, and then suddenly it wasn't. 'I'll have to check with Chris, though,' Jeanette added, and I realised she had a boyfriend.

I spent the rest of the afternoon alternating between trying to calm myself down and violently but silently cursing. I should have known that someone like her would already be taken—after all, they always are. Of course, it didn't mean it was a no-go area. People sometimes leave their partners. I know, I've done it myself. And people have left me. But suddenly it had changed, morphed from something that might—in my dreams, at least— have developed smoothly into a Nice Thing. Instead it become a miasma of potential grief which was unlikely to even start.

For about half an hour I was furious, with what I don't know. With myself, for letting my feelings grow and complicate. With her, for having a boyfriend. With life, for always being that bit more disappointing than it absolutely has to be.

Then, because I'm an old hand at dealing with my inner conditions, I talked myself round. It didn't matter. Jeanette could simply become a pleasant aspect of a month-long contract, someone I could chat to. Then the job would end, I'd move on, and none of it would matter. I had to nail that conclusion down on myself pretty hard, but thought I could make it stick.

I decided that I might as well go out for the drink anyway. There was another party I could go to but it would involve trekking halfway across town. Nick was busy. I might as well be sociable, now that they'd made the offer.

So I went, and I wish I hadn't.

The evening was okay, in the way that they always are when people from the same office get together to drink and complain about their boss. Morehead wasn't there, thankfully, and Cremmer quickly got sufficiently drunk that he didn't qualify as a Morehead substitute. The evening was fine, for everyone else. It was just me who didn't have a good time.

Jeanette disappeared just before we left the office, and I found myself walking to the pub with everyone else. I sat drinking Budweisers and making conversation with John and Sarah, wondering where she was. She'd said she'd meet everyone there. So where was she?

At about half-past-eight the question was answered. She walked into the pub and I started to get up, a smile of greeting on my face. Then I realised she looked different somehow, and I noticed the man standing behind her.

The man was Chris Ayer. He was her boyfriend. He was also the nastiest man I've met in quite some time. That's going to sound like sour grapes, but it's not. He was perfectly presentable, in that he was good-looking and could talk to people, but everything else about him was wrong. There was something odd about the way he looked at people, something both arrogant and closed off. There was an air of restrained violence about him that I found unsettling, and his sense of his possession of Jeanette was complete. She sat at his side, hands in her lap, and said very little throughout the evening. I couldn't get over how different she looked to the funny and confident woman I'd had lunch with the day before, but nobody else seemed to notice it. After all, she joined in the office banter as usual, and smiled with her lips quite often. Nobody apart from me was looking for any more than that.

As the evening wore on I found myself feeling more and more uncomfortable. I exchanged a few tight words with Ayer, mainly concerning a new computer he'd bought, but wasn't bothered when he turned to talk to someone else. The group from the office seemed to be closing in on itself, leaning over the table to shout jokes which they understood and I didn't. Ayer's harsh

laugh cut across the smoke to me, and I felt impotently angry that someone like him should be able to sit with his arm around someone like Jeanette.

I drank another couple of beers and then abruptly decided that I simply wasn't having a good enough time. I stood up and took my leave, and was mildly touched when Tanya and Sarah tried to get me to stay. Jeanette didn't say anything, and when Ayer's eyes swept vaguely over me I saw that for him I didn't exist. I backed out of the pub smiling, and then turned and stalked miserably down the road.

***

BY SUNDAY EVENING I was fine. I met my ex-girlfriend-before-last for lunch on the Saturday, and we had a riotous time bitching and gossiping about people we knew. In the evening I went to a restaurant that served food only from a particular four square mile region of Nepal, or so Nick claimed, such venues being his speciality. It tasted just like Indian to me, and I didn't see any sherpas, but the food was good. I spent Sunday doing my kind of thing, wandering round town and sitting in cafés to read. I called my folks in the evening, and they were on good form, and then I watched a horror film before going to bed when I felt like it. The kind of weekend that only happily single people can have, in other words, and it suited me just fine.

Monday was okay too. I was regaled with various tales of drunkenness from Friday night, as if for the first time I had a right to know. I had all the information I needed from Jeanette for the time being, so I did most of my work at a different machine. We had a quick chat in the kitchen while I made some coffee, and it was more or less the same as it had been the week before—because she'd always *known* she had a boyfriend, of course. I caught myself sagging a couple of times on the afternoon, but bullied my mood into holding up. In a way it was kind of a relief, not to have to care.

The evening was warm and sunny, and I took my time walking home. Then I rustled myself up a chef's salad, which is my only claim to culinary skill. It has iceberg lettuce, black olives, grated cheese, julienned ham (that's 'sliced', to you and me), diced tomato and two types of home-made dressing: which is more than enough ingredients to count as cooking in my book.

When I was sufficiently gorged on roughage I sat in front of the computer and tooled around, and by the time it was dark outside found myself cruising round the net.

And, after a while, I found myself accessing alt.binaries.pictures.erotica. I was in a funny sort of mood, I guess. I scrolled through the list of files, not knowing what I was after. What I found was the usual stuff, like '-TH2xx. jpg-{m/f}-hot sex!'. Hot sex wasn't really what I was looking for, especially if it had an exclamation mark after it. Of all the people who access the group, I suspect it's less than about 5% who actually put pictures up there in the first place. It seems to be a matter of intense pride with them, and they compete with each other on the volume and 'quality' of their postings. Their tragically sad bickering is often more entertaining than the pictures themselves.

It's complete pot luck what is available at any given time, and no file stays on there for more than about two days. The servers which hold the information have only limited space, and files get rolled off the end pretty quickly in the high volume groups. I was about to give up when something suddenly caught my attention.

'j1.gif-{f}-"Young_woman, fully_clothed (part 1/3)".

Fuck *me*, I thought: that's a bit weird. The group caters for a wide spectrum of human sexuality, and I'd seen titles which promised fat couples, skinny girls, interracial bonding and light S&M. What I'd never come across was something as perverted as a woman with all her clothes *on*. Intrigued, I did the necessary to download the picture's three segments onto my hard disk.

By the time I'd made a cup of coffee they were there, and I severed the Net connection and stitched the three files together. Until they were converted they were just text files, which is one of the weird things about the newsgroups. Absolutely anything, from programs to articles to pictures, is up there as plain text. Without the appropriate decoders it just looks like nonsense, which I guess is as good a metaphor as any for the Net as a whole. Or indeed for life. Feel free to use that insight in your own conversations.

When the file was ready, I loaded up a graphics package and opened it. I was doing so with only half an eye, not really expecting anything very interesting. But when, after a few seconds of whirring, the image popped onto the screen, I dropped my cup of coffee and it teetered on the desk before falling to shatter on the floor.

It was Jeanette.

The image quality was not especially high, and looked as if it had been taken with some small automatic camera. But the girl in the picture was Jeanette, without a shadow of a doubt. She was perched on the arm of an anonymous armchair, and with a lurch I realised it was probably taken in her flat. She was, as advertised, fully clothed, wearing a short-ish skirt and a short-sleeved top which buttoned up at the front. She was looking in the general direction of the camera, and her expression was unreadable. She looked beautiful, as always, and somehow much, much more appealing than any of the buck-naked women who cavorted through the usual pictures to be found on the net.

After I'd got over my jaw-dropped surprise, I found I was feeling something else. Annoyance, possibly. I know I'm biased, but I didn't think it right that a picture of her was plastered up in cyberspace for everyone to gawk at, even if she was fully clothed. I realise that's hypocritical in the face of all the other women up there, but I can't help it. It was different.

Because I knew her.

I was also angry because I could only think of one way it could have got there. I'd mentioned a few net-related things in Jeanette's presence at work, and she'd showed no sign of recognition. It was a hell of a coincidence that I'd seen the picture at all, and I wasn't prepared to speculate about stray photos of her falling into unknown people's hands. There was only one person who was likely to have uploaded it. Her boyfriend.

The usual women (and men) in the pictures are getting paid for it. It's their job. Jeanette wasn't, and might not even know the picture was there.

I quickly logged back onto the Net and found the original text files. I extricated the uploader information and pulled it onto the screen, and then swore.

Remember a while back I said it was possible to hide yourself when posting up to the net? Well, that's what he'd done. The email address of the person who'd uploaded the picture was listed as 'anon99989@penet.fi'. That meant that rather than posting it up in his real name, he'd routed the mail through an anonymity server in Finland called PENET. This server strips the journey information out of the posting and assigns a random address which is held on an encrypted database. I couldn't tell anything from it at all. Feeling my lip curl with distaste, I quit out.

By the time I got to work the next day I knew there wasn't anything I could say about it. I could hardly pipe up with 'Hey! Saw your pic on the Internet porn board last night!' And after all, it was only a picture, the kind that people have plastic folders stuffed full of. The question was whether Jeanette knew Ayer had posted it up. If she did then, well, it just went to show that you didn't know much about people just because you worked with them. If she didn't, then I think she had a right both to know, and to be annoyed.

I dropped a few net-references into the conversations we had, but nothing came of them. I even mentioned the newsgroups, but got mild interest and nothing more. It was fairly clear she hadn't heard of them. In the end I sort of mentally shrugged. So her unpleasant boyfriend had posted up a picture. There was nothing I could do about it, except bury still further any feelings I might have entertained for her. She already had a life with someone else, and I had no business interfering.

In the evening I met up with Nick again, and we went and got quietly hammered in a small drinking club we frequented. I successfully fought off his ideas on going and getting some food, doubtless the cuisine of one particular village on the top of Kilimanjaro, and so by the end of the evening we were pretty far gone. I stumbled out of a cab, flolloped up the stairs and mainlined coffee for a while, in the hope of avoiding a hangover the next day. And it was as I sat, weaving slightly, on the sofa, that I conceived the idea of checking a certain newsgroup.

Once the notion had taken hold I couldn't seem to dislodge it. Most of my body and soul was engaged in remedial work, trying to save what brain cells they could from the onslaught of alcohol, and the idea was free to romp and run as it pleased. So I found myself slumped at my desk, listening to my hard disk doing its thing, and muttering quietly to myself. I don't know what I was saying. I think it was probably a verbal equivalent of that letter I never gave to someone, an explanation of how much better off Jeanette would be with me. I can get very maudlin when I'm drunk.

When the newsgroup appeared in front of me I blearily ran my eye over the list. The group had seen serious action in the last twenty-four hours, and there were over 300 titles to contend with. I was beginning to lose heart and interest when I saw something about two thirds of the way down the list.

'j2.gif-{f}-"Young_woman"', one line said, and it was followed by 'j3. gif-{f}-"Young_woman"'.

These two titles started immediately to do what half a pint of coffee hadn't: sober me up. At a glance I could tell that there were two differences from the description of the first picture of Jeanette I'd seen. The numerals after the 'j' were different, implying they were not the same picture. Also, there were two words missing at the end of the title: the words 'fully clothed'.

I called the first few lines of the first file onto the screen, and saw that it too had come from anon99989@penet.fi. Then, reaching shakily for a cigarette, I downloaded the rest. When my connection was over I slowly stitched the text files together and then booted up the viewer.

It was Jeanette, again. Wincing slightly, hating myself for having access to photos of her under these circumstances when I had no right to know what they might show, I looked briefly at first one and then the other.

j2.gif looked as if it had been taken immediately after the first I'd seen. It showed Jeanette, still sitting on the arm of the chair. She was undoing the front of her top, and had got as far as the third button. Her head was down, and I couldn't see her face. Trembling slightly from a combination of emotions, I looked at j3.gif. Her top was now off, showing a flat stomach and a dark blue lacy bra. She was steadying herself on the chair with one arm, and her position looked uncomfortable. She was looking off to one side, away from the camera, and when I saw her face I thought I had the answer to at least one question. She didn't look very happy. She didn't look as if she was having fun.

She didn't look as if she wanted to be doing this at all.

I stood up suddenly and paced around the room, unsure of what to do. If she hadn't been especially enthralled about having the photos taken in the first place, I couldn't believe that Jeanette condoned or even knew about their presence on the net. Quite apart from anything else, she wasn't that type of girl, if that type of girl indeed existed at all.

This constituted some very clear kind of invasion by her boyfriend, something that negated any rights he may have felt he had upon her. But what could I do about it?

I copied the two files onto a floppy, along with j1.gif, and threw them off my hard disk. It may seem like a small distinction to you, but I didn't want them on my main machine. It would have seemed like collusion.

I got up the next morning with no more than a mild headache, and before I left for work decided to quickly log onto the net. There were no more pictures, but there was something that made me very angry indeed. Someone had posted up a message whose total text was the following.

'Re: j-pictures {f}: EXCELLENT! More pleeze!'.

In other words, the pictures had struck a chord with some nameless net-pervert, and they wanted to see some more.

I spent the whole morning trying to work out what to do. The only way I could think of broaching the subject would involve mentioning the alt.binaries.pictures.erotica group itself, which would be a bit of a nasty moment—I wasn't keen on revealing the fact that I was a nameless Net pervert myself. I hardly got a chance to talk to her all morning anyway, because she was busy on the phone. She also seemed a little tired, and little disposed to chat on the two occasions we found ourselves in the kitchen together.

It felt as if parts of my mind were straining against each other, pulling in different directions. If she didn't know about it, it was wrong, and she should be put in the picture. If I did so, however, she'd never think the same of me again. There was a chance, of course, that the problem might go away: despite the net-loser's request, the expression on Jeanette's face in j3.gif made it seem unlikely there *were* any more pictures. And ultimately the whole situation probably wasn't any of my business, however much it felt like it was.

In the event, I missed the boat. About four thirty I emerged from a long and vicious argument with the server software to discover that Jeanette had left for the day. 'A doctor's appointment'. In most of the places I've worked that phrase translates directly to 'A couple of hours off from work, *obviously* not spent at the doctors', but that didn't seem to be the general impression at the VCA. She'd probably just gone to the doctor's. Either way she was no longer in the office, and I was slightly ashamed to find myself relaxing now that I could no longer talk to her.

At eight thirty that evening, after my second salad of the week, I logged on and checked the group again. There was nothing there. I fretted and fidgeted around the apartment for a few hours, and then tried again at eleven o'clock. This time I found something. Two things. j4.gif, and j5.gif, both from the anonymous address.

In the first picture Jeanette was standing. She was no longer wearing her skirt, and her long legs led up to underwear that matched the bra I'd already seen. She wasn't posing for the picture. Her hands were on her hips, and she looked angry. In j5 she was leaning back against the arm of the chair, and no longer wearing her bra. Her face was blank.

I stared at the second picture for a long time, mind completely split in two. If you ignored the expression on her face, she looked gorgeous. Her breasts were small but perfectly shaped, exactly in proportion to her long, slender body. It was, undeniably, an erotic picture. Except for her face, and the fact that she obviously didn't want to be photographed, and the fact that someone was doing it anyway. Not only that, but broadcasting it to the planet.

I decided that enough was enough, and that I had to do something. After a while I came up with the best that I could. I loaded up my email package, and sent a message to anon99989@penet.fi. The double-blind principle the server operated on meant that the recipient wouldn't know where it had come from, and that was fine by me. The message was this:

'I know who you are'.

It wasn't much, but it was something. The idea that someone out there on the information superhighway could know his identity *might* be enough to stop him. It was only a stop-gap measure, anyway. I now knew I had to do something about the situation. It simply wasn't on.

And I had to do it soon. When I checked the next morning there were no more pictures, but two messages from people who'd downloaded them. 'Keep 'em cumming!' one wit from Japan had written. Some slob from Texas had posted in similar vein, but added a small request: 'Great, but pick up the pace a little. I want to see more FLESH!'

All the way to work I geared myself up to talking to Jeanette, and I nearly punched the wall when I heard she was out at a venue meeting for the whole morning and half the afternoon. I got rid of the morning by concentrating hard on one of her databases, wanting to bring at least something positive into her life. I know it's not much, but all I know is computers, and that's the best that I could do.

At last three o'clock rolled round, and Jeanette reappeared in the office. She seemed tired and a little preoccupied, and sat straight down at her desk to work. I loitered in the main office area, willing people to fuck off out of it so hard my head started to ache. I couldn't get anywhere near the topic if there were other people around. It would be hard enough if we were alone.

Finally, bloody, *finally* she got up from her desk and went into the kitchen. I got up and followed her in. She smiled faintly and vaguely on seeing me, and, seeing that she had a bandage on her right forearm, I used that to start a conversation. A small mole, apparently, hence the visit to the doctor. I let her finish that topic, keeping half an eye out to make sure that no one was approaching the kitchen.

'I bought a camera today,' I blurted, as cheerily as I could. It wasn't great, but I wanted to start slowly. She didn't respond for a moment, and then looked up, her face expressionless.

'Oh yes?' she said, eventually. 'What are you going to photograph?'

'Oh, you know, buildings, landscape. Black and white, that kind of thing.' She nodded distantly, and I ran out of things to say.

I ran out because in retrospect the topic didn't lead anywhere, but I stopped for another reason too. I stopped because as she turned to pick up the kettle, the look on her face knocked the wind out of me. The combination of unhappiness and loneliness, the sense of helplessness. It struck me again that despite the anger in her face in j4, in j5 she had not only taken her bra off but looked resigned and defeated. Suddenly I didn't care how it looked, didn't care what she thought of me.

'Jeanette,' I said, firmly, and she turned to look at me again. 'I saw a pict...'

'Hello boys and girls. Having a little tea party, are we?'

At the sound of Morehead's voice I wanted to turn round and smash his face in. Jeanette laughed prettily at her employer's sally, and moved out of the way to allow him access to the kettle. Morehead asked me some balls-achingly dull questions about the computer system, obviously keen to sound as if he had the faintest conception of what it all meant. By the time I'd finished answering him Jeanette was back at her desk.

The next hour was one of the longest of my life. I'd gone over, crossed the line. I knew I was going to talk to her about what I'd seen. More than that, I'd realised that it didn't have to be as difficult as I'd assumed.

The first picture, j1.gif, simply showed a pretty girl sitting on a chair. It wasn't pornographic, and could have been posted up in any number of places on the Net. All I had to do was say I'd seen *that* picture. It wouldn't implicate me, and she would know what her boyfriend was up to.

I hovered round the main office, ready to be after her the minute she looked like leaving, having decided that I'd walk with her to the tube and tell her then. So long as she didn't leave with anyone else, it would be perfect. While I hovered I watched her work, her eyes blank and isolated. About quarter to five she got a phone call. She listened for a moment, said 'Yes, alright' in a dull tone of voice, and then put the phone down. There was nothing else to distract me from the constant cycling of draft gambits in my head.

At five she started tidying her desk, and I slipped out and got my jacket. I waited in the hallway until I could hear her coming, and then went downstairs in the lift. I walked through the lobby as slowly as I could, and then went and stood outside the building. My hands were sweating and I felt wired and frightened, but I knew I was going to go through with it. A moment later she came out.

'Hi,' I said, and she smiled warily, surprised to see me, I suppose. 'Look Jeanette, I need to talk to you about something.'

She stared at me, looked around, and then asked what.

'I've seen pictures of you.' In my nervousness I blew it, and used the plural rather than singular.

'Where?' she said, immediately. She knew what I was talking about. From the speed with which she latched on I realised that whatever fun and games were going on between her and Ayer were at the forefront of her mind.

'The newsgroups. It's…'

'I know what they are,' she said. 'What have you seen?'

'Five so far,' I said. 'Look, if there's anything I can do…'

'Like what?' she said, and laughed harshly, her eyes beginning to blur. 'Like what?'

'Well, anything. Look, let's go talk about it. I could…'

'There's no use,' she said hurriedly, and started to pull away. I followed her, bewildered. How could she not want to do anything about it? I mean, all right, I may not have been much of a prospect, but surely some help was better than none.

'Jeanette…'

'Let's talk tomorrow,' she hissed, and suddenly I realised what was happening. Her boyfriend had come to pick her up. She walked towards the curb where a white car was coming to a halt, and I rapidly about-faced and started striding the other way. It wasn't fear, not purely. I also didn't want to get her in trouble.

As I walked up the road I felt as if the back of my neck was burning, and at the last moment I glanced to the side. The white car was just passing, and I could see Jeanette sitting bolt upright in the passenger seat. Her boyfriend was looking out of the side window. At me. Then he accelerated and the car sped away.

That night brought another two photographs. j6 had Jeanette naked, sitting in the chair with her legs slightly apart. Her face was stony. In j7 she was on all fours, photographed from behind. As I sat in my chair, filled with impotent fury, I noticed something in both pictures, and blew them up with the magnifier tool. In j6 one side of her face looked a little red, and when I looked carefully at j7 I could see that there was a trickle of blood running from a small cut on her right forearm.

And suddenly I realised, with help from memories of watching her hands and arms as she worked, that there had never been a mole on her arm. She hadn't got the bandage because of the doctor.

She had it because of him.

———

I HARDLY SLEPT that night. I stayed up till three, keeping an eye on the newsgroup. Its denizens were certainly becoming fans of the 'j' pictures, and I saw five requests for some more. As far as they knew all this involved was a bit more scanning originals from some magazine. They didn't realise that someone I knew was having them taken against her will. I considered trying to do something within the group, like posting a message telling what I knew. While its frequenters are a bit sad, they tend to have a strong moral stance about such things. It's not like the alt.binaries.pictures.tasteless group—where anything goes, the sicker the better. If the a.b.p.erotica crowd were convinced the pictures were being taken under coercion, there was a strong chance they might mailbomb Ayer off the Net. It would be a big war to start, however, and one with potentially damaging consequences. The mailbombing would have to go through the anonymity server, and would probably crash it. While I couldn't give a fuck about that, it would draw the attention of all manner of people. In any event, because of the anonymity, nothing would happen directly to Ayer apart from some inconvenience.

I decided to put the idea on hold, in case talking to Jeanette tomorrow made it unnecessary. Eventually I went to bed, where I thrashed and turned for hours. Some time just before dawn I drifted off, and dreamt about a cat being caught in a lawnmower.

I was up at seven, there being no point in me staying in bed. I checked the group, but there were no new files. On an afterthought I checked my email, realising that I'd been so out of it that I hadn't done so for days. There were about thirty messages for me, some from friends, the rest from a variety of virtual acquaintances around the world. I scanned through them quickly, seeing if any needed urgent attention, and then slap in the middle I noticed one from a particular address.

anon99989@penet.fi.

Heart thumping, I opened the email. In the convention of such things, he'd quoted my message back at me, with a comment. The entire text of the mail read:

'> I know who you are.

>Maybe. But I know where you live.'

WHEN I GOT to work, at the dot of nine, I discovered Jeanette wasn't there. She'd left a message at eight thirty announcing she was taking the day off. Sarah was a bit sniffy about this, though she claimed to be great pals with Jeanette. I left her debating the morality of such cavalier leave-taking with Tanya in the kitchen, as I walked slowly out to sit at Jeanette's desk to work. After five minutes' thought I went back to the kitchen and asked Sarah for Jeanette's number, claiming I had to ask her about the database. Sarah seemed only too pleased to provide the means of contacting a friend having a day off. I grabbed my jacket, muttered something about buying cigarettes, and left the office.

Round the corner I found a public phone box and called her number. As I listened to the phone ring I glanced at the prostitute cards which liberally covered the walls, but soon looked away. I didn't find their representation of the female form amusing any more. After six rings an answering machine cut in. A man's voice, Ayer's, announced that they were out. I rang again, with the same result, and then left the phone box and stood aimlessly on the pavement.

There was nothing I could do.

I went back to work. I worked. I ran home.

At six thirty I logged on for the first time, and the next two pictures were already there. I could tell immediately that something had changed. The wall behind her was a different colour, for a start. The focus of the action seemed to have moved, to the bedroom, presumably, and the pictures were getting worse. j8 showed Jeanette spread-eagled on her back. Her legs were very wide open, and both her hands and feet were out of shot. j9 was much the same, except you could see that her hands were tied. You could also see her face, with its hopeless defiance and fear. As I erased the picture from my disk I felt my neck spasming.

Too late I realised that what I should have done was get Jeanette's address while I was at work. It would have been difficult, and viewed with suspicion, but I might have been able to do it. Now I couldn't. I didn't know the home numbers of anyone else from the VCA, and couldn't trace her address from her number. The operator wouldn't give it to me. If I'd had the address I could have gone round. Maybe I would have found myself in the worst situation of my life, but it would have been something to try. The idea of her being in trouble somewhere in London, and me not knowing where, was almost too much to bear. Suddenly I decided that I had to do the one small thing I could. I logged back onto the erotica group and prepared to start a flame war.

The classic knee-jerk reaction that people on the Net use to express their displeasure is known as 'flaming'. Basically it involves bombarding the offender with massive mail messages until their virtual mailbox collapses under the load. This draws the attention of the administrator of their site, and they get chucked off the net. What I had to do was post a message providing sufficient reason for the good citizens of pornville to dump on anon99989@penet.fi.

So it might cause some trouble. I didn't fucking care.

I had a mail slip open and my hands poised over the keyboard before I noticed something which stopped me in my tracks.

There were two more files. Already. The slob from Texas was getting his wish: the pace was being picked up.

In j10 Jeanette was on her knees on a dirty mattress. Her hands appeared to be tied behind her, and her head was bowed. j11 showed her lying awkwardly on her side, as if she'd been pushed over. She was glaring at the camera, and when I magnified the left side of the image I could see a thin trickle of blood from her right nostril.

I leapt up from the keyboard, shouting. I don't know what I was saying. It wasn't coherent. Jeanette's face stared up at me from the computer and I leant wildly across and hit the switch to turn the screen off. Just quitting out didn't seem enough. Then I realised that the image was still there, even though I couldn't see it. The computer was still sending the information to the screen, and the minute I turned it back on, it would be there. So I hard-stopped the computer by just turning it off at the mains. Suddenly what had always been my domain felt like the outpost of someone very twisted and evil, and I didn't want anything to do with it.

Then, like a stone through glass, two ideas crashed into each other in my head.

Gospel Oak.

Police.

From nowhere came a faint half-memory, so tenuous that it might be illusory, of Jeanette mentioning Gospel Oak station. In other words, the rail-station in Gospel Oak. I knew where that was.

An operator wouldn't give me an address from a phone number. But the police would be able to get it. They had reverse directories.

I couldn't think of anything else.

I rang the police. I told them I had reason to believe that someone was in danger, and that she lived at the house with this phone number. They wanted to know who I was and all manner of other shit, but I rang off quickly, grabbed my coat and hit the street.

Gospel Oak is a small area, filling up the gap between Highgate, Chalk Farm and Hampstead. I knew it well because Nick and I used to go play pool at a pub on Mansfield Road, which runs straight through it. I knew the entrance and exit points of the area, and I got the cab to drop me off as near to the centre as possible. Then I stood on the pavement, hopping from foot to foot and smoking, hoping against hope that this would work.

Ten minutes later a police car turned into Mansfield Road. I was very pleased to see them, and enormously relieved. I hadn't been particularly sure about the Gospel Oak part. I shrank back against the nearest building until it had gone past, and then ran after it as inconspicuously as I could. It took a left into Estelle Road and I slowed at the corner to watch it pull up outside number 6. I slipped into the doorway of the corner shop and watched as two policemen took their own good time about untangling themselves from their car.

They walked up to the front of the house. One leant hard against the doorbell, while the other peered around the front of the house as if taking part in an officiousness competition. The door wasn't answered, which didn't surprise me. Ayer was hardly going to break off from torturing his girlfriend to take social calls. One of the policemen nodded to the other, who visibly sighed, and made his way round the back of the house.

'Oh come on, come *on*,' I hissed in the shadows. 'Break the fucking door down.'

About five minutes passed, and then the policeman reappeared. He shrugged flamboyantly at his colleague, and pressed the doorbell again.

A light suddenly appeared above the door, coming from the hallway behind it. My breath caught in my throat and I edged a little closer. I'm not sure what I was preparing to do. Dash over there and force my way in, past the policemen, to grab Ayer and smash his head against the wall? I really don't know.

The door opened, and I saw it wasn't Ayer or Jeanette. It was an elderly man with a crutch and grey hair that looked like it had seen action in a hurricane. He conversed irritably with the policemen for a moment and then shut the door in their faces. The two cops stared at each other for a moment, clearly considering busting the old tosser, but then turned and made their way back to the car. Still looking up at the house, the first policeman made a report into his radio, and I heard enough to understand why they then got into the car and drove away.

The old guy had told them that the young couple had gone away for the weekend. He'd seen them go on Thursday evening. I was over twenty-four hours too late.

When the police car had turned the corner I found myself panting, not knowing what to do. The last two photographs, the one with the dirty mattress, hadn't been taken here at all. Jeanette was somewhere in the country, but I didn't know where, and there was no way of finding out. The pictures could have been posted from anywhere.

Making a decision, I walked quickly across the road towards the house. The policemen may not have felt they had just cause, but I did, and I carefully made my way around the back of the house. This involved climbing over a gate and wending through the old guy's crowded little garden, and I came perilously close to knocking over a pile of flower-pots. As luck would have it there was a kind of low wall which led to a complex exterior plumbing fixture, and I quickly clambered on top of it. A slightly precarious upward step took me next to one of the second floor windows. It was dark, like all the others, but I kept my head bent just in case.

When I was closer to the window I saw that it wasn't fastened at the bottom. They might have gone, and then come back. Ayer could have staged it so the old man saw them go, and then slipped back when he was out.

It was possible, but not likely. But on the other hand, the window was ajar. Maybe they were just careless about such things. I slipped my fingers under the pane and pulled it open. Then I leant with my ear close to the open space and listened. There was no sound, and so I boosted myself up and quickly in.

I found myself in a bedroom. I didn't turn the light on, but there was enough coming from the moon and streetlights to pick out a couple of pieces of Jeanette's clothing, garments that I recognised, strewn over the floor. She wouldn't have left them like that, not if she'd had any choice in the matter. I walked carefully into the corridor, poking my head into the bathroom and kitchen, which were dead. Then I found myself in the living room.

The big chair stood in front of a wall I recognised, and at the far end a computer sat on a desk next to a picture scanner. Moving as quickly but quietly as possible, I frantically searched over the desk for anything that might tell me where Ayer had taken her. There was nothing there, and nothing in the rest of the room. I'd broken—well, *opened*—and entered for no purpose. There were no clues. No sign of where they'd gone. An empty box under the table confirmed what I'd already guessed: Ayer had a laptop computer as well. He could be posting the pictures onto the Net from anywhere that had a phone socket. Jeanette would be with him, and I needed to find her. I needed to find her soon.

I paced around the room, trying to pick up speed, trying to work out what I could possibly do. No one at VCA knew where they'd gone—they hadn't even known Jeanette wasn't going to be in. The old turd downstairs hadn't known. There was nothing in the flat that resembled a phone book or personal organiser, something that would have a friend or family member's number. I was prepared to do anything, call anyone, in the hope of finding where they'd gone. But there was nothing, unless…

I sat down at the desk, reached behind the computer and turned it on. Ayer had a fairly flash deck, together with a scanner and laser printer. He knew the Net. Chances were he was wirehead enough to keep his phone numbers somewhere on his computer.

As soon as the machine was booted up I went rifling through it, grimly enjoying the intrusion, the computer-rape. His files and programs were spread all over the disk, with no apparent system. Each time I finished looking through a folder, I erased it. It seemed the least I could do.

Then after about five minutes I found something, but not what I was looking for. I found a folder named 'j'.

There were files called j12 to j16 in the folder, in addition to all the others that I'd seen. Wherever Jeanette was, Ayer had come back here to scan the pictures. Presumably that meant they were still in London, for all the good that did me.

I'm not telling you what they were like, except that they showed Jeanette, and in some she was crying, and in j15 and j16 there was blood running from the corner of her mouth. A lot of blood. She was twisted and tied, face livid with bruises, and in j16 she was staring straight at the camera, face slack with terror.

Unthinkingly I slammed my fist down on the desk. There was a noise downstairs and I went absolutely motionless until I was sure the old man had lost interest. Then I turned the computer off, opened up the case and removed the hard disk. I climbed out the way I'd come and ran out down the street, flagged a taxi by jumping in front of it and headed for home.

I was going to the police, but I needed a computer, something to shove the hard disk into. I was going to show them what I'd found, and fuck the fact it was stolen. If they nicked me, so be it. But they had to do something about it. They had to try and find her. If he'd come back to do his scanning he had to be keeping her somewhere in London. They'd know where to look, or where to start. They'd know what to do.

They had to. They were the police. It was their job.

I ran up the stairs and into the flat, and then dug in my spares cupboard for enough pieces to hack together a compatible computer. When I'd got them I went over to my desk to call the local police station, and then stopped and turned my computer on. I logged onto the Net and kicked up my mail package, and sent a short, useless message.

'I'm coming after you,' I said.

It wasn't bravado. I didn't feel brave at all. I just felt furious, and wanted to do anything which might unsettle him, or make him stop. Anything to make him stop.

I logged quickly onto the newsgroups, to see when anon99989@penet.fi had most recently posted. A half-hour ago, when I'd been in his apartment, j12-16 had been posted up. Two people had already responded: one hoping the blood was fake and asking if the group really wanted that kind of picture—the other asking for more. I viciously wished a violent death upon the second person, and was about to log off, having decided not to bother phoning but to just go straight to the cops, when I saw another text-only posting at the end of the list.

'Re: j-series' it said. It was from anon99989@penet.fi.

I opened it. 'End of series,' the message said. 'Hope you all enjoyed it. Next time, something tasteless.'

'And I hope,' I shouted at the screen, 'that you enjoy it when I ram your hard disk down your fucking throat.'

Then suddenly my blood ran cold.

'Next time, something tasteless.'

I hurriedly closed the group, and opened up alt.binaries.pictures.tasteless. As I scrolled past the titles for road-kills and people crapping I felt the first heavy, cold tear roll out onto my cheek. My hand was shaking uncontrollably, my head full of some dark mist, and when I saw the last entry I knew suddenly and exactly what Jeanette had been looking at when j16 was taken.

'j17.gif,' it read. '{f} Pretty amputee'.

MICHAEL MARSHALL SMITH is a novelist and screenwriter. Under this name he has published nearly 100 short stories, and five novels— *Only Forward*, *Spares*, *One of Us*, *The Servants* and *Hannah Green and her Unfeasibly Mundane Existence*—winning the Philip K. Dick, International Horror Guild, and August Derleth awards, along with the Prix Bob Morane in France. He has also won the British Fantasy Award for Best Short Fiction four times, more than any other author. Writing as 'Michael Marshall', he has published seven thrillers including *The Straw Men* series, *The Intruders* (adapted by BBC America into a TV series starring John Simm and Mira Sorvino), *Killer Move* and *We Are Here*. Under the name 'Michael Rutger', he has additionally published the adventure thriller *The Anomaly* and a sequel, *The Possession*. Currently co-writing and executive producing development of *The Straw Men* for television, Smith is also Creative Consultant to The Blank Corporation, Neil Gaiman's production company in Los Angeles. He lives in Santa Cruz, California, with his wife, son, and two cats. The author is somewhat reticent about 'More Tomorrow', except to say that the information within the story came not from him, but from a…friend. 'People should be very careful of the Internet—it's an easier way of wasting time than even a Sega Megadrive,' he advises. For a story written more than a quarter of a century ago, that observation now seems very prescient!

I'VE COME TO TALK WITH YOU AGAIN

Karl Edward Wagner

THEY WERE ALL in the Swan. The music box was moaning something about 'everybody hurts sometime' or was it 'everybody hurts something'. Jon Holsten couldn't decide. He wondered, why the country-western sound in London? Maybe it was 'everybody hurts somebody'. Where were The Beatles when you needed them? One Beatle short, to begin with. Well, yeah, two Beatles. And Pete Best. Whatever.

'Wish they'd turn that bloody thing down.' Holsten scowled at the offending speakers. Coins and sound effects clattered from the fruit machine, along with bonks and flippers from the Fish Tales pinball machine. The pub was lusty with mildew from the pissing rain of the past week and the penetrating stench of stale tobacco smoke. Holsten hated the ersatz stuffed trout atop the pinball machine.

Mannering was opening a packet of crisps, offering them around. Foster declined: he had to watch his salt. Carter crunched a handful, then wandered across to the long wooden bar to examine the two chalk-on-slate menus: Quality Fayre was promised. He ordered prime pork sausages with chips and baked beans, not remembering to watch his weight. Stein limped down the treacherous stairs to the Gents. Insulin time. Crossley helped himself to the crisps and worried that his round was coming up. He'd have to duck it. Ten quid left from his dole cheque, and a week till the next.

There were six of them tonight, where once eight or ten might have foregathered. Over twenty years, it had become an annual tradition: Jon Holsten over from the States for his holiday in London, the usual crowd around for pints and jolly times. Cancer of the kidneys had taken McFerran last year; he who always must have his steak and kidney pie. Hiles had decamped to the Kentish coast, where he hoped the sea air would improve his chest. Marlin was somewhere in France, but no one knew where, nor whether he had kicked his drug dependence.

So it went.

'To absent friends,' said Holsten, raising his pint. The toast was well received, but added to the gloom of the weather with its memories of those who should have been here.

Jon Holsten was an American writer of modest means but respectable reputation. He got by with a little help from his friends, as it were. Holsten was generally considered to be the finest of the later generation of writers in the Lovecraftian school—a genre mainly out of fashion in these days of chainsaws and flesh-eating zombies, but revered by sufficient devotees to provide for Holsten's annual excursion to London.

Holsten tipped back his pint glass. Over its rim he saw the yellow-robed figure enter the doorway. He continued drinking without hesitation, swallowing perhaps faster now. The pallid mask regarded him as impassively as ever. An American couple entered the pub, walking past. They were arguing in loud New York accents about whether to eat here. For an instant the blue-haired woman shivered as she brushed through the tattered cloak.

Holsten had fine blond hair, brushed straight back. His eyes were blue and troubled. He stood just under six feet, was compactly muscled beneath his blue three-piece suit. Holsten was past the age of sixty.

'Bloody shame about McFerran,' said Mannering, finishing the crisps. Carter returned from the bar with his plate. Crosley looked on hungrily. Foster looked at his empty glass. Stein returned from the Gents.

Stein: 'What were you saying?'

Mannering: 'About McFerran.'

'Bloody shame.' Stein sat down.

'My round,' said Holsten. 'Give us a hand, will you, Ted?' The figure in tattered yellow watched Holsten as he arose. Holsten had already paid for *his* round.

Ted Crosley was a failed writer of horror fiction: some forty stories in twenty years, mostly for non-paying markets. He was forty and balding and worried about his hacking cough.

Dave Mannering and Steve Carter ran a bookshop and lived above it. Confirmed bachelors adrift from Victorian times. Mannering was thin, dark, well-dressed, scholarly. Carter was red-haired, Irish, rather large, fond of wearing Rugby shirts. They were both about forty.

Charles Stein was a book collector and lived in Crouch End. He was show-ing much grey and was very concerned about his diabetes. He was about forty.

Mike Foster was a tall, rangy book collector from Liverpool. He was wearing a leather jacket and denim jeans. He was concerned about his blood pressure after a near-fatal heart attack last year. He was fading and about forty.

The figure in the pallid mask was seated at their table when Holsten and Crosley returned from the bar with full pints. No need for a seventh pint. Holsten sat down, trying to avoid the eyes that shone from behind the pallid mask. He wasn't quick enough.

The lake was black. The towers were somehow behind the moon. The moons. Beneath the black water. Something rising. A shape. Tentacled. Terror now. The figure in tattered yellow pulling him forward. The pallid mask. Lifted.

'Are you all right?' Mannering was shaking him.

'Sorry?' They were all looking at Holsten. 'Jet lag, I suppose!'

'You've been over here for a fortnight,' Stein pointed out.

'Tired from it all,' said Holsten. He took a deep swallow from his pint, smiled reassuringly. 'Getting too old for this, I imagine.'

'You're in better health than most of us,' said Foster. The tattered cloak was trailing over his shoulders. His next heart attack would not be near-fatal. The figure in the pallid mask brushed past, moving on.

Mannering sipped his pint. The next one would have to be a half: he'd been warned about his liver. 'You will be sixty-four on November the 18th.' Mannering had a memory for dates and had recently written a long essay on Jon Holsten for a horror magazine. 'How do you manage to stay so fit?'

'I have this portrait in my attic.' Holsten had used the joke too many times before, but it always drew a laugh. And he was not going on sixty-four, despite the dates given in his books.

'No. Seriously.' Stein would be drinking a Pils next round, worrying about alcohol and insulin.

The tentacles were not really tentacles—only something with which to grasp and feed. To reach out. To gather in those who had foolishly been drawn into its reach. Had deliberately chosen to pass into its reach. The promises. The vows. The laughter from behind the pallid mask. Was the price worth the gain? Too late.

'Jon? You sure you're feeling all right?' Stein was oblivious to the pallid mask peering over his shoulder.

'Exercise and vitamins,' said Holsten. He gave Stein perhaps another two years.

'It must work for you, then,' Mannering persisted. 'You hardly look any older than when we first met you here in London some ages ago. The rest of us are rapidly crumbling apart.'

'Try jogging and only the occasional pint,' Holsten improvised.

'I'd rather just jog,' said Carter, getting up for another round. He passed by the tattered yellow cloak. Carter would never jog.

'Bought a rather good copy of *The Outsider*,' said Foster, to change the subject. 'Somewhat foxed, and in the reprint dust jacket, but at a good price.' It had been Crosley's copy, sold cheaply to another dealer.

Holsten remembered the afternoon. Too many years ago. New York. Downstairs book shop. Noise of the subway. Cheap shelf. *The King in Yellow*, stuffed with pages from some older book. A bargain. Not cheap, as it turned out. He had never believed in any of this.

The figure in the pallid mask was studying Crosley, knowing he would soon throw himself in front of a tube train. Drained and discarded.

'Well,' said Holsten. 'I'd best be getting back after this one.'

'This early in the day?' said Mannering, who was beginning to feel his pints. 'Must be showing your age.'

'Not if I can help it.' Holsten sank his pint. 'It's just that I said I'd meet someone in the hotel residents' bar at half three. He wants to do one of those interviews, or I'd ask you along. Boring, of course. But...'

'Then come round after,' Mannering invited. 'We'll all be here.'

But not for very much longer, thought Holsten; but he said: 'See you shortly, then.'

Crosley was again coughing badly, a stained handkerchief to his mouth. Jon Holsten fled.

———

THE KID WAS named Dave Harvis, he was from Battersea, and he'd been waiting in the hotel lobby of the Bloomsbury Park for an hour in order not to be late. He wore a blue anorak and was clutching a blue nylon bag with a cassette recorder and some books to be signed, and he was just past twenty-one. Holsten picked him out as he entered the lobby, but the kid stared cluelessly.

'Hello. I'm Jon Holsten.' He extended his hand, as on so many such meetings.

'Dave Harvis.' He jumped from his seat. 'It's a privilege to meet you, sir. Actually, I was expecting a much older...that is...'

'I get by with a little help from my friends.' Holsten gave him a firm American handshake. 'Delighted to meet you.'

The tentacled mouths stroked and fed, promising whatever you wanted to hear. The figure in its tattered yellow cloak lifted its pallid mask. What is said is said. What is done is done. No turning back. Some promises can't be broken.

'Are you all right, sir?' Harvis had heard that Holsten must be up in his years.

'Jet lag, that's all,' said Holsten. 'Let's go into the bar, and you can buy me a pint for the interview. It's quiet there, I think.'

Holsten sat down, troubled.

Harvis carried over two lagers. He worked on his cassette recorder. The residents' bar was deserted but for the barman.

'If you don't mind, sir.' Harvis took a gulp of his lager. 'I've invited a few mates round this evening to meet up at the Swan. They're great fans of your work. If you wouldn't mind…'

'My pleasure,' said Holsten.

The figure in tattered yellow now entered the residents' bar. The pallid mask regarded Harvis and Holsten as Harvis fumbled with a micro-cassette tape.

Holsten felt a rush of strength.

He mumbled into his pint: 'I didn't mean for this to happen this way, but I can't stop it.'

Harvis was still fumbling with the tape and didn't hear. Neither did any gods who cared.

KARL EDWARD WAGNER was one of the genre's finest practitioners of horror and fantasy tales. His untimely death in 1994 robbed the field of a major talent. Creator of 'Kane, the Mystic Swordsman', Wagner's early writing included a series of fantasy novels and stories featuring the flame-haired sorcerer-warrior. For fourteen years he was the editor of the renowned *The Year's Best Horror Stories* anthology series from DAW Books, while his own short horror tales have been collected in *In a Lonely Place, Why Not You and I?* and *Unthreatened by the Morning Light*. At the time of his death, he had just finished compiling a new collection, *Exorcisms and Ecstasies* (eventually published posthumously), from which we selected the semi-autobiographical 'I've Come to Talk With You Again' as our own personal tribute to a fine writer and a good friend.

A REALLY GAME BOY

Brian Lumley

YES, YOU'RE RIGHT, Sheriff, Willy Jay *is* a real game boy, and I counts myself lucky he's my friend. And I really do 'preciate the point that he ain't been home for more'n a week, (a whole week! Dun't that beat all?) but iffen we was to stop him now—why, he'd never fergive us!

As to the folks sayin' *I* got somethin' to do with him bein' missin'—why, I really dun't believe that. Everyone knows how much I love that boy! He's the onliest kid 'round here has anythin' to do with me. Hell, most o' the kids is even a mite scared o' me! Well, they shouldn't do the things they do and then I wouldn't git mad.

And you know as well as I do how many heads Willy's rattled 'cause he heard them a-callin' me. *That's* how close Willy Jay and me is, Sheriff, and you can believe it. And that's why I cain't tell you where he's at.

Now listen, Sheriff, you dun't scare me none. My Paw says that iffen I dun't want to talk to you I sure dun't have to, and that dang him but it might be best iffen I dun't say nothin' anyhow. And anyways, Willy made me promise.

See, it's a kind o' endurance test—that's what Willy called it, a endurance test—and he wouldn't thank me none for lettin' you break it up. Not now he's gone this long. Sure is a game boy, that Willy...

Tell you all about it?

Well, I s'pose I could. I mean, that's not like tellin' you where he's at. See, I cain't do that. 'Cause iffen you stopped him he'd surely blame me, and I values his friendship too much to lose it just 'cause I shot my mouth off to the town Sheriff. I mean, Sheriff—what did you ever do for me, eh?

Hey, I knows you laugh at me behind my back. Paw told me you do. He says that you're the two-facedest Sheriff he ever knowed.

What's that you say? Well what's that got to do with it, Willy bein' just thirteen and me eighteen and all? He's a real big kid for thirteen, and he treats me just like a brother. Why, I could tell you secrets me and Willy knows that would—

—But I wun't...

There you go again, blamin' me for that little Emmy-May kid what drowned. You think I did that? Why, it was me drug her out the water! And Willy with me. It was a accident she fell in the crick, that's all, and I never did take her clothes offen her like some tried to say I did. That was just Willy foolin' about with her. He didn't mean her no real harm, but—

Aw, see? I promised him I'd never say a word 'bout that, and there you go trickin' me into shootin' off my mouth again. Well, okay, I'll tell you—but you got to promise me you'll never tell Willy.

Okay...

It was like this:

See, Willy took a shine to that little Emmy-May girl and he wanted to sort of kiss her and do things! Aw, shucks, Sheriff, you *knows* what sort o' things! Anyways, she bein' a Sunday school girl and all, he figures maybe she ain't much for that kind o' thing. So bein' a game boy and all, and not lettin' nothin' stop him once he's set hissen mind on somethin', Willy works out a little trick to play on her. So this Sunday Willy gets re-ligion and off he goes to Sunday school. When it's over and all the kids is a-leavin', he catches up to Emmy-May and asks her iffen he can see her home. See, she's seen him hangin' back, and she's sort o' hung back too, so maybe she's taken a shine to him like he has to her.

Anyways, their walkin' takes 'em close to Fletcher's Spinney where the crick bends, and this was part o' Willy's plan. I was a-waitin' in the spinney, all crouchin' down and out o' sight like he told me to be, and I seen and heard it all.

'I knows a secret place,' says Willy, his face all eyes and teeth and smiles.

'Oh?' says Emmy-May, and she laughs. 'You're just foolin' about, Willy Jay,' she tells him. 'Why, there ain't no secret places 'round here!'

'Is so,' he says. 'C'mon and I'll show you—but you got to keep it a secret.'

'Sure thing!' she says, all big-eyed, and they runs into the spinney.

Anyways, sure 'nough there is a secret place: a clearin' where the grass is kind o' cropped under a big old oak that leans right out over the crick. Me and Willy had fixed up a rope there and used to swing right out over the crick and back. And sometimes we'd take our clothes off and splash down into the water off the rope. O' course, me and Willy can swim like we was born to the water…

So there they are in the secret place, and me creepin' close in the shrubs and listenin' and a-watchin' it all.

'See,' says Willy, 'this here's my secret place. And that's my swing. Why, I can swing right over the crick on that there rope!'

'Can you really, Willy?' says Emmy-May.

'Sure 'nough. Watch!' says he. And he takes a run at the rope, grabs it and swings right over the crick and back. 'Iffen I'd let go I could've landed on the other side,' he says. 'Would you like to try the swing, Emmy-May?'

'Oh, no!' she holds back. 'I cain't swim, and iffen I fell—'

Willy, he nods and lets it be. 'Anyways,' says he, 'it's just a pre-caution, is all.'

'A what? What sort of precaution, Willy?' she asks.

'Why, the rope!' says he. 'In case I got to run.'

'From what?' she laughs. 'Ain't nothin' here'bouts to be a-feared of.'

'Oh?' says he. 'What about wood spirits, eh? Surely you knows about them? My Paw says your Maw and Paw is full o' superstition from the old country.'

'Oh, I *knows* about them,' she answers, 'but like you say, them's just old wives' tales.' But still she looks around the clearin' real careful like.

By now they's a-sittin' under the old oak and this is where I'm to play my part in this joke. See, Sheriff, Willy had it all figured out. I just rustled a bush a little and let out a low sort o' groan, like a hant might make.

'What was that?' asks Emmy-May, and she creeps real close to Willy and puts her arms around his neck.

'Did you hear 'im?' says Willy, actin' all s'prised. 'Ordinary folk dun't hear 'im, mostly.'

'Hear who?' she whispers, her blue eyes big and round.

'That mean old wood spirit,' says Willy. 'But dun't you worry none. Oh, he's ugly and he's mean, but iffen you're a good friend o' mine he wun't hurt you. He's only ever real bad on full moon nights.'

She hugs his neck tighter. 'Tonight's a full moon, Willy Jay,' she whispers.

'Is it?' again he looks s'prised. 'Why, so it is! But that's okay. Just be still and quiet. As long as you're with me he wun't hurt you none. We gets along just fine, me and the wood spirit—mostly.' And he gives her a kiss full on her mouth.

Now she pulls back from him and stands up—just like he'd told me she might. I rustles the bush some more and makes a angry sort of grunt, and Willy says, 'I *told* you to stay still, Emmy-May! Dun't you know them wood spirits is dangerous? Now come back down here.'

So she gets down again, all shivery like, and Willy pulls the bow at her neck and loosens her buttons. Well, Sheriff, by now I'm all excited. I mean me?—I'd never *ever* dare do any sech a thing, but dang me iffen Willy ain't the gamest boy. But…that Emmy-May is sort o' game, too. She slaps him real hard. And me, watchin', I sees his face go all red from the slap.

'So,' he says, breathin' real hard. 'That's how it's a-goin' to be, is it? Well, I warned you, Emmy-May.' And he calls out: 'Wood spirit, you see this here girl, Emmy-May?' I gives a big grunt and shakes my bush. 'Well, she dun't like me and she dun't believe in you. There,' he says to her. 'Serves you right, Emmy-May, for slappin' me. Your folks'll sure miss you tonight!'

That was my signal to make some real angry growlin' and snarlin', and to beat on the ground with a fallen branch. And I set the bushes a-shakin' like they was full of rattlers as I crept closer, pantin' like a wild animal.

'Call 'im off, Willy Jay!' Emmy-May cries. She hugs Willy tight and sobs, and this time when he kisses her she dun't protest none. And when he puts his hand up her dress she sobs a little but she dun't stop him none. Then he stands up, real slow like, and takes off his clothes, every last stitch. And his pecker is big as my own, Sheriff, I swear it. He's a real big boy for thirteen…

'What you a-doing', Willy Jay?' she says, all breathless like.

'Wood spirit,' he calls out. 'Iffen she's good to me you just stay quite—but iffen she ain't…'

Emmy-May starts in a-sobbin' real loud.

'And iffen she dun't stop her snivellin' right this minute—then she's all your'n!'

'Willy! Willy!' she cries, crawlin' to his feet.

'Take off your clothes,' he says, his voice all broke up like. 'All of 'em, and do it slow.'

'But Willy,' she gasps, 'I—'

'Wood spirit!' he calls, and I gives a real loud howl, so like a wolf it scares even me!

So she takes her clothes off and stands there all pink and sweet and shivery and a-tryin' to cover herself up with her hands, and even the hot summer sun comin' through the oak's branches cain't warm her none. And Willy, he lies her down in the grass and touches, pokes, strokes and kisses her here and there and everywhere, and—

Well, I'm *a-comin'* to that, Sheriff!

Finally, he's all worked up and his face is red and his hands a-shakin'. He says: 'Open your legs real wide, Emmy-May, so's I can put my pecker in you.'

'I'll tell, I'll tell!' she screams, and she jumps up.

Quick as a flash Willy yells: 'Sic 'er, wood spirit—sic 'er good!' But she ain't listenin' none.

That was when the accident happened. See, she made a run at the rope, jumped, fell…

Well, I sprung up out o' hidin' and was all fixed to dive right in after her, but Willy grabs me and says: 'Dun't fret yourself, Zeb,' he says. 'She swims real good…' Only he was mistook, 'cause she couldn't. And the crick bein' pretty fast water just there and all…

Down she went and swept away, and her head bobbin' in the current as she's whirled out of sight. Willy, he tosses her clothes in after her and gets hisself dressed real quick. 'C'mon, Zeb,' he says, 'and I'll tell you what we'll do. We'll say we was walkin' by the crick and we saw her in the water. Mind, we dun't know as to how she got there.'

Then we races near a mile to the big swimmin' hole where the kids is all splashin' and a-yellin'. And Willy shouts, 'There's a girl in the water, comin' down the crick! We seen her!' And as Emmy-May comes driftin' into view we both go in full-dressed and drag her out. But by then she's a goner.

So you see, Sheriff, it were a accident. Just Willy's little trick gone a mite wrong, is all.

Now I done *told* you he ain't run away! What, because o' what happened to Emmy-May, you mean? Shucks, why that weren't nothin' compared to the other things. I mean, it were a accident. But then there was your prize hens, and—

Oh. My! I didn't *ever* mean to mention them hens, Sheriff, I surely did not. Well, you shouldn't whacked his ear that time he gave Jason Harbury a bloody nose. That really made him sore, Sheriff. Oh, it were Willy, all right. He pizzened 'em good! And then there's Old Miss Littlewood...

Why sure, Sheriff, I knows she's dead.

Well, see, Willy had this thing he'd do with worms. It tickled me pink and made the girls all throw up, and Willy—heh! heh!—such a *game* boy, that one!

See, he'd find a big, juicy worm and pop it in his mouth, then let it just sort o' dribble out, all wrigglin', when someone'd stop to speak to him—'specially girls.

One day he'd trapped Old Miss Littlewood's cat and tied a can to his tail, then let him loose over the old lady's fence. Why, that cat was madder'n all hell! Finally she grabbed him and got the can off of him, and she came over to the fence where we was hidin' in the bushes.

She sees us and says: 'Zeb, I just knows you wouldn't do a thing like that. But you, Willy Jay—'bout you I ain't so sure. You are one mean, cruel, unpleasant boy, Willy—and you'll end up in a sorry mess sure as shootin'!'

And Willy, he just stands up all slow like, and he opens his mouth and grins, and a big fat worm glides over his bottom lip and falls plop onto the grass!

Well, she screams! She really screams!—and Willy just standin' there laughin'. Until she reaches across that fence and brings him such a smack as I never heard. That did it. Willy bein' such a game boy and all, he wa'n't a-goin' to let no old spinster lady get away with that! No sir!

We spent the next hour or two diggin' out the biggest, fattest, juiciest worms we could find, and when Old Miss Littlewood left her house and walked off down the street and into town with her basket, then that Willy he snuck into the house and put worms in her bed, and her kitchen, in her preserves, her butter, her milk…worms everywhere!

T'ward dusk she comes home, goes in, lights her lamp, and for a while we can hear her a-hummin' through the open window. Then—she starts a-screamin'. And she keeps right on a-screamin', each scream higher'n the last. Woke all the neighbours, and all their lights goin' on, and me and Willy watchin' the house and a-sniggerin' fit to bust. Then she comes staggerin' out in her nightdress, trips and falls in the garden—and lies still. Me and Willy, we gits out o' there fast!

Yes, I know folks said she'd had a stroke or heart attack or suthin', and so she did. But what *caused* it, eh?

Now, Sheriff, I allow I didn't much care for that one. I mean, when I saw Willy the next day and he laughed at her bein' dead and all. But when he saw I wa'n't too happy 'bout it he soon dried up and said yes, I was right. But it had been a accident, just like Emmy-May, and iffen folks found out I'd be in real trouble 'cause I helped him dig them worms. But, him bein' my friend and all, he said not to worry my head none—he wouldn't tell on me. I was just to fergit the whole thing…

Now Sheriff, I done told you already I cain't—

What?

Just tell you what the endurance test is all about? Well, I suppose that'd be okay. So long as you dun't ask me where it's at.

See, Willy has this thing 'bout ropes and climbin' and a-swingin'—a reg'lar Tarzan, he is. Well, one day we was at—the place. No, sir, not the secret place in Fletcher's Spinney, the place o' the endurance test. And there's this rope a-hangin', see. And Willy says, 'Hey, Zeb, you're pretty big and strong. Iffen that rope was round your feet, how long you reckon you could hang up there, all upside down like, afore you had to stop?'

'Why, I really cain't say as I knows that, Willy Jay,' says I.

'I reckon,' says he, 'I could beat your time whatever.'

'Now Willy,' says I, 'you're a real game boy and no question, but I beat you at runnin', swimmin', wrestlin' and swingin'—so what makes you think you could outlast me on that there rope?'

Willy, I dun't think he liked bein' reminded I could beat him at them things. He got that stubborn look on his face and said: 'But I could beat you this time, Zeb, I knows I could.'

'Willy, you're a real winner,' says I, 'and my onliest true friend, too—but I'm older, bigger and stronger'n you. Now you think real clever and no question, but you're just thirteen and—'

'I can beat you!' he says.

'Okay,' says I. 'I believe it.'

'No,' says he, 'that ain't no proof. This here's a endurance test, Zeb, and we got to try it out.'

'Now, Willy,' says I, 'I got a good many chores to do for Paw. Iffen I'm not home an hour from now, he'll—'

'You first,' says Willy.

See, it makes no matter no how arguin' with him when he's in that there stubborn mood o' hissen. So we climbs up and hauls up the rope and he ties it round my feet in a noose. Then I climbs back down and lets go and swings to and fro 'til I'm all still, and Willy Jay sits up there lookin' down at me and a-grinnin'. 'There you go,' says he, and he keeps the time.

Now then, Sheriff, after 'bout an hour or so Willy says, 'Hey, Zeb! You all right down there?'

'Sure,' says I. 'My ears is a mite poundin', and I got pins and needles in my legs—but I'm okay, Willy Jay.'

'Sure?'

'Sure, I'm sure!'

'Well, enough is enough,' he says, soundin' a bit sore at me. I can't say why he's sore, but he sounds it. 'You better come on up now, 'cause it's time you was a-startin' home to them chores o' your'n.'

'But what about the endurance test?' says I.

'Well, we'll finish it another day,' he says.

So I clumb up—but truth to tell I nearly didn't make it, my arms and legs was so stiff and all. And I got the rope off and staggered about and stamped my feet 'til I could feel 'em again. 'How long'd I do?' I asks.

'Oh, an hour and three and a half minutes,' says Willy, sort of half-sneerin' like.

'Hey!' says I. 'I could go a lot longer but for them chores. Why, I could go another ten or twenty minutes easy!'

'Oh, sure!' says he. 'Listen,' he says, 'I beat you hands down, Zeb. I could stay up that there rope a whole week iffen I wanted to...'

Now that was boastin' pure and simple and I knowed it.

'Willy,' says I, 'ain't nobody—but nobody—could do that! Why, you'd git all hungry, and how'd you sleep?'

'Hell!' he says. 'There's meat enough on my bones, Zeb. I'd not crave fee-din'. And as for sleepin'—well, bats do it, dun't they? They spends all winter a-hangin' and a-sleepin'. Hell, I bet I could do that too, iffen I put my mind to it.'

'Well all I knows,' says I, 'is that I'm real glad I'm down after only one hour, three and a half minutes, that's all.'

'You're you and I'm me, Zeb,' he says, 'but I can see you needs convincin'. Okay, how long's them chores o' your'n a-goin' to take?'

'Oh, 'bout an hour, I reckon.'

'Okay,' says he. 'I'm a-goin' to tie up my feet right now and hang here 'til you gets back.' And he did. And hangin' there, he says: 'Now this is stric'ly 'tween you and me, our secret. Dun't you dare tell a soul 'bout this, hear? See, I'm a-goin' to stick my thumbs in my belt, like this—' and he did, '—and just rest here easy like. And I'm a-goin' to concentrate. Now dun't you go breakin' my concentration nohow, Zeb, hear?'

And I said, 'Okay.'

'Iffen I feels like hangin' here a week, you just let me hang, right?'

'Right,' says I. But o'course, I dun't believe he can do it.

'So off you go and do your chores, Zeb Whitley, and I'll be right here when you gits back.'

'Okay,' I says again, and I scoots.

Well, I was late home and Paw gives me some talkin' to. Then I did my chores—chopped firewood, fetched-n'-carried, this and that—until I figured I was all through. A good hour was up by then, but Paw saw me a-headin' off and says: 'Hey, boy! Where you a-goin'?'

'Why, nowheres, Paw.'

'Danged right!' says he. 'You was late, and so you can do some more chores. I got a whole list for you.' And he kept me right at it all evenin' 'til dark come in. After that—well, I ain't allowed out after dark, Sheriff. Paw says he dun't want no trouble, and people bein' ready to lay the blame too quick and all, it's best he knows where I'm at after dark. So off I goes to bed.

But when I hears him a-snorin', up I jumps and runs to...to the place o' the endurance test. And wouldn't you know it? There he is a-hangin' in the dark, quiet as a bat, all concentratin', his thumbs tucked in his belt just like afore. And Lord, he's been there all of five or six hours! And him so quiet, I figures maybe he's a-sleepin' just like he said he could. So I just tippy-toed out o' there and snuck home and back to bed.

Anyhow, next mornin' Paw gets a note from Uncle Zach over the hill, sayin' please come and bring big Zeb, 'cause Uncle Zach's a-clearin' a field and there's work a-plenty. And hey!—that was excitin'! I mean, I really do like Uncle Zach and him me. So Paw hitches up the wagon and off we goes, and we're all the way to Uncle Zach's place afore I remembers Willy.

By now he'll be down off of that rope for sure and madder'n all hell, I reckon, 'cause I wa'n't there to check his time. But heck!—he beat me every which ways anyhow...

And we was at Uncle Zach's six days.

This mornin' we comes home, and soon's Paw's done with me I gits on over to...to the place o' the endurance test, and—

That's right, Sheriff! Now how'd you guess that? Sure 'nough, he's still up there. Nearly a week, and that spunky boy still a-hangin' by his feet. So I goes up to him—but not too close, 'cause it's all shut in and hot and all, and the summer flies is bad and the place stinks some—and I says: 'Willy, you been here six days and seven nights and some hours, and you sure beat the hell out o' me! You see that old clock out there over the schoolhouse? It's near noon o' the seventh day. Dun't you reckon you should come on down now, Willy Jay?' And I reaches up and gives him a little prod.

Sheriff, are you okay? You sure do look groggy, Sheriff...

Well, I shouldn't prodded Willy like that 'cause I guess it spoils his concentration. Down comes a arm real slow and creaky like, and it points to the door. He's a tellin' me to git out, he ain't finished yet! So off I goes, and I'm a-comin' up the street when you grabs me and—

Why, yes, I did say I could see the schoolhouse clock from the place o' the endur—

Aw, Sheriff! You're just too danged clever for your own good. You guessed it. That's right, Old Man Potter's livery—and him away visitin' and all. His old barn, sure—but dun't you go disturbin' Willy none, or—

Okay, okay, I'm a-comin'—but I just knows there'll be trouble. He told me not to say a word, and there I goes blabbin' and a-blabbin'. And he wun't thank me none for bringin' you down on him, Sheriff, and that's a fact. Okay, I'll be quiet...

———

OH, SURE, I knows the door's shut and bolted, Sheriff, but there's a loose board there, see? Yes, sir, you're right, it is a danged hot summer. And did you ever see so many flies? Only quiet now, or you'll disturb Willy.

See him there? Yes sir, Sheriff, I knows it's gloomy, but—

Hey! Lookit them flies go when you touched him! And...Sheriff? Are you sure you're feelin' okay, Sheriff?

What?

The rope was too tight 'round his ankles? His blood pooled and swelled up his belly? His belt got wedged under his ribs, you say, and trapped his thumbs? And he's...he's...

No! You must be mistook, Sheriff Tuttle. Just give him another little shake and you'll see how wrong you are. Why, he'll go up that rope like a monkey up a stick, all a laughin' and—

But he *cain't* be dead, not Willy! He's just a-concentratin', that's all. Maybe he's a-sleepin' even, like them bats do. What, Willy Jay—dead?

See! See! I'm right. I done *told* you, Sheriff. See what he's a-doin' now? That there's his worm trick!

Dang me, Willy Jay, but I never seen you get *that* many in your mouth afore—you really *game* boy!

BRIAN LUMLEY BEGAN writing in the 1960s with stories, and later novels, set in the milieu of the 'Cthulhu Mythos'; but later he turned his attention to more contemporary horror. His output was necessarily limited because he was a serving Royal Military Policeman—a twenty-two-year man—until December 1980, when he handed in his uniform and became a full-time author. In the 1980s he began to write his best-selling, multi-reprinted *Necroscope®* series, an 'alleged trilogy', which now runs to seventeen volumes in English, with translations in fourteen countries! Among other literary awards, the author received a Grand Master Award from the World Horror Convention, a Lifetime Achievement Award from the Horror Writers Association, and another Lifetime Achievement Award from the World Fantasy Convention. As for the preceding story: 'A Really Game Boy' was originally written in 1981 but…'Was laid aside and forgotten, and only came to light among a pile of old manuscripts when the editors asked my agent if there was anything available…' With what we imagine is a monstrous grin, Lumley adds: 'Now we find ourselves wondering what else may be in there—"rotting down", as it were—among those old manuscripts…'

(MELODRAMA)

David J. Schow

MONSTROUS, WAS THE countenance staring back from the mirror at Robert Blake. Its colourless mat of hair resembled a scrap of shag throw in which rats had nested. A glob of scar tissue occluding the left eye had stratified into layers, like wax melting floorwards, to fuse with the cheekbone due south of a black eye-patch. There was beard stubble and burn-flesh and gapped, rotten teeth; spider-webs were hung up in the hair and lingered on the funereal clothing. The left shoulder drooped to accommodate some spinal inadequacy, and a shabby three-quarter cloak failed to conceal or contour the hump that bulged there, like some failed, half-metastasised twin.

Robert Blake smiled, and the monster smiled back. It was all part of what had become a personal, private ritual. He did the Gravely Grimace. Maybe some more blackout stick for the teeth, but overall, not bad for a fifteen-minute job by a non-professional.

Perfect.

Sherry dropped off formatted pages for the prompter and Blake watched her ass in the mirror as she slid sideways into soundstage blackness. The pages were part of the ritual: He would hand over his scrawl on yellow legal sheets (always neatly calved from the notebook perforations, never torn free in haste), she would transcribe his shotgun cursive into machine jive, and her printer would burp out real words in readable English. Nobody used formal script style for a gig such as this. In the half-hour before they got the use of the stage, she would drop off his so-called 'script' without a word; her silent delivery, in turn, helped Robert Blake, program director of KMAQ-TV (and her boss), ease into the persona of Gravely, late-night host of that station's *Friday Night at the Frights*—a more blatantly avuncular role which permitted all sorts of safe, de-fanged innuendo between them, as sort of a private fringe-benefit never incorporated into his job summary.

He doubted whether Sherry could ever appreciate the subtlety of their relationship-by-default. He paused to ponder, instead, whether her brassieres appeared several sizes too small on purpose; whether that low-slung, saucy lope was unconscious or calculated. She was quite the anatomical master-work, despite being a gum cracker and what was called a 'bottle blonde' in the 1950s. Her mien and manner screamed *sex* no matter what she actually intended or did. She was at least thirty years younger than Robert, yet still over two inches taller. The *concept* of women bigger than him was still a pleasant surprise. His late wife, Marion, had remained a neat five-one until the cancer had shrunken, then stolen her…about the time sweet Sherry Malone had been celebrating her sweet sixteen.

Had Sherry been a virgin at sixteen? Was anyone still unplucked at that advanced age, any more?

Eyes in the mirror. Contacts are too uncomfortable, too costly. The nose is fake; he had bought the very first one mail-order. Later jazzed up in latex by a kid whose ambition was to change the world with make-up effects—fired, long ago. Robert had not seen the boy's credit anywhere lately. Ever.

His wobble had always been a mimic of poor old Karloff's arthritic gait. Awaiting him onstage was a two-camera set-up a handbreadth shy of local access. Sherry usually loitered long enough to see Gravely do his stuff for another week. She never watched the movies. Reverie on that topic was like a foreign language to her.

Wilson, at Camera One, handed him his cigarette in its trademark long-stem holder. Show intro was a bit of tape featuring clay animation of a zombie-looking critter clawing its way out of a mulchy plot. When the camera went live, Wilson would reach around and slide back a foreground model gate with gargoyles on it. It was on top of a stack of milk crates right in front of the lens. Through the viewfinder—and onscreen—the POV would appear to push into the cemetery set as an *enormous* iron gate withdrew to frame left; it was cheesy but effectively atmospheric, and sound effects helped sell it. Above them, in the spider-web of the light rigging, a KMAQ gofer named Will Folke waited to drop a prop tentacle, his historical precedent being Groucho's duck on *You Bet Your Life*. The teleprompter began to scroll Sherry's rearranged text. On the cue, Robert was gone and Gravely, cradling a real film can, was live-on-tape, in a world where he knew monsters personally, and whatever outlandish supernatural pun he uttered, referenced something real.

(*roll / gate / cue Gravely*)

'According to my ghost-writer's his-and-hearse horror-scope—he's in the spook-of-the-month club, don't you know—our venue this week is drama. No, not the living ends of a fairly grim tale, like *Jerk the Giant Killer*, or a game-show like *Tooth or Consequences*, but a classic—you know, like *Sales of a Deathman*.'

(*cackle / puff cigarette*)

'We received tonight's fright feast C.O.D.—Corpse on Delivery. Part of the die-nasty of some son-of-a-witch who slipped me this philtre-tip.'

(*puff / cue Will F. / tentacle uncoils from the ceiling / sign on tentacle reads: NOT ME / Gravely Grimace*)

'No, Dora dearest—not you.'

(*pat tentacle / tentacle retreats*)

'Before you could say, "dig that crazy grave," I become the soul proprietor of an edifice complex.'

(*pat nearby tombstone / muffled voice says: 'LET ME OUT!'*)

'Tonight, haunters of the dark, I would love to show you Lon Chaney, Jr. in *The Wolf Man*…but that never had the chance of a ghost. I'm the man who cried wolf.'

(*fling film can / OS 'crash' / Stump howls*)

'But it's the play that's the thing, as some Brit once said, eh, Stump? And our play is also the Thing—*The Thing That Wouldn't Die*, dug up for your midnight pleasure here on *Friday Night at the Frights*.'

(*puff* / *Gravely Grimace* / DISSOLVE *to bumper*)

He squinted past the glare of key lights aimed at his face, past the boundaries of Gravely's domain, this gutter-budget boneyard of *papier-mâché*. Past Wilson, and Camera One. They'd sail through the whole routine a second time, top to bottom, half an hour from now, which was how they managed cutaways with only one cameraman. Sherry had already left.

By the time they wrapped, it was past eleven thirty. And, while they had not been looking, Robert Blake and Gravely had missed two decades and change, and all of a sudden the fans of films fantastic, or horrific, or science fictional had become much younger—a generation of such youth that *Star Wars* was both a watershed and a fond memory of early childhood, a vast crowd who could access obscure movies via rental tape or cable or dish, and conduct searches for rarities on something called the Internet. Unseen, they *watched*, staring at screens for everything important to them, to whom Gravely's antique medicine show was a curiosity, a byte of pop kitsch to be ridiculed and forgotten by people to whom the TV tripe of the 1960s counted as nostalgia, or worse, culture.

'I can still remember when we actually got the movies shipped in on reels,' Wilson told him, during their post-show ritual of shots in the imaginary graveyard. Robert, in Gravely drag, sat on one side of an enormous fake sepulchre engraved with the name TALBOT. Most of Gravely's repertoire was spun from behind this prop, which provided a 'surface' to fill the bottom of the frame and permitted him to produce or exhibit other wild bits of business. Just now, it made an excellent bar. Wilson poured Old Crow into paper cups. No ice, no water; everything beyond the phoney cemetery gate of balsa wood and spray-paint was, give or take, straight-up. 'Getting those Mexican cheapies from the film rental joints for fifteen bucks a feature. Tossing up a PLEASE STAND BY card while we spliced the breaks in the film manually.'

'Jesus,' Robert muttered, Gravely. 'What I remember was that *The Brainiac* held the all-time record for on-air breaks—'

Wilson finished the line for him: '—because the reels were full of hot glue splices that had dried out and turned to brown dust that looked a lot like heroin. It got all over the projection bed.' He smoothed his palm back over the dome of his head until he hit what little hair he had left. Robert could only see the whites of scoop lamps, sharply reflected in the lozenge-shaped lenses of Wilson's glasses. Wilson was the only person at KMAQ-TV who still wore new plaid shirts, and two innovations of the 1970s to which he had really cottoned were hi-tech running shoes (for work) and fanny packs worn front-wise (for gear related to work). He held in his free hand a VHS cassette—the air-check of tonight's taping, cut as a regular courtesy to Robert. 'You know, I wouldn't take away tapes and laserdiscs and cable and all of it from anybody. But you know something?' He waved the cassette; Robert's eyes followed its arc. '*This* is too damned easy.'

'I like movies,' said Robert, sipping. 'Moreover, I like film. I mean the actual printed film-stock. Spooled on reels. Any gauge. I like looking at reels of film, whether they're being projected or not. I enjoy holding the damned reels, Wilson. They have weight and substance, a heft that suggests what you're holding is not just a representation of a movie—like a book of plot synopses, or that videotape—but the movie itself. Every foot of every 16-millimetre film contains three little pictures per inch; forty per foot. Presume a ninety-minute movie and that's somewhere in the neighbourhood of 130,000 tiny photographs, and you can hold each one of them up to the light and see it without the help of a videocassette player, which is basically an interpreter of rust…that is, iron oxide particles stuck on plastic.'

'Like I said,' said Wilson, toasting semi-obliviously. 'Too damned easy.'

'I am attempting, my good man, to elucidate a passion most irrational and increasingly obscure, yet not without arguable merit.' He burped softly; the whiskey burned in his gorge.

'Thank you, Gravely.'

'You know, people are going to look at old movies a hundred years from now and be totally lost. They won't comprehend *Frankenstein* because they won't be able to see what product the movie was pushing. What line of toys. What action figure.'

'Know what happened to the stock-in-trade of your scare show, since the bad old days?'

'Do tell. No puns, please.'

'It all got legitimate.' Wilson paused in his pronouncement long enough to pour new doubles and encompass Gravely Manor and the Gravely Grounds with a sweep of his hand. 'All this. Monster movies. Scary actors. Special effects. Cruise your ass over to World Book and News and check out how many individual magazines there are on aliens and monsters and recycled serial junk from the dawn of cinema time.' He performed the expansive gesture again, looking rather lordly. 'It got legit. What was once fringe has now been assimilated, my friend, into the mainstream. And lo, there shall come forth a day when even Gravely—much as I love him—won't be able to compete with some bimbo in Vampira drag with deep-dish cleavage and double scoops.

'So get over it.'

'Doom-crier,' Gravely said, gravely.

'Simple truth, then,' Wilson countered. 'You know how they're always saying that ninety per cent of the movies made during the Silent Era don't even exist any more? They're dust; goo and nitrate flecks.'

'They died in the great plague,' said Gravely. 'Latin name, *autocatalytic nitrocellulose* decomposition. Vinegar sickness.'

'People *expect* silent films to be ancient history, like Roman ruins. But half the films made before 1950 *don't exist* any more, and that's strident, but it's a fact. Every collector enjoys the delusion that they are insurance against apocalypse. That's why you hang on; it's the way one rationalises any collecting obsession—the gentle lie that you are the last hope, the only one who genuinely cares.'

'Except, in my case, I don't have the collection to prove it.'

'It's there.' Wilson pointed at Gravely's head. 'In your case, it isn't a physical thing, or quantifiable, but it exists because you keep it alive, and I help you do it.'

'I was wondering why we enact this desperate pageant every week, unto death.' Robert was joking, of course. 'My slang is dated, my references

outmoded, and my only cheer is in the thought that the same fate will befall everything that's new *this* year.'

'I thought you were just a plain, ordinary guy who likes to scare the hell out of people.'

'I no longer *scare* anyone, dear boy. Not in an age of slash-and-bash, slice-and-dice, rut-and-cut, chew-and-spew.'

'For you, it's a love of art. You'd be lost without your work.'

'Correction: *Art* is too highfalutin a word, and *work* is too low-brow. I love *craft*. There's a difference.'

It was all part of the ritual, such talk between them after shows. Two men in the process of ageing beyond their youthful exuberance, trying to figure out how to ride the waves that crashed towards them. Generally, Wilson wrapped first, pleading wife, kids, chores, the obligations of the day-to-day, leaving Robert, as Gravely, to kill the last lingering lights, prime the alarms, and lock down. Just a back-end task performed by rote by any other programming director moonlighting as the station's resident ghoul emcee. It was Robert's habit to sit quietly in the imaginary cemetery by himself, expending his store of contemplation points in (you should pardon the expression) grave reflection. Funny—he always removed the Gravely make-up and costume last. Every time.

Tonight, when Wilson slapped on his ball-cap and bid the empty stage *adieu*, he joked about how maybe Robert should clear a space in his living room for that big TALBOT tombstone soon…for the second time. Once, it was a rib. Twice, and it was some kind of obscure point *maybe* Wilson would get around to the specifying in the next week or so…*if* Robert was wily enough to ask the right question, the right way.

Robert finished his whiskey and scrutinised the monument. He could see the flaking seams and patches of paint-over. Black-and-white would not have forced it to pass such severe muster. A drum of the fingertips would betray it as hollow, untenanted. The moony pall of his good-old-days reveries lingered suffocatingly, thick as Spanish moss on a humid evening. Moving through Gravely by rote had begun to leave a repellent tang of decay in his mouth. Wilson was gone. Sherry had left the building. Will F. the tentacle-boy and

that nameless make-up maven were history. Robert Blake felt like spitting. Instead, he would lumber home and pop a sleeping pill, which was the only way he could guarantee himself more than twenty minutes of uninterrupted slumber. Each day was an arc of pills, from the round headache tablets in the morning, to the medications and vitamins taken with or without meals, and terminating in two oval sleeping pills at bedtime. Pills dried a person out. Perhaps that was why he could work up no spit.

He decided to answer the letter he had received. Just one; the only component of his end-of-week mail stack that did not bear a corporate return address or a cellophane window. The correspondent was one Master John Sheldon, aged eleven, and he was writing to thank Gravely for showing *I Married a Monster from Outer Space* two weeks ago, and that movies that weren't in colour were sometimes pretty good.

Oh, yes, and did Gravely have an email address?

According to custom, Master John Sheldon would receive an autographed Gravely 8x10 and a hand-written note on Gravely stationery. The task was not that time-consuming; very few fan letters came in at all these days. What Robert needed was some way for Gravely to thank this young stranger for the note of hope on which he had closed—time marched on, and there were still some people who believed in the romantic, and kids weren't all aliens, and sometimes movies in black-and-white could be, well, pretty good.

Robert flicked on lights as he returned to his office, unconsciously maintaining the lop-sided Gravely gait. It was so quiet the fluoro-tubes could be heard to hum. He slotted this week's air-check onto the bookshelf with its fellows. The tapes bore a long-standing down of dust on their top edges; they had lived on the shelf for years, rarely played back. In the file drawer of Gravely stuff he discovered that the folder of 8x10s was empty. He had mailed off the last one a long time back—so long that if he were to order another 100 printed, the dent would probably hit his own pocket.

There were clippings in that drawer, stirred in amid crumpled promo posters, press releases, and the odd film clip—the whole history of a cadaverous wiseass named Gravely, from the heyday of the Screen Gems *Shock Theatre* package in the late 1950s, to the last gasp period, late 1970s, when

the nation's eccentric, weird and just plain regional TV horror hosts dropped out of sight more quickly than shooting-gallery wildlife. Born amid shameless hype, Gravely and his fellows were an anachronistic hangover, ill-designed to outlast the explosion of microchip media. Robert Blake understood evolution, especially natural selection.

In the eyes of someone like the ebullient Sherry, he thought, *all* his days were halcyon. No wonder she had left. Nobody relishes hanging around a funeral when the ghoul is bombing. The world had no need for him as a repository of classic fright-film lore; his goldmine of myth had petered into common coin. Even Wilson could see it.

He wanted to pretend that Master John Sheldon's fan letter was a message from the past—a telegram bearing special powers from a time that mattered.

There came a thud on the office door, accompanied by a clotted voice: '*Master!*'

Robert tried to stand and turn all at once, but his hump constricted him. He had been genuinely startled since, as had been established by the worst of slasher-flicks, he was supposed to be alone. He smiled the first honest smile of the night. *How about that; I'm having the horror movie host version of a 'Nam flashback.*

'*Master!*'

It was impossible not to recollect the character of Stump, since Stump seemed to be speaking to him from the distant past. Stump was a fur-ball, one of the tamer breeds of lycanthrope, pudgy, savvy enough to cross the street if the traffic wasn't too fast, rather like Michael Landon's Teenage Werewolf in the wake of a decade of bad chow (Gravely Train, of course) and two of senescence, utterly devoted to Gravely's needs yet only capable of fulfilling entry-level monster sidekick duties. If there was a gruesome gag to be had at someone's expense, the all-purpose butt was always Stump, so-called because of the bear-trap incident. His right hand was a big coat-hook attached to a leather wristlet, and yes, Stump had chewed off his own hand after waking up that night in Tijuana with a brand-new wife-wolf.

Stump had been portrayed on *Friday Night at the Frights* by Jim Kjelgaard, by day a KMAQ accountant whose deep operatic basso kept him in *à la carte* announcing gigs, as well. If you had ever heard a KMAQ public service announcement, then you had experienced Jim at his most resonant. Stump had been phased out in June of '78, during the budget tightening. Kjelgaard had moved to Hawaii and, as far as Robert knew, was still using his voice to make a living.

'*Master!*' *Thud-thud-thud.*

It was so much like the old routine that Robert automatically responded in the Gravely voice. 'Oh, who goes there, a wolf?'

'Not there-wolf, Master. *Were*-wolf!'

'Were? Ware?'

'Right here, Master.'

'Oh, what is it, you flea-bitten nincompoop?!' Automatically, the corn was flying.

The door was nosed open, and there stood Stump in his perpetual half-crouch, as though undecided between biped and quadruped. 'Master! I have it! I have brought it for you!' Stump held out a stack of linen-grain writing note-cards emblazoned with the Gravely Crest. 'For the epistle you so needed to dispatch!'

'For christ sake,' Gravely muttered, still in character. 'Who sent you—Wilson or Sherry?' He stopped, focused his eyes on the surface of the desk, and when he looked up, Stump was still there, dammitall. 'Epistle?'

Stump cocked his head and scratched, using his hook gingerly. A flea popped. 'You needed paper, Master. And the photographs.' From his lupine armpit Stump shook an equivalent stack of fresh Gravely glossies.

Standing up abruptly forced a plunging vertigo to slam through Gravely's eyes and sinuses. How much of Wilson Kane's Old Crow had he pounded down? It was never in his interest to actually count shots. Don't drink and jive. He steadied himself against the desk and succeeded in making the action resemble an executive point-making gesture. 'Look—'

Stump went *yipe*, turned tail, and fled in a cloud of floating stationery and photos.

Robert was disgusted. It didn't even make sense as a practical joke; the punch line was not pushing its spoilage date so much as dragging it. He

yanked the door open, expecting a *boo!* and getting none. 'Come *on*,' he said, more to establish presence than ask questions.

The cemetery and Gravely Grounds were full of fog. He could see the vapour swirls of Stump's hasty passage towards Gravely Manor. The fog was damp, but it did not have the distinct odour of the CO2 stuff.

All right, Gravely thought. *Actual real fog has invaded our stage. Accidentally.*

Three steps in, he added: *Keep your wits. You don't know everything. You can be tricked.*

Stump was capering in little wee-wee circles before the iron (plywood) door of the Film Vault (styro veneer and spray ageing). 'It's time, Master, it's time! Time to choose!'

The normal show routine would have Gravely selecting some sterling-silver horror classic—*Frankenstein*, say, with all the cut footage restored. He would hold the film can to his breast, sigh wistfully…then toss the movie aside—(*crash*)—in favour of some spool of schlock that classified as a movie only because it had sprocket holes and used up ninety minutes of air-time. At the off-screen impact of the discarded classic, Stump would always howl.

Since its inception, this gag had been Gravely's backhanded dig at KMAQ, which would rarely budget for monster movies of genuine pedigree. Instead, Gravely's imaginary Film Vault filled up with the leftovers of barter deals and low-end booking. It had not been much different in 1957, when the first *Shock* package of Universal Studios' horror films had been unleashed. Over 600 of the studio's pre-1948 films went hunting for TV adoption, and to get the scary stuff an enterprising programmer had to eat a generous portion of turkey. Just the year before, a TV broadcast of *King Kong* pulled in viewership at a whopping ninety per cent of the people who owned television sets. The *Chiller Theatre*-style shows that sprang up in response to the *Shock* and *Son of Shock* film packages could have *Dracula*, *The Mummy* and *Man-Made Monster*…if they also took *Sealed Lips*, *Destination Unknown* and *Danger Woman*.

Gravely's joke on KMAQ had been to first name the film he would *prefer* to screen, then plod onwards with the business of what he was *forced* to screen, whatever creature feature they'd been able to dig up for cheap *that* week.

Stump eagerly pushed open the vault door, which shrieked on corroded hinges—a sound effect Robert Blake had selected and dubbed personally.

Had he promised to dance this dance for someone's birthday, was that it? Certainly never on the for-real set; there were insurance risks to consider. Maybe it was *his* birthday, that was the gag, and everyone was going to leap from the fog and scream surprise, causing him to remember that it was actually his anniversary or something. Maybe Sherry would slither up from a cake, wearing only diet frosting and sprinkles.

'Master! Time to choose!' Stump danced around. Up close he smelled, well, like a wet police dog needing a bath and breath-freshening biscuits. Gravely's eyes itched. He sneezed, once, twice, concussively. He had not suffered an allergic reaction this strong and swift since Marion's boxer, Lefty. Lefty had last made Robert Blake sneeze a very long time ago.

The whiskey was still stroking the furrows in his brain, permitting him to indulge whatever madness this might be. But it had just crossed over into being irritating.

'Look, Stump, or is it…it can't be Jim Kjelgaard, I mean, whoever you are—'

Gravely got an eyeful of what was revealed when Stump swung the Film Vault door full back, squeak and all. He executed a mid-course correction in his speech: '—holy fucking *christ*, what have we got here?'

This made Stump jolly. He proceeded to doggy-dance around the interior of the Vault…

…which was lined with cubist ranks and files of films, films on reels, well-maintained and labelled films on reels. *Good* films, on reels. *Attack of the Mushroom People* and *The Strange Island of Dr Nork* were nowhere to be glimpsed, even by accident.

'This wasn't here.' Under normal circumstances, the Film Vault was a false front with just enough room for Gravely or Stump to reach inside. It had no interior; it ended a foot short of the background cyclorama for the cemetery, which featured a painting of Gravely Manor in the far distance, at the end of a winding uphill path dotted with tilting headstones.

'Always was here,' countered Stump, who cringed at the appropriate moment. Best not to contradict the Master. 'You are the Master! Only you

choose!' Stump waved his hook towards the film racks, which looked to be mahogany, and twelve feet high. The gesture reminded him of Wilson's, in another life. 'You give them a home, take care of them, only you, like you take care of Stump!'

Gravely was ignoring his mascot, gazing at the spines of the film cans. He extracted one. No corrosion. Not a whiff of vinegar sickness. In black ink, in a steady hand—the way his handwriting *used* to look—was the title: *London After Midnight*. It was on two big 2000-foot reels and one smaller pick-up reel. Gravely slid it back.

Odd.

Since entering the Film Vault he had not looked back, nor bothered to reassure himself of his own passage into this hallucinatory state. Now he turned around. Where Camera One had been an hour earlier was now just a tombstone, and more fog. He could not recall passing either camera. When he looked up he saw no lights and no rigging. Just a full moon, costumed in cirrocumulus.

The next logical conclusion at which a man like Robert Blake would arrive was: *I've tipped over, or, in Gravely-speak, I'm marble-less. I've gone insane and out-sane.*

Time-delay extrapolation slapped him in the side of the head. *London After Midnight* was a silent. No way KMAQ would ever permit it to be shown...not even with a laugh track.

He shook his head. Stump had apparently lit off to pee on Dora the Tentacle's prop tree.

Being intended for short hauls only, Gravely's patience was already down to fumes. Normally, the mystery resurgence of Stump would have already used up most of an entire show.

Gravely's weekly assignment was to occupy ten minutes per show, which in theory left ninety minutes for the movie and twenty for commercials. When KMAQ decided to bunk-bed the ad blocs during each half-hour bridge (after ten p.m. nobody gave an honest damn about ratings and focus polls), they cut Gravely down to five minutes per show for *everything*—intro, outro, shtick and viewer mail, plus a set of bumpers to book-end the

commercials. If that wasn't enough, then the movies were easy to shave. Ridiculously easy.

Apart from Stump and Folke, the tentacle operator, the closest the show got to actual guest appearances could be counted on two fingers. In early 1974, Forrest J Ackerman had done a walk-on, toting an issue of *Famous Monsters of Filmland* featuring the Creature from the Black Lagoon on the cover. In 1976, Jim Kjelgaard had busted his leg, and so for four shows in a row his Stump duties were handled by an East Coast monster delinquent named Jarvis; Gravely could not recall a first name. On the spot they conceived the twisted saga of Stump's courtly cousin, Count Ludarca, supposedly a bluesman from the Transylvania bayous. They coasted the rest of the way, gooning Lugosi.

Then whatsisname-Jarvis lit back to New York to endure some sort of comic book job, and *Friday Night at the Frights* commenced its twilight period.

'Enough.'

That was remotely decisive. It was too easy, to get lost in the maze of past events; too easy to distract his attention from the precipitous weirdness of Stump, bounding out of the past to dog him. He marched towards the head of the cemetery path—down-frame, cameras or no—repeating 'enough' to himself, keeping his eyes on his feet and the tamped earth of the trail.

He almost collided with the flagstone wall, which had not been there before, either. The only place there had ever been such a wall was in the imagination of Robert Blake, when idealising how the Gravely Grounds would look, given proper funding. This wall was supposed to lead to a vast mausoleum, where Gravely was known to picnic. If memory served, the concept included a vaulted arch of skulls, decorated with bone grotesques.

Inside, he found a corridor of marble, dark, cool, monochromatic. One of the plaque-stones at eye level read:

COLLIER YOUNG
HE SCREWED UP BIG-TIME

He remembered when he had first proposed that inscription for one of the foamcore tombstones on the Gravely Grounds. KMAQ had shot him down on the grounds that 'screwed up' was invective too harsh for what the affiliate considered a kiddie show. Next from on high would come the objection that Gravely's smoking sent a bad message to the kids. That was the sort of anal, blinkered complaint could burrow beneath the skin of his conscience, to fester. It was all kid stuff, no matter how it was dressed up. Wilson had been right about its legitimisation; the youngsters who liked it simply grew up and found a civilised way to hang onto it—the imprimatur of camp. All through the 1960s, the tale had been different. Monsters were sub-par entertainment, derided as spook-fests, always cited with that knowing elbow-to-the-ribs. *TV Guide* listings told the tale whenever it sub-headed Gravely's weekly offerings not as drama, horror, thriller or suspense, but as melodrama—meaning extravagant theatricality, plot and physical action over characterisation, sensational trifles aiming for the gut rather than the head. Such flip categorisations caused a special alchemy to start bubbling away, independently, in its own secret corner, where responsible grown-ups could not watchdog. It happened when that word, *melodrama*, suddenly shape-shifted to mean *monster movies*. If you were a kid reading any programme listing and your eyes skidded past that magic word, you knew without looking further that you had hit pay dirt.

Gravely heard noise from the far end of the mausoleum. A clanking of chain-links echoed, a soft, almost porcelain sound.

Scrolled, wrought stanchions held black tapers. Gravely lifted the nearest one to see.

Sherry, she of the Ilona Massey bosom and endless legs, goddess of watermelon-flavoured sugarless gum and lipstick-by-the-pound, was shackled to the far wall, clad in the nightgowny rags of a serial heroine after about four chapters of thrills. Her artfully-shredded clothing was precariously close to non-existent.

'Oh, Master, it's you, Stump told me you would come, you never forget your Lenore, I'm so happy, you don't know how happy I am, how I look forward to your visits.'

Whatever else cascaded through his mind at that moment, it was handily conquered by this clear vision of a woman in heat.

'Sherry—' He faltered. Bad form. Try to be strong. 'Eh… Sherry, this is way beyond what either of us would call irregular—'

'Sherry, yes!' she overrode him. 'I'll be Sherry for you tonight. Any name! Just promise me the cat, after the movie!'

'The—*what?*'

'And the leather paddles, yes, and promise your Sherry you'll use the quirt and the signal whip! Save the strop for my ass, and I'm yours, darling!'

It was totally berserk, but so was the erection inside his spacious Gravely trousers. The temperature in the mausoleum seemed to be skyrocketing. Hot wax from the candle stung his wrist. Pheromones were zizzing around his system like bubbles in seltzer, dissolving his inhibitions in fast-forward.

'Master! The movie! The movie!' It was Stump, back at the arch with a film can crooked against his hook.

Gravely turned and shuffled towards the arch, imagining his enrobed penis slicing through the heavy atmosphere like the prow of a clipper through choppy seas. 'Can't you see I'm *busy*, dog breath?!'

Stump flinched. 'Yes, Master! But they're all waiting.' He numbly indicated something outside.

'Get out of my way.' He shoved past Stump, who was accustomed to the casual abuse. He looked out into the cemetery. In terms of the extremely limited set, he would be looking roughly from the Camera Two position towards the Gravely Manor back-drop, with its painted extension of the cemetery.

He saw thousands and thousands of headstones. No, not headstones, but *heads*—a whole Woodstock of milling people seen only in shadow, but for the calm glow of their waiting eyes. The crowd began in the darkness beyond the Film Vault, stretched unbroken to the top of the hill, and kept going, like all the armies of Rome on standby, all awaiting him.

Gravely's first response was to recoil. He took an involuntary backwards step, away from the mausoleum. Conceivably, he could just limp away double-time, if not run like hellfire. But the gate was closed. It was solid wrought iron, and the topmost spikes jutted five feet higher than he could reach on tiptoe. The gargoyles were full-sized, as menacing as his conception of them had originally been.

He moved for the TALBOT sepulchre from which all of his presentations had emanated. Even though he was on the opposite side, facing the wrong way, it felt right and spurred his courage. It had always been his rock, his anchor.

'Unholy smokes!' he belted out. 'I won't say the movies are in a bad way, but Garland has wilted, John has waned, and Andy's no longer very Hardy, either. Tonight's fear-feast might have been the immortal—' he paused to peer at the film can Stump had handed off—'*Thanksgiving VII*—so called because it's the sequel to six other turkeys. The producer lit off to Bermuda to make some shorts, and in view of the cow flops he squeezes out, we can only hope the future is better than the pasture!' He flung the film can in the prescribed manner, and Stump jitterbugged when it splashed down and was engulfed by quickmud.

Vamping here, now, was no more difficult than the average *a cappella* personal appearance at some supermarket opening, and he had sailed through plenty of *those* during his tenure. Dora's tentacle dropped in at the appropriate moment for Gravely to deploy the 'tree's a crowd' gag.

Right on cue, Stump slammed the big Strickfaden knife-switch home. Contact. Blue neon sparks leapt away from the prongs as an unseen projector started to grind celluloid. A fan of mote-laden light sprayed over the multitude, and every single head turned to watch it. Comparisons to religious mob behaviour were unavoidable.

Stump panted. Gravely saw him at ease near the sepulchre, as though awaiting the command to sit.

'Who are they?'

'Master?'

He gestured. 'All of them. Those watchers in the darkness.'

Stump shrugged exaggeratedly, inadequate to the demands of plot arcs or pinpoint irony. 'They just come.'

'Why?'

Stump brightened. Here was something he could answer. 'Because of… that!' He pointed at the projection light with something like beatific idiocy

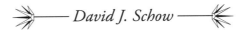

softening the point of his snout. His hook indicated the Film Vault. 'Because Master is the only one who…you are the keeper. Only you.'

Stump was mesmerised by the flicker, the only kind of light that would ever matter in a realm such as this. Gravely took advantage of his distraction to snatch his hook, which came free like a leather chap off a wooden leg.

'Master!' Stump instantly cowered, his furry arms crossed before his face. At the end of one was a black-nailed were-hand. Only one.

'Sorry, Stump, it's okay.' Fortunately, as well as his other canine attributes, Stump had the guilt-span of a puppy, and by the time Gravely had reattached the hook and patted him on the head—which cost him another wet sneeze—all feelings were bandaged. 'It's all right, boy.'

He leaned against the rough granite, graven with TALBOT for as long as he could remember, and, for the first time in quite a long time, he was fulfilled and content. Yonder waited Lenore. But Gravely still had a performance to get out of the way.

He returned to the office and took his seat before the mirror. This was a private ritual for him—the way he sat, the order in which his cosmetics remained arranged from the previous session, the mirror he promised himself he would wipe clean before the next time.

He re-did his nose with care. Spirit gum was used to attach it, then he smeared a base-coat for the preliminary blends. Unlike his earlier application, this was no fifteen-minute quickie. The custom-made dentures had to be specially bonded. Once his wig was affixed, he combed loose strands to hide the clips. He stowed the long-stemmed cigarette holder in a jewellery drawer.

Perfect.

Then he rose, just as the sun was doing likewise, to be the first person into work, as Robert Blake, programme director of KMAQ-TV.

DAVID J. SCHOW is a multiple-award-winning West Coast writer. The latest of his ten novels is a hardboiled extravaganza called *The Big Crush*, while the newest of his ten short story collections is a 'greatest hits' anniversary compendium titled *DJStories*. He has been a contributor to Storm King Comics' *John Carpenter's Tales for a Halloween Night* since its very first issue, and in 2018 Storm King released his five-issue series for *John Carpenter's Tales of Science Fiction: The Standoff*. Schow has written extensively for movies (*The Crow, Leatherface: Texas Chainsaw Massacre III, The Hills Run Red*) and television (*Masters of Horror, Mob City, Creepshow*). His non-fiction works include *The Art of Drew Struzan* and *The Outer Limits at 50*. He can be seen on various DVDs and Blu-rays as expert witness or documentarian, on everything from *Creature from the Black Lagoon* to *Psycho* and *I, Robot*, not to mention the Rondo- and Saturn Award-winning discs of *The Outer Limits* (Seasons 1 and 2) from Kino-Lorber. Thanks to him, the word 'splatterpunk' has been in the *Oxford English Dictionary* since 2002. About his contribution to this anthology, the author says: '(Melodrama)' is dedicated to Jeff Rovin, my friend of some forty-five years, and owes its existence to a number of others, some of them imaginary—Robert Downey, Hattie the Witch, Tom Weaver, Dennis Daniel, Jeepers Keeper, John Bloom, John Stanley, Bob Stephens, Vincent Di Fate, Jack Jacobsen, Bill Warren, and kindly, loveable Dr Scar. Grateful acknowledgement is also made to Elena M. Watson's *Television Horror Movie Hosts* (McFarland & Co., 1991). The story also provides the third act to a trilogy written over an eight-year period. The two previous pieces investigating variants on the same arc are 'Monster Movies' (1988, published in *Lost Angels*) and 'Last Call for the Sons of Shock' (1990, in *The Mammoth Book of Frankenstein*). But most of all, those who pay attention to what they read will realise that this story belongs to Robert Bloch (1917–94) as well. Besides the obvious referents (all

the players except Gravely himself being named after Bloch's assorted pseudonyms and alter-egos) or the abstract homages (think *structure),* much of Bloch's cunning punnage, from story rides to odd quotations, has been worked into (or wreaked upon) the dialogue directly.'

TO THIS WATER
(JOHNSTOWN, PENNSYLVANIA 1889)

Caitlín R. Kiernan

HARDLY DAWN, AND already Magda had made her way through the forest into the glittering frost at the foot of the dam. When the sun climbed high enough, it would push aside the shadows and set the hollow on fire, sparkling crystal fire that would melt gently in the late spring sunrise and drip from hemlock and aspen branches, glaze the towering thickets of mountain laurel, later rise again as gauzy soft steam. Everything, ice-crisped ferns and everything else, crunched beneath her shoes, loud in the cold, still air; no sound but morning birds and the steady gush from the spillway into South Fork Creek, noisy and secretive, like careless whispers behind her back.

Winded, her breath puffing out white through chapped lips and a stitch nagging her side, she rested a moment against a potato-shaped boulder, and the moss there frost-stiffened too, ice-matted green fur and grey lichens like scabs. Back down the valley towards South Fork, night held on, a lazy thing curled in the lee of the mountain. Magda shivered and pulled her shawl tighter about her shoulders.

All the way from Johnstown since nightfall, fifteen miles or more since she'd slipped away from the darkened rows of company houses on Prospect Hill, following the railroad first and later, after the sleeping streets of South Fork, game trails and finally the winding creek, yellow-brown and swollen with the runoff of April thaw and heavy May rains. By now her family would be awake, her father already gone to the mill and twelve hours at the furnaces, her mother and sister neglecting chores and soon they would be asking from house to house, porches and back doors.

But no one had seen her go, and there would be nothing but concerned and shaking heads, shrugs and suspicion for their questions and broken English. And when they'd gone, there would be whispers, like the murmur and purl of mountain streams.

As the sky faded from soft violet, unbruising, Magda turned and began to pick her way up the steep and rocky face of the dam.

———

THIS IS NOT memory, this is a pricking new thing, time knotted, cat's cradled or snarled like her sister's brown hair and she is always closing her eyes, always opening them again and always the narrow slit of sky is red, wound red slash between the alley's black walls and rooftops, pine and shingle jaws. And there is nothing left of the men but calloused, groping fingers, the scalding whiskey soursweetness of their breath. Sounds like laughter from dog throats and the whiskery lips of pigs, dogs and pigs laughing if they could.

And Magda does not scream, because they have said that if she screams, if she cries or even speaks they will cut her tongue out, will cut her hunkie throat from ear to ear and she knows that much English. And the big Irishman has shown her his knife, they will all show her their knives, and cut her whether she screams or not.

The hands pushing and she turns her face away, better the cool mud, the water puddled that flows into her mouth, fills her nostrils, that tastes like earth and rot and the alcohol from empty barrels and overflowing crates of bottles stacked high behind the Washington Street saloon. She grinds her teeth, crunching grit, sand sharp against her gums.

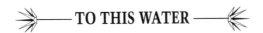

And before she shuts her eyes, last thing before there is only raw pain and the sounds she won't ever shut out, Magda catches the dapper man watching from the far away end of the alley, surprised face peering down the well. Staring slack-jawed and light from somewhere safe glints coldly off his spectacles, moonlight on thin ice.

The demons growl and he scuttles away and they fold her open like a cockleshell.

———

BY THE WAVERING orange oil light, her mother's face had glowed warm, age and weariness softened almost away, and she had been speaking to them in Magyar, even though Papa said that they'd never learn that way. And she had leaned over them, brushing her sister Emilia's hair from her face. Her mother had set the lamp carefully down on the wobbly little table beside their bed, herself in the wobbly chair, and it had still been winter then, still dirty snow on the ground outside, the wind around the pine-board corners of the house, howling for its own misfortunes. And them bundled safe beneath quilts and rag-swaddled bricks from the hearth at their feet.

Magda had watched the shadows thrown across the walls, bare save for knotholes stuffed with old newspapers and the crucifix her mother had brought across from Budapest, blood-dark wood and tortured pewter. And the lamp-light had danced as her mother had spoken, had seemed to follow the rise and fall of her words, measured steps in a pattern too subtle for Magda to follow.

So she had closed her eyes tight, buried her face in pillows and Emilia's back, and listened to her mother's stories of childhood in the mountain village of Tatra Lomnitz and the wild Carpathians, listening more to her soothing voice than the words themselves. She knew all the old stories of the house elves, the hairy little *domovoy* that had lived in the dust and sooty corner behind her grandmother's stove, and the river people, the *Vodyaniyie* and *Rusalky;* the comfort her sister drew from the fairy tales, she took directly from the music of timbre and tender intonation.

'And in the autumn,' her mother had said, 'when a fat gander was offered to the people who lived under the lake, we would first cut off its

head and nail it to the barn door so that our *domovoy* would not know that one of his geese had been given away to another.' And then, sometime later, the lamp lifted from the wobbly table and her mother had kissed them both, Magda pretending to sleep, and whispered, her voice softer than the bed, *'Jo ejszakat,'* and her bare footsteps already moving away, sounding hollow on the floor, when Emilia had corrected her, 'Good night, Mama.'

'Good night, Emilia,' her mother had answered and then they had been alone with the night and the wind and the sky outside their window that was never quite black enough for stars, but always stained red from the belching foundry fires of Johnstown.

IT WAS FULL morning by the time Magda reached the top, and her eyes stung with her own sweat and when she licked her lips she tasted her own salt; not blood but something close. Her dress clung wetly to her back, clammy damp armpits, and she'd ripped her skirt and stockings in blackberry briars and creeper vines. Twice she'd slipped on the loose stones and there was a small gash on her left palm, purpling bruise below her thumb. Now she stood a moment on the narrow road that stretched across the breast of the dam, listening to her heart, fleshpump beneath cotton and skin, muscle and bone. Watching the mist, milky wisps curling up from the green-grey water, burning away in the sun.

Up here, the morning smelled clean, pine and the silent lake, no hint of the valley's pall of coal dust or factory smoke. There were clouds drifting slowly in from the south-west, scowling, steelbellied thunderheads, and so the breeze smelled faintly of rain and ozone as well.

Magda stepped across the road, over deep buggy ruts, pressing her own shallow prints into the clay. The pockets of her skirt bulged with the rocks she'd gathered as she climbed, weather-smoothed shale and gritty sandstone cobbles the colour of dried apricots. Four steps across, and on the other side, the bank dropped away sharply, steep, but only a few feet down to water, choked thick with cattails and weeds.

Quickest glance, then, back over her shoulder, not bothering to turn full and play Lot's wife proper. The fire burned *inside* her, scorching, righteous flame shining through her eyes, incapable of cleansing, scarring and salting her brain. And, careful, Magda went down to the cold water.

AND WHEN THEY have all finished with her, each in his turn, when they have carved away at her insides and forced their fat tongues past her teeth and so filled her with their hot seed that it leaks like sea salt pus from between her bloodied thighs, they slosh away through the mud and leave her; not for dead, not for anything but discarded, done with. For a long time, she lies still and watches the sky roiling above the alley, and the pain seems very, very far away, and the red clouds seem so close that if she raises her hand she might touch them, might break their blister-thin skins and feel the oily black rain hiding inside. Gazing up from the pit into the firelight her own Papa stokes so that the demons can walk the streets of Johnstown.

But the demons have kept their promises, and her throat is not sliced ear to ear, and she can still speak, knows this because she hears the animal sounds from her mouth, distant as the pain between her legs. She is not dead, even if she is no longer alive.

'TELL US ABOUT the *Rusalky*, Mama,' her sister had said, and her mother had frowned, looked down at hands folded on her lap like broken wings.

'Nem, Emilia,' her mother had answered firmly, gently, *'Rusalky* is not a good story for bedtime.'

And as her sister pleaded, Magda had sat straightbacked on the edge of the bed, silent, watching the window, watching the red and starless sky, and already, that had been two weeks after the men with the buckboard and the white mare had brought her home, two weeks after her mother had cried and washed away the dirt and blood, the clinging semen. Two weeks since her father had stormed down from Prospect Hill with his deer rifle and had spent a night in jail, had been reminded by the grave-jowled constable that they were, after all, Hungarians, and what with all the talk of the Company taking on bohunkie contract workers, cheap labour depriving honest men with families of decent wages, well, it wouldn't do to look for more trouble, would it? And in the end, he'd said, it would have been the girl's word against anyone he might have brought in, anyway.

In that space of time, days stacked like broken dishes, not a word from Magda and no tears from her dark and empty eyes. When food was pressed to her lips, a spoonful of soup or *gulyas*, she'd eaten, and when the sun went down and the lamps were put out, she had lain with her eyes open, staring through the window at the seething sky.

'Please, Mama, *kérem*,' her sister had whined, whined and Magda turned then, had turned on them so furiously that a slat cracked gunshot-loud beneath the feather mattress. Emilia had cried out, reached for their startled mother. And Magda had pulled herself towards them, hands gone to claws, tetanus snarl and teeth bared like a starving dog. And all that furnace glow gathered, hoarded from the red nights, and spilling from her eyes.

'*Magda, stop this*,' and her mother had pulled Emilia to her, 'you're frightening your sister! You're frightening me!'

'No, Mama. She wants to hear a story about the *Rusalky*, then I will *tell* her about the *Rusalky*. I will *show* her about the *Rusalky*.'

But her mother had stumbled to her feet, too-big Emilia clutched awkwardly in her arms, and the wobbly chair tumbled over and kicked aside. Backing away from the sagging bed and Magda, burning Magda, Emilia's face hidden against her chest. Backing into the shadows crouched in the doorway.

'She wants to hear, Mama, she *wants* to hear my story.'

Her mother had stepped backwards into the hall gloom, had slammed the bedroom door shut behind her, and Magda had heard the key rattle in the lock, bone rattle, death rattle, and then she'd been alone. The oil lamp still bright on the wobbly table, and a train had wailed, passing down in the valley, and when the engineer's whistle and the rattle and throb of boxcars had faded away, there had been only her mother's sobs from the other side of the door and the distant clamour of the mills.

Magda had let the lamp burn, stared a while into its tiny flame haloed safe behind blackened chimney glass, and then she'd turned back to the window, the world outside framed safe within, and she'd held fingers to her mouth and between them whispered her story to the sympathetic night.

ALL THE LOST and pretty suicides, all the girls in deep lakes and swirling rivers, still ponds, drowned or murdered and their bodies secreted in fish-silvered palaces. Souls committed to water instead of consecrated earth, and see her on Holy Thursday, on the flat rocks combing out her long hair, grown green and tangled with algae and eels? See her sitting in the low branches of this willow, bare legs hanging like pale fruit, toes drawing ripples in the stream, and be kind enough this sixth week past Easter to leave a scrap of linen, a patch or rag. Come back, stepping quiet through the tall grass, to find it washed clean and laid to dry beneath the bright May sky.

And there is more, after that, garlands for husbands and the sound of clapping hands from the fields, voices like ice melting, songs like the moment before a dropped stone strikes unseen well water.

Carry wormwood in your pockets, young man, and bathe with a cross around your neck.

Leave her wine and red eggs.

And when she dances under the summer moon, when the hay is tall and her sisters join hands, pray you keep yourself behind locked doors, or walk quickly past the waving wheat; stay on the road, watch your feet.

Or you'll wind up like poor Jozef; remember Jozef, Old Viktor's son? His lips were blue, grain woven in his hair, and how do you think his clothes got wet, so muddy, so far from the river?

And see her there, on the bank beneath the trees, her comb of stickly fish bones? Watch her, as she pulls the sharp teeth through her green hair, and watch the water rise.

THIS IS WHAT *it's like to drown,* Magda thought, *like stirring salt into water,* as she drifted, dissolving, just below the lake, sinking slowly into twilight the colour of dead moss, the stones in her pockets only a little help. Her hair floated, wreathed her face and the last silver bubbles rose from her open mouth, hurrying towards the surface. Just the faintest, dull pressure in her chest, behind her eyes, and a fleeting second's panic, and then there was a quiet more perfect than anything she had ever imagined. Peace folding itself thick around her, driving back the numbing cold and the useless sun filtering down from above, smothering doubt and fear and the crushing regret that had almost made her turn around, scramble back up the slippery bank when the water had closed like molasses around her ankles.

Magda flowed into the water, even as the water flowed into her, and by the time she reached the bottom, there was hardly any difference any more.

THURSDAY, WET DREGS of Memorial Day, and Mr Tom Givens slipped quietly away from the talk and cigar smoke of the clubhouse front rooms. Talk of the parade down in Johnstown and the Grand Army Veterans and the Sons of Veterans, the amputees on their crutches and in faded Union blues; twenty-four years past Appomattox, and Grant was dead, and Lee was dead, and those old men, marching clear from Main to Bedford Street despite the drizzling sky. He'd sat apart from the others, staring out across the darkening lake, the docks and the clubfleet, the canoes and sailboats and Mr Clarke's electric catamaran moored safe against the threat of a stormy night.

And then someone, maybe Mr D.W.C. Bidwell, had brought up the girl, and faces, smoke-shrouded, brandy-flushed, had turned towards him, curious, and

Oh, yes, didn't you know? Why, Tom here saw her, saw the whole damnable thing, and so politely he'd excused himself. Had left them mumbling before the crackle and glow of the big sandstone fireplace, and by the time he'd reached the landing and the lush path of burgundy carpet that would carry him back to his room, the conversation had turned inevitably to iron and coke, the new Navy ironclads for which Carnegie, Phipps and Co. had been contracted to produce the steel plating. Another triumph for Pittsburgh, another blow to the Chicago competition.

Now he shut the door behind him and the only light was dim grey through the windows; for a moment he stood in the dark before reaching for the chain. Above the lake, the clouds were breaking apart, hints of stars and moonshine in the rifts, and the lake almost glimmered, out in the middle seemed to ripple and swirl.

It's only wind on the water, Tom Givens told himself as he pulled the lamp chain hard and warm yellow drenched the room, drove the black outside and he could see nothing in the windows except the room mirrored and himself, tall and very much needing a shave. By the clock on his dresser, it was just past nine, and *At least*, he thought, *maybe there'll be no storms tonight*. But the wind still battered itself against the clubhouse, and he sat down in a chair, back to the lake, and poured amber whiskey. He drank it quickly and quickly refilled the glass, tried not to hear the gusting wind, the shutter rattle, the brush of pine boughs like old women wringing their bony hands.

By ten the bottle was empty and Tom Givens was asleep in the chair, stocking feet propped on the bed.

An hour later, the rain began.

THE STORM WAS as alive as anything else, as alive as the ancient shale and sandstone mountains and the wind; as alive as the scorch and burn of the huge Bessemer converters and the slag-scabbed molten iron that rolled like God's blood across the slippery steel floors of the Cambria mills. And as perfectly mindless, as passionately indifferent. It had been born somewhere over Nebraska two days before, had swept across the plains and in Kansas spawned twister children who danced along the winding Cottonwood River and wiped away roads and farms. It had seduced Arctic air spilling off the Great Lakes and sired blizzards across Michigan and Indiana, had spoken its throaty poetry of gale and thunder throughout the Ohio River Valley, and finally, with its violent arms, would embrace the entire Mid-Atlantic seaboard.

As Tom Givens had listened distractedly to the pomp and chatter of the gentlemen of the club, the storm had already claimed western Pennsylvania, had snubbed the sprawling scar of Pittsburgh for greener lovers further east. And as he'd slept, it had stroked bare ridges and stream-threaded valleys, rain-shrouding Blairsville and Bolivar, New Florence and Ninevah, had followed the snaky railroad through Conemaugh Gap into the deep and weathered folds of Sang Hollow.

And then, Johnstown, patchwork cluster of boroughs crowded into the dark hole carved in the confluence of two rivers. The seething Cambria yards and the tall office buildings, the fine and handsome homes along Main Street. The storm drummed tin and slate shingled roofs, played for the handful of mill workers and miners drinking late inside California Tom's, for the whores in Lizzie Thompson's sporting house on Frankstown Hill. George and Mathilde Heiser, closing up for the night, paused in the mercantile clutter of their store to watch the downpour, and inside St Joseph's parsonage, Reverend Chapman, who'd been having bad dreams lately, was awakened by his wife, Agnes, and they lay together and listened to the rain pounding Franklin Street.

Unsatisfied, insatiable, the storm had continued east, engulfing the narrow valley, Mineral Point and the high arch of the Pennsylvania Railroad viaduct, and, finally, sleeping South Fork.

As alive as anything it touched.

———

THE GIRL ON the dam doesn't know he's watching, of that much he's certain. He sits by open windows and the early morning air smells like the lake, like fish and mud, and something sharper. He's been drunk more than he's been sober since the night down in Johnstown, the night he sat in the balcony of the Washington Street Opera House, *Zozo the Magic Queen* on stage and some other fellows from the club with him, talking among themselves.

The girl from the dam is walking on the water.

He leans forwards, head and shoulders out the window because he can't hear, Irwin braying like a goddamned mule from the seat behind and he can't hear the words, the players' lines, can only hear Irwin repeating the idiot joke over and over again. Beneath the window of his room, the audience is seated, and he stares down at men's heads and ladies' feathered hats, row after row on the front lawn of the South Fork Hunting and Fishing Club.

Somewhere, far away still but rushing like locomotive wheels, thunder, like applause and laughter and the footlights like lightning frozen on her face.

'Ask Tom,' the usher says, 'Tom saw the whole damnable thing,' and Irwin howls.

And then she's gone, if she was ever really there, and the crowd is on its feet, flesh smacking flesh in frenzied approval; if she was ever there. Lake Conemaugh is as smooth as varnished wood, and he knows it's all done with trapdoors and mirrors and that in a moment she'll rise straight up from the stage planks to take her bows. But the roses fall on the flat water and lie there and now the curtains are sweeping closed, velvet the colour of rain rippling across the sky.

'...Saw the *whole* thing,' Irwin echoes, so funny he wants to say it over and over, and they're all laughing, every one, when he gets up to go, when it's obvious that the show's over and everyone else is leaving their seats, the theatre emptying into the front porch of the clubhouse.

Sidewalk boards creak loud beneath his shoes, thunk and mould-rotten creak; after the evening showers the air smells cleaner at least, coal dust and factory soot washed from the angry industrial sky into the black gutters, but the low clouds hold in the blast furnace glow from Cambria City and the sky is bloodier than ever.

Spring buggies and lacquered wagon wheels, satin skirts and petticoats held above the muddy street. The pungent musk of wet horsehair.

And he knows that he's only stepped out of his room, that he stands in the hall, second floor, and that if he walks straight on he'll pass three rooms, three numbered doors, and come to the stairs, the oak banister, winding down. But it's dark, the sputtering white arc streetlights not reaching this narrow slit, inverted alley spine between Washington and Union, and the carpet feels more like muck and gravel, and he turns, starts to turn when thunder rumbles like animal whispers and cloth tearing and

Why, Tom here saw her, saw the whole damnable thing

the shadow things hunched, claws and grunts and breath exhaled from snot wet nostrils, and she turns her head, hair mired in the filth and standing water, face minstrel smudged, but eyes bright and she sees him, and he knows she's begging him to help, to stop this, to pull the shadows off her before there's nothing left to save.

But a shaggy head rises ox-slow from the space between her breasts and these eyes are nothing but the red sky, molten pools of stupid hunger, and Tom turns away, lost for a moment, feeling his way along the silken-papered walls, until his fumbling hands find the brass cool doorknob and the thunder splits apart that world. Splits the alley girl like an overripe peach, and he steps across the threshold, his bare feet sinking through the floor into the icy lake, and she's waiting, dead hand shackle-tight around his ankle to pull him down into the fishslime and silting night.

MR TOM GIVENS woke up, sweat-soaked, eyes wide, still seeing white-knuckled hands clasped, sucking air in shuddering gulps, air that seemed as thick, as unbreathable, as dark lake water. The crystal-cut whiskey glass tumbled from his hands, rolled away beneath the bed. And still the pain, fire twisting his legs, and outside the thunder rumbled across the Allegheny night like artillery fire and Old Testament judgement.

Both legs were still propped up on the four-poster and, as he shifted, the Charley horse began slowly, jealously, to relax its grip, and he realised there was no feeling at all in his left leg. Outside, furious rain pounded the windows, slammed the shutters against the clubhouse wall. Tom Givens cursed his stupidity, nodding off in the chair like a lousy drunkard, and carefully, he lowered his tortured legs on to the floor. Fresh pain in bright and nauseating waves as the blood rushed back into droughty capillaries; the room swam, lost its precious substance for a moment and the dream still so close, lingering like crows around the grey borders.

Lightning then, blinding sizzle that eclipsed the electric lamp, and the thunder clamoured eager on its heels.

He sat in the chair, waited for the last of the pins and needles stab to fade, listened to the storm. A wild night on the mountain, and that went a long way towards explaining the nightmare, that and the bourbon, that and the things he'd seen since he'd arrived at the lake two weeks before. He'd come out early, before the June crowds, hoping for rest and a little time to recover from the smoky bustle of Pittsburgh.

The loose shutters banged and rattled like the wind knocking to come inside, and he got up, cautious, legs still uncertain, but only two steps, three, to the window. And even as he reached for the latch, thumbed it back, even as he pushed against the driving rain, knowing that he'd be soaked before it was done, he heard the roar, not thunder, but something else, something almost alive. Immediate and stinging cold and the sashes were ripped from his hands, slammed back and panes shattered against the palsied shutters.

And through the darkness and the downpour he saw the white and whirling thing, impossibly vast, moving past the docks, dragging itself across the lake. Silvered clockwise, and the deafening roar and boom, and Tom Givens forgot the broken windows, the frantic drapery flutter, the shutters, ignored the rain blowing in, soaking him through, drenching the room. He watched as the waterspout passed by, and the girl, the girl standing there, her long dark hair whipped in the gale, her body an alabaster slash in the black night. She raised her bare arms, worshipping, welcoming, granting passage, and turning, her white gown a whirling echo of the thing, and her arms were opened to him now, and he knew the face.

The face that had turned to him, helpless, pleading, in the Johnstown alleyway, but changed, eyes swollen with bottomless fury and something that might be triumph, if triumph could be regret. And he knew as well that this was also the girl that he'd watched drown herself off South Fork Dam barely a week back.

Her lips moved but the wind snatched the words away.

And then lightning splashed the docks in noonday brilliance, and she was gone, nothing but bobbing canoes and the waves, and the trees bending down almost to the ground.

⸻

HE PASSED THE night downstairs, hours sobering into headache and listening to the storm from the huge main living room. He sat on pebble-grained calfskin and paced the Arabian carpeted floors, thumbed nervously through the new Mark Twain novel someone had left, finished or merely forgotten, on an end table. Occasionally, he glanced at the windows, towards the docks and the lake. And already the sensible, nineteenth century part of his mind had begun to convince itself that he'd only been dreaming, or near enough; drunk and dreaming.

Finally, others awake and moving, pot and pan noise and cooking smells from the kitchen, and the warm scents of coffee and bacon were enough to stall the argument, rational breakfast, perfect syllogism against the fading night. He smoothed his hair, straightened his rumpled shirt and vest with hands that had almost stopped shaking and rose to take his morning meal with the others.

Then young Mr Parke, resident engineer, shaved and dressed as smartly as ever, came quickly down the stairs, walked quickly to the porch door and let in the dawn, light like bad milk and the sky out there hardly a shade lighter than the night had been. And something roaring in the foggy distance.

John Parke stepped outside and Tom Givens followed him, knowing that he was certainly better off heading straight for the dining room, finding himself shivering on the long porch anyway. Before them, the lawn was littered with branches and broken limbs, with unrecognisable debris, and the lake was rough and brown.

'It's up a ways, isn't it?' and Tom's voice seemed magnified in the soppy air.

John Parke nodded slowly, contemplative, spoke without looking away from the water. 'I'd say it's up at least two feet since yesterday evening.'

'And that awful noise, what is that?'

Parke pointed south-east, towards the head of the lake, squinted as if by doing so he might actually see through the fog and drizzle.

'That awful noise, Mr Givens, is most likely Muddy Run coming down to the lake from the mountains.' Pause, and, 'It must be a blessed torrent after so much rain.'

'Doesn't sound very good, does it? Do you think that the dam is, ah, I mean, do you…'

'Let's see to our breakfasts, Mr Givens,' John Parke said, weak smile, pale attempt at reassurance, 'and then I'll see to the lake.'

The door clanged shut and he was alone on the porch, rubbing his hands together against the gnawing damp and chill. After breakfast, he would go upstairs and pack his bags, find a carriage into South Fork; from there, he could take the 9:15 back to Pittsburgh. More likely than not, there would be others leaving, and it would be enough to say he was sick of the weather, sick of this dismal excuse for a holiday.

Whatever else, that much certainly was true.

Tom Givens turned his back on the lake, on the mess the night had made of the club grounds, and as he reached for the door he heard what might have been laughter or glass breaking or just the wind whistling across the water. Behind him one loud and sudden splash, something heavy off docks but he kept his eyes on the walnut dark wood-grain, gripped the brass handle and pulled himself inside.

———

A WEEK DROWNED, and what was left of her, bloated flesh sponge like strawberry bruise and whitest cheese, pocked by nibbling, hungry black bass mouths, this much lay knitted into the pine log tangle and underbrush jamming the big iron fish screens. The screens that strained the water, that kept the lake's expensive stock inside (one dollar apiece, the fathers and grandfathers of these fish, all the way from Lake Erie by special railroad car) and now sieved the cream-and-coffee brown soup before it surged, six feet deep, through the spillway; and the caretaker and his Italians, sewer diggers with their shovels and pickaxes, watched as the lake rose, ate away the mounds of dirt heaped all morning along the breast of the dam.

Blackened holes that were her eyes, grub-clogged sockets haloed in naked bone and meaty tatter, cribs for the blind and new-born maggots of water beetles and dragonflies.

Some minutes past grey noon, the lake spread itself into a wide and glassy sheet and spilled over the top, began its slice and carve, bit by bit, sand and clay and stone washed free and tumbled down the other side. And now the morning's load of cautious suggestions, desperate considerations and shaken heads, gambles passed on, the things that might have been done, didn't matter any more; and the workmen and the bystanders huddled, the dutiful and the merely curious, all rain-drenched, on either hillside, bookends for a deluge.

—————

TOM GIVENS SAT alone, safe and almost drunk again within the shelter of the South Fork depot, sipping Scotch whisky from his silver flask and trying not to watch the nervous faces, not to overhear the hushed exchanges between the ticket agent and the yardmaster. During the night, almost a quarter mile of track washed out between South Fork and Johnstown, and so there had been no train to Pittsburgh or anywhere else that morning, and by afternoon the tracks were backed up; the *Chicago Limited* stretched across Lamb's Bridge like a rusty fat copperhead and a big freight from Derry, too common for names, steamed rainslick and sullen just outside the station.

He'd come from the club in Bidwell's springboard, but had lost track of him around noon, shortly after John Parke had ridden down from the dam. Soaked through to the skin, quite a sorry sight, really, drowned rat of a man galloping in on a borrowed chestnut filly; Parke had gathered a small crowd outside Stineman's supply store, had warned that there was water flowing across the dam, that, in fact, there was real danger of its giving way at any time.

Bidwell had snorted, practised piggy snort of authority and money, had busied himself immediately, contradicting the dripping engineer, assuring everyone who'd listen (and everyone listens to the undespairing cut of those clothes, the calm voice that holds itself in such high esteem) that there was nothing for them to get excited about. Mr Parke had shrugged, duty done, had known better than to argue. He'd sent two men across the street to wire Johnstown from the depot's telegraph tower, had climbed back on to the mud-spattered horse, and then he'd gone, clopping up the slippery road towards the lake.

Tom Givens' ass ached from the hardwood bench, torturous church pew excuse for comfort, and the rain was coming down hard again, hammering at the tin roof. He closed his eyes and thought briefly about dozing off, opened them again and checked his watch instead; twenty minutes past three, nearly three hours sitting, waiting. Tom Givens snapped the watch shut, slipped it back into his vest pocket. And he knew that the sensible thing to do was return to the club, return to its amenities and cloister, and he knew he'd sooner spend the night sleeping on this bench.

When he stood, his knees popped loud as firecrackers and the yardmaster was yelling to someone out on the platform; the ticket agent looked up from his paper and offered a strained and weary smile. Tom Givens nodded and walked slowly across the room, paused to warm his hands at the squat, pot-bellied stove before turning to stare out rainstreaky windows. Across the tracks, Railroad Street, its tidy row of storefronts, the planing mill and the station's coal tipple; further along, the Little Conemaugh and South Fork Creek had twined in a yellow-brown ribbon swallowing the flats below the depot, had claimed the ground floors of several houses out there. Along the banks, oyster-barked aspens writhed and whipped in the wind and current.

There were people in the street, men and women standing about like simple idiots in the downpour, shouting, some running, but not back indoors.

And he heard it too, then, the rumbling thunder growl past thunder, past even the terrible whirl and roar from his nightmare, and the trembling earth beneath his feet, the floorboards and walls and window panes of the depot, resonating with sympathetic tremor.

Run, Thomas, run away.

One, two quickened heartbeats and it rolled into view, very close, fifty feet high and filling in the valley from side to side, an advancing mountain of foam and churning rubbish. Every stump and living tree and fence post between the town and the dam, ripped free, oak and birch and pinewood teeth set in soil-frothy mad dog gums, chewing up the world as it came.

Run, Thomas, run fast. She's coming.

But there was no looking away, even as he heard footsteps and some-one grabbed, tugged roughly at his shoulder, even as he pissed himself and felt the warm spread at his crotch. He caught a fleeting glimpse of a barn roof thrown high on the crest before it toppled over and was crushed to splinters underneath.

She's here, Tom, she's here.

And then Lake Conemaugh and everything it had gathered in its rush down to South Fork slammed into the town and in the last moment before the waters reached Railroad Street and the depot, Tom Givens shut his eyes.

Beneath the red sky, he has no precise memory of the long walk down to this particular hell, slippery cantos blurred with shock and wet, does not even remember walking out on to the bridge.

Dimmest recollection of lying on the depot floor, face down as it pitched and yawed, moored by telegraph cable stitchings; window shards and the live coals spilling from the fallen stove, steam and sizzle in the dirty water, grey-black soot shower from the dangling pendulum stove pipe; dimmer, the pell-mell stumble through the pitchy dark, leaf-dripping, hemlock slap and claw of needled branches and his left arm has stopped hurting, finally, and hangs useless numb at his side; falling again and falling again, and unseen dogs howling like paid mourners, the Negro boy, then, sobbing and naked and painted with blood the sticky-slick colour of molasses, staring down together at the scrubbed raw gash where Mineral Point should have been,

Where is it? Tell me where it's gone.

Mister, the water just came and washed it off.

and his eyes follow the boy's finger and howling dogs like mourners and

Mister, your arm is broke, ain't it?

There is nothing else, simply nothing more, and above him the sky is fur-nace red and he sits alone on the bridge. Sandstone and mortar arches clogged with the shattered bones of the newly dead, South Fork and Mineral Point, Woodvale and Franklin, Johnstown proper, the flood's jumbled vomit, piled higher than the bridge itself. Boxcars and trees, hundreds of houses swept neatly off foundations and jammed together here, telegraph poles and furni-ture. Impossible miles of glinting barbed wire from the demolished Gautier wireworks, vicious garland strung with the corpses of cows and horses and human beings.

And the cries of the living trapped inside.

And everything burns.

Tar black roil, oily exhalation from the flames, breathed crackling into the sky, choking breath that reeks of wood smoke and frying flesh. Embers spiral up, scalding orange and yellow-white, into the dark and vanish overhead, spreading the fire like sparkling demon seeds.

Around him, men and women move, bodies bend and strain to wrestle the dead and dying and the barely bruised from the wreckage. And if anyone notices that he makes no move to help, no one stops to ask why.

From somewhere deep inside the pyre, hoarse groan of steel, lumber creak, wood and metal folded into a single shearing animal cry, rising ululation, and the wreckage shudders, shivers in its fevered dreams; and for *this* they stop, for this they spare fearful seconds, stare into the fuming night, afraid of what they'll see, that there might still be something worse left, held back for drama, for emphasis. But the stifling wind carries it away, muffles any chance of echo, and once again there are only the pain sounds and the burning sounds.

And he is the only one who sees her, the only one still watching, as she walks between the jutting timbers, steps across flaming pools of kerosene-scummed water. One moment, lost inside the smoke and then she steps clear again. Her hair dances in the shimmering heat and her white gown is scorched and torn, hangs in linen tatters. And the stain blooming at her crotch, rust-brown carnation unfolding itself, blood rich petals, blood shiny on the palms of the hands she holds out to him.

Dead eyes flecked with fire and dead lips that move, shape soundless words, and *Oh, yes, didn't you know? Why, Tom here saw her,* and what isn't there for him to hear is plain enough to see; she spreads her arms and in another moment there is only the blazing rubbish.

...saw the whole damnable thing.

He fights the clutching grip of their hands, hands pulling him roughly back from the edge, hands grown as hard as the iron and coke they've turned

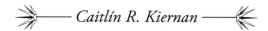

for five or ten or fifteen years, forcing him down on to the smooth and corpse-cold stones, pinning him, helpless, to the bridge.

Above him, the sky is red and filled with cinders that sail and twinkle and finally fall like stars.

'If there were such a thing as ghosts, the night was full of them.'
—David McCullough, *The Johnstown Flood*

for Melanie Tem

CAITLÍN R. KIERNAN is a two-time recipient of both the World Fantasy and World Horror awards, and has been nominated for the Nebula, Shirley Jackson, Mythopoeic, and British Fantasy awards. Their critically acclaimed novels include *The Red Tree* and *The Drowning Girl: A Memoir,* and their short fiction has been collected in multiple collections, including *The Ape's Wife and Other Stories, Dear Sweet Filthy World, The Dinosaur Tourist,* and *The Very Best of Caitlín R. Kiernan.* Kiernan is also a vertebrate palaeontologist and is currently a research associate at the McWane Science Center in Birmingham, Alabama. Their accomplishments in that field include the discovery and description of the a new mosasaur, *Selmasaurus russelli,* studies on mosasaur biostratigraphy, the discovery and description of the first velociraptorinae dinosaur from the south-eastern United States, and, mostly recently, co-authoring the description of a new fossil sea turtle, *Asmodochelys parhami.* The author explains that their stories occur by a gradual, mostly unconscious, accumulation of images: '"To This Water (Johnstown, Pennsylvania 1889)" was written during June and July of 1994, as Tropical Storm Alberto was passing over Georgia, and it seemed like it rained the entire time I was working on the piece; there were terrible floods all across the south-east. Also, I'd just seen a particular painting for the first time, Constantin Makovski's *The Roussalkas,* and Sarah McLachlan's song "Possession", another influence, was getting a lot of radio play. The ending of the story came to me first, or, rather, the image of the fire in the flood came to me, while I was hearing that song and then, a little later, other images coalesced into what would eventually become this story.'

THE MUSEUM ON CYCLOPS AVENUE

Harlan Ellison®

THE JAUNTY FEATHER in my hatband? I knew you'd ask. Makes my old Tyrolean look rather natty, don't it? Yeah, well, I'll tell you about this flame-red feather some time, but not right now.

What about Agnes? Mmm. Yeah. What *about* Agnes.

No, hell no, I'm not unhappy, and I'm certainly not bitter. I *know* I promised to bring her home with me from Sweden, but, well, as we say here in Chapel Hill, *that* dog just ain't gonna hunt.

I'm sorry y'all went to the trouble of settin' up this nice coming-home party, and it truly is a surprise to walk back into my own humble bachelor digs and find y'all hidin' behind the sofas, but to be absolutely candid with myself and with y'all... I'm about as blind tired as I've ever been, fourteen and a half hours riding coach on SAS, customs in New York, missing two connector flights, almost an hour in traffic from Raleigh-Durham...you see what I'm sayin'? Can I beg off this evenin' and I *promise* just as soon as I get my sea-legs under me again with the new semester's classes and the new syllabus, I swear I *promise* we'll all do this up right!

Oh, God bless you, I *knew* you'd understand! Now, listen, Francine, Mary Katherine, Ina...y'all take this food with you, because as soon as the door closes behind you, I'm going to hit my bed and sleep for at least twenty-four hours, so all these here now goodies will gonna rot if you don't take 'em and make y'self a big picnic t'night. Y'all wanna do that now? Excellent! Just excellent.

Thank ya, thank ya *ever* so much! Y'all take care now, y'heah? I'll see you bunch in a few days over to the University. Bye! Bye now! See ya!

(Henry, you want to hold on for just a few minutes? I do need someone to talk to for a spell. You don't mind? Excellent.) Bye! Drive carefully, you be sure to do it! Bye, William; bye, Cheryl an' Simon! Thank you again, thank you ver—

(Thank God they're gone. Hold on just about a minute, Henry, just in case someone forgot a purse or something.)

Okay, street's clear. Damn, Henry, thought I'd croak when I walked into the house and y'all popped out of the walls. Whose dumbshit idea was this, anyway? Don't tell me yours, I cannot afford to lose any respec' for you at the moment. I need a friend, and I need an open mind, an' *most* of all I need a smidge outta that fifth of Jack black sittin' up there on the third shelf 'tween Beckwith's *Hawaiian Mythology* and Bettelheim's *Uses of Enchantment*.

I'd get up and fetch it myself, but I'm shanxhausted, and you're the one just had the angioplasty, so I figger you got lots more energy in you, right at the moment.

They's a coupla clean glasses right there in the cabinet, unless the cleanin' woman saw fit to move things around while I was gone. Asked her not to, but you know nobody listens.

Yeah, right. *While I was gone.* Just decant me about thirty millimetres of that Tennessee sippin', and I'll regale your ageing self with the source of my truly overwhelmin' anomie.

No, I'm not cryin', it's the strain and the long trip and everything that happened in Stockholm. Truly, Henry. I'm sad, I own to it; but it's been four days since the street signs changed, and I'm reconciled to it…say what…?

All right, sorry sorry, didn't mean to get ahead of it. I'll tell you. It's a not terribly complicated saga, so I can tell you everything in a short space. But hold off makin' any judgements till I finish, we agree on that?

Fine. Then: my paper was scheduled for the second day of the Conference, I wanted a few days to see the sights, and when SAS put that Boeing 767 down at Arlanda International, my sponsor, John-Henri Holmberg, was waiting with his new wife Evastina, and John-Henri's son, Alex. And they'd brought along a Dr Richard Fuchs, a very strange little man who writes incredibly obscure books on bizarre illnesses that no one, apparently, either buys or reads. It was quite warm; John-Henri's shirt was open and he carried his jacket; Evastina kept daubing at her moist upper lip; and Alex, who's too old for them now, he was wearing short pants; it was *quite* warm. Fuchs wore gloves. Milky-white latex gloves, the kind you'd put on to examine specimens. But he was effusive in his greetings. Said he wanted me to see a monograph he'd translated into English on some quisquous aspect of Swedish mythology. Why an' wherefore this odd little man should be such a slavish devotee of my work, the semiotics of mythology, by an obscure Professor of Classics from the English Department of the University of North Carolina, is somethin' I was unable to discover. But since it was he—of everyone I met over theah—was the cause of everything that happened to me…I do suspect his bein' there at the airport was considerable more than merest happenstance. I'm gettin' ahead of myself. Patience, Henry.

They took me to the Royal Viking Hotel, and I unpacked and showered and napped for about an hour. But I was still restless; I was aching for sleep, but I couldn't fall off. My legs kept twitching. I couldn't stop worrying about my paper. Two days, I was supposed to deliver it to a major international conference on the latest academic rigours, an' you *know* I've never been comfortable with all this 'deconstructionise' criticism. So I was dog-tired, but instead of taking a Q-Vel for the leg cramps and catching up on some sleep, I fiddled with the manuscript. Even wound up putting a new sub-title on it: *Post-Structuralist Hermeneutics of the Theseus-Minotaur Iconography.* I could barely get my tongue around all that. Imagine what I'd've done somebody asked me what the hell it *meant.* But I knew it'd look impressive in *The Journal.*

So by the time they came to get me for the opening day's dinner reception, I was pretty well goggle-eyed. Maybe that's why I didn't think what was happening was all that distressin'. What Shakespeare called 'how strange or odd'.

I had fourteen and a half hours on the flight back to mull it, an' I can tell you *now* that it was indeed, oh my yes, it was *indeed* distressin', strange, *and* odd.

NOW TAKE IT easy! I'll skip all the local colour, what it's like ridin' over cobblestone streets, and the hoe-ren-duss cost of livin' in Sweden—y'know how much it costs for a roll of Scotch Tape? About seven *dollars*, that's what it costs, can you believe it—and I'll cut right to the reception, and meeting Agnes. And Fuchs. And the sepulchre on Osterlanggatan. And the flame feather I brought home from Stockholm instead of the most beautiful woman who ever walked the face of the earth.

We were sitting around at this big table at the reception, with a classical pianist named Baekkelund playing all sorts of twentieth-century Swedish compositions—Blomdahl, Carlid, Back, Lidholm, that whole 'Monday Group'—and Fuchs was sitting next to me, looking at me as if I might start blowing bubbles at any moment, and I thanked him again for runnin' to get me a champagne refill, 'bout the third or fourth time he'd done it, like as if he wanted to come into my employ as a manservant, and he smiled at me with a little face full of nasty brown teeth, and he said, 'I notice it is that you concern over my wearing of gloves.'

I hadn't realised I'd been oglin' his li'l rubber mittens, but I was just bubbly-happy enough to smart him, 'stead of just answering polite. I said, 'Well, Dr Foowks, it *has* attended my attention that the warm factor in this jammed ballroom is very possibly running towards ninety or so, and the rest of us are, how do they say it in Yiddish, we are all *schvitzin'* like sows, whilst you are covered fingertip to neck-bone. Why *do* you think that is so, suh?'

John-Henri looked uncomfortable. It was just the three of us had come to the reception—Evastina was home with the new baby, Fnork, who had reached the infant stage of catching and eating flies—and though there were others who'd come to sit at that big round table, it was more a matter of expediency in a jammed room with limited seating, than it was a desire to mingle with the three of us. (It had seemed to me, without too close an examination of the subject, that though a few people knew John-Henri, and greeted him saucily, not only did no one *speak* to Dr Fuchs, but there were several who seemed to veer clear when they espied him.)

Dr Fuchs grew tolerably serious, and soft spoke, an' he replied to what instantly became obvious to me had been an incredibly stupid, rude, and champagne-besotted remark: 'I live with a bodily condition known as hyperhidrosis, Professor Stapylton. Abnormally excessive sweating. As you have said it, *schvitzing*. I perspire from hands, feet, my underarms. I must wear knitted shirts to absorb the moisture. Underarm dress shields, of a woman's kind. I carry pocket towels, in the ungood event I must actually shake hands flesh on flesh with someone. Should I remove my latexwear, and place my palm upon this tablecloth, the material would be soaked in a widened pool in moments.' He gave me a pathetic little smile that was meant to be courageous, and he concluded, 'I see revulsion in people's faces, Professor. So I wear the gloves, is it not?'

I felt like thirty-one kinds of a blatherin' damnfool, an' I suppose it was because I had no way of extricatin' my size 11M Florsheim from my mouth, that I was so susceptible when Fuchs humiliated me even more by introducin' me to this utter vision of a woman who came blowin' by the table.

Without even a *hesitation* on his part, springs right off this 'I make people sick 'cause I'm soakin' wet all the time,' right into, 'Oh, Agnes! Come, my dear, come meet the famous American scholar and authority of mythic matters, Professor Gordon Stapylton of Chapel Hill, North Carolina, a most brilliant colleague of our friend John-Henri.'

We took one look at each other, and I knew what it was to endure hyperhidrosis. Every pore in my body turned Niagara. Even half stupored on good French champagne, I was sober enough to know I had, at last, finally, unbelievably, met the most beautiful woman in the world, the one woman I would marry and, failing that liaison, would never be able to settle for anyone else.

Her hair was the colour of the embers when the fire has died down and the companions have snuggled into their sleeping bags and you cannot fall asleep and lie there looking into that moving breathing susurrating crimson at the bottom of the campfire. Her eyes were almond-shaped, and tilted, and green. Not murky, dirty green, but the shade of excellent Chinese jade pieces,

Shang dynasty, Chou dynasty. Describing more, I'd sound even more the idiot than I do right now. I tried to tell y'all what she was like, when I called the next morning, remember? When I said I was bringing home the woman I loved, her name was Agnes? Well, I was tipsy with her, then…and I'm tipsy all over again now, just describin' her, But the im*port*ant part of all this, is that we took one look t'each other, an' we couldn't keep our hands off!

Fuchs was tryin' to tell me that Agnes Wahlstrom was, herself, a noted scholar, a student of mythology, and curator of the *Magasinet for sällsamma väsen*, some kind of a museum, but I wasn't much listening by that time. We were swimming in each other's eyes; and the next thing I knew, I'd gotten up and taken her hand—which had a wonderful strong independent kind of a grip—and we were outside the two hundred-year-old building with the reception up those marble staircases; and we were in a narrow service alley that ran back from the cobble-stoned street into darkness alongside the hulking ugliness of the assembly hall; and I barely had an instant to speak her name before she bore me back against the alley wall, her lips on mine.

She fumbled her dress up around her hips, and undid my belt, almost batting away my hands as I tried to undress *her*.

And there, in that alley, Henry, there in the darkness I found what I'd never been able to locate in nearly forty years of believing it existed: I found utter and total passion, I-don't-give-a-damn lust, a joining and thrashing that must have made steam come off us, like a pair of rutting weasels. Look, I'm sorry to be embarrassin' you, Henry, my old friend, but under this pleasant, gregarious, buttoned-down academic pose, I have been nothin' but a *lonely* sonofabitch all my life. You *know* how it was between my parents, an' you know how few relationships I've had with women who counted. So, now, you have *got* to understan' that I was crazy with her, drunk with her, inside her and steam comin' off us. Migawd, Henry, I think we banged against that alley wall for an hour, maybe more. I have *no* idea why some Swedish cop didn't hear us growlin' and pantin' and yellin' moremoremore, and come in there an' arrest us. Oh, jeezus, lemme catch mah breath. Lawd, Henry, you are the colour of Chairman Mao's Little Book! We never got back to the reception the Conference was hostin'.

We spent the night at the Royal Viking, and the next morning she was as beautiful as the night before, except the sun loved touchin' her, Henry; and we ate breakfast in the room, and her eyes were that green, and made love again for another hour or so. But then she said she had to go home and change because she had to be at the Museum, she was late already, but she'd find me at the Conference in the afternoon and we'd, well, we'd be *together*.

Can you understand what that word meant to me? We'd be *together*. That was when I called you and told you I'd be bringin' back the greatest mythic treasure ever. I had to share it with *some*one, Henry. That was four days ago, before the street signs changed.

———

JOHN-HENRI IS a decent man, and an absolutely great friend, so his chiding me on my behaviour was maximum softly-spoke; but I was given to understand that walkin' off like Night of the Livin' Dumbbells with some gorgeous museum curator, right in the middle of where I was *supposed* to be, was unacceptable. He also confided that he'd been stuck with Dr Fuchs all night, nearly, and he was not overwhelmin'ly thrilled by *that*, either. Turned out he was less acquainted with the man in the moist mittens than I'd thought. Out of nowhere, a few weeks before I was scheduled to fly in, he suddenly showed up, ingratiating, charming, knowledgeable about John-Henri's background, very complimentary, workin' ever so hard to become Evastina's and John-Henri's best new buddy-chum. Just so, just that way, out of nowhere, he suddenly appeared in the antechamber of the Conference Hall, right in the middle of John-Henri's polite, with-clenched-teeth admonition that I not pull a repeat of the previous evening's gaucherie.

Fuchs kept smilin' at me with that scupperful of brown bicuspids, just smarmily enquiring, had I had a pleasant evening, but not gettin' any closer to questions I'd've had to tell him were none of his damned business.

But I couldn't get rid of him. He dogged my every step.

And I attended the sections I'd wanted to drop in on, and my mind wasn't focused for a second on such arcane trivia. All I could think of was sliding my hands up between Agnes' legs.

Finally, about three in the afternoon, she arrived. Looking absolutely wonderful, wearing a summery dress and sandals, in defiance of the chill that was in the air. She found me at the rear of the auditorium, slid in beside me, and whispered, 'I have nothing on under this'.

We left not more than three heartbeats later.

All right, Henry, I'll skip all that. But now pay close attention. Five or six hours later, she seemed distracted, an' I suggested we go get some dinner. I was goin' to pop the question. Oh, yes, Henry, I *see* that expression. But the only reason you got it on you, is that you know somethin' was amiss. But if you didn't *know* that, then you wouldn't think I was bein' precipitous, you'd agree that once having been in the embrace of such a woman, a man would be a giant fool to let her slip away. So just pretend you're as innocent as I was, at that moment, and go along with me on this.

She said no, she wasn't hungry, she'd had a big salad before she came to fetch me at the Conference, but would I be interested in seeing the Museum? Where she was curator. I said that would be charming. Or somesuch pseudo phrase so she wouldn't suspect all I could think about was makin' love to her endlessly. As if she weren't smart enough to know *all* that; and she laughed, and I looked sheepish, and she kissed me, and we went to get the car in the hotel structure, and we drove out, about nine or so.

It was a chilly night, and very dark. And she drove to the oldest section of Stockholm, blocky ribbed-stone buildings leaning over the narrow, winding streets, fog or mist trailing through the canyons, silvery and forlorn. It was, well, not to make a cliché of it…it was melancholy. Somehow sad and winsome at the same time. But I was on a cloud. I had found the grail, the crown, the sceptre, the very incarnation of True Love. And I would, very soon now, pop the question.

She parked on a side-street, cobbled and lit fitfully by old electric brazier lamps, and suggested we should walk, it was invigorating. I worried about her in that thin dress. She said, 'I am a sturdy Scandinavian woman, dear Gordon. Please.' And the *please* was neither cajoling nor requesting. It was 'Give me a break, I can outwalk you any day, son'. And so we strode off down the street.

We turned a number of times, this side-street, that little alley, pausing every once in a while to grope each other, usually on my pretext that certain parts of her body needed to be warmed against the sturdy Scandinavian chill. And finally, we turned on to an absolutely shadow-gorged street down which I could not see a solitary thing. I glanced up at the street sign, and it read: *Cyklopavenyn*. Cyclops Avenue.

Now isn't that remarkable, I thought.

She took me by the hand, and led me into the deep shadow pool of the narrow, claustrophobic, fog-drenched Cyclops Avenue. We walked in silence, just the sound of our hollow footsteps repeating our progress.

'Agnes,' I said, 'where the hell are we going? I thought you wanted me to see—'

Invisible beside me, but her flesh warm as a beacon, she said, 'Yes. *Magasinet for sälsamma väsen.*'

I asked her if we were nearly there, and she said, with a small laugh, 'I told you to tinkle before we left.' But she didn't say 'tinkle'. She used the Swedish equivalent, which I won't go into here, Henry, because I can see that you think I'm leading this story towards her giving me a vampire bite, or trying to steal my soul and sell it to flying saucer people…well, it wasn't anything sick or demented, absolutely no blood at all, and as you can see I'm sittin' right here in front'cher face, holdin' up my glass for a splash more of Mr Jack Daniel's.

Thank'ya. So we keep walkin', and I ask her to translate for me what *Magasinet* etcetera et-cet-era means, and she said, it's hard to translate into English. But she tried, and she said Museum wasn't quite the right word, more rightly something not quite like Sepulchre. I said that gave me chills, and she laughed and said I could call it The Gatherum of Extraordinary Existences—as we reached a brooding shadowy shape darker than the darkness filling Cyclops Avenue, a shape that rose above us like an escarpment of black rock, something hewn from obsidian, and she took a key from a pocket of the thin summery dress, and inserted it in the lock, and turned the key—or you could call it The Repository of Unimaginable Creatures—and she pushed open a door that was three times our height, and I'm six one, and

Agnes is just under six feet—or the Cyklopstrasse Keep of Rare and Extinct Beasts—and as the door opened we were washed by pure golden light so intense I shielded my eyes. Where the door had snugged against the jamb and lintel so tightly there had been no leakage of illumination, now there was an enormous rectangle three times our height of blazing burning light. I could see *nothing*, not a smidge, but that light. And Agnes took me by the elbow, and walked me into the light, and I was *inside* the most breathtaking repository of treasures I'd ever seen.

Greater than the Prado, more magnificent than the Louvre, dwarfing the Victoria and Albert, more puissant than the Hermitage, enfeebling the image of Rotterdam's Museum Boymans-van Beuningen, it rose above us till the arching ceilings faded into misty oblivion. I could see room after room after channel after salon after gallery stretching away in a hundred different directions from the central atrium where we stood, mah mouth open and my wits havin' fled.

Because the Museum that my Agnes tended, the Sepulchre that my Agnes oversaw, the Gallery my Agnes captained...it was filled with the dead and mounted bodies of every creature I'd read about in the tomes of universal mythology.

In niches and on pedestals, in crystal cases and suspended by invisible wires from the invisible ceilings, ranked in shallow conversation-pit-like depressions in the floor and mounted to the walls, in showcases and free-standing in the passageways:

The Kurma tortoise that supported Mt Mandara on its back during the churning of the ocean by the Devas and Asuras. A matched set of unicorns, male and female, one with silver horn, the other with golden spike. The bone-eater from the Ani papyrus. Behemoth and Leviathan. Hanuman the five-headed of the Kalighat. A Griffin. And a Gryphon. Hippogryph and Hippocamp. The Kimura bird of Indian mythology, and the thousand-headed snake Kalinaga. Jinn and Harpy and Hydra; yeti and centaur and minotaur; the holy feathered serpent Quetzalcoatl and a winged horse and a Ryu dragon. Hundreds and thousands of beasts of all worlds and all nations, of all beliefs and all ages, of all peoples and of all dreams and nightmares. There, in the stunning Sepulchre on the Verg Cyklop, was amassed and arrayed and ranked all the impossible creatures that had never made it on to Noah's leaky tub. I wandered gallery to gallery, astounded, impossible sights choking my throat and making me weep with amazement that it was all, all, *all of it* absolutely true. There was even a Boogeyman and his mate. They looked as if they had lived their lives under beds and in dark closets.

'But how...?' I could barely find words, at long last.

'They are here, assembled all. And I am the one who caught them.'

Of all I had seen, of all she might say, *that* was the most astonishin'. *She* had brought these beasts to heel. I could not believe it. But no, she insisted, she trekked out, and she stalked them, and she caught them, and killed them, and brought them back here for display. 'For whom?' I asked. 'Who comes to this place?' And she smiled the sweetest smile, but did not reply. *Who*, I wondered, assaying the size of the rooms, the height of the ceilings, *who did the tour of this repository of miracles?*

Hours later, she took me away, and we went back to the Royal Viking, and I was too aswirl in magic and impossibilities to drench myself in her scented skin. I could not fathom or contain what I had seen. Her naked body was muscular, but more feminine than Aphrodite and Helen of Troy and the Eternal Nymph all combined. She was gorgeous, but she was the hunter of them all. Of course she had had a strong grip. From holding machete, and crossbow, and Sharps rifle, and bolas, and gas-gun. She told me of the hunts, the kills, the scent of the track, the pursuits in far lands: Petra and Angkor, Teotihuacan and Tibet, Djinnistan and Meszria, Skull Island and Malta and Knossos.

And then she said to me, 'I am very much drawn to you, Gordon, but I know you're going to ask me to come away with you, to live in America and be your wife. And I truly, deeply, am mad about even the thought of making love to you endlessly...but...'

————

THE NEXT DAY, I went looking for Cyclops Avenue. I have a skunk-sniffin' dog's sense of direction, you know that, Henry; and I actual found the street again. I recognised all the twisty turns we'd made, even lookin' different in the daylight. But I got there. And, of course, the street signs had changed. Cyclops Avenue was now Österlinggatan. The Museum was not there. Oh, it likely *was* there, but I didn't have either the proper guide or a key taken from the pocket of a summery dress to help me find it. So I went away, and I came back here, and that's my story. Except for a couple of loose ends...

One: What of the peculiar Dr Fuchs? Well, Agnes never said it in so many words, but I got the impression that she had taken pity on the poor little man, that he had been someone who had loved her and followed her, and whose existence meant nothing without her in it, and so she had allowed him to assist her. She said he was her 'spotter'. I didn't ask what that meant, nor what it was he spotted. (Before I left Stockholm, John-Henri called to say goodbye, and he told me he had found a pair of gloves, apparently the property of Fuchs, half-filled with foul-smelling water or sweat or some fishy liquid, but that Dr Fuchs, himself, had vanished, leaving an enormous hotel bill for John-Henri and the Conference to pay.)

And two: I'll bet you haven't forgotten, have you?

That's right, Henry, the feather.

I plucked it from the flank of an enormous roc that she had stalked and bagged and killed and stuffed. It hung from the ceiling in the Museum of Unimaginable Creatures, hung low enough so I could pluck one memento. I think, I guess, I, well I *suppose* I knew somewhere in my head or my heart, certainly not in my pants, that I was never going to get this prize, this treasure, this woman of all women. And so, in some part of my sense, I stole a token to keep my memory warm. It's all I have, one flame-red feather from the flank of the roc that tried to carry off Sinbad the Sailor.

And do you know *why* she renounced me, gave me a pass, shined me on, old Henry? I guess I begged a little, told her how good we were together and, yes, she admitted, that was so; but it was never gonna work. Because, Henry, she said...

I was too easy a catch. I didn't nearly put up the fight it would take to keep her hunter's interest pinned.

What's that? Do I think I'll ever see her again?

Henry, I see her all the time. This world of you and the University and houses and streets and mail-boxes and a drink in my hand…it's all like a transparent membrane on which a movie picthuh is bein' cast. And behind it, I see *her*. My Agnes, so fabulous. She's in a rough-bark coracle, with a canvas sail ripped by terrible winds caused by the beating of a devil roc's great feathered wings, as its spiked tail thrashes the emerald water into tidal spires. She holds a scimitar, and her jade-green eyes are wild; and I know the flame-feathered monster that seeks to devour her, capsize her, drag her down and feast on her delicious flesh—I know that poor dumb ravening behemoth hasn't got the chance of a snowball in a cyclotron. In her path, in the fury of her flesh, *no* poor dumb beast has a chance. Not even—pardon the pun—the Roc of Agnes.

Do I see her? Oh my, yes. I see her clearly, Henry. I may never see *my* world clearly again after walking the halls and galleries of the Cyclops Avenue Museum…but I'll always see her.

For a poor dumb beast, that vision and a goddam red feather is almost enough to get by on. Wouldja kindly, that Jack Daniel's beside you. And then maybe I will go upstairs and try to catch a little sleep.

Thank ya kindly, Henry.

HARLAN ELLISON® WAS called 'one of the greatest living American short story writers' by the *Washington Post*, while the *Los Angeles Times* said, 'It's long past time for Harlan Ellison to be awarded the title: 20th Century Lewis Carroll'. In a career spanning more than sixty years, he won more awards than any other living fantasist—including multiple Hugo, Nubula, Writers Guild of America, Edgar Allan Poe and P.E.N. International Silver Pen awards, along with the SFWA Grandmaster and World Fantasy and HWA Bram Stoker Lifetime Achievement awards. After his first SF story was published in 1956, he became a prolific writer of stories and novels (in various genres and under a number of pseudonyms and house names), non-fiction and screenplays. Some of his best short fiction is collected in *Ellison Wonderland, I Have No Mouth and I Must Scream, Love Ain't Nothing But Sex Misspelled, Deathbird Stories, Strange Wine, Shatterday, Stalking the Nightmare, Angry Candy* and *Slippage*. As an editor, he is best known for the groundbreaking anthologies *Dangerous Visions* (1967) and *Again, Dangerous Visions* (1972), although a planned third volume, *The Last Dangerous Visions*, was compiled but controversially never published. About the origin of 'The Museum on Cyclops Avenue', the author had the following to say (written, amazingly, from his recovery bed four days after quadruple heart-bypass surgery in April 1996): 'As much as any story I've written—and I find that I am as secretly fond of this story as the best of the more than 1,700 stories I've written over the past forty-plus years—this speaks to the lovely quote from Bernard Malamud: "Art lives on surprise. A writer has to surprise himself to be worth reading". Susan and I were Guests of Honour (along with ex-KGB chief Boris Pankin) at the prestigious International Book Fair in Göteberg in 1992. During the trip, I wrote large portions of what became my short novel *Mefisto in Onyx*. And I realised, much later, that whether writing on the floor of the huge convention before hundreds of bewildered attendees who couldn't understand that creation occurs everywhere and doesn't always need a velvet-lined closet, or on pillows in a hotel room, that Sweden was a particularly salutary venue to produce contemporary fantasy, light or dark. So it was with a *frisson* of familiarity that I found myself, as I started writing this story, three years later...returning to a memory of Stockholm. Had no idea as I sat down to write, to do this "story behind the cover" to fit an existing painting by Ron Brown for the fifth issue of my comic book, *Harlan Ellison's Dream Corridor* (quarterly, from Dark Horse), that I was embarking on a story to be told entirely in dialect by a tenured Professor of Classics from the University of North Carolina Chapel Hill (where I'd lectured some years earlier), recollecting incidents that had happened to him in Sweden. Most peculiar. The voice, the venue, the congeries of disparate elements, the use of my close friends John-Henri Holmberg and Richard Fuchs, all in the service of explaining what was going on in this "heroic" painting Ron Brown had done for my comic. (Every issue, I'd pick some piece of specially-painted or already-existing unpublished Fine Art, and write a story from scratch to fit the vision that would be used as a cover for the comic. It was a great game. I enjoyed it immensely). Incidentally, only the name "Dr Richard Fuchs" bears relation to the real, extremely charming Dr Fuchs, who is a Swedish best-selling author and a swell guy, who permitted me to make him odd and ominous for this tale. I had no idea where I was going when I started. That I began with the feather is to me another example of how secure I've become—as all writers must become, I believe—in trusting the talent. The onboard expertise and cleverness of the unconscious are the best helpmeets to integrating the elements of a story...particularly if you begin *tabula rasa*. This is one of those stories that truly told itself. I just went along for the ride.' Like David J. Schow's story earlier in this volume, 'The Museum on Cyclops Avenue' also stands as a tribute to the late Robert Bloch. As Ellison noted at the time: 'I have always written my stories on Olympia office standard or portable typewriters. Bob Bloch also wrote on Olympias. When Bob died, he passed on to me two of his machines. This story was written on one of those typewriters, completed on July 5, 1995. The work goes on.'

FREE DIRT

Ray Bradbury

THE CEMETERY WAS in the centre of the city. On four sides, it was bounded by gliding streetcars on glistening blue tracks and cars with exhaust fumes and sound. But, once inside the wall, the world was lost. For half a mile in four directions, the cemetery raised midnight trees and headstones that grew from the earth, like pale mushrooms, moist and cold. A gravel path led back into darkness and within the gate stood a Gothic Victorian house with six gables and a cupola. The front porch light showed an old man there alone, not smoking, not reading, not moving, silent. If you took a deep breath, he smelled of the sea, of urine, of papyrus, of kindling, of ivory, and of teak. His false teeth moved his mouth automatically when it wanted to talk. His tiny yellow seed eyes twitched and his poke-hole nostrils thinned as a stranger crunched up the gravel path and set foot on the porch step.

'Good evening!' said the stranger, a young man, perhaps twenty.

The old man nodded, but his hands lay quietly on his knees.

'I saw that sign out front,' the stranger went on. '"Free Dirt", it said.'

The old man almost nodded.

The stranger tried a smile. 'Crazy, but that sign caught my eye.'

There was a glass fan over the front door. A light shone through this glass fan, coloured blue, red, yellow, and touched the old man's face. It seemed not to bother him.

'I wondered, free dirt? Never struck me you'd have much left over. When you dig a hole and put the coffin in and refill the hole, you haven't much dirt left, have you? I should think...'

The old man leaned forward. It was so unexpected that the stranger pulled his foot off the bottom step. 'You *want* some?' said the old man.

'Why, no, no, I was just curious. Signs like that make you curious.'

'Set down,' said the old man.

'Thanks.' The young man sat uneasily on the steps. 'You know how it is, you walk around and never think how it is to own a graveyard.'

'And?' said the old man.

'I mean, like how much time it takes to dig graves.'

The old man leaned back in his chair. 'On a cool day, two hours. Hot day, four. Very hot day, six. Very cold day, not cold so it freezes, but *real* cold, a man can dig a grave in one hour so he can head in for hot chocolate, brandy in the chocolate. Then again you get a good man on a hot day, he's no better than a bad man in the cold. Might take eight hours to open up, but there's easy digging soil here. All loam, no rocks.'

'I'm curious about winter.'

'In blizzards we got a ice-box mausoleum to stash the dead—undelivered mail—until spring and a whole month of shovels and spades.'

'Seeding and planting time, eh?' The stranger laughed.

'You might say that.'

'Don't you dig in winter anyhow? For special funerals? *Special* dead?'

'Some yards got a hose-shovel contraption. Pump hot water through the blade; shape a grave quick, like placer mining, even with the ground an ice pond. We don't cotton to that. Use picks and shovels.'

The young man hesitated. 'Does it bother you?'

'You mean, I get scared ever?'

'Well...yes.'

The old man took out and stuffed his pipe with tobacco, tamped it with a calloused thumb, lit it, and let out a small stream of smoke.

'No,' he said at last.

The young man's shoulders sank.

'Disappointed?' said the old man.

'I thought maybe once...?'

'Oh, when you're young maybe. One time...'

'Then, there *was* a time!' The young man shifted up a step.

The old man glanced at him sharply. 'One time.' He stared at the marbled hills and the dark trees. 'My grandpa owned this yard. I was born here. A gravedigger's son learns to ignore things.'

The old man took a number of deep puffs and said, 'I was just eighteen, folks off on vacation, me left to tend things alone, mow the lawn, dig holes, and such. Alone, four graves to dig in October and a cold came hard off the lake, frost on the graves, tombstones like snow, ground froze solid.

'One night I walked out. No moon. Hard grass underfoot, could see my breath, hands in my pockets, walking, listening.'

The old man exhaled frail ghosts from his thin nostrils. 'Then I heard this sound, deep under. I froze. It was a voice, screaming. Someone woke up buried, heard me walk by, cried out. I just *stood*. They screamed and screamed. Earth banged. On a cold night, ground's like porcelain, rings, you see?

'Well.' The old man shut his eyes to remember. 'I stood like the wind off the lake stopped my blood. A joke? I searched around and thought, Imagination! No, it was underfoot, sharp, clear. A woman's voice. I *knew* all the gravestones.' The old man's eyelids trembled. 'Could recite them alphabetical, year, month, day. Name any year, and I'll tell. 1899? Jake Smith departed. 1923? Betty Dallman lost. 1933? P.H. Moran! Name a month. August? August last year, buried Henrietta Wells. August 1918? Grandma Hanlon, whole family! Influenza! Name a day. August fourth? Smith, Burke, Shelby carried off. Williamson? He's on that hill. Douglas? By the creek...'

'The *story*,' the young man urged.

'Eh?'

'The story you were telling.'

'Oh, the voice below? Well, I knew all the stones. Standing there I guessed that voice out of the ground was Henrietta Fremwell, fine girl, twenty-four years, played piano at the Elite Theatre. Tall, graceful, blonde. How did I know her voice? I stood where there was only men's graves. Hers was the only woman's. I ran to put my ear on her stone. Yes! Her voice, way down, screaming!

'"Miss Fremwell!" I shouted.

'"Miss Fremwell!" I yelled again.

'Deep down I heard her, only weeping now. Maybe she heard me, maybe not. She just cried. I ran downhill so fast I tripped and split my head on a stone, got up, screamed myself. Got to the tool shed, all blood, dragged out the tools, and just stood there with one shovel. The ground was ice solid. I fell back against a tree. It would take three minutes to get back to her grave and eight hours to dig to her box. The ground was like glass. A coffin is a coffin; only so much space for air. Henrietta had been buried two days before the freeze, been asleep all that time, using up air, and it rained just before the cold spell and the earth over her, soaked with rainwater, now froze. I'd have to dig maybe eight hours. And the way she cried, there wasn't another hour of air left.'

The old man's pipe had gone out. He rocked in his chair, back and forth, back and forth, silently.

'But,' said the young man, 'what did you do?'

'Nothing,' said the old man.

'Nothing?'

'Nothing I *could* do. That ground was solid. Six men couldn't have dug that grave. No hot water near. And she might've been screaming hours before I heard, so...'

'You did...nothing?'

'Something. Put the shovel back in the tool shed, locked it, and went back to the house and built a fire and drank some hot chocolate, shivering and shivering. Would you have done different?'

'I…'

'Would you have dug for eight hours in hard ice rock so's to reach her when she was truly dead of exhaustion, cold, smothered, and have to bury her all over again? Then call her folks and *tell* them?'

The young man was silent. On the porch, the mosquitoes hummed about the naked light bulb.

'I see,' said the young man.

The old man sucked his pipe. 'I think I cried all night because there was nothing I could do.' He opened his eyes and stared about, surprised, as if he had been listening to someone else.

'That's quite a story,' said the young man.

'No,' said the old man. 'God's truth. Want to hear more? See that big stone with the ugly angel? That was Adam Crispin's. Relatives fought, got a writ from a judge, dug him up hoping for poison. Found nothing. Put him back, but by that time, the dirt from his grave mixed with other dirts. We shovelled in stuff from all around. Next plot, the angel with broken wings? Mary Lou Phipps. Dug her up to lug her off to Elgin, Illinois. More relatives. Where she'd been, the pit stayed open, oh, three weeks. No funerals. Meanwhile, her dirt got cross-shovelled with others. Six stones over, one stone north, that was Henry Douglas Jones. Became famous sixty years after no one paid attention. Now he's planted under the Civil War monument. His grave lay wide two months, nobody wanted to utilise the hole of a Southerner, all of us leaning North with Grant. So his dirt got scattered. That give you some notion of what that "Free Dirt" sign means?'

The young man eyed the cemetery landscape. 'Well,' he said, 'where is that dirt you're handing out?'

The old man pointed with his pipe, and the stranger looked and, indeed, by a nearby wall was a sizeable hillock some ten feet long by about three feet high, loam and grass tufts of many shades of tan, brown, and burnt umber. 'Go look,' said the old man.

The young man walked slowly over to stand by the mound. 'Kick it,' said the old man. 'See if it's real.'

The young man kicked, and his face paled. 'Did you hear that?' he said.

'What?' said the old man, looking somewhere else.

The stranger listened and shook his head. 'Nothing.'

'Well, now,' said the old man, knocking out the ashes from his pipe. 'How much free dirt you need?'

'I hadn't thought.'

'Yes, you have,' said the old man, 'or you wouldn't have driven your light-weight delivery truck up by the gate. I got cat's ears. Heard your motor just when you stopped. How much?'

'Oh,' said the young man uneasily. 'My backyard's eighty feet by forty. I could use a good inch of topsoil. So…?'

'I'd say,' said the old man, 'half of that mound there. Hell, take it. Nobody wants it.'

'You mean…'

'I mean, that mound has been growing and diminishing, diminishing and growing, mixtures up and down, since Grant took Richmond and Sherman reached the sea. There's Civil dirt there, coffin splinters, satin casket shreds from when Lafayette met the honour guards. Edgar Allan Poe. There's funeral flowers, blossoms from ten hundred obsequies. Condolence card confetti for Hessian troopers, Parisian gunners who never shipped home. That soil is so laced with bone meal and casket corsages I should charge *you* to buy the lot. Grab a spade before I do.'

'Stay right there.' The young man raised one hand.

'I'm not going anywhere,' said the old man. 'Nor is anyone else nearby.'

***

THE HALF-TRUCK was pulled up by the dirt mound and the young man was reaching in for a spade, when the old man said, 'No, I think not.'

The old man went on.

'Graveyard spade's best. Familiar metal, familiar soil. Easy digging, when like takes to like. So…'

The old man's head indicated a spade half-stuck in the dark mound. The young man shrugged and moved.

The cemetery spade came free with a soft whispering. Pellets of ancient mound fell with similar whispers.

He began to dig and shift and fill the back of his half-truck as the old man, from the corners of his eyes, observed, 'It's more than dirt, as I said. War of 1812, San Juan Hill, Manassas, Gettysburg, October flu epidemic 1918, all strewn from graves filled and evicted to be refilled. Various occupants leavened out to dust, various glories melted to mixtures, rust from metal caskets, coffin handles, shoelaces but no shoes, hairs long and short. Ever see wreaths made of hair saved to weave crowns to fix on mortal pictures? All that's left of a smile or that funny look in the eyes of someone who knows she's not alive any more, ever. Hair, epaulettes, not whole ones, but one strand of epaulettes, all there, along with blood that's gone to silt.'

The young man finished, sweating, and started to thrust the spade back in the earth when the old man said:

'Take it. Cemetery dirt, cemetery spade, like takes to like.'

'I'll bring it back tomorrow.' The young man tossed the spade into the mounded truck.

'No. You got the dirt, so keep the spade. Just don't bring that free dirt back.'

'Why would I do that?'

'Just don't,' said the old man, but did not move as the young man climbed in his truck to start the engine.

He sat listening to the dirt mound tremble and whisper in the flatbed.

'What're you waiting for?' asked the old man.

———

THE FLIMSY half-truck ran towards the last of the twilight, pursued by the ever-encroaching dark. Clouds raced overhead, perturbed by the invisible. Back on the horizon, thunder sounded. A few drops of rain fell on the windshield, causing the young man to ram his foot on the gas and swerve into his home street even as the sun truly died, the wind rose, and the trees around his cottage bent and beckoned.

Climbing out, he stared at the sky and then his house and then the empty garden. A few drops of cold rain on his cheeks decided him; he drove the rattling half-truck into the empty garden, unlatched the metal back flap, opened it just an inch so as to allow a proper flow, and then began motoring back and forth across the garden, letting the dark stuffs whisper down, letting the strange midnight earth shift and murmur, until, at last, the truck was empty and stood in the blowing night, watching the wind stir the black soil.

Then he locked the truck in the garage and went to stand on the back porch thinking, I won't need water. The storm will soak the ground.

He stood for a long while simply staring at the graveyard mulch waiting for rain until he thought, *What am I waiting for? Jesus!* And went in.

At ten o'clock, a light rain tapped on the windows and sifted over the dark garden. At eleven, it rained so steadily that the gutter drains swallowed and rattled. At midnight, the rain grew heavy. He looked to see if it was eroding the new dark earth, but only saw the black muck drinking the downpour, like a great black sponge, lit by distant flares of lightning.

Then, at one in the morning, the greatest Niagara of all shuddered the house, rinsed the windows to blindness, and shook the lights.

And then, abruptly, the downpour ceased, followed by one great downfall blow of lightning, which ploughed and pinioned the dark earth close by, near, outside, with explosions of light as if ten thousand flashbulbs had been fired off. Then darkness fell in curtains of thunder, cracking the heart, breaking the bones.

In bed, wishing for the merest dog to hold, for lack of human company, hugging the sheets, burying his head, then rising full to the silent air, the dark air, the storm gone, the rain shut, and a silence spread in whispers as the last drench melted into the trembling soil. He shuddered and then shivered and then hugged himself to stop the shivering of his cold flesh, and he was thirsty, but could not make himself move to find the kitchen and drink water, milk, leftover wine, anything. He lay back, dry-mouthed, with unreasonable tears filling his eyes.

Free dirt, he thought. My God what a damn fool night.

Free dirt!

At two o'clock he heard his wristwatch ticking softly.

At two-thirty he felt his pulse in his wrists and ankles and neck and then in his temples and inside his head.

The entire house leaned in the wind, listening.

Outside in the still night, the wind failed and the yard lay soaking and waiting.

And at last...*yes.* He opened his eyes and turned his head towards the window.

He held his breath. What? Yes? What?

Beyond the window, beyond the wall, beyond the house, outside somewhere, a whisper, a murmur, growing louder and louder. Grass growing? Blossoms opening? Soil shifting, crumbling?

A great whisper, a mix of shadows and shades. Something rising. Something moving.

Ice froze beneath his skin. His heart ceased.

Outside in the dark, in the yard. Autumn had arrived.

October was there.

His garden gave him...

A *harvest.*

RAY BRADBURY WAS, without any doubt, our most distinguished and influential fantasy writer. Cutting his literary teeth in the memorable pages of *Weird Tales* in the 1940s, his early stories from that pulp magazine were reprinted in the Arkham House collection *Dark Carnival*, published in 1947. Known principally for his short fiction, he sold his work to all the major magazines in the intervening sixty-five years, until his death in 2012. His many tales of science fiction, fantasy and horror have been widely collected, and *The Martian Chronicles*, *The Illustrated Man*, *The Golden Apples of the Sun*, *The October Country*, *A Medicine for Melancholy*, *I Sing the Body Electric* and *Long After Midnight* are just some of the evocative titles that hint at the equally atmospheric prose to be found in the author's timeless fiction. He was also the author of several classic novels, including *Something Wicked This Way Comes*, *Fahrenheit 451*, *Dandelion Wine*, *The Halloween Tree*, *Death Is a Lonely Business* and *A Graveyard for Lunatics*. 'I took a couple of years off, and did sixty-five teleplays for my TV series, plus a couple of screenplays,' recalled Bradbury. 'But I wanted to get back to my root system—because I started as a short story writer when I was twelve. I had a lot of ideas put away, just old scribbled notes I started going through.' The result was a number of new short stories, including 'Free Dirt', which were eventually collected in *Quicker Than the Eye*.

SELF-MADE MAN

Poppy Z. Brite

JUSTIN HAD READ *Dandelion Wine* seventeen times now, but he still hated to see it end. He always hated endings.

He turned the last page of the book and sat for several minutes in the shadows of his bedroom, cradling the old thumbed paperback by Ray Bradbury, marvelling at the world he held in his hands. The hot sprawl of the city outside was forgotten; he was still lost in the cool green Byzantium of 1928.

Within these tattered covers, dawning realisation of his own mortality might turn a boy into a poet, not a dark machine of destruction. People only died after saying to each other all the things that needed to be said, and the summer never truly ended so long as those bottles gleamed down the cellar, full of the distillate of memory.

For Justin, the distillate of memory was a bitter vintage. The summer of 1928 seemed impossibly long ago, beyond imagining, forty years before blasted sperm met cursed egg to make him. When he put the book aside and looked at the dried blood under his fingernails, it seemed even longer.

An artist who doesn't read is no artist at all, he had scribbled in a notebook he once tried to keep, but abandoned after a few weeks, sick of his own thoughts. *Books are the key to other minds, sure as bodies are the key to other souls. Reading a good book is a lot like sinking your fingers up to the second knuckle in someone's brain.*

In the world of the story, no one left before it was time. Characters in a book never went away; all you had to do was open the book again and there they'd be, right where you left them. He wished live people were so easy to hold onto.

You could hold onto *parts* of them, of course; you could even make them part of yourself. That was easy. But to keep a whole person with you forever, to stop just one person from leaving or gradually disintegrating as they always did…to just *hold* someone. *All* of someone.

There might be ways. There had to be ways.

Even in Byzantium, a Lonely One stalked and preyed.

Justin was curled up against the headboard of his bed, a bloodstained comforter bunched around his bare legs. This was his favourite reading spot. He glanced at the nightstand, which held a Black & Decker electric drill, a pair of scissors, a roll of paper towels, and a syringe full of chlorine bleach. The drill wasn't plugged in yet. He closed his eyes and allowed a small slow shudder to run through his body, part dread, part desire.

There were screams carved on the air of his room, vital fluids dried deep within his mattress, whole lives sewn into the lining of his pillow, to be taken out and savoured later. There was always time, so long as you didn't let your memories get away. He had kept most of his. In fact, he'd kept seventeen; all but the first two, and those he didn't want.

Justin's father had barely seen him out of the womb before disappearing into the seamy nightside of Los Angeles. His mother raised him on the continent's faulty rim, in an edging-toward-poor neighbourhood of a city that considered its poor a kind of toxic waste: ceaselessly and unavoidably churned out by progress, hard to store or dispose of, foul-smelling and ugly and dangerous. Their little stucco house was at the edge of a vast slum, and Justin's dreams were peppered with gunfire, his play permeated with the smell of piss and garbage. He was often beaten bloody just for being a scrawny white boy carrying a book. His mother never noticed his hands scraped raw on concrete, or the thin crust of blood that often formed between his oozing nose and mouth by the time he got home.

She had married again and moved to Reno as soon as Justin turned eighteen, as soon as she could turn her painfully awkward son out of the house. *You could be a nice-looking young man if you cleaned yourself up. You're smart, you could get a good job and make money. You could have girlfriends,* as if looks and money and girlfriends were the sweetest things he could ever dream of.

Her new husband had been a career Army man who looked at Justin the way he looked at their ragged old sofa, as leftover trash from her former life. Now they were both ten years dead, their bones mummified or scattered by animals somewhere in the Nevada desert, in those beautiful blasted lands. Only Justin knew where.

He'd shot his stepfather first, once in the back of the head with his own Army service pistol, just to see the surprise on his mother's face as brain and bone exploded across the glass top of her brand-new dinner table, as her husband's blood dripped into the mashed potatoes and the meat loaf, rained into her sweating glass of tea. He thought briefly that this surprise was the strongest emotion he had ever seen there. The sweetest, too. Then he pointed the gun at it and watched it blossom into chaos.

Justin remembered clearing the table, noticing that one of his mother's eyes had landed in her plate, afloat on a thin patina of blood and grease. He tilted the plate a little and the glistening orb rolled onto the floor. It made a small satisfying squelch beneath the heel of his shoe, a sound he felt more than heard.

No one ever knew he had been out of California. He drove their gas-guzzling luxury sedan into the desert, dumped them and the gun. He returned to L.A. by night, by Greyhound bus, drinking bitter coffee and reading at rest stops, watching the country unspool past his window, the starlit desert and highway and small sleeping towns, the whole wide-open landscape folding around him like an envelope or a concealing hand. He was safe among other human flotsam. No one ever remembered his face. No one considered him capable of anything at all, let alone murder.

After that he worked and read and drank compulsively, did little else for a whole year. He never forgot that he was capable of murder, but he thought he had buried the urge. Then one morning he woke up with a boy strewn across his bed, face and chest battered in, abdomen torn wide open. Justin's hands were still tangled in the glistening purple stew of intestines. From the stains on his skin he could see that he had rubbed them all over his body, maybe rolled in them.

He didn't remember meeting the boy, didn't know how he had killed him or opened his body like a big wet Christmas present, or why. But he kept the body until it started to smell, and then he cut off the head, boiled it until the flesh was gone, and kept the skull. After that it never stopped again. They had all been boys, all young, thin, and pretty: everything the way Justin liked it. Weapons were too easy, too impersonal, so he drugged them and strangled them. Like Willy Wonka in the Technicolor bowels of his chocolate factory, *he* was the music maker, and *he* was the dreamer of dreams.

It was a dark and lonely revelry, to be sure. But so was writing; so was painting or learning music. So, he supposed, was all art when you penetrated to its molten core. He didn't know if killing was art, but it was the only creative thing he had ever done.

He got up, slid *Dandelion Wine* back into its place on his crowded bookshelf, and left the bedroom. He put his favourite CD on shuffle and crossed his small apartment to the kitchenette. A window beside the refrigerator looked out on a brick wall. Frank Sinatra was singing 'I've Got You Under My Skin'.

Justin opened the refrigerator and took out a package wrapped in foil. Inside was a ragged cut of meat as large as a dinner plate, deep red, tough and fibrous. He selected a knife from the jumble of filthy dishes in the sink and sliced off a piece of meat the size of his palm. He wasn't very hungry, but he needed something in his stomach to soak up the liquor he'd be drinking soon.

Justin heated oil in a skillet, sprinkled the meat with salt, laid it in the sizzling fat and cooked it until both sides were brown and the bottom of the pan was awash with fragrant juices. He slid the meat onto a saucer, found a clean fork in the silverware drawer, and began to eat his dinner standing at the counter.

The meat was rather tough, but it tasted wonderful, oily and salty with a slight undertone of musk. He felt it breaking down in the acids of his saliva and his stomach, felt its proteins joining with his cells and becoming part of him. That was fine. But after tonight he would have something better. A person who lived and stayed with him, whose mind belonged to him. A homemade zombie. Justin knew it was possible, if only he could destroy the right parts of the brain. If a drill and a syringeful of bleach didn't work, he would try something else next time.

The night drew like a curtain across the window, stealing his wall view brick by brick. Sinatra's voice was as smooth and sweet as cream. *Got you... deep in the heart of me...* Justin nodded reflectively. The meat left a delicately metallic flavour on his tongue, one of the myriad tastes of love. Soon it would be time to go out.

Apart from the trip to Reno and the delicious wallow in the desert, Justin had never left Los Angeles. He longed to drive out into the desert, to find again the ghost towns and nuclear moonscapes he had so loved in Nevada. But he never had. You needed a car to get out there. If you didn't have a car in L.A., you might as well curl up and die. Los Angeles was a city with an enormous central nervous system, but no brain.

Since being fired from his job at an orange juice plant for chronic absenteeism—too many bodies demanding his time, requiring that he cut them up, preserve them, consume them—Justin wasn't even sure how much longer he would be able to afford the apartment. But he didn't see how he could move out with things the way they were in here. The place was a terrible mess. His neighbours had started complaining about the smell.

Justin decided not to think about all that now. He still had a little money saved, and a city bus would get him from his Silver Lake apartment to the garish carnival of West Hollywood; that much he knew. It had done so countless times.

If he was lucky, he'd be bringing home company.

SUKO RAN FINGERS the colour of sandalwood through haphazardly cut black hair, painted his eyes with stolen drugstore kohl, and grinned at himself in the cracked mirror over the sink. He fastened a string of thrift-shop beads round his neck, studied the effect of the black plastic against torn black cotton and smooth brown skin, then added a clay amulet of the Buddha and a tiny wooden penis, both strung on leather thongs.

These he had purchased among the dim stalls at Wat Rajanada, the amulet market near Klong Saensaep in Bangkok. The amulet was to protect him against accidents and malevolent ghosts. The penis was to increase his potency, to make sure whoever he met up with tonight would have a good time. It was supposed to be worn on a string around his waist, but the first few times he'd done that, his American lovers gave him strange looks.

The amulets were the last thing Suko bought with Thai money before boarding a California-bound jet and bidding farewell to his sodden homeland, most likely forever. He'd had to travel a long way from Patpong Road to get them, but he didn't know whether one could buy magical amulets in America. Apparently one could: attached to his beads had once been a round medallion stamped with an exaggerated Negro face and the word ZULU. He'd lost the medallion on a night of drunken revelry, which was as it should be. *Mai pen rai. No problem.*

Suko was nineteen. His full name was unpronounceable by American tongues, but he didn't care. American tongues could do all sorts of other things for him. This he had learned at fourteen, after hitching a midnight ride out of his home village, a place so small and so poor that it appeared on no map foreign eyes would ever see.

His family had always referred to the city by its true name, Krung Thep, the Great City of Angels. Suko had never known it by any other name until he arrived there. Krung Thep was only an abbreviation for the true name, which was more than thirty syllables long. For some reason, *farangs* had never gotten used to this. They all called it Bangkok, a name like two sharp handclaps.

In the streets, the harsh reek of exhaust fumes was tinged with a million subtler perfumes: jasmine, raw sewage, grasshoppers frying in peppered oil, the odour of ripe durian fruit that was like rotting flesh steeped in thick sweet cream. The very air seemed spritzed with alcohol, soaked with neon and the juices of sex.

He found his calling on Patpong 3, a block-long strip of gay bars and nightclubs in Bangkok's famous sleaze district. In the village, Suko and his seven brothers and sisters had gutted fish for a few *baht* a day. Here he was paid thirty times as much to drink and dance with *farangs* who told him fascinating stories, to make his face prettier with makeup, to be fondled and flattered, to have his cock sucked as often as he could stand it. If he had to suck a few in return, how bad could that be? It was far from the worst thing he had ever put in his mouth. He rather liked the taste of sperm, if not the odd little tickle it left in the back of his throat.

He enjoyed the feel of male flesh against his own and the feel of strong arms enfolding him, loved never knowing what the night would bring. He marvelled at the range of body types among Americans and English, Germans and Australians. Some had skin as soft and pale as rice-flour dough; some were covered with thick hair like wool matting their chests and arms. They might be fat or emaciated, squat or ponderously tall, ugly, handsome, or forgettable. All the Thai boys he knew were lean, light brown, small-boned and smooth-skinned, with sweet androgynous faces. So was he. So was Noy.

From the cheap boom box in the corner of the room, Robert Smith sang that Suko made him feel young again. Suko scowled at the box. Noy had given him that tape, a poor-quality Bangkok bootleg of the Cure, right after Suko first spoke of leaving the country. Last year. The year Suko decided to get on with his life.

The rest of them, these other slim raven-haired heartbreakers, they thought they would be able to live like this forever. They were seventeen, fifteen, younger. They were in love with their own faces in the mirror, jet-coloured eyes glittering with drink and praise, lips bruised from too many rough kisses, too much expert use. They could not see themselves at thirty, could not imagine the roughening of their skin or the lines that bar life would etch into their faces. Some would end up hustling over on Soi Cowboy, Patpong's shabby cousin where the beer was cheaper and the tinsel tarnished, where the neon flickered fitfully or not at all. Some would move to the streets.

And some would simply disappear. Suko intended to be one of those.

Noy was just his age, and smart. Suko met him onstage at the Hi-Way Bar. They were performing the biker act, in which two boys sat facing each other astride the saddle of a Harley-Davidson, wearing only leather biker caps, tongue-kissing with sloppy abandon and masturbating each other while a ring of sweaty *farang* faces gathered around them.

Immediately afterward, while the come was still oozing between the thrumming saddle and the backs of their skinny thighs, Noy murmured into Suko's mouth, 'Wouldn't they be surprised if we just put this thing in gear and drove it into the crowd?'

Suko pulled back and stared at him. Noy's left arm was draped lazily around Suko's neck; Noy's right hand cupped Suko's cock, now tugging gently, now relaxing. Noy smiled and lifted one perfect eyebrow, and Suko found himself getting hard again for someone who wasn't even paying him.

Noy gave him a final squeeze and let go. 'Don't make a date when you get done working,' he told Suko. 'Take me home with you.'

Suko did, and even after a night on Patpong, they puzzled out one another's bodies like the streets of an unfamiliar city. Soon they were the undisputed stars of the Hi-Way's live sex shows; they knew how to love each other in private and how to make it look good in public. They made twice as much money as the other boys. Suko started saving up for a plane ticket.

But Noy spent his money on trinkets: T-shirts printed with obscene slogans, little bags of pot and pills, even a green glow-in-the-dark dildo to use in their stage show. In the end, Noy was just smart enough to make his stupidity utterly infuriating.

I'm really leaving, Suko would tell him as they lay entwined on a straw pallet in the room they rented above a cheap restaurant, as the odours of *nam pla* and chilli oil wafted through the open window to mingle with the scent of their lovemaking. *When I save up enough, I'm going to do it. You can come, but I won't wait for you once I have the money, not knowing how many ways I could lose this chance.*

But Noy never believed him, not until the night Suko showed him the one-way ticket. And how Noy cried then, real tears such as Suko had never thought to see from him, great childish tears that reddened his smooth skin and made his eyes swell to slits. He clutched at Suko's hands and slobbered on them and begged him not to go until Suko wanted to shove him face-first into the Patpong mud.

This is all you want? Suko demanded, waving a hand at the tawdry neon, the ramshackle bars, the Thai boys and girls putting everything on display with a clearly marked price tag: their flesh, their hunger, and if they stayed long enough, their souls. *This is enough for you? Well, it isn't enough for me.*

Noy had made his choices, had worked hard for them. But Suko had made his choices too, and no one could ever take them away. The city where he lived now, Los Angeles, was one of his choices. Another city of angels.

He had left Noy sobbing in the middle of Patpong 3, unable or unwilling to say goodbye. Now half a world lay between them, and with time, Suko's memories of Noy soured into anger. He had been nothing but a jaded, fiercely erotic, selfish boy, expecting Suko to give up the dreams of a lifetime for a few more years of mindless pleasure. *Asshole*, Suko thought, righteous anger flaring in his heart. *Jerk. Geek.*

Now Robert Smith wanted Suko to fly him to the moon. As reasonable a demand, really, as any Noy had handed him. Suko favoured the boom box with his sweetest smile and carefully shaped his mouth round a phrase:

'Get a life, Robert!'

'I will always love you,' Robert moaned.

Suko kept grinning at the box. But now an evil gleam came into his black eyes, and he spat out a single word.

'NOT!'

JUSTIN HIT THE bars of West Hollywood hard and fast, pounding back martinis, which he couldn't help thinking of as martians ever since he'd read *The Shining.* Soon his brain felt pleasantly lubricated, half-numb.

He had managed to find five or six bars he liked within walking distance of each other, no mean feat in L.A. Just now he was leaning against the matte-grey wall of the Wounded Stag, an expensive club eerily lit with blue bulbs and blacklights. He let his eyes sweep over the crowd, then drift back to the sparkling drink in his hand. The gin shattered the light, turned it silver and razor-edged. The olive bobbed like a tiny severed head in a bath of caustic chemicals.

Something weird was happening on TV. Justin had walked out of Club 312, a cosy bar with Sinatra on the jukebox that was normally his favourite place to relax with a drink before starting the search for company. Tonight 312 was empty save for a small crowd of regulars clustered around the flickering set in the corner. He couldn't tell what was going on, since none of the regulars ever talked to him, or he to them.

But from the scraps of conversation—*eaten alive, night of the living dead*—and edgy laughter he caught, Justin assumed some channel was showing a Halloween horror retrospective. The holiday fell next week and he'd been meaning to get some candy. You ought to have something to offer trick-or-treaters if you were going to invite them in.

He heard a newscaster's voice saying, 'This has been a special report. We'll keep you informed throughout the evening as more information becomes available...' Could that be part of a horror filmfest? A fake, maybe, like that radio broadcast in the 1930s that had driven people to slit their wrists. They'd been afraid of Martians, Justin remembered. He downed the last of his own martian and left the bar. He didn't care about the news. He would be making his own living dead tonight.

The Wounded Stag had no TV. Pictures were passé here, best left to that stillborn golden calf that was the *other* Hollywood. Sound was the thing, pounds and pounds of it pushing against the eardrums, saturating the brain, making the very skin feel tender and bruised if you withstood it long enough. Beyond headache lay transcendence.

The music at the Stag was mostly psycho-industrial, Skinny Puppy and Einsturzende Neubaten and Ministry, the Butthole Surfers and Nine Inch Nails and My Bloody Valentine. Justin liked the names of the bands better than he liked the music. The only time they played Sinatra here was at closing hour, when they wanted to drive people out.

But the Stag was where the truly beautiful boys came, the drop-dead boys who could get away with shaving half their hair and dyeing the other half dead black or lurid violet, or wearing it long and stringy and filthy, or piercing their faces twenty times. They swept through the door wrapped in their leather, their skimpy fishnet, their jangling rings and chains as if they wore precious jewels and ermine. They allowed themselves one contemptuous glance around the bar, then looked at no one. If you wanted their attention, you had to make a bid for it: an overpriced drink, a compliment that was just ambiguous enough to be cool. Never, ever a smile.

Like as not, you would be rejected summarily and without delay. But if even a spark of interest flared in those coldly beautiful black-rimmed eyes, what sordid fantasy! What exotic passion! What delicious viscera!

He had taken four boys home from the Stag on separate nights. They were still in his apartment, their organs wrapped neatly in plastic film inside his freezer, their hands tucked within easy reach under his mattress, their skulls nestled in a box in the closet. Justin smiled at them all he wanted to now, and they grinned right back at him. They had to. He had boiled them down to the bone, and all skulls grinned because they were so happy to be free of imprisoning flesh.

But skulls and mummified hands and salty slices of meat weren't enough any more. He wanted to keep the face, the thrilling pulse in the chest and guts, the sweet slick inside of the mouth and anus. He wanted to wrap his mouth around a cock that would grow hard without his having to shove a finger up inside it like some desiccated puppet. He wanted to keep a boy, not a motley collection of bits. And he wanted that boy to smile at him, for him, for *only* him.

Justin dragged his gaze away from the swirling depths of his martian and glanced at the door. The most beautiful boy he had ever seen was just coming in. And he was smiling: a big, sunny, unaffected and utterly guileless smile.

SUKO LEANED HIS head against the tall blond man's shoulder and stared out the window of the taxi. The candy panorama of West Hollywood spread out before them, neon smeared across hot asphalt, marabou cowboys and rhinestone drag queens posing in the headlights. The cab edged forward, parting the throng like a river, carrying Suko to whatever strange shores of pleasure still lay ahead of him this night.

'Where did you say you were from?' the man asked. As Suko answered, gentle fingers did something exciting to the inside of his thigh through his ripped black jeans. The blond man's voice was without accent, almost without inflection.

Of course, no one in L.A. had an accent. Everyone was from somewhere else, but they all strove to hide it, as if they'd slid from the womb craving flavoured mineral water and sushi on Melrose. But Suko had met no one else who spoke like this man. His voice was soft and low, nearly a monotone. To Suko it was soothing; any kind of quiet aimed at him was soothing after the circuses of Patpong and West Hollywood, half a world apart but cut from the same bright cacophonous cloth. Cities of angels: *yeah, right*. Fallen angels.

They pulled up in front of a shabby apartment building that looked as if it had been modelled after a cardboard box sometime in the 1950s. The man—*Justin*, Suko remembered, his name was *Justin*—paid the cab driver but didn't tip. The cab gunned away from the curb, tyres squealing rudely on the cracked asphalt. Justin stumbled backward and bumped into Suko. 'Sorry.'

'Hey, no problem.' That was still a mouthful—his tongue just naturally wanted to rattle off a *mai pen rai*—but Suko got all the syllables out. Justin smiled, the first time he'd done so since introducing himself. His long skinny fingers closed around Suko's wrist.

'Come on,' he said. 'It's safer if we go in the back way.' They walked around the corner of the building, under an iron stairwell and past some garbage cans that fairly shimmered with the odour of decay. Suko's foot hit something soft. He looked down, stopped, and backed into Justin. A young black man lay among the stinking cans, his head propped at a painful angle against the wall, his legs sprawled wide.

'Is he dead?' Suko clutched for his Buddha amulet. The man's ghost might still be trapped in this mean alley, looking for living humans to plague. If it wanted to, it could suck out their life essences through their spinal columns like a child sipping soda from a straw.

But Justin shook his head. 'Just drunk. See, there's an empty bottle by his leg.'

'He looks dead.'

Justin prodded the black man's thigh with the toe of his loafer. After a moment, the man stirred. His eyes never opened, but his hands twitched and his mouth gaped wide, chewing at the air.

'See?' Justin tugged at Suko's arm. 'Come on.'

They climbed the metal stairs and entered the building through a fire door wedged open with a flattened Old Milwaukee can. Justin led the way down a hall coloured only by shadow and grime, stopped in front of a door identical to all the others but for the number 21 stamped on a metal plate small as an egg, and undid a complicated series of locks. He opened the door a crack and ushered Suko inside, then followed and turned to do up all the locks again.

At once Suko noticed the smell. First there was only the most delicate tendril, like a pale brown finger tickling the back of his throat; then a wave hit him, powerful and nauseating. It was the smell of the garbage cans downstairs, increased a hundredfold and overlaid with other smells: cooking oil, air freshener, some caustic chemical odour that stung his nostrils. It was the smell of rot. And it filled the apartment.

Justin saw Suko wrinkling his nose. 'My refrigerator broke,' he said. 'Damn landlord says he can't replace it till next week. I just bought a bunch of meat on sale and it all went bad. Don't look in the fridge, whatever you do.'

'Why you don't—' Suko caught himself. 'Why *don't you* throw it out?'

'Oh...' Justin looked vaguely surprised for a moment. Then he shrugged. 'I'll get around to it, I guess. It doesn't bother me much.'

He pulled a bottle of rum from somewhere, poured a few inches into a glass already sitting on the countertop and stirred in a spoonful of sugar. Justin had been impressed by Suko's taste for straight sugared rum back at the Stag, and said he had some expensive Bacardi he wanted Suko to try. Their fingertips kissed as the glass changed hands, and a tiny thrill ran down Suko's spine. Justin was a little weird, but Suko could handle that, no problem. And there was a definite sexual charge between them. Suko felt sure the rest of the night would swarm with flavours and sensations, fireworks and roses.

Justin watched Suko sip the rum. His eyes were an odd, deep lilac-blue, a colour Suko had never seen before in the endless spectrum of American eyes. The liquor tasted faintly bitter beneath the sugar, as if the glass weren't quite clean. Again, Suko could deal; a clean glass at the Hi-Way Bar on Patpong 3 was a rare find.

'Do you want to smoke some weed?' Justin asked when Suko had polished off an inch of the Bacardi.

'Sure.'

'It's in the bedroom.' Suko was ready to follow him there, but Justin said, 'I'll get it,' and hurried out of the kitchen. Suko heard him banging about in the other room, opening and shutting a great many drawers.

Suko drank more rum. He glanced sideways at the refrigerator, a modern monolith of shining harvest gold, without the cosy clutter he had seen decorating the fridges of others: memo boards, shopping lists, food-shaped magnets trapping snapshots or newspaper cartoons. It gave off a nearly imperceptible hum, the sound of a motor running smoothly. And the smell of decay seemed to emanate from all around the apartment, not just the fridge. Could it really be broken?

He grabbed the door handle and tugged. The seal sucked softly back for a second; then the door swung wide and the refrigerator light clicked on.

A fresh wave of rot washed over him. Maybe Justin hadn't been lying about meat gone bad. The contents of the fridge were meagre and depressing: a decimated twelve-pack of cheap beer, a crusted jar of Gulden's Spicy Brown mustard, several lumpy packages wrapped in foil. A residue of rusty red on the bottom shelf, like the juice that might leak out of a meat tray. And pushed far to the back, a large Tupperware cake server, incongruous among the slim bachelor pickings.

Suko touched one of the beer cans. It was icy cold.

Something inside the cake server was moving. He could just make out its faint shadowy convulsions through the opaque plastic.

Suko slammed the door and stumbled away. Justin was just coming back in. He gripped Suko's arms, stared into his face. 'What's wrong?'

'Nothing—I—'

'Did you open the fridge?'

'No!'

Justin shook him. The strange lilac eyes had gone muddy, the handsome features twisted into a mean mask. *'Did you open the fucking fridge?'* Suko felt droplets of spit land on his face, his lips. He wished miserably that they could have gotten there some other way, any way but this. He had wanted to make love with this man.

'Did you—'

'No!!!'

Suko thought he might cry. At the same time he had begun to feel remote, far away from the ugly scene, as if he were floating in a corner watching it but not caring much what happened. It must be the rum. But it wasn't like being drunk; that was a familiar feeling. This was more like the time Noy had convinced him to take two Valiums.

An hour after swallowing the little yellow wafers, Suko had watched Noy suck him off from a million miles away, wondering why anyone ever got excited about this, why anyone ever got excited about anything.

He had hated the feeling then. He hated it more now, because it was pulling him down.

He was afraid it might be the last thing he ever felt.

He was afraid it might not be.

———

JUSTIN HALF-DRAGGED, half-carried Suko into the bedroom and dumped him on the mattress. He felt the boy's delicate ivory bones shifting under his hands, the boy's exquisite mass of organs pressing against his groin. He wanted to unzip that sweet sack of skin right now, sink his teeth into that beating, bleeding heart…but no. He had other plans for this one.

He'd closed the door to the adjacent bathroom in case he brought the boy in here still conscious. Most of a body was soaking in a tub full of ice water and Clorox. Suko wouldn't have needed to see that. Justin almost opened the door for the extra light, but decided not to. He didn't want to leave the bedside even for a second.

His supplies were ready on the nightstand. Justin plugged the drill's power cord into the socket behind the bed, gently thumbed up one of Suko's make-up-smudged eyelids and examined the silvery sclera. The sleeping pills had worked fine, as always. He ground them up and put them in a glass before he left. That way, when he brought home company, Justin could simply pour him a drink in the special glass.

He used the scissors to slice off Suko's shirt, which was so artfully ripped up that Justin hardly had to damage it further to remove it. He cut away the beads and amulets, saving the tiny wooden penis, which had caught his eye back at the Stag. His own penis ached and burned. He pressed his ear against the narrow chest, heard the lungs pull in a deep slow breath, then release it just as easily. He heard blood moving unhurried through arteries and veins, heard a secret stomach sound from down below. Justin could listen to a boy's chest and stomach all night, but reluctantly he took his ear away.

He crawled onto the bed, positioned Suko's head in his lap, and hefted the drill, which was heavier than he remembered. He hoped he would be able to control how far the bit went in. A fraction of an inch too deep into the brain could ruin everything. It was only the frontal lobes he wanted to penetrate, the cradle of free will.

Justin parted the boy's thick black hair and placed the diamond-tipped bit against the centre of the pale, faintly shiny scalp. He took a deep breath, bit his lip, and squeezed the trigger. When he took the drill away, there was a tiny, perfect black hole near the crown of the boy's head.

He picked up the syringe, slid the needle in and forward, toward the forehead. He felt a tiny resistance, as if the needle was passing through a

hair-thin elastic membrane. He pushed the plunger and flooded the boy's brain with chlorine bleach.

Three things happened at once.

Suko's eyes fluttered open.

Justin had an explosive orgasm in his pants.

Something heavy thudded against the bathroom door.

———

SUKO SAW THE blond man's face upside down, the lilac eyes like little slices of moon, the mouth a reverse smile or grimace. A whining buzz filled his skull, seemed to jar the very plates of his skull, as if hornets had built a nest inside his brain. A dull ache spread spider-like over the top of his head.

He smelled roses, though he had seen none in the room. He smelled wood shavings, the sharp stink of shit, the perfume of ripe oranges. Each of these scents was gone as quickly as it had come. Lingering was a burnt metallic flavour, a little like the taste that had lingered in his mouth the time he'd had a tooth filled in Bangkok.

Shavings. Roses. Cut grass. Sour milk. And underneath it all, the smell of rotting flesh.

Suko's field of vision went solid screaming chartreuse, then danger red. Now Justin was back, a negative of himself, hair green, face inky purple, eyes white circles with pinholes at their centres like tiny imploding suns. And suddenly something else was in the frame as well. Something all black, with holes where no holes should be. A face swollen and torn, a face that could not be alive, but whose jaw was moving.

A hand missing most of its fingers closed on the back of Justin's hair and yanked. A drooling purple mouth closed on Justin's throat and tore away a chunk.

Suko managed to sit up. His vision spun and yawed. The reek of rot was dizzying, and overlying it was a new stinging smell, a chemical smell he could not identify. Something salty ran into his eyes. He touched his face, and his fingers came away slicked with a thin clear substance.

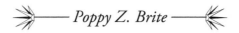
The thing wrapped skeletal arms around Justin and pulled him off the bed. They rolled on the floor together, Justin's blood fountaining out of his throat, the thing grunting and lapping at it.

Ragged flesh trailed from its mouth.

Justin wasn't screaming, Suko realised.

He was *smiling*.

IT WAS THE boy from the bathtub. Justin couldn't see his face, but he could smell the Clorox, raw and fresh. He had carved a great deal of flesh off of this one, as well as removing the viscera. But he had not yet cut off the head. Now it was snuggled under his chin, tongue burrowing like a worm into his wounded throat. He felt the teeth tearing at him, chunks of his skin and muscle disappearing down the boy's gullet. He felt one of the bones in his neck crack and splinter.

The pain was as shocking as an orgasm, but cleaner. The joy was like nothing he had known before, not when he watched his mother die, not when he tasted the flesh of another person for the first time. It had worked. Not only was the Asian boy still alive, but the others had come back as well. They had never left Justin at all. They had only been waiting.

He got his arms around the hollow body, pulled it closer. He cupped the cold rubbery buttocks, entwined his legs with the thrusting bones of its thighs. When its jaws released his throat, he pressed his face against the voracious swollen one, pushed his tongue between the blackened lips and felt the teeth rip it out. His mouth filled with blood and rot. He swallowed, gagged, swallowed again.

A head rolled out from under the bed, pushing itself by frantic motions of jaw and tongue. The severed ends of the neck muscles twitched, trying to help it along. Its nose and left eyebrow were pierced with silver rings, its empty eye-sockets crusted with blood and greasy black makeup. It reached Justin and bit deep into one of his thighs. He kicked once, in surprise, then bent his leg so that the teeth could more easily get at the soft muscle of his groin. He felt his flesh peeling away.

The upper half of a body was pulling itself out of the closet. Its black-lacquered nails dug into the carpet. Ropes of intestine trailed behind it, coming apart, leaving a trail of shit and ichor on the rug. This one had been, possibly, a Mexican boy. Now its skin was the colour of decaying eggplant, and very few teeth were left in its gaping mouth. Dimly Justin remembered extracting them with a pair of pliers after the rigor mortis had slackened.

It tore Justin's belly open with its hands and sank its face into his guts. He arched his back, felt its fingers plunging deep, its mouth lapping at the very core of him.

The small pleasures of his life—reading, listening to the music of another time, choking the life out of boys and playing with their abandoned shells—were nothing compared to this. He wanted it to go on forever.

But, eventually, he died.

The corpse from the bathtub chewed at Justin's throat and chest. Half-chewed pieces of Justin slid down its gullet, into the great scooped-out hollow of its abdomen, out onto the floor. The corpse from the closet sucked up the liquor and partly digested meat it found in Justin's stomach. The head bit into Justin's scrotum and gulped the savoury mass of the testicles like a pair of tender oysters.

They seemed to know when to stop feeding, to refrain from pulling him completely apart, to leave enough of him. When he came back, Justin knew exactly what to do.

After all, he had been doing it long before most of the others.

———

SUKO STUMBLED OUT of the bedroom and slammed the door behind him. Something was rolling around and around in the refrigerator, banging against the inside of the door. He almost went over to open it, only caught himself at the last second. He wasn't thinking very clearly. His head felt wrong somehow, his brain caught in a downward spiral. He did not understand what he had just seen. But he knew he had to get out of the apartment.

No problem, a voice yammered in his head. *Stay cool. Chill out. Don't have a cow, man.* He barely knew the meaning of the words. The American voice seemed to be receding down a long black tunnel; already it was so tiny and faint he could hardly hear it. He realised he was thinking in Thai for the first time in years. Even his native language was strange, a flurry of quick sharp syllables like little whirling razorblades slicing into the meat of his brain.

He fumbled with the complicated series of locks, yanked the door open and nearly fell into the hall. How had he entered the building...? Up a metal staircase, through a door at the end of the long dark hall. He reached it and let himself out. The hot October night seared his lungs. He could smell every poisonous particle of exhaust blanketing the city, every atom of shit and filth and blood baked onto the streets. Not like the ripe wet kiss of Bangkok, but so arid, so mercilessly dry. He felt his way down the fire escape and around the corner of the building.

The empty street seemed a mile wide. There was no sidewalk, only a steep curb and a long grey boulevard stretching away toward some other part of the city. There were no cars; he could hear no traffic anywhere. Even with his head feeling so strange, Suko knew something was wrong. L.A. streets were often empty of people, but always there were cars.

Far away at the next intersection, he made out a small group of figures straggling in his direction, bathed in a traffic light's red glow. For a long moment he watched them come, trying to be sure they were really there, wondering what he should do. Then he started toward them. The blond man had done something awful to his head; he needed help. Maybe the figures would be able to help him.

But when he got closer, he saw that they were like the things he had seen in the bedroom. One had a long fatty slash wound across its bare torso. One had been gouged in the face with something jagged; its nose was cloven in half and an eyeball hung out of the socket, leaking yolky fluid. One had no wounds, but looked as if it had starved to death; its nude body was all bone-ends and wasted hollows, its genitals shrivelled into the pelvic cavity, its blue-white skin covered with huge black and purple lesions.

When they saw him, the things opened their mouths and widened their nostrils, catching his scent. It was too late to get away. He couldn't run,

didn't think he would even be able to stand up much longer. He stumbled forward and gave himself to them.

The little group closed around Suko, keeping him on his feet, supporting him as best they could. Gouged Eyeball caught him and steadied him. Slash Wound mouthed his shoulder as if in comfort, but did not bite. Lesions nudged him, urged him on. Suko realised they were *herding* him. They recognised him as one of their own, separated from the flock somehow. They were welcoming him back in.

Miserably, Suko wondered what would happen when they met someone alive.

Then the hunger flared in his belly, and he knew.

POPPY Z. BRITE is the author of eight novels, several short story collections and some non-fiction, as well as editing two volumes of the vampire anthologies *Love in Vein*. Now known as Billy Martin, he lives in New Orleans and is married to the visual artist Grey Cross. 'The greatest horror of "Self-Made Man",' reveals the author, 'is that it was originally written for *Book of the Dead 3*, an anthology that went through a series of delays, scandals, intrigues and near-lawsuits before sinking under the weight of editorial and publishing idiocy. As for the story itself, it was written when I was mid-way through my novel *Exquisite Corpse*, and I just had to get some of the Jeffrey Dahmer-mania out of my system before I could go on. Readers have said my characters in the novel are too influenced by Dahmer—wait 'til they get a load of this baby.'

THE WEDDING PRESENT

Neil Gaiman

AFTER ALL THE joys and the headaches of the wedding, after the madness and the magic of it all (not to mention the embarrassment of Belinda's father's after-dinner speech, complete with family slide-show), after the honeymoon was literally (although not yet metaphorically) over and before their new suntans had a chance to fade in the English autumn, Belinda and Gordon got down to the business of unwrapping the wedding presents and writing their thank-you letters—thank-yous enough for every towel and every toaster, for the juicer and the bread-maker, for the cutlery and the crockery and the Teasmaid and the curtains.

'Right,' said Gordon. 'That's the large objects thank-you'd. What've we got left?'

'Things in envelopes,' said Belinda. 'Cheques, I hope.'

There were several cheques, a number of gift tokens, and even a £10 book token from Gordon's Aunt Marie, who was poor as a church mouse, Gordon told Belinda, but a dear, and who had sent him a book token every birthday for as long as he could remember. And then, at the very bottom of the pile, there was a large, brown business-like envelope.

'What is it?' asked Belinda.

Gordon opened the flap and pulled out a sheet of paper the colour of two-day-old cream, ragged at top and bottom, with typing on one side. The words had been typed with a manual typewriter, something Gordon had not seen in some years. He read the page slowly.

'What is it?' asked Belinda. 'Who's it from?'

'I don't know,' said Gordon. 'Someone who still owns a typewriter. It's not signed.'

'Is it a letter?'

'Not exactly,' he said, and he scratched the side of his nose and read it again.

'Well,' she said, in an exasperated voice (but she was not really exasperated; she was happy. She would wake in the morning and check to see if she was still as happy as she had been when she went to sleep the night before, or when Gordon had woken her in the night by brushing up against her, or when she had woken him. And she was). 'Well, what is it?'

'It appears to be a description of our wedding,' he said. 'It's very nicely written. Here,' and he passed it to her.

———

IT WAS A crisp day in early October when Gordon Robert Johnson and Belinda Karen Abingdon swore that they would love each other, would support and honour each other as long as they both should live. The bride was radiant and lovely, the groom was nervous, but obviously proud and just as obviously pleased.

———

THAT WAS HOW it began. It went on to describe the service and the reception clearly, simply and amusingly.

'How sweet,' she said. 'What does it say on the envelope?'

'*Gordon and Belinda's Wedding*,' he read.

'No name? Nothing to indicate who sent it?'

'Uh-uh.'

'Well, it's very sweet, and it's very thoughtful,' she said. 'Whoever it's from.'

She looked inside the envelope to see if there was something else in there that they had overlooked, a note from whichever one of her friends (or his, or theirs) had written it, but there wasn't. So, vaguely relieved that there was one less thank-you note to write, she placed the cream sheet of paper back in its envelope, which she placed in the box-file along with a copy of the Wedding Banquet menu, and the invitations, and the contact sheets for the wedding photographs, and one white rose from the bridal bouquet.

———

GORDON WAS AN architect, and Belinda was a vet. For each of them what they did was a vocation, not a job. They were in their early twenties. Neither of them had been married before, nor even seriously involved with anyone else. They met when Gordon brought his thirteen-year-old golden retriever, Goldie, grey-muzzled and half-paralysed, to Belinda's surgery to be put down. He had had the dog since he was a boy, and insisted on being with her at the end. Belinda held his hand as he cried, and then, suddenly and unprofessionally, she hugged him, tightly, as if she could squeeze away the pain and the loss and the grief. One of them asked the other if they could meet that evening in the local pub for a drink, and afterwards neither of them was sure which of them had proposed it.

The most important thing to know about the first two years of their marriage was this: they were pretty happy. From time to time they would squabble, and every once in a while they would have a blazing row about nothing very much that would end in tearful reconciliations, and they would make love and kiss away the other's tears, and whisper heartfelt apologies into each other's ears. At the end of the second year, six months after she came off the pill, Belinda found herself pregnant.

Gordon bought her a bracelet studded with tiny rubies, and he turned the spare bedroom into a nursery, hanging the wallpaper himself. The design was covered with nursery rhyme characters, with Little Bo Peep, and Humpty Dumpty, and the Dish Running Away With the Spoon, over and over and over again.

Belinda came home from the hospital with little Melanie in her carrycot, and Belinda's mother came to stay with them for a week, sleeping on the sofa in the lounge.

It was on the third day that Belinda pulled out the box-file, to show her wedding souvenirs to her mother, and to reminisce. Already their wedding seemed like such a long time ago. They smiled at the dried, brown thing that had once been a white rose, and clucked over the menu and the invitation. At the bottom of the box was a large brown envelope.

'*Gordon and Belinda's Marriage*,' read Belinda's mother.

'It's a description of our wedding,' said Belinda. 'It's very sweet. It even has a bit in it about Daddy's slide-show.'

Belinda opened the envelope and pulled out the sheet of cream paper. She read what was typed upon the paper, and made a face. Then she put it away, without saying anything.

'Can't I see it, dear?' asked her mother.

'I think it's Gordon playing a joke,' said Belinda. 'Not in good taste, either.'

———

BELINDA WAS SITTING up in bed that night, breast-feeding Melanie, when she said to Gordon, who was staring at his wife and new daughter with a foolish smile upon his face, 'Darling, why did you write those things?'

'What things?'

'In the letter. That wedding thing. You know.'

'I don't know.'

'It wasn't funny.'

He sighed. 'What are you talking about?'

Belinda pointed to the box-file, which she had brought upstairs and placed upon her dressing-table. Gordon opened it and took out the envelope. 'Did it always say that on the envelope?' he asked. 'I thought it said something about our wedding.' Then he took out and read the single sheet of ragged-edged paper, and his forehead creased. 'I didn't write this.' He turned the paper over, staring at the blank side as if expecting to see something else written there.

'You didn't write it?' she asked. 'Really you didn't?' Gordon shook his head. Belinda wiped a dribble of milk from the baby's chin. 'I believe you,' she said. 'I thought you wrote it, but you didn't.'

'No.'

'Let me see that again,' she said. He passed the paper to her. 'This is so weird. I mean, it's not funny, and it's not even true.'

Typed upon the paper was a brief description of the previous two years for Gordon and Belinda. It had not been a good two years, according to the typed sheet. Six months after they were married Belinda had been bitten in the cheek by a Pekingese, so badly that the cheek needed to be stitched back together. It had left a nasty scar. Worse than that, nerves had been damaged, and she had begun to drink, perhaps to numb the pain. She suspected that Gordon was revolted by her face, while the new baby, it said, was a desperate attempt to glue the couple together.

'Why would they say this?' she asked.

'They?'

'Whoever wrote this horrid thing.' She ran a finger across her cheek: it was unblemished and unmarked. She was a very beautiful young woman, although she looked tired and fragile now.

'How do you know it's a *they?*'

'I don't know,' she said, transferring the baby to her left breast. 'It seems a sort of *they*-ish thing to do. To write that and to swap it for the old one and to wait until one of us read it... Come on, little Melanie, there you go, that's such a fine girl...'

'Shall I throw it away?'

'Yes. No. I don't know. I think...' She stroked the baby's forehead. 'Hold on to it,' she said. 'We might need it for evidence. I wonder if it was something Al organised.' Al was Gordon's youngest brother.

Gordon put the paper back into the envelope, and he put the envelope back into the box-file, which was pushed under the bed and, more or less, forgotten.

Neither of them got much sleep for the next few months, what with the nightly feeds and the continual crying, for Melanie was a colicky baby. The box-file stayed under the bed. And then Gordon was offered a job in Preston, several hundred miles north, and since Belinda was on leave from her job and had no immediate plans to go back to work, she found the idea rather attractive. So they moved.

They found a terraced house in a cobbled street, high and old and deep. Belinda filled in from time to time at a local vet's, seeing small animals and house pets. When Melanie was eighteen months old Belinda gave birth to a son, whom they called Kevin, after Gordon's late grandfather.

Gordon was made a full partner in the firm of architects. When Kevin began to go to kindergarten, Belinda went back to work.

The box-file was never lost. It was in one of the spare rooms at the top of the house, beneath a teetering pile of copies of the *Architects' Journal* and *The Architectural Review*. Belinda thought about the box-file, and what it contained, from time to time, and, one night when Gordon was in Scotland overnight consulting on the remodelling of an ancestral home, she did more than think.

Both of the children were asleep. Belinda went up the stairs into the undecorated part of the house. She moved the magazines and opened the box, which (where it had not been covered by magazines) was thick with two years of undisturbed dust. The envelope still said *Gordon and Belinda's Marriage* on it, and Belinda honestly did not know if it had ever said anything else.

She took out the paper from the envelope, and she read it. And then she put it away, and sat there, at the top of the house, feeling shaken and sick.

According to the neatly-typed message, Kevin, her second child, had not been born; the baby had been miscarried at five months. Since then Belinda had been suffering from frequent attacks of bleak, black depression. Gordon was home rarely, it said, because he was conducting a rather miserable affair with the senior partner in his company, a striking but nervous woman ten years his senior. Belinda was drinking more, and affecting high collars and scarves, to hide the spider-web scar upon her cheek. She and Gordon spoke little, except to argue the small and petty arguments of those who fear the big arguments, knowing that the only things that were left to be said were too huge to be said without destroying both their lives.

Belinda said nothing about the latest version of *Gordon and Belinda's Marriage* to Gordon. However, he read it himself, or something quite like it, several months later, when Belinda's mother fell ill and Belinda went south for a week to help look after her.

On the sheet of paper that Gordon took out of the envelope was a portrait of a marriage similar to the one that Belinda had read, although, at present, his affair with his boss had ended badly, and his job was now in peril.

Gordon rather liked his boss, but could not imagine himself ever becoming romantically involved with her. He was enjoying his job, although he wanted something that would challenge him more than it did.

Belinda's mother improved, and Belinda returned within the week. Her husband and children were relieved and delighted to see her come home.

It was Christmas Eve before Gordon spoke to Belinda about the envelope.

'You've looked at it too, haven't you?' They had crept into the children's bedrooms earlier that evening and filled the hanging Christmas stockings. Gordon had felt euphoric as he had walked through the house, as he stood beside his children's beds, but it was a euphoria tinged with a profound sorrow: the knowledge that such moments of complete happiness could not last; that one could not stop Time.

Belinda knew what he was talking about. 'Yes,' she said. 'I've read it.'

'What do you think?'

'Well,' she said. 'I don't think it's a joke any more. Not even a sick joke.'

'Mm,' he said. 'Then what is it?'

They sat in the living room at the front of the house with the lights dimmed, and the log burning on the bed of coals cast flickering orange and yellow light about the room.

'I think it really is a wedding present,' she told him. 'It's the marriage that we aren't having. The bad things are happening there on the page, not here, in our lives. Instead of living it, we are reading it, knowing it could have gone that way and also that it never did.'

'You're saying it's magic, then?' He would not have said it aloud, but it was Christmas Eve, and the lights were down.

'I don't believe in magic,' she said, flatly. 'It's a wedding present. And I think we should make sure it's kept safe.'

On Boxing Day she moved the envelope from the box-file to her jewellery drawer, which she kept locked, where it lay flat beneath her necklaces and rings, her bracelets and her brooches.

Spring became summer. Winter became spring.

Gordon was exhausted: by day he worked for clients, designing, and liaising with builders and contractors; by night he would sit up late, working for his own self, designing museums and galleries and public buildings for competitions. Sometimes his designs received honourable mentions and were reproduced in architectural journals.

Belinda was doing more large animal work, which she enjoyed, visiting farmers and inspecting and treating horses, sheep and cows. Sometimes she would bring the children with her on her rounds.

Her mobile phone rang when she was in a paddock trying to examine a pregnant goat who had, it turned out, no desire to be caught, let alone examined. She retired from the battle, leaving the goat glaring at her from across the field, and thumbed the phone open. 'Yes?'

'Guess what?'

'Hello darling. Um. You've won the lottery?'

'Nope. Close, though. My design for the British Heritage Museum has made the shortlist. I'm up against some pretty stiff contenders, though. But I'm on the shortlist.'

'That's wonderful!'

'I've spoken to Mrs Fulbright and she's going to have Sonja baby-sit for us tonight. We're celebrating.'

'Terrific. Love you,' she said. 'Now got to get back to the goat.'

They drank too much champagne over a fine celebratory meal. That night in their bedroom as Belinda removed her earrings, she said, 'Shall we see what the Wedding Present says?'

He looked at her gravely from the bed. He was only wearing his socks. 'No, I don't think so. It's a special night. Why spoil it?'

She placed her earrings in her jewellery drawer and locked it. Then she removed her stockings. 'I suppose you're right. I can imagine what it says, anyway. I'm drunk and depressed and you're a miserable loser. And meanwhile we're...well, actually I *am* a bit tiddly, but that's not what I mean. It just sits there at the bottom of the drawer, like the portrait in the attic in *The Picture of Dorian Gray.*'

'"And it was only by his rings that they knew him." Yes. I remember. We read it in school.'

'That's really what I'm scared of,' she said, pulling on a cotton night-dress. 'That the thing on that paper is the real portrait of our marriage at present, and what we've got now is just a pretty picture. That it's real and we're not. I mean,' she was speaking intently now, with the gravity of the slightly drunk, 'don't you ever think that it's too good to be true?'

He nodded. 'Sometimes. Tonight, certainly.'

She shivered. 'Maybe really I *am* a drunk with a dog-bite on my cheek, and you fuck anything that moves and Kevin was never born and—and all that other horrible stuff.'

He stood up, walked over to her, put his arms around her. 'But it isn't true,' he pointed out. 'This is real. You're real. I'm real. That wedding thing is just a story. It's just words.' And he kissed her, and held her tightly, and little more was said that night.

It was a long six months before Gordon's design for the British Heritage Museum was announced as the winner, although it was derided in *The Times* as being too 'aggressively modern' and in various architectural journals as being too old-fashioned, and it was described by one of the judges, in an interview in the *Sunday Telegraph,* as 'a bit of a compromise candidate—everybody's second choice'.

They moved to London, letting their house in Preston to an artist and his family, for Belinda would not let Gordon sell it. Gordon worked intensively, happily, on the museum project. Kevin was six and Melanie was eight. Melanie found London intimidating, but Kevin loved it. Both of the children were initially distressed to have lost their friends and their school. Belinda found a part-time job at a small animal clinic in Camden, working three afternoons a week. She missed her cows.

Days in London became months and then years, and, despite occasional budgetary setbacks, Gordon was increasingly excited. The day approached when the first ground would be broken for the museum.

One night Belinda woke in the small hours, and she stared at her sleeping husband in the sodium yellow illumination of the street-lamp outside their bedroom window. His hairline was receding, and the hair at the back was thinning. Belinda wondered what it would be like when she was actually married to a bald man. She decided it would be much the same as it always had been. Mostly happy. Mostly good.

She wondered what was happening to the *them* in the envelope. She could feel its presence, dry and brooding, in the corner of their bedroom, safely locked away from all harm. She felt, suddenly, sorry for the Belinda and Gordon trapped in the envelope on their piece of paper, hating each other and everything else.

Gordon began to snore. She kissed him, gently, on the cheek, and said, 'Shhh.' He stirred and was quiet, but did not wake. She snuggled against him and soon fell back into sleep herself.

After lunch the following day, while in conversation with an importer of Tuscan marble, Gordon looked surprised, and reached a hand up to his chest. He said, 'I'm frightfully sorry about this,' and then his knees gave way, and he fell to the floor. They called an ambulance, but Gordon was dead when it arrived. He was thirty-six years old.

At the inquest the coroner announced that the autopsy showed Gordon's heart to have been congenitally weak. It could have gone at any time.

For the first three days after his death, Belinda felt nothing, a profound and awful nothing. She comforted the children, she spoke to her friends and to Gordon's friends, to her family and to Gordon's family, accepting their condolences gracefully and gently, as one accepts unasked-for gifts. She would listen to other people cry for Gordon, which she still had not done. She would say all the right things, and she would feel nothing at all.

Melanie, who was eleven, seemed to be taking it well. Kevin abandoned his books and computer games, and sat in his bedroom, staring out of the window, not wanting to talk.

The day after the funeral her parents went back to the countryside and they took both the children with them. Belinda refused to leave London. There was, she said, too much to do.

On the fourth day after the funeral she was making the double bed that they had shared when she began to cry, and the sobs ripped through her in huge, ugly spasms of grief, and tears fell from her face onto the bedspread and clear snot streamed from her nose, and she sat down on the floor suddenly, like a marionette whose strings have been cut, and she cried for the best part of an hour, for she knew that she would never see him again.

She wiped her face. Then she unlocked her jewellery drawer and pulled out the envelope. She opened it and pulled out the cream-coloured sheet of paper, and ran her eyes over the neatly-typed words. The Belinda on the paper had crashed their car while drunk, and was about to lose her driving licence. She and Gordon had not spoken for days. He had lost his job, almost eighteen months earlier, and now spent most of his days sitting around their house in Salford. Belinda's job brought in what money they had. Melanie was out of control: Belinda, cleaning Melanie's bedroom, had found a cache of five and ten pound notes. Melanie had offered no explanation for how an eleven-year-old girl had come by the money, had just retreated into her room and glared at them, tight-lipped, when quizzed. Neither Gordon nor Belinda had investigated further, scared of what they might have discovered. The house in Salford was dingy and damp, such that the plaster was coming away from the ceiling in huge, crumbling chunks, and all three of them had developed nasty, bronchial coughs.

Belinda felt sorry for them.

She put the paper back in the envelope. She wondered what it would be like to hate Gordon, to have him hate her. She wondered what it would be like not to have Kevin in her life, not to see his drawings of aeroplanes or hear his magnificently tuneless renditions of popular songs. She wondered where Melanie—the other Melanie, not *her* Melanie but the there-but-for-the-grace-of-God Melanie—could have got that money from, and was relieved that her own Melanie seemed to have few interests beyond ballet and Enid Blyton books.

She missed Gordon so much it felt like something sharp being hammered into her chest, a spike, perhaps, or an icicle, made of cold and loneliness and the knowledge that she would never see him again in this world.

Then she took the envelope downstairs to the lounge, where the coal fire was burning in the grate, because Gordon had loved open fires. He said that a fire gave a room life. She disliked coal fires, but she had lit it this evening out of routine and out of habit, and because not lighting it would have meant admitting to herself, on some absolute level, that he was never coming home.

Belinda stared into the fire for some time, thinking about what she had in her life, and what she had given up; and whether it would be worse to love someone who was no longer there, or not to love someone who was.

And then, at the end, almost casually, she tossed the envelope onto the coals, and she watched it curl and blacken and catch, watched the yellow flames dancing amidst the blue.

Soon, the Wedding Present was nothing but black flakes of ash which danced on the updraughts and were carried away, like a child's letter to Santa Claus, up the chimney and off into the night.

Belinda sat back in her chair, and closed her eyes, and waited for the scar to blossom on her cheek.

NEIL GAIMAN IS credited with being one of the creators of modern comics, as well as an author whose work crosses genres and reaches audiences of all ages. He is listed in the *Dictionary of Literary Biography* as one of the top ten living post-modern writers, and is a prolific creator of works of prose, poetry, film, journalism, comics, song lyrics, and drama. He is the author of the international best-sellers *Norse Mythology* and *The Ocean at the End of the Lane*, the award-winning *The Graveyard Book*, as well as *Coraline, Neverwhere*, the essay collection *The View from the Cheap Seats* and *The Sandman* series of graphic novels, amongst many other works. His fiction has received numerous awards, including the Carnegie and Newbery medals, and the Hugo, Nebula, World Fantasy and Eisner awards. Originally from England, Gaiman now divides his time between the UK, where he recently turned *Good Omens*, originally a novel that he wrote with Terry Pratchett, into a television series for Amazon/BBC, and the US, where he is professor in the arts at Bard College. 'I had the idea for "The Wedding Present" several years before I wrote it,' Gaiman recalls. 'Some friends were getting married, and I thought "wouldn't it be an interesting thing to give them a short story as a present?" Then I went out and bought them a toaster instead, because I knew what the story would be about, and suspected that it might not be the most welcome of wedding gifts. Each time I was invited to a wedding I'd wonder if finally the bride and groom would be right for this story, and, on reflection, I would get them a toaster, or a coffee-maker, or towels. Years passed, and the story remained unwritten. Then I began writing the Introduction to my short fiction collection, *Smoke & Mirrors*. In discussing where the stories came from, I used as an example that unwritten story idea. And then I thought, "Why don't I write it now?" I had imagined it would be very short and fable-like, but it grew in the telling as the people came to life, and took over. My computer was off being repaired that week, so this was written in fountain pen in a blank notebook.'

FAMILY HISTORY

Stephen Baxter

THE WALL RAN to the left of the road. It was a long, hummocky earthwork, like a line of beasts buried in the intense green that blanketed the ground. After two thousand years the mortar had crumbled to dust, and unruly life sprouted from the stones' every frost-cracked crevice. The Wall itself was flanked by partially filled ditchwork, and punctuated by the remains of turrets and milecastles and forts; the surviving buildings were reduced to their foundations, which were moulded into eerie stone ripples by centuries of subsidence.

The Wall marched for seven hundred miles, across the neck of the country, from Carlisle to Newcastle.

Beyond the Wall there was only moorland waste: rowan trees clinging to rock outcrops, scattered farmsteads, knots of cattle diminished by the sweep of the landscape. The cattle seemed to glare, challenging, into Valler's warm BMW. As if some remnant of their ancient wildness had yet to be bred out of them.

Sunday morning in Northumberland. The February sky was a grey lid, betraying no hint of the sun.

Valler had grown up here, but he had always felt out of place, lost in this huge time-steeped landscape.

Somehow threatened.

After the encounter with his father this morning Valler had intended to drive by the most direct route back to London, back to his life. But frustration and aggression were still fizzing in his blood.

In fact his hand still hurt.

And some impulse had made him swing off the A road to follow this minor route, the Roman road that tracked the line of the Wall. He was heading east; sooner or later he would hit the southbound A1, around Newcastle.

He came to a church.

He knew it, in fact: it was called Saint Andrew's, and it was a squat, ugly Anglo-Saxon pile. He'd spent every Sunday morning of his youthful life here, dragged along by his mother.

After fourteen centuries the church looked like an eroded, crouching animal.

He slowed.

There was a pub opposite the church.

It used to be called something appropriate—the Wilfrid Arms?—but now it was part of a chain, meaninglessly renamed the Frog and Firkin. But it was brightly lit, replete with chalkboards offering satellite football and COUNTRY-STYLE HOT FOOD.

And it was open, of course. Sunday morning.

Six, seven hours to London from here, Valler. A quick one would calm him down. And it would be a kind of triumph, to drink in sight of his mother's church.

He pulled into the pub car park.

Outside the BMW, the air was profoundly cold: not freezing, but laden with a moisture that seemed to work into his lungs. But he relished the sudden discomfort. The distraction.

…It had come to a head this morning.

The whole point of Valler's weekend visit was to get his father to sign the papers that would get him, at last, out of his miner's cottage and into sheltered accommodation.

And then they could sell the cottage.

And so release the money Valler found he needed.

Simple. Valler had everything prepared, had rehearsed what he would say.

But when Valler had called, he found the old man in all his Mithraic finery: the absurd red tunic with its piped sleeves and yellow belt, and the Superman cloak hanging off that wizened remnant of a body, and the *patera* and sword in those arthritic hands. He was the Father of the Temple: the highest Grade, the earthly counterpart of the Unconquered God himself.

The old fool was trying, one last time, to recruit Valler. To make him stay here, as the last of the line.

Family history, he'd said. Two thousand years. Valler should put aside the middle class claptrap he surrounded himself with in London. He should come back here, to what was, in the end, all that mattered.

Family and blood.

But Valler hadn't come here for this tired old bullshit.

He'd said so.

And one thing had led to another.

And then—

…He found he'd crossed the road, to the church. There were a few cars here, bumped onto the road's dark green verge.

He walked along a gravel path to the back of the church, to the heavy wooden door. It was propped open with a wedge. Walking in was like being swallowed by a dry old mouth.

He let his eyes dark-adapt. There was a battered wooden chair here, notices about services, a box for restoration donations.

He passed through a second door, and entered the body of the church. There was a sharp, warm smell of incense and flower perfume, and just for a moment Valler was a child again, holding his mother's hand.

There were people here, mostly women and children. A brightly robed vicar was reading at a candle-lit altar.

It was a service, some kind of modern happy-clappy thing for simple minds.

Of course it's a service. It's Sunday, Valler.

Nobody had noticed him.

The church's enclosing, womb-like darkness was barely relieved by the sparsely placed candles.

Valler found himself standing on the gravestone of a Roman soldier. INTERFECTUS IN BELLUM—killed in the war. It was a warrior's memorial slab, recycled as a paving stone.

The women were dowdy, overweight and slumped. The men wore track-suit tops stretched over beer bellies. The restless kids were of all ages. There was a group of older girls, huddling together like young heifers, whispering and giggling.

Heifers, yes.

These people were like cattle, most of them without jobs, without purpose or function or beauty, the fight bred out of them. Like the cattle in the fields outside.

Like his father.

Brittunculi. The little Brits. That was what the Romans had contemptuously called those they had conquered.

Valler despised them all.

One of the older girls turned and looked directly at Valler.

She was slim, but he could see the curve of hips, the push of small breasts under the striped football shirt she wore. Her oval, perfectly symmetrical face seemed to shine against the drab background. She looked at him as a child would, without calculation or mockery, her eyes blue windows. But her lips were full.

She could have been as old as seventeen, as young as fourteen.

He felt his mouth dry. He was dismayed by the power of his lust for this girl.

The girl turned away. Somehow he found it hard to pick her out again.

Now the ancient, reworked stones seemed enclosing, oppressive.

He walked out of the church. Outside, the sky was unbroken cloud. He sucked in the damp, cold air.

He headed back over the road. He hesitated at the BMW, then went on to the pub, blood swirling.

The redeveloped bar was too big, too cold. There were a couple of old men drinking pints of thick black local beer with a steady, practised purpose. A TV mounted in an upper corner carried a rattling, noisy cartoon.

Valler ordered a bitter from the bored landlord. And then another. He drank his beer quickly. It was pumped, gassy. He could feel it working on his head, but its taste was sour.

He lit up a cigarette, filling his nose and mouth with the smoke.

…The girl, though.

He'd never been able to understand how such beauty was able to emerge from the herds of *Brittunculi*, with their lousy diet and precocious smoking and drinking. But emerge it did, in every generation, and the girls bloomed like etiolated flowers for their few short years. Long enough for them to attract the fumbling hands and stiff dicks of the local boys. Pretty little heifers.

With mothers who were probably younger than he was.

And the boys who were like he used to be, awkward and useless, aching with lust.

But it was different *now,* for him.

Valler worked in computers in the City.

He had made a lot of money out of the year 2000 panic. Selling the work of underpaid Third World programmers to lazy, scared corporations. His world was lit by bright fluorescents, indifferent to weather or season, textured by an unceasing social buzz of wine and cigarettes and videos and sex. More wine than sex nowadays, now he was forty and his belly and hair showed it…

He hated to come back *here*, from where he'd escaped, hated to have to handle all this family history bullshit, the business with his father.

But the year 2000 bubble was bursting, and Valler had a lifestyle to keep up.

He needed his father's money.

He wished he was in London now, surrounded by the press of people and traffic noise and the stale stink of cigarette smoke and car exhaust.

The girl, though.

He imagined touching her.

Her hands would be weak, the bones fragile, unable to match his greater strength. The muscles of her belly would be flat, lean. Like an animal's.

He turned his thoughts away, disturbed by their intensity.

He looked out of the grimy window, across the road towards the church.

...He thought he saw the girl—the same girl—standing on the far side of the road. That oval face like a coin, turned to him.

She was gone, lost in the grime of the glass.

He drained his pint and walked out of the pub.

He found himself back at the church, without conscious intent. The service was over; the cars had gone.

He was out of breath just from walking across the road. He could feel the beer inside him, too much this early, sour and flat. The world was sour too, just blocks of greasy light, livid green and dun sandstone and the sky's pervasive dull grey.

He reached the door of the church. It was locked.

Behind the church was a small stand of trees, leafless and stark. And there was movement, against the background of the trees. Black and white stripes.

He turned that way, panting. He stepped off the path. He could feel long, dead grass crushing under his leather shoes, lapping at his heels.

Soon he was out of sight of the road, and the BMW.

He pushed through the damp undergrowth at the back of the church, on the fringe of the copse. There was rubbish, plastic bags and lager cans. He was probably walking over layers of old graves here, he thought, strata of ancient mouldering corpses.

He couldn't see the girl. He felt a frustrated tightness in his lower belly.

...But what if you do find her, Valler? What do you want?

He should just walk back to the pub, take a piss, get in the BMW.

He felt pulled apart—by the road to London, the girl—his father in his ridiculous robe, cowering when Valler had approached him.

To stop the clamour in his head he plunged through the grass, ignoring the dew soaking into his shoes.

He found a hole in the ground.

It wasn't railed off or marked: it was just a gaping mouth in the damp, worked earth.

He remembered this now. Another piece of his childhood mythology. This was the crypt: even older than the rest of the church, long abandoned.

He bent, wheezing a little, and peered inside.

There were steps: steep, awkward-looking blocks. There was no sign of a light.

He looked around. The girl was nowhere to be seen. She could only be in the crypt.

He couldn't find his lighter in his pockets. He pictured it sitting on the sticky pub table.

He shouldn't go down there. If he fell—

The first step was the hardest, a good two feet deep and no handholds.

Bracing his hands on the slimy walls, he worked his way down, from step to step. He had to tuck in his arms to force his shoulders and head into the hole. It was like some bizarre inverted birth.

Deeper still. His head sank beneath the level of the turf.

There was a stink of dampness and moss, of half-digested things. The sky shrank to a rectangle of silver-grey.

A face, in the deeper darkness below. Shining like an oval medallion at the bottom of a pond.

Then it was gone.

He pushed on, breathing hard, impatiently working his way down the worn, slick steps.

He reached the bottom. It was so unexpected he stumbled.

There was no light save a dim greyness behind him, no sound save the scratch of his own breath. He raised his arms and stepped forward.

Walls, damp and slick, to either side. He was in a tunnel.

He took a step forward. Then another.

He could scarcely get lost, darkness or not. It wasn't even cold. It was like climbing through some rocky intestine.

The last murky daylight glimmer died. He walked on, deeper.

The beer seemed to be working at his temples now, filling his head with a banging pulse, obscuring the darkness with splashes of retinal blood.

He didn't have any firm intention. Nothing planned.

He was strong. She was weak. He had money. Fifty quid was nothing to him, but would be a hell of a lot to a girl like that. Enough for—

Enough for what, Valler?

Nobody knew he was here.

Those old boys in the pub wouldn't remember him. He could be back in the BMW and gone in five minutes. After—

After what?

She was just a pretty heifer.

On he walked. Obscurely tempted.

He could feel a texture in the blocks that made up the walls. Parallel grooves, the characteristic of Roman-dressed stone. But, when he explored the joins in the walls, he found the stone blocks had been crudely cut, jammed together with gritty, crumbling mortar. This was stone mined by the *Brittunculi* from the abandoned towns of the Empire. Like gulls pecking over corpses.

Valler's fluttering fingers found a wall, ahead of his face. To his right, an open space. A corner, then.

He stepped forward—

Light.

He threw his hands over his eyes and cried out.

—But had there been just a glimpse of movement—a slim form, an oval face—ducking out of sight?

He forced himself to open his blinking, streaming eyes.

He was in a small chamber: an arched roof of stone blocks, a roughly levelled floor. The only light came from cressets—wicks floating in what smelled like tallow, set in recesses that were stained black with soot.

The *only* light.

And yet those primitive lamps had seemed, briefly, as bright as the sun.

It was just dark-adaptation. He'd been taken in by a medieval special effect.

He laughed, deliberately, out loud.

His voice returned no echo.

He walked forward.

There was an altar here, just a crude block of dressed stone. Before it was a pit, dug in the earth, the size of a coffin.

It looked to him like an ordeal pit.

Aside from the tunnel, there was no way out of the chamber.

He turned, letting his eyes become accustomed to the light. The cut-up Roman stones contained fragments of friezes, inscriptions, even bas-relief carving, sliced apart and jammed together.

They were fragments of an image.

As he looked round the room he could piece it together, like assembling a jigsaw.

A young man kneeling on the back of a bull, which he had forced to its knees. Some kind of incised starburst effect around the man's head. With one hand he was forcing back the bull's head, and with the other he drove a sword into the bull's body. A dog and a serpent leapt up to the wound to drink the blood, and a scorpion was collecting the bull's semen.

There was an inscription, in three pieces. DEO INVICTO SOLI MITHRAE.

Valler, startled, knew the image. He had grown up with it, thanks to his father.

This was the primeval bull: the source of all brute force and untamed vitality, the first creation of Ahura Mazda, Lord of Creation. And the god was releasing that flood of primordial, beneficial energy into the world.

The god was Mithras: Lord of Light, protecting, avenging.

The emperors had manned their Wall with dark-skinned men from the eastern provinces. The soldiers, far from home, had brought their own old gods to protect them from whatever untamed beasts lay to the unyielding north here.

They had brought Mithras. DEO INVICTO, the Unconquered God.

But the early bishops had reviled Mithras, Christ's dark, ancient twin. They had banned his rites, burned his books, desecrated his temples. And thus, here was this image, a *tauroctony*, once found in every *mithraeum* in the Empire: a sacred tableau sliced to pieces to make up the walls of the crypt of this dismal church. A demonstration of Christ's triumph.

But maybe, in the end, the bishops had failed. Maybe Christ hadn't prevailed here after all.

His father told Valler he'd understand when he was old enough to join the Temple as a Raven, the lowest of the seven Grades. Old enough to descend into some dank cave like this one, and undergo the initiation ordeal.

But Valler had understood already.

He hated what he had glimpsed of the exclusively male, secretive, unforgivingly strict cult. He hated his father's absences and distance. He hated his dead mother's bemused, tolerant Christianity, her readiness to forgive her husband's eccentricities.

…Or maybe, Valler, you just hate your own weakness. You could never survive a Mithraic initiation, could you? And maybe you just hated to witness your parents' relationship, more flexible and more subtle than any you've proven capable of…

His father's disapproving, disappointed face superimposed itself on Mithras's stone glare.

His father's face: filled with stubbornness, his refusal to give up the Temple, to move into the sheltered flat, to start waiting to die.

His father's face: as Valler drove his fist into it.

His father used to be a big man: strict, always disappointed, always punishing. But he wasn't big any more.

His father's face, at last: fixed with a glare. An unspoken promise of revenge. A look that had presaged a beating for the child Valler.

But that didn't matter a cold damn now. What could he do? Valler was the strong one now, and would take what he wanted.

Valler had taunted him.

Where is Mithras now, old man? Where is your protector, the Unconquered God? Gone. Dead two thousand years. As you will be, soon.

His father's face—

He heard footsteps. Remote, echoing.

It must be the girl.

He felt blood surge in his loins. He stood in the middle of the crypt, hands huge and clammy at his sides.

He must be crazy to have got himself in so deep. His car was separated from him by fifty feet of earth, London by three hundred miles.

…But he'd seen the way she'd *looked* at him.

His father's face.

His father would probably warn him off.

Valler blood ran deep and wide here.

For—it was said—a Mithraic Temple had survived in this lost corner of Northumberland, its small flames kept alive for two thousand years, by the descendants of a Sixth Legion centurion. A man who had never gone home.

A man called Valerius.

That was the family history, anyhow, the reason it mattered so much to his father.

She might be your cousin.

But even if she was, it didn't matter. He had money. He would be gone in an hour.

He had condoms.

Footsteps at the base of the stairs.

Heavy.

It was the girl. It must be.

But if not—

It struck him suddenly that he was trapped here, in this crypt.

The lights went out.

In darkness, Valler cried out.

He had to hide.

He could only think of the ordeal pit.

He stepped into the pit and lay down. It had no cover. He could feel mud working into his shirt collar. The mud was cold, and stank of blood, of old meat.

He crossed his arms over his chest.

The footsteps were still approaching, still getting louder.

Heavier.

Clattering.

Not a girl's steps.

Valler screamed.

Clattering, like the tread of some huge, monstrously heavy man.

Or of an animal.

A wild, untamed animal.

Like a bull.

STEPHEN BAXTER IS the winner of a number of prestigious science fiction swards, including the Philip K. Dick Award, the John W. Campbell Memorial Award, the British Science Fiction Association Award, the Kurd Lasswitz Award (Germany) and the Seiun Award (Japan). He has also received nominations for several others, including the Arthur C. Clarke Award, the Hugo Award and Locus awards. The author of more than 100 short stories and around forty novels, including collaborations with Sir Arthur C. Clarke, Sir Terry Pratchett, Eric Brown and Alastair Reynolds, his most recently published books are the sequels *Xeelee: Redemption* and *World Engines: Destroyer*. 'My wife's family come from Northumberland and this story was inspired by a visit to the area over Christmas 1997,' explains Baxter. 'We explored the ruins of the Wall and visited Hexham Abbey, whose crypt—of recycled Roman stone—is very like that in the story. I was struck by the depth and strangeness of the region's history, and since this story was first published we've moved to the area. The past is a foreign country—and Britain's past is darker and more foreign than most.'

//

INSIDE THE CACKLE FACTORY

Dennis Etchison

UNCLE MILTIE DID not look very happy. Someone had left a half-smoked cigar on his head, and now the wrapper began to come unglued in the rain. A few seconds more and dark stains dripped over his slick hair, ran down his cheeks and collected in his open mouth, the bits of chewed tobacco clinging like wet sawdust to a beaver's front teeth.

'Time,' announced Marty, clicking his stopwatch.

Lisa Anne tried to get his attention from across the room, but it was too late. She saw him note the hour and minute on his clipboard.

'Please pass your papers to the right,' he said, 'and one of our monitors will pick them up...'

On the other side of the glass doors, Sid Caesar was even less amused by the logjam of cigarette butts on his crushed top hat. As the water rose they began to float, one disintegrating filter sloshing over the brim and catching in the knot of his limp string tie.

She forced herself to look away and crossed in front of the chairs to get to Marty, scanning the rows again. There, in the first section: an empty seat with a pair of Ray-Bans balanced on the armrest.

'Sixteen,' she whispered into his ear.

'Morning, Lisa.' He was about to make his introductory spiel before opening the viewing theatre, while the monitors retrieved and sorted the questionnaires. 'Thought you took the day off.'

'Number Sixteen is missing.'

He nodded at the hallway. 'Check the men's room.'

'I think he's outside,' she said, 'smoking.'

'Then he's late. Send him home.'

As she hurried toward the doors, the woman on the end of row four added her own questionnaire to the pile and held them out to Lisa Anne.

'Excuse me,' the woman said, 'but can I get a drink of water?'

Lisa Anne accepted the stack of stapled pages from her. 'If you'll wait just a moment—'

'But I have to take a pill.'

'Down the hall, next to the restrooms.'

'Where?'

She handed the forms to one of the other monitors. 'Angie, would you show this lady to the drinking fountain?'

Then she went on to the doors. The hinges squeaked and a stream of water poured down the glass and over the open toes of her new shoes.

Oh great, she thought.

She took the shoes off and stood under the awning while she peered through the blowing rain. The walkway along the front of the AmiDex building was empty.

'Hello?'

Bob Hope ignored her, gazing wryly across the courtyard in the direction of the adjacent apartment complex, while Dick Van Dyke and Mary Tyler Moore leaned so close to each other that their heads almost touched, about to topple off the bronze pedestals. They had not been used for ashtrays yet today, though their nameplates were etched with the faint white tracks of bird droppings. She hoped the rain would wash them clean.

'Are you out here? Mister...?'

She had let Angie check them in this morning, so she did not even know Number Sixteen's name. She glanced around the courtyard, saw no movement and was about to go back inside, when she noticed someone in the parking lot.

It was a man wearing a wet trench coat.

So Number Sixteen had lost patience and decided to split. He did not seem to be looking for his car, however, but walked rapidly between the rows on his way to—what? The apartments beyond, apparently. Yet there was no gate in this side of the wrought-iron fence.

As she watched, another man appeared as if from nowhere. He had on a yellow raincoat and a plastic-covered hat, the kind worn by policeman or security guards. As far as she knew the parking lot was unattended. She could not imagine where had he come from, unless there was an opening in the fence, after all, and the guard had come through from the other side. He stepped out to block the way. She tried to hear what they were saying but it was impossible from this distance. There was a brief confrontation, with both men gesturing broadly, until the one in the trench coat gave up and walked away.

Lisa Anne shook the water out of her shoes, put them on and turned back to the glass doors.

Marty was already into his speech. She had not worked here long enough to have it memorised, but she knew he was about to mention the cash they would receive after the screening and discussion. Some of them may have been lured here by the glamour, the chance to attend a sneak preview of next season's programs, but without the promise of money there was no way to be sure anyone would show up.

The door opened a few inches and Angie stuck her head out.

'Will you get *in* here, girl?'

'Coming,' said Lisa Anne.

She looked around one more time.

Now she saw a puff of smoke a few yards down, at the entrance to Public Relations.

'Is anybody there?' she called.

An eyeball showed itself at the side of the building.

Maybe this is the real Number Sixteen, she thought. Trying to get in that last nicotine fix.

'I'm sorry, but you'll have to come in now...'

She waited to see where his cigarette butt would fall. The statues were waiting, too.

As he came toward her his hands were empty. What did he do, she wondered, eat it?

She recognised him. He had been inside, drinking coffee with the others. He was a few years older than Lisa Anne, late twenties or early thirties, good looking in a rugged, unkempt way, with his hair tied back in a ponytail and a drooping moustache, flannel shirt, tight jeans and steel-toed boots. A construction worker, she thought, a carpenter, some sort of manual labour. Why bother to test him? He probably watched football games and not much else, if he watched TV at all.

As he got closer she smelled something sweet and pungent. The unmistakable odour of marijuana lingered in his clothes. So that's what he was up to, she thought. A little attitude adjustment. I could use some of that myself right about now.

She held out her hand to invite him in from the rain, and felt her hair collapse into wet strings over her ears. She pushed it back self-consciously.

'You don't want to miss the screening,' she said, forcing a smile, 'do you?'

'What's it about?' he asked.

'I don't know. Honest. They don't tell me anything.'

The door swung open again and Angie rolled her eyes.

'Okay, okay,' said Lisa Anne.

'He can sign up for the two o'clock, if he wants.'

Number Sixteen shook his head. 'No way. I gotta be at work.'

'It's all right, Angie.'

'But he missed the audience prep...'

Lisa Anne looked past her. Marty was about finished. The test subjects were already shifting impatiently, bored housewives and tourists and retirees with nothing better to do, recruited from sidewalks and shopping malls and the lines in front of movie theatres, all of them here to view the pilot for a new series that would either make it to the network schedule or be sent back for retooling, based on their responses. There was a full house for this session.

Number Sixteen had not heard the instructions, so she had no choice. She was supposed to send him home.

But if the research was to mean anything, wasn't it important that every demographic be represented? The fate of the producers and writers who had laboured for months or even years to get their shows this far hung in the balance, to be decided by a theoretical cross-section of the viewing public. Not everyone liked sitcoms about young urban professionals and their wacky misadventures at the office. They can't, she thought. I don't. But who ever asked me?

'Look,' said Number Sixteen, 'I drove a long ways to get here. You gotta at least pay me.'

'He's late,' said Angie. She ignored him, speaking as though he were not there. 'He hasn't even filled out his questionnaire.'

'Yes, he has,' said Lisa Anne and ushered him inside.

The subjects were on their feet now, shuffling into the screening room. Lisa Anne went to the check-in table.

'Did you get Number Sixteen's?' she asked.

The monitors had the forms laid out according to rows and were about to insert the piles into manila envelopes before taking them down the hall.

Marty came up behind her. 'Which row, Miss Rayme?' he said officiously.

'Four, I think.'

'You think?' Marty looked at the man in the plaid shirt and wrinkled his nose, as if someone in the room had just broken wind. 'If his form's not here—'

'I know where it is,' Lisa Anne told him and slipped behind the table.

She flipped through the pile for row four, allowing several of the questionnaires to slide onto the floor. When she knelt to pick them up, she pulled a blank one from the carton.

'Here.' She stood, took a pencil and jotted *16* in the upper right-hand corner. 'He forgot to put his number on it.'

'We're running late, Lees...' Marty whispered.

She slid the forms into an envelope. 'Then I'd better get these to the War Room.'

On the way down the hall, she opened the envelope and withdrew the blank form, checking off random answers to the multiple-choice quiz on the first page. It was pointless, anyway, most of it a meaningless query into personal habits and lifestyle, only a smokescreen for the important questions about income and product preferences that came later. She dropped off her envelope along with the other monitors, and a humourless assistant in a short-sleeved white shirt and rimless glasses carried the envelopes from the counter to an inner room, where each form would be tallied and matched to the numbered seats in the viewing theatre. On her way back, Marty intercepted her.

'Break time,' he said.

'No, thanks.' She drew him to one side, next to the drinking fountain. 'I got one for you. *S.H.A.M.*'

'*M.A.S.H.*,' he said immediately.

'Okay, try this. *Finders.*'

He pondered for a second. '*Friends?*'

'You're good,' she said.

'No, I'm not. You're easy. Well, time to do my thing.'

At the other end of the hall, the reception room was empty and the doors to the viewing theatre were already closed.

'Which thing is that?' she said playfully.

'That thing I do, before they fall asleep.'

'Ooh, can I watch?'

She propped her back against the wall and waited for him to move in, to pin her there until she could not get away unless she dropped to her knees and crawled between his legs.

'Not today, Lisa.'

'How come?'

'This one sucks. Big time.'

'What's the title?'

'I don't know.'

'Then how do you know it sucks?'

'Hey, it's not my fault, okay?'

For some reason he had become evasive, defensive. His face was now a smooth mask, the skin pulled back tautly, the only prominent features his teeth and nervous, shining eyes. Like a shark's face, she thought. A residue of deodorant soap rose to the surface of his skin and vaporised, expanding outward on waves of body heat. She drew a breath and knew that she needed to be somewhere else, away from him.

'Sorry,' she said.

He avoided her eyes and ducked into the men's room.

What did I say? she wondered, and went on to the reception area.

A list of subjects for the next session was already laid out on the table, ninety minutes early. The other monitors were killing time in the chairs, chatting over coffee and snacks from the machines.

Lisa Anne barely knew them. This was only her second week and she was not yet a part of their circle. One had been an editorial assistant at the *L.A. Weekly,* two were junior college students, and the others had answered the same classified ad she had seen in the trades. She considered crashing the conversation. It would be a chance to rest her feet and dry out. The soggy new shoes still pinched her toes and the suit she'd had to buy for the job was damp and steamy and scratched her skin like a hair shirt. She felt ridiculous in this uniform, but it was necessary to show people like Marty that she could play by their rules, at least until she got what she needed. At home she would probably be working on yet another sculpture this morning, trying to get the face right, with a gob of clay in one hand and a joint in the other and the stereo cranked up to the max. But living that way hadn't gotten her any closer to the truth. She couldn't put it off any longer. There were some things she had to find out or she would go mad.

She smiled at the monitors.

Except for Angie they barely acknowledged her, continuing their conversation as though she were not there.

They know, she thought. They must.

How much longer till Marty saw through her game? She had him on her side, but the tease would play out soon enough unless she let it go further, and she couldn't bear the thought of that. She only needed him long enough to find the answer, and then she would walk away.

She went to the glass doors.

The rain had stopped and soon the next group would begin gathering outside. The busts of the television stars in the courtyard were ready, Red Buttons and George Gobel and Steve Allen and Lucille Ball with her eyebrows arched in perpetual wonderment, waiting to meet their fans. It was all that was left for them now.

Angie came up next to her.

'Hey, girl.'

'Hey yourself.'

'The lumberjack. He a friend of yours?'

'Number Sixteen?'

'The one with the buns.'

'I never saw him before.'

'Oh.' Angie took a bite of an oatmeal cookie and brushed the crumbs daintily from her mouth. 'Nice.'

'I suppose. If you like that sort of thing.'

'Here.' She offered Lisa Anne the napkin. 'You look like you're melting.'

She took it and wiped the back of her neck, then squeezed out the ends of her hair, as a burst of laughter came from the theatre. That meant Marty had already gone in through the side entrance to warm them up.

'Excuse me,' she said. 'It's showtime.'

Angie followed her to the hall. 'You never miss one, do you?'

'Not yet.'

'Aren't they boring? I mean, it's not like they're hits or anything.'

'Most of them are pretty lame,' Lisa Anne admitted.

'So why watch?'

'I have to find out.'

'Don't tell me. What Marty's really like?'

'Please.'

'Then why?'

'I've got to know why some shows make it,' she said, 'and some don't.'

'Oh, you want to get into the biz?'

'No. But I used to know someone who was. See you.'

I shouldn't have said that, she thought as she opened the unmarked door in the hall.

The observation booth was dark and narrow with a half-dozen padded chairs facing a two-way mirror. On the other side of the mirror, the test subjects sat in rows of theatre seats under several thirty-six-inch television sets suspended from the ceiling.

She took the second chair from the end.

In the viewing theatre, Marty was explaining how to use the dials wired into the armrests. They were calibrated from zero to ten with a plastic knob in the centre.

During the screening the subjects were to rotate the knobs, indicating how much they liked what they saw. Their responses would be recorded and the results then analysed to help the networks decide whether the show was ready for broadcast.

Lisa Anne watched Marty as he paced, doing his shtick. He had told her that he once worked at a comedy traffic school, and she could see why. He had them in the palm of his hand. Their eyes followed his every move, like hypnotised chickens waiting to be fed. His routine was corny but with just the right touch of hipness to make them feel like insiders. He concluded by reminding them of the fifty dollars cash they would receive after the screening and the discussion. Then, when the lights went down and the tape began to roll, Marty stepped to the back and slipped into the hall. As he entered the observation booth, the audience was applauding.

'Good group this time,' he said, dropping into the chair next to hers.

'You always know just what to say.'

'I do, don't I?' he said, leaning forward to turn on a tiny twelve-inch set below the mirror.

She saw their faces flicker in the blue glow of the cathode ray tubes while the opening titles came up.

The show was something called *Dario, You So Crazy!* She sighed and sat back, studying their expressions while keeping one eye on the TV screen. It wouldn't be long before she felt his hand on her forearm as he moved in, telling her what he really thought of the audience, how stupid they were, every last one, down to the little old ladies and the kindly grandfathers and the working men and women who were no more or less ordinary than he was under his Perry Ellis suit and silk tie. Then his breath in her hair and his fingers scraping her pantyhose as if tapping out a message on her knee and perhaps today, this time, he would attempt to deliver that message, while she offered breathless quips to let him know how clever he was and how lucky she felt to be here. She shuddered and turned her cheek to him in the dark.

'Who's that actor?' she said.

'Some Italian guy. I saw him in a movie. He's not so bad, if he could learn to talk English.'

She recognised the co-star. It was Rowan Atkinson, the slight, bumbling everyman from that British TV series on PBS.

'Mr Bean!' she said.

'Roberto Begnino,' Marty corrected, reading from the credits.

'I mean the other one. This is going to be good…'

'I thought you were on your break,' said Marty.

'This is more important.'

He stared at her transparent reflection in the two-way mirror.

'You were going to take the day off.'

'No, I wasn't.'

The pilot was a comedy about an eccentric Italian film director who had come to America in search of fame and fortune. Mr Bean played his shy, inept manager. They shared an expensive rented villa in the Hollywood Hills. Just now they were desperate to locate an actress to pose as Dario's wife, so that he could obtain a green card and find work before they both ran out of money.

She immediately grasped the premise and its potential.

It was inspired. Benigno's abuse of the language would generate count-less hilarious misunderstandings; coupled with his manager's charming incompetence, the result might be a television classic, thanks in no small measure to the brilliant casting. How could it miss? All they needed was a good script. She realised that her mind had drifted long enough to miss the screenwriter's name. The only credit left was the show's creator/producer, one Barry E. Tormé. Probably the son of that old singer, she thought. What was his name? Mel. Apparently he had fathered a show-business dynasty. The other son, Tracy, was a successful TV writer; he had even created a science fiction series at Fox that lasted for a couple of seasons. Why had she never heard of brother Barry? He was obviously a pro.

She sat forward, fascinated to see the first episode.

'*Me, Dario!*' Benigno crowed into a gold-trimmed telephone, the third time it had rung in less than a minute. It was going to be his signature bit.

'*O, I Dream!*' she said.

'Huh?'

'The line, Marty. Got you.'

The letters rearranged themselves automatically in her mind. It was child's play. She had almost expected him to come up with it first. They had kept the game going since her first day at AmiDex, when she pointed out that his full name was an anagram for *Marty licks on me*. It got his attention.

'You can stop with the word shit,' he said.

He sounded irritated, which surprised her. 'I thought you liked it.'

'What's up with that, anyway?'

'It's a reflex,' she said. 'I can't help it. My father taught me when I was little.'

'Well, it's getting old.'

She turned to his profile in the semidarkness, his pale, clean-shaven face and short, neat hair as two-dimensional as a cartoon cut-out from the back of a cereal box.

'You know, Marty, I was thinking. Could you show me the War Room sometime?' She moved her leg closer to his. 'Just you and me, when everybody's gone. So I could see how it works.'

'How what works?'

She let her hand brush his knee. 'Everything. The really big secrets.'

'Such as?'

'I don't know.' Had she said too much? 'But if I'm going to work here, I should know more about the company. What makes a hit, for example. Maybe you could tell me. You explain things so well.'

'Why *did* you come here?'

The question caught her off-guard. 'I needed a job.'

'Plenty of jobs out there,' he snapped. 'What is it, you got a script to sell?'

The room was cold and her feet were numb. Now she wanted to be out of here. The other chairs were dim, bulky shapes, like half-reclining corpses, as if she and Marty were not alone in the room.

'Sorry,' she said.

'I told you to stay home today.'

No, he hadn't. 'You *want* me to take the day off?'

He did not answer.

'Do you think I need it? Or is there something special about today?'

The door in the back of the room opened. It connected to the hall that led to the other sections of the building and the War Room itself, where even now the audience response was being recorded and analysed by a team of market researchers. A hulking figure stood there in silhouette. She could not see his features. He hesitated for a moment, then came all the way in, plunging the room into darkness again, and then there were only the test subjects and their flickering faces opposite her through the smoked glass. The man took a seat at the other end of the row.

'That you, Mickleson?'

At the sound of his voice Marty sat up straight.

'Yes, sir.'

'I thought so. Who's she?'

'One of the girls—Annalise. She was just leaving.'

Then Marty leaned close to her and whispered:

'*Will you get out?*'

She was not supposed to be here. The shape at the end of the row must have been the big boss. Marty had known he was coming; that was why he wanted her gone. This was the first time anyone had joined them in the booth. It meant the show was important. The executives listened up when a hit came along.

'Excuse me,' she said, and left the observation booth.

She wanted very much to see the rest of the show. Now she would have to wait till it hit the airwaves. Was there a way for her to eavesdrop on the discussion later, after the screening?

In the hall, she listened for the audience reaction. Just now there must have been a lull in the action, with blank tape inserted to represent a commercial break, because there was dead silence from the theatre.

She was all the way to the reception area before she realised what he had called her.

Annalise.

It was an anagram for Lisa Anne, the name she had put on her application—and, incredibly, it was the right one. Somehow he had hit it. Had he done so naturally, without thinking, as in their word games? Or did he know?

Busted, she thought.

She crossed to the glass doors, ready to make her break.

Then she thought, so he knows my first name. So what? It's not like it would mean anything to him, even if he were to figure out the rest of it.

She decided that she had been paranoid to use a pseudonym in the first place. If she had told the truth, would anybody care? Technically AmiDex could disqualify her, but the family connection was so many years ago that the name had probably been forgotten by now. In fact she was sure it had. That was the point. That was why she was here.

Outside, the rain had let up. A few of the next hour's subjects were already wandering this way across the courtyard. Only one, a woman with a shopping bag and a multi-coloured scarf over her hair, bothered to raise her head to look at the statues.

It was disturbing to see the greats treated with such disrespect.

All day long volunteers gathered outside at the appointed hour, smoking and drinking sodas and eating food they had brought with them, and when they went in they left the remains scattered among the statues, as if the history of the medium and its stars meant nothing to them. Dinah Shore and

Carol Burnett and Red Skelton with his clown nose, all nothing more than a part of the landscape now, like the lamp-posts, like the trash cans that no one used. The sun fell on them, and the winds and the rains and the graffiti and the discarded wads of chewing gum and the pissing of dogs on the place where their feet should have been, and there was nothing for any of them to do but suffer these things with quiet dignity, like the fallen dead in a veterans' cemetery. One day the burdens of their immortality, the bird shit and the cigarette butts and the McDonald's wrappers, might become too much for them to bear and the ground would shake as giants walked the earth again, but for now they could only wait, because that day was not yet here.

'How was it?' said Angie.

'The show? Oh, it was great. Really.'

'Then why aren't you in there?'

'It's too cold.' She hugged her sides. 'When does the grounds crew get here?'

'Uh, you lost me.'

'Maintenance. The gardeners. How often do they come?'

'You're putting me on, right?'

She felt her face flush. 'Then I'll do it.'

'Do—?'

'Clean up. It's a disgrace. Don't you think so?'

'Sure, Lisa. Anything you say...'

She started outside, and got only a few paces when the sirens began. She counted four squad cars with the name of a private security company stencilled on the doors. They screeched to a halt in the parking lot and several officers jumped out. Did one of them really have his gun drawn?

'Oh, God,' said Angie.

'What's going on?'

'It's the complex. They don't like people taking pictures.'

Now she saw that the man in the dark trench coat had returned. This time he had brought a van with a remote broadcasting dish on top. The guards held him against the side, under the call letters for a local TV station and the words EYEBALL NEWS. When a cameraman climbed down from the back to object they handcuffed him.

'Who doesn't like it?'

'AmiDex,' Angie said solemnly. 'They own it all.' She waved her hand to include the building, the courtyard, the parking lot and the fenced-in apartments. 'Somebody from *Hard Copy* tried to shoot here last month. They confiscated the film. It's off-limits.'

'But why?'

'All I know is, there must be some very important people in those condos.'

'In *this* neighbourhood?'

She couldn't imagine why any VIP's would want to live here. The complex was a lower-middle-class housing development, walled in and protected from the deteriorating streets nearby. It had probably been on this corner since the fifties. She could understand AmiDex buying real estate in the San Fernando Valley instead of the overpriced Westside, but why the ageing apartments? The only reason might be so that they could expand their testing facility one day. Meanwhile, why not tear them down? With its spiked iron fences the complex looked like a fortress sealed off against the outside world. There was even barbed wire on top of the walls.

Before she could ask any more questions, the doors to the theatre opened. She glanced back and saw Marty leading the audience down the hall for the post-screening discussion.

She followed, eager to hear the verdict.

The boys in the white shirts were no longer at the counter. They were in the War Room, marking up long rolls of paper like doctors charting the vital signs in an intensive care ward. Lights blinked across a bank of electronic equipment, as many rack-mounted modules as there were seats in the theatre, with dials and connecting cables that fed into the central computer. She heard circuits humming and the ratcheting whirr of a wide-mouthed machine as it disgorged graphs that resembled polygraph tests printed in blood-red ink.

She came to the next section of the hall, as the last head vanished through a doorway around the first turn.

The discussion room was small and bright with rows of desks and acoustic tiles in the ceiling. It reminded her of the classrooms at UCLA, where she had taken a course in Media Studies, before discovering that they didn't have any answers, either. She merged with the group and slumped down in the back row, behind the tallest person she could find.

Marty remained on his feet, pacing.

'Now,' he said, 'it's your turn. Hollywood is listening! How many of you would rate—' He consulted his clipboard. '—*Dario, You So Crazy!* as one of the best programmes you've ever seen?'

She waited for the hands to go up. She could not see any from here. The tall man blocked her view and if she moved her head Marty might spot her.

'Okay. How many would say "very good"?'

There must not have been many because he went right on to the next question.

'"Fair"?'

She closed her eyes and listened to the rustle of coat sleeves and wondered if she had heard the question correctly.

'And how many "poor"?'

That had to be everyone else. Even the tall man in front of her raised his arm. She recognised his plaid shirt. It was Number Sixteen.

Marty made a notation.

'Okay, great. What was your favourite scene?'

The silence was deafening.

'You won't be graded on this! There's no right or wrong answer. I remember once, when my junior-high English teacher…'

He launched into a story to loosen them up. It was about a divorced woman, an escaped sex maniac and a telephone call to the police. She recognised it as a very old dirty joke. Astonishingly he left off the punch-line. The audience responded anyway. He had his timing down pat. Or was it that they laughed *because* they knew what was coming? Did that make it even funnier?

The less original the material, she thought, the more they like it. It makes them feel comfortable.

And if that's true, so is the reverse.

She noticed that there was a two-way mirror in this room, too, along the far wall. Was anyone following the discussion from the other side? If so, there wasn't much to hear. Nobody except Marty had anything to say. They were bored stiff, waiting for their money. It would take something more than the show they had just seen to hold them, maybe *Wrestling's Biggest Bleeps, Bloopers and Bodyslams* or *America's Zaniest Surveillance Tapes*. Now she heard a door slam in the hall. The executives had probably given up and left the observation room.

'What is the matter with you people?'

The woman with the multi-coloured scarf hunched around to look at her, as Marty tried to see who had spoken.

'In the back row. Number...'

'You're right,' she said too loudly. 'It's not poor, or fair, or excellent. It's a *great* show! Better than anything I've seen in years. Since—'

'Yes?' Marty changed his position, zeroing in on her voice. 'Would you mind speaking up? This is your chance to be heard...'

'Since *The Fuzzy Family*. Or *The Funnyboner*.' She couldn't help mentioning the titles. Her mouth was open now and the truth was coming out and there was no way to stop it.

Marty said, 'What network were they on?'

'CBS. They were cancelled in the first season.'

'But you remember them?'

'They were brilliant.'

'Can you tell us why?'

'Because of my father. He created them both.'

Marty came to the end of the aisle and finally saw her. His face fell. In the silence she heard other voices, arguing in the hall. She hoped it was not the people who had made *Dario, You So Crazy!* If so, they had to be hurting right now. She felt for them, bitterness and despair and rage welling up in her own throat.

'May I see you outside?' he said.

'No, you may not.'

The hell with Marty, AmiDex and her job here. There was no secret as to why some shows made it and other, better ones did not. Darwin was wrong. He hadn't figured on the networks. They had continued to lower their sights until the audience devolved right along with them, so that any ray of hope was snuffed out, overshadowed by the crap around it. And market research and the ratings system held onto their positions by telling them what they wanted to hear, that the low-rent talent they had under contract was good enough, by testing the wrong people for the wrong reasons, people who were too numb to care about a pearl among the pebbles. It was a perfect, closed loop.

'*Now*, Miss Rayme.'

'That isn't my name.' Didn't he get it yet? 'My father was Robert Mayer. The man who wrote and produced *Wagons, Ho!*'

It was TV's first Western comedy and it made television history. After that he struggled to come up with another hit, but every new show was either cancelled or rejected outright. His name meant nothing to the bean-counters. All they could see was the bottom line. As far as they were concerned he owed them a fortune for the failures they had bankrolled. If he had been an entertainer who ran up a debt in Vegas, he would have had to stay there, working it off at the rate of two shows a night, forever. The only thing that gave her satisfaction was the knowledge that they would never collect. One day when she was ten he had a massive heart attack on the set and was whisked away in a blue ambulance and he never came home again.

'Folks, thanks for your time,' Marty said. 'If you'll return to the lobby...'

She had studied his notes and scripts, trying to understand why he failed. She loved them all. They were genuinely funny, the very essence of her father, with his quirky sense of humour and extravagant sight gags—as original and inventive as *Dario, You So Crazy!* Which was a failure, too. Of course. She lowered her head onto the desktop and began to weep.

'Hold up,' said Number Sixteen.

'Your pay's ready. Fifty dollars cash.' Marty held the door wide. 'There's another group coming in...'

The lumberjack refused to stand. 'Let her talk. I remember *Wagons, Ho!* It was all right.'

He turned around in his seat and gave her a wink as she raised her head.

'Thank you,' she said softly. 'It doesn't matter, now.'

She got to her feet with the others and pushed her way out. Farther down the hall, another door clicked shut. It was marked GREEN ROOM. She guessed that the executives from the other side of the mirror had decided to finish their argument in private.

Marty grabbed her elbow.

'I told you to stay home.'

'You're hurting me,' she said.

'But you just wouldn't take the hint, would you?'

'About what?'

'You can pick up your cheque in Payroll.'

'Get your hands off me.'

Number Sixteen came up next to her. 'You got a problem here?'

'Not anymore,' she said.

'Your pay's up front, cowboy,' Marty told him.

'You sure you're okay?' asked Number Sixteen.

'I am now.'

Marty shook his head sadly.

'I'll tell them to make it for the full two weeks. I liked you, you know? I really did.'

Then he turned and walked the audience back to the lobby.

Farther down the hall, she saw HUMAN RESOURCES, where she had gone the first day for her interview, and beyond that PUBLIC RELATIONS and PAYROLL. She didn't care about her cheque but there was a security door at the end. It would let her out directly into the courtyard.

Number Sixteen followed her.

'I was thinking. If you want some lunch, I've got my car.'

'So do I,' she said, walking faster.

Then she thought, Why not? Me, with a lumberjack. I'll be watching Martha Stewart while he hammers his wood and lays his pipe or whatever he does all day, and he'll come home and watch hockey games and I'll stay loaded and sit up every night to see *Wagons, Ho!* on the Nostalgia Channel and we'll go on that way, like a sitcom. He'll take care of me. And in time I'll forget everything. All I have to do is say yes.

He was about to turn back.

'Okay,' she said.

'What?'

'This way. There's an exit to the parking lot, down here.'

Before they could get to it the steel door at the end swung open.

The rain had stopped and a burst of clear light from outside reflected off the polished floor, distorting the silhouette of the figure standing there. A tall woman in a designer suit entered from the grounds. Behind her, the last of the private security cars drove off. The Eyeball News truck was gone.

'All set,' the woman said into a flip-phone, and went briskly to the door marked GREEN ROOM.

Voices came from within, rising to an emotional pitch. Then the voices receded as the door clicked shut.

There was something in the tone of the argument that got to her. She couldn't make out the words but one of the voices was close to pleading. It was painful to hear. She thought of her father and the desperate meetings he must have had, years ago. When the door whispered open again, two men in grey suits stepped out into the hall, holding a third man between them.

It had to be the producer of the pilot.

She wanted to go to him and take his hands and look into his eyes and tell him that they were wrong. He was too talented to listen to them. What did they know? There were other networks, cable, foreign markets, features, if only he could break free of them and move on. He had to. She would be waiting and so would millions of others, an invisible audience whose opinions were never counted, as if they did not exist, but who were out there, she was sure. The ones who remembered *Wagons, Ho!* and *The Funnyboner* and *The Fuzzy Family* and would faithfully tune in other programs with the same quirky sensibility, if they had the choice.

He looked exhausted. The suits had him in their grip, supporting his weight between them, as if carrying a drunk to a waiting cab. What was his name? Terry Something. Or Barry. That was it. She saw him go limp. He had the body of a middle-aged man.

'Please,' he said in a cracking voice, 'this is the one, you'll see. *Please...*'

'Mr Tormé?' she called out, remembering his name.

The letters shuffled like a deck of cards in her mind and settled into a new pattern. It was a reflex she could not control, ever since she had learned the game from her father so many years ago, before the day they took him away and told his family that he was dead.

Barry E. Tormé, she thought.

You could spell a lot of words with those letters.

Even...

Robert Mayer.

He turned slightly, and she saw the familiar nose and chin she had tried so many times to reproduce, working from fading photographs and the shadow pictures in her mind. The two men continued to drag him forward. His shoes left long black skid-marks on the polished floor. Then they lifted him off his feet and he was lost in the light.

Outside the door, a blue van was waiting.

They dumped him in and locked the tailgate. Beyond the parking lot lay the walled compound, where the razor wire gleamed like hungry teeth atop the barricades and forgotten people lived out lives as bleak as unsold pilots and there was no way out for any of them until the cameras rolled again on another hit.

Milton Berle and Johnny Carson and Jackie Gleason watched mutely, stars who had become famous by speaking the words put into their mouths by others, by men who had no monuments to honour them, not here or anywhere else.

Now she knew the real reason she had come to this place. There was something missing. When she finished her sculpture there would be a new face for the courtyard, one who deserved a statue of his own. And this time she would get it right.

The steel door began to close.

Sorry, Daddy! she thought as the rain started again outside. I'm sorry, sorry...

'Wait.' Number Sixteen put on his Ray-Bans. 'I gotta get my pay first. You want to come with me?'

Yes, we could do that. Simple. All we do is turn and run the other way, like Lucy and Desi, like Dario and Mr Bean, bumbling along to a private hell of our own. What's the difference?

'No,' she said.

'I thought—'

'I'm sorry. I can't.'

'Why not?'

'I just…can't.'

She ran instead toward the light at the end, hoping to see the face in the van clearly one last time as it drove away, before the men in the suits could stop her.

DENNIS ETCHISON WAS a recipient of both the World Fantasy and the British Fantasy awards. His short fiction appeared in many magazines and anthologies and is collected in *The Dark Country, Red Dreams, The Blood Kiss, The Death Artist, Got to Kill Them All & Other Stories, Talking in the Dark* and *Fine Cuts*. Along with such movie novelisations as *The Fog, Halloween II* and *III*, and *Videodrome*, his novels include *Darkside, Shadowman, California Gothic* and *Double Edge*. He was also the editor of the landmark anthologies *Cutting Edge, MetaHorror* and *Masters of Darkness*. About the preceding story, the author explained: 'One evening in 1997, my wife Kris and I ran into Peter and Dana Atkins at Dark Delicacies bookstore, a favourite haunt of horror writers in Southern California. The occasion was a street fair sponsored by the local merchants along Burbank's Magnolia Boulevard. At some point Dana and I decided to search out a shop called It's a Wrap, featuring clothes worn only once or twice in movies and TV shows filmed at the studios nearby, much of it with expensive designer labels and offered for resale at ridiculously low prices. There were rumours of Armani suits for $150. Before we got there, a woman with a clipboard sidled up to us and asked if we would like to attend the screening of a new television pilot. Dana had already spotted It's a Wrap. I needed her advice about the women's clothing inside so that I'd know whether to go back for Kris. 'No, thanks,' I said. 'It pays fifty dollars,' said the woman. That sounded like a painless way to cover the cost of some Oscar-winning threads. We both signed on, and a month later I found myself in a theatre owned by a market research company. The dreary sitcom I saw that day was soon forgotten, and the cash I received was quickly squandered, but certain details remained with me. The two-way mirrors, for example. The hi-tech monitoring equipment I glimpsed on the way out. And the unreadable expressions of the young women who worked at the testing facility. What sort of

person, I wondered, takes such a job—and why? Was it only for the salary? Or were there other, more secret reasons? Dana never followed up, and her husband, who is a horror writer, wasn't offered the gig. A pity. I can't guess what story he might have written, but I'm sure it would have been a good one, very different from mine and worth a lot more than fifty bucks. The reasons to be afraid are all around, if you make it your business to look for such things.'

MY PATHOLOGY

Lisa Tuttle

IT MAY NOT be a truth universally acknowledged, but people value more that which is not easily won. Challenge and difficulty add to the appeal. As I once said to Saskia, unavailable men are always more attractive. I'd never known Saskia to fall for a man who wasn't already committed elsewhere— but she just said, '*If* that's your pathology.'

Certainly it was hers. The way she ignored perfectly nice men in favour of bastards belonging to someone else...

But love is a basic human need. Does it make sense to call it a disease?

DANIEL AND I were attracted to each other from the start, and there didn't seem to be anything difficult or inherently unavailable about him. The one slight little hitch—that the woman he described as his ex-girlfriend hadn't *quite* let him go—probably added to his attraction; I was touched by his tender concern for her feelings.

As he explained it: 'We were together for nearly three years. At one time I thought we'd get married. But... We had a major disagreement, one of those things where there can be no compromise. I won't go into the details.

Anyway, she knows it's over, knows we don't have a future together, and we're not…not sleeping together, you know, but she's afraid of being alone. She needs to know that I'm still her friend. I don't love her anymore, but I feel responsible. She's had a hard time lately.'

He told me about her (Michele, her name was) before we'd actually become lovers, on an evening when the possibility was quivering between us, so I knew his intentions toward me must be serious.

'Are you going to tell her about me?'

'I've already told her I've met someone.'

My heart leapt and I went to kiss him, this unknown woman's man who was now mine.

DANIEL WORKED IN an office in central London, as did I, but he lived out in Metroland—nearest station, Rayner's Lane—where the dear old London Underground emerges above ground, transformed into a suburban commuter train. The rails ran behind his house, so we were treated to a view of his back garden a good quarter hour before we could expect to arrive at the front door, on foot, from the station. Once, on his way home, Daniel had seen someone entering by the back door, and even though he phoned the police immediately on his mobile, the burglars managed to get away with the TV and VCR.

These were easily replaced. Daniel kept little that he valued on the ground floor of his narrow, two-bedroomed turn-of-the-century terraced cottage. Practically everything that mattered to him was kept locked in his 'workroom', otherwise the spare bedroom.

Daniel was a chartered accountant in his ordinary life, but in his workroom he was an alchemist.

He told me this, as he'd told me about Michele, early in our relationship. It meant nothing to me then. If asked to define alchemy, I'd have said it was a sort of primitive, magical chemistry, bearing about the same relationship to modern chemistry as astrology did to astronomy. It seemed a very strange hobby for someone as sane and successful as Daniel, but I kept my mouth shut as he unlocked his workshop to show me the shelves filled with ancient, leather-bound volumes, sealed jars with Latin labels, beakers and retorts, a Bunsen burner, vessels of copper and of glass. The smells were what most struck me: half a dozen different odours lingering in the air. Sulphur, roses, hot metal, burnt sugar, tar, and something pricklingly acidic which made me cough.

'What do you do here, exactly?'

'Do you really want to know, "exactly"?'

'Generally, then.'

'Search. Explore. Study. Experiment. I'm looking for the Philosopher's Stone—does that mean anything to you?'

I shook my head apologetically. 'Afraid not.'

He kissed me. 'Never mind. If you are interested, I can help you learn, but it doesn't matter; we can't share everything.'

As I watched him lock the door to his workshop, I wondered if it would matter. Of course couples couldn't share all their interests, but this hobby seemed less like stamp collecting, more like a religion.

We didn't talk about alchemy and we didn't talk about Michele, and as the weeks and the months passed, and my love for Daniel became more deeply rooted, those two 'untouchable' areas of his life became irritants, and I wondered if there was a connection. I finally asked him if Michele had shared his interest in alchemy.

He tensed. 'She pretended that she did, for a while, but she didn't. It was my fault as much as hers. I let her know how important it was to me… but it's not as important as honesty. If she'd just had faith in me, instead of pretending she understood… She lied to me.'

I held his hand. 'I won't lie to you. I won't pretend. But I would like to know more about something so important to you. You said you could teach me…'

But the shutters were down; I was trespassing. He shook his head firmly. 'No. I won't make that mistake again. It's better if you don't know, and you won't be put in an insidious position. If you don't know anything about The Work, we can't possibly argue about it.'

I wished I'd never mentioned Michele. I began to hate the invisible woman who still hovered on the periphery of my life, attached to my lover like a parasite, barring certain possibilities from me forever.

It was harder for me now to leave those two sore subjects alone, but at least I didn't speak to Daniel about them. I found a bookshop in Cecil Court which specialised in esoteric learning, and bought an armload of books about alchemy. On the evenings Daniel did his duty by his ex-girlfriend, I went back to my rented room and got into bed with his ancient philosophy.

The fact that I was still shelling out money for a room of my own, although I scarcely spent any time there, was a sore point. I wanted to live with Daniel and found his arguments against it pretty feeble. If he really felt that his two-bedroomed house wasn't big enough for the two of us, then he should sell it, and we could buy something else together. I'd been looking for something to buy when I met him, but I didn't want to commit myself to mortgage payments on some tiny flat if there was any future in our relationship.

We had been lovers for nearly nine months when I began to suspect I was pregnant.

I'd been careless about contraception. The truth was, I wanted to have a baby; I wanted to force the issue of our relationship to a crisis, even if I hadn't admitted it to myself. When my period didn't arrive bang on time, my first response was an inward clutch of sheer joy. I was ready to change my life.

I didn't tell him straight away. When I got on the train for Rayner's Lane one evening, two weeks later, I was still happy keeping my secret. I watched out the window for his house, as I always did. In the slanting, pre-dusk light and shade the view of row upon row of narrow back gardens was like the unspooling of a film, one I found inexhaustibly absorbing. Occasionally I saw people, either through windows or outside, children playing, men or women mowing their little carpet-strips of lawn or taking washing from a line, but more often there were no people to be seen, only the signs, ordinary and cryptic, of their invisible occupation.

The back of Daniel's house was normally almost exactly like its neighbours on either side, but not that evening.

That evening there was something growing out of it. It was a pale, whitish blister, a sort of bubble, or a cocoon, the size of a small room. I sensed it was organic, something which had grown rather than been added on. It was as if Daniel's house was a living organism, a body which could extrude a tissue-like substance.

I was astonished, and then it was out of sight. My mind immediately set to work revising and editing the memory of what I'd seen. It must have been something else, something ordinary, like a sheet of plastic or PVC. If there'd been an accident, fire, or explosion (my throat tightened with the memory of those smells, those volatile substances locked in his workroom) or even a break-in, it might have been necessary to shroud the back of the house in some protective material.

Alighting at the station, I ran practically the whole way back to his house, gulping and weeping in fearful suspense. If only Daniel were all right...

Daniel opened the door to my hysterical pounding and I threw myself into his arms. 'Thank God! Oh, Daniel, what happened? When I saw the back of your house—'

'What are you talking about?'

I broke away and hurried through to the kitchen. The window offered me an unobstructed view of the fig tree at the very bottom of the garden. The back door was locked and bolted, but I got the keys from the top of the fridge and let myself out.

I could find nothing out of the ordinary. No protrusion, no growth, only the weathered grey paint beginning to peel away from the wall in a few places. Everything looked exactly as it always had. I touched it to be sure. I listened to a bird singing, and the distant wind-rush of traffic. Another train rattled by, and when I looked up a few pale faces gazed at me blankly over the fence. It was obvious that none of them saw anything to get excited about. I started to feel like an idiot.

Slowly I went back inside to offer Daniel some lame excuse for my excitement. 'I thought I saw something. I don't know what—a sort of hallucination, I guess it must have been. I don't know why...'

He laid a cool hand caressingly on my hot face and looked at me very tenderly. 'Excitement, maybe? Hormones?'

I realised then that he must have known, or at least started to suspect, about the pregnancy as soon as I did. Even though we didn't live together, we'd never spent more than a night or two apart.

I started crying. Daniel wrapped his arms around me and held me close. He murmured his love in my ear. 'When will you move in? This weekend?'

I gaped, sobs shuddering to a halt. 'But…if this place isn't big enough for the two of us…'

'But it's not just the two of us anymore. Everything's changed.' He smiled joyfully. 'My workroom can be the nursery.'

I DON'T LIKE doctors, and I can't stand hospitals. I don't even like visiting people in them, and my one experience as a patient—after a burst appendix at the age of eight—was enough to put me off for life. I knew that even if I was to have a home birth (Daniel agreed that was best) I would still have to visit a doctor, but I kept putting it off, and somehow got through the whole of my first trimester, grimly putting up with the sickness and the pains, still avoiding the evil day.

Daniel, who had become very protective—ensuring that alcohol, caffeine, French cheeses, and shellfish did not pass my lips, constantly querying my emotional, mental, and physical health—accepted my fear of hospitals and didn't push. When I finally, with great reluctance, decided that I'd have to go register with the local GP, he shook his head. 'Really, that's not necessary. I know how you feel, Bess, so I've asked my mother to come 'round and have a look at you.'

'Your mother?' He'd never mentioned this personage before; from the way he shrugged off my questions about his background I'd gathered only that he and his parents were not close. 'Is she a doctor, then?'

He looked oddly embarrassed. 'Well, yes, of course. She's a specialist in, you know…in private practice, of course, but she won't charge us.'

And, for me, she would make house calls. I was relieved.

Her appearance surprised me. She had aquiline features very like Daniel's, but she looked far too young to be his mother. Except for her hair, which was coarse and heavily streaked with grey, I'd have thought her not much older than I was. She seemed uncomfortable with her own attractiveness, dressed in a frumpy, ill-fitting suit and wearing heavy, dark-framed spectacles.

She had a chilly, distant manner, never meeting my eyes, hardly even looking at me properly. Her examination of me seemed cursory; I didn't even have to undress. She prodded my barely-showing 'bump', took my blood pressure, which she pronounced excellent, got me to stand on the scales, asked me a few medical questions, and announced her pleasure at learning that I was 'giving Daniel a child'.

'Hang on,' I said. 'It's my baby. I'm not "giving" anybody anything!'

'It's only a manner of speaking,' said Daniel. He was standing behind me, stroking my hair, and I hoped he was shooting poison with his eyes at his mother.

'I'm sorry if I've disturbed you,' she said awkwardly. 'I didn't mean anything wrong by it. I'm sure you must understand how pleased I am that Daniel will be a father.'

Well, fair enough. After all, I thought, she hardly knew me; why should she feel pleased that I was to be a mother? And she might have preferred someone else as her son's partner. Yet I noticed she seemed almost as uncomfortable with Daniel as she was with me. Watching them as they stood, uneasily close, by the door, hesitating over whether and how to kiss goodbye, I wondered what had come between them.

Daniel's mother showed me how to take my own blood pressure, gave me some guidelines for monitoring my weight gain, and promised to send along a midwife in good time. Meanwhile, I read books about natural childbirth, drank herbal teas, and slept a lot. I was so tired all the time. Around about the sixth month I started suffering from backache in addition to everything else and decided to take my maternity leave earlier than planned.

One good thing about not going out to work anymore was that I didn't have to deal with seeing that thing on the back of the house so often. Because

I hadn't stopped seeing it. Maybe it was hormonal—at any rate, whether it was a trick of the eye or of the brain, it bothered me.

I knew that Daniel didn't see it, but another time I took Saskia with me on the train. I didn't try to warn her or set her up; I just pointed out the house from the train window and waited, trembling with nerves, for her response. The thin, pale growth had become a huge bubble with the passage of time, inescapably strange, and I could hardly believe that I was the only person to see it.

'Which one?' asked Saskia, peering out at the monstrosity. 'Oh, there? With the red geranium in the kitchen window? My pot! Is that what you wanted me to see?'

Saskia had made me a lovely blue pot when I'd told her I was pregnant. I couldn't see it from the train; the whole of the kitchen window was blocked from my view by the sinister, gently bobbing growth.

I knew there was nothing 'really' there on the back of the house; what I saw came from within me.

It was in me.

I had nightmares about the baby.

Usually, in my dreams, I gave birth to a perfectly normal, sweet, much wanted little baby…then I'd lose it by doing something criminally insane: I put it in the oven to keep it warm, and only realised what I'd done hours later; I wrapped it in newspaper and absent-mindedly dropped it in a bin; I left it on a tube train.

But there were other dreams in which I gave birth to things which were not babies. Sometimes it was a deformed creature, armless and legless, or looking like a foetal pig; once it was a wizened, evil-looking old man who bit off my breast; another time it was an egg-shaped thing, glowing red-hot, the passage of which woke me screaming in pain.

One night I dreamed that I was inside the cocoon, Daniel and his mother on either side of me, holding down my arms and shouting at me to push. The struggle to give birth was inextricably bound with the struggle to breathe properly, and as I inhaled, gasping, I became aware that I'd used up nearly all the air in the room, and also that the soft, tissue-like walls were collapsing.

They fell upon me (Daniel and his mother had vanished), enveloping me like vast sheets of cling film, incredibly strong, binding my limbs and closing off my mouth and nostrils, suffocating me.

With a snort and gasp I woke. Heart pounding, I sat up, breathing deeply in and out. I was alone in bed. The room felt horribly close and hot. I rolled out of bed and staggered across to the window with the idea of opening it, but then I looked out, and froze.

There below me, rising to just below the window ledge and ballooning out to fill nearly half the back garden, was that thing which before I had only seen from a distance, from the train window. Now, so close, I could appreciate its size and solidity. It gave off a glow; after a moment, I realised that the source of the glow was an inner-light, and then I saw movement, like fish deep beneath murky water. I stared, concentrating so intensely that I forgot to breathe, until I was certain that the moving shapes I saw were human.

I screamed for Daniel. Below, the two figures stopped moving.

I stumbled across the room, calling his name, and out onto the landing. Light rose up from below, light from the kitchen, and as I started downstairs, leaning heavily on the rail, I saw the two of them: Daniel and a woman. She looked like his mother except for her hair, which was short, fair, and curly, and the fact that she was making no effort to hide the fact that she was young and attractive. All of a sudden I understood: I had never met Daniel's mother, only Michele in disguise.

The next thing I knew I was lying on the couch in the sitting room and Daniel was holding my hand.

'Where is she?'

'There's no one here.' He told me I'd been dreaming. According to him, he'd been asleep in bed beside me when I started screaming his name. He'd been unable to stop me from stumbling downstairs, although he had managed to catch me when I collapsed at the bottom.

I believed him. What I had seen had been 'only' a dream. But that didn't make it unimportant.

One of the strongest memories I have from my childhood is also the memory of a dream; more real to me than much that 'really' happened.

I was eight years old, asleep in my bed, when a strange, high, buzzing sound awoke me. I sat up and looked over at my sister, peacefully sleeping in her matching bed. The noise seemed to be coming from directly below us, from the kitchen. I got up to investigate.

As I came down the stairs I could hear my parents talking in the kitchen, but I couldn't make out their words. The hall was dark, and I arrived at the kitchen door unnoticed. There was a strong light on at one end of the kitchen which cast my parents' shadows on the wall. I had noticed the effect before, but this time it was different. This time the shadows on the wall did not correspond to the two familiar people. I could see my mother and father sitting at the table, but on the wall behind them were the shadows of monstrous insects.

Mum turned her head and saw me. She didn't seem surprised. She opened her arms. 'Come here, darling.'

I went to her, nervously watching the wall. Nightmares usually fled at the arrival of grown-ups, but the shadows didn't change as I'd expected. The one behind my Mum moved, becoming three-dimensional, an inky-black, gigantic insect which emerged from the pale wall and came for me. I began to scream and wriggle, trying to get away, but my mother held me tight, her face stiff, implacable. She held me fast as the shadow-creature's long, black proboscis snaked out and struck my pyjama-clad tummy. It pierced the cloth and then my skin, sinking deep into me. It hurt worse than anything I'd ever known. I screamed in agony before passing out.

The cocoon-thing on the outside of the house belonged to the same level of reality as the shadow insects of my childhood. Lying awake beside Daniel for what remained of that night, I let myself think, for the first time, about all the things which can go wrong with a pregnancy, let myself recall, clearly, those sections of my pregnancy-and-childbirth books which I'd skimmed so nervously. Because there had been signs that all was not well—signs which Daniel and his mother (if she was his mother) had dismissed as unimportant. The pains. The occasional show of blood. The fact that I had yet to feel my baby move.

I didn't tell Daniel what I had decided. For once, I didn't want him to soothe away my fears. In the morning, after he'd gone to work, I took the bus to Northwick Park Hospital.

At the maternity unit there I was scolded for not coming in sooner, my fears—both about hospitals and about the baby—reassuringly brushed away. I was given forms to fill out, and taken along for an ultrasound scan. Although I was dry-mouthed and twitchy with nerves, I thought the end of the nightmare was in sight, but in fact it was only the beginning.

There was no baby in my womb. It was a tumour.

In a state of shock, I was whisked from Maternity to Oncology where a grave-faced physician informed me that although many, perhaps most, ovarian cysts were benign, the size of this one did not incline him to be optimistic. It would have to be removed in either case; if it proved malignant, a complete hysterectomy would follow. He invited me to return three days later, perhaps with my partner or another family member, to discuss the prognosis further.

I had expected Daniel to be upset. What I did not expect was his rage.

'What have you done?' His voice was a vicious, strangled whisper. He looked as if he would have killed as soon as touched me. My tears dried up, misery overwhelmed by baffled fear. I wished it could have been a dream, like the one in which my mother held me still to receive the insect-man's terrifying attack.

'I didn't do anything, Daniel,' I said carefully. 'I'm telling you what they said at the hospital—'

He was in a fury. 'Why did you go to the hospital? Why? Why? Why couldn't you trust me? How could you do this to me?'

'What are you talking about? Are you crazy? This is happening to me, if you hadn't noticed! I had to go to the hospital—your bloody mother was no bloody use at all. She couldn't tell a baby from a tumour. That's what it is—a tumour, not a baby. And the doctor said it's so big that it's probably malignant, and if it is they'll have to take out my whole womb, my ovaries, everything!' I began to weep again.

'No they won't,' said Daniel, relaxing a little. He no longer looked so angry. 'I won't let them. We won't let them.'

'But they'll have to operate. Even if it's not malignant—'

'It's not malignant.'

'You can't know that.'

'I do know that.' His eyes drilled into mine with the intensity, the absolute certainty which I'd always found irresistibly sexy. 'I know what it is, and they don't. They think it's cancer. I know it's not.'

'What is it, then?'

'It's the Philosopher's Stone.'

I WANTED SO much to believe him. Who would choose cancer, surgery, a possibly fatal illness, over magic? Daniel, impassioned, was a convincing advocate. The so-called Philosopher's Stone, although sometimes identified with various gems or minerals, was also described as an elixir, a water, a dragon, and a 'divine child'. I'd thought it a symbol for the knowledge sought by alchemists, but Daniel told me that although symbolic, it was also very real. It was the stuff of creation, a kind of super-DNA, created, replicated, by life itself. By us. Our union was the rare and perfect Alchemical Marriage; my womb was the alembic in which the dragon, stone, or divine child was now growing. When perfect it would be born, and I would be transformed in the process.

'If you'll think about it, you'll realise your own transformation has already started,' he said. 'You can see things other people can't. The thing you saw on the back of the house—don't you realise what that is? It's an amniotic sac, indicating the impending mystical birth of knowledge.'

He'd been transformed himself by his wonder and joy; there was no doubt that he believed everything he told me. How I struggled, to join him in his magical belief-system. For a little while, that evening, I managed to convince us both that I did believe—but the next day, alone in the house, the effort was too great, and I collapsed into dull despair. Daniel was the alchemist, not me. In my world, a lump in the womb couldn't be both child and stone; it was one or the other, and I knew which mine was.

As the days passed, I went on struggling to believe in Daniel's reality while the horror of mine threatened to overwhelm me. I was too frightened to go back to the hospital, anyway. Daniel believed that all was well. He shared his books, his notes, his experiments and fantasies with me: finally, every secret corner of his life was revealed to me. I was his partner now in what he called The Great Work.

I felt that I would burst with the secret and the stone inside me. Finally, I confessed all—or nearly all—to Saskia, who immediately arranged for me to see her own doctor.

'I had a cyst five years ago the size of a large grapefruit. It turned out to be benign. Lots of women get them. I lost one ovary…but I've still got the other *and* my womb, just in case.' She made a face. I knew already about the tipped cervix, the doctor who'd reckoned her chances of conceiving normally, without medical intervention, at less than ten percent, but the idea that she, too, had once carried a stone inside was new to me.

'I never knew that!'

'Sure you did. Remember, when I was in the hospital?'

'Oh.' Ancient guilt swept over me. I was her best friend, but I'd never visited her in the hospital.

'It's all right; it was always all right.' Telepathic, she patted my arm. 'I knew how you felt. I had enough visitors and enough chocolates—I was really grateful for the books you sent, a new one every day! Did I ever tell you what they found inside the cyst?'

I shook my head.

'Six tiny baby teeth, bits of bone and tissue, and a huge hair-ball. It was like a giant owl pellet!'

'Teeth?'

'It sounds creepy, but my doctor said it's not that unusual. The cyst is formed from ovarian cells gone wrong, and after all, that's where babies come from, teeth and bone and hair and all.'

I imagined our divine child a mass of skin and hair and bone and teeth all jumbled up together in the wrong order. What would Daniel say if he could see it?

'Could I keep it, do you think? I mean, after they take it out, would they save it for me?'

Saskia's face revealed no horror or dismay at my suggestion. 'I don't see why not. It's yours, after all.'

I TOLD DANIEL I was going to Lincolnshire to stay with my mother for a few days, and Saskia took me in to the hospital. She was with me nearly the whole time, comforting, advising, taking control when I couldn't cope.

'If I ever have a baby, Sask, I want you with me,' I said, gripping her hand just before I was wheeled into the operating room.

'Of course you'll have a baby. You'll have as many as you want, and I'll be godmother,' she promised.

But Saskia was wrong. There would be no babies for me. The surgeon removed both ovaries, my fallopian tubes, my entire womb. I was left with nothing except the cyst I had asked them to save.

It was a disgusting thing to have carried around inside me, to have imagined as a living child: a fleshy lump covered in hair. I cut it open with my Swiss army knife, balancing it on my bed tray.

A foul-smelling semi-solid liquid dripped out, and I gagged, but kept on sawing.

There was more hair inside, more disgusting pus, and soft, baby flesh. No teeth, no bones, but, right at the centre, one hard, tiny nugget the size of a pea.

I picked it out with my bare fingers and wiped it on a tissue. It was a deep, reddish brown in colour and felt like stone. I rapped it against the bedside table and scraped at it with a fingernail. I felt a strong urge, which I resisted, to put it in my mouth and swallow it.

Holding it tightly between the thumb and forefinger of one hand, I rang for the nurse with the other, to ask her to please get rid of the grisly, oozing thing on my tray.

I FELT MUCH weaker than I'd anticipated, and I knew I would not be able to deceive Daniel, or to face him. He would be angry, I knew; he would be furious, at first, but then, I hoped, he would get over his disappointment and understand. Eager for his forgiveness, for the enveloping love which I needed to help me recover, I sent Saskia to break the news to him. I thought it would be easier for her, and that he would hide his true feelings from a relative stranger. I was wrong.

Afterward, when she told me about it, she was shaking.

'He's grieving. He's like you've had an abortion. Didn't you tell him you weren't pregnant? Didn't you tell him what it was?'

'Of course I did!'

'Well, you didn't make him understand. The poor, sad man… I explained about the cancer, but he couldn't get the idea of a child out of his head, and the notion that you'd destroyed it. Oh, Bess!'

She looked at me with tears in her eyes and, horrified, I saw that she, like Daniel, blamed me. It was all my fault that I could only produce a malignant, hairy lump instead of a wanted child.

'But I didn't! I wanted a baby, too, as much as ever he did!'

Saskia put her arms around me and, not for the first time or the last, we cried together.

WHEN IT CAME time for me to leave the hospital it turned out I had no home. Saskia took me by taxi to the house in Rayner's Lane where I found that Daniel had changed the locks. Saskia was furious, but it was so over-the-top that I had to laugh. She took me to Muswell Hill to stay in her flat until something else could be sorted.

Saskia went on being my intermediary with Daniel. He grudgingly agreed to meet me, to talk, and I spent hours hurling myself at his stony indifference. Saskia felt that as Daniel was so intransigent I should simply accept that the affair was over and get on with my own life. But I couldn't do that. I'd lost far more than he had, and it was his fault.

Guilt worked better on Daniel than reason; he could see what a state I was in, and he knew he owed me something. He tried to buy me off, but although I took his money I always let him know it wasn't enough. Given time, I felt I could win him back, until the day he told me, over the phone, that he was 'seeing' someone else.

In a panic, I played my last card and told him I had the Philosopher's Stone. 'I found it inside the, the thing they cut out of me. I kept it.'

'Why didn't you tell me before?'

For the first time since before the operation I felt the flutter of hope inside. 'Well, you know, Daniel, you haven't been very nice to me. If we're not partners anymore, then what business is it of yours what I have?'

'What does it look like?' When I described it, he said flatly, 'That's not very big.'

'When Helvetius complained that a piece the size of a mustard-seed was too small to be of use he was given a piece only half that size, and used it to make several ounces of gold.'

'What do you know about Helvetius?'

He spoke as if he'd completely forgotten that he'd once shared the Great Work with me.

'Daniel, are you interested or not?'

No alchemist could have refused. I took the Metropolitan Line out to his house that very evening, for the first time since leaving the hospital.

Although it was still light and I was looking out for it, I didn't see his house on the journey. I realised why later: with the strange, shroud-like growth gone from the back of the house there was nothing to distinguish it from its neighbours. I wondered, had I dwindled back into the ordinary, too, now, my special-ness cut out of me? Or would the tiny stone I kept clamped between finger and thumb redeem me?

The ancient texts advised a variety of methods for testing the Stone, each more lengthy than the last. We opted for the quickest. I managed to shave off a bit of the stone with a razor-knife and introduced it into a pan containing twelve ounces of lead, which we melted down over one of the gas burners on the kitchen cooker. Before morning dawned we had our result: two ounces of pure gold.

For a moment I saw euphoria and greed mingled undisguised on Daniel's face. 'We've done it!' I cried, thinking, *I've got you!*

But his face closed up at the sound of my voice. He shook his head.

'Big deal. Two ounces of gold. Worth about three hundred dollars per ounce on today's market.'

'We can make more.'

'Oh, yes. At *least* another six ounces.'

'I can't win, can I? The only reason you want me is to produce your precious Philosopher's Stone, and when I do—at huge cost to myself!—you turn me away.' In a withering tone I finished, 'It's not big enough!'

'You don't understand anything,' he said fiercely. 'It's not to do with size, or with gold. It's not the product, it's the process. Our child wasn't ready—and now we'll never know what might have been because you let them cut it out. You let them kill it.'

'It would have killed me!'

'Oh, you know that, do you? If you believe everything they tell you, you'd have to believe that's not real gold, that what we just did was impossible.' He sighed, becoming calmer. 'Pregnancy is a journey fraught with danger. Women do still die in childbirth, but is that a justification for abortion? You wouldn't have died, only changed, if you'd waited and let it be born.'

'Daniel, that was not a child. I saw it, remember?'

'You saw what they took out of you: the *magna mater*, the basic material of life, alive and growing until it was ripped from you. Oh, Bess.' He groaned. 'It's not about making gold—that's just one aspect. What you had inside you—it could have been all knowledge; it could have been eternal life, a transformation for both of us...' He looked stricken. 'It's my fault, isn't it? My fault, not yours. If I'd been a proper teacher, if I'd made you understood the risks and the rewards, you'd never have gone near that hospital.' He began to weep as nakedly and helplessly as a child, and I put my arms around him and tried to give him comfort.

Finally I realised that I was not the only victim in this. I recognised just how seriously I had hurt him.

'Poor, poor,' I murmured, and stroked his head and kissed away his tears. For the first time in ages I began to feel aroused, and when his tears were gone, I unfastened his trousers and snaked a hand inside.

He did nothing to encourage me. He stood very still, utterly passive, while in my hand he quickly grew hard. I pulled down his pants. Looking at his face I saw a familiar shy, boyish, slightly guilty smile quivering about his lips. In a rush of affection and desire I sank to my knees and sucked him, and when he came, I swallowed his semen. It was something I had never done before, but it felt right, a symbol of a new beginning, my new and utter commitment to him. I had let him down once, but would never do so again.

I went off to the bathroom for a wash, debating whether to take the day off. I wondered what Daniel planned to do, and thought what a warm and welcome relief it would be to spend the day in bed with him. When I came out, I found he'd made a pot of coffee.

I smiled at him as he poured me a cup, but lost the smile when he put the lump of gold into my saucer.

'Oh, no.'

'It's yours.'

'Ours.'

'Bess, it's over.'

'Oh, yeah? What was that just then?'

'That was sex. And it was your idea.'

I felt sick. 'You're saying you didn't enjoy it?'

'Enjoyment isn't the point. One sexual…spasm…can't revive a dead relationship.'

'Are you so sure it's dead?'

'You're the one who killed it.' He saw my face, and his own crumbled into grief. 'Oh, Bess! I'm not blaming you.'

'Like hell!'

'It was my fault, too, I see that now. Naturally, you were afraid, you didn't understand. How could you? The Work was still new to you. Never mind all that. Whatever happened, it's over now.'

'You hate me.'

'No, of course not.'

'Then why can't we forget the past and start over?'

'Because we can't.' He closed his eyes briefly, then looked straight into mine. 'Look, we can't even communicate. We live in different worlds. Where I see something wonderful, you see something terrible. A tumour instead of the Philosopher's Stone. It's not your fault; I was wrong to try to change you.'

'I will change.' I'd lost all shame, all sense of myself. I can't explain it. I would be whatever he wanted.

'It's too late for that.'

'Because you don't love me anymore.'

'No!' Tears rose to his eyes again; I felt I was looking through their clarity straight into his soul. He put out his hand and I gripped it. 'I love you, Bess. God help me, I do. Forever. But I can't give up The Work, not even for you. It would be like giving up my life.'

'I'm not asking you to. I'll help.'

'You can't.' He watched me warily as he pronounced my death sentence. 'I know you mean well, but you're no good to me without a womb. I must have a woman in my life, for The Work—a complete woman.'

Strangely enough, I did understand. And accepted what I know many would find unacceptable. I had entered into his alchemical world far enough for that. I saw the impasse before me, but still I refused to give up. I could not grow another womb, but there must still be a way to keep him.

'We can still be friends,' I tried.

'If—if you can bear it.'

I would have to. 'I can if you'll be honest with me. You mustn't try to protect me, or control me, by keeping secrets. This woman you're seeing…?'

'It might not work out,' he said swiftly.

'If it doesn't, there'll be someone else. You'll need your other woman, for the physical side. She'll be your crucible. I can accept that as long as I know that I'm your real partner, spiritually and intellectually. As long as you still love me, ours will be the real sacred marriage.'

Was it love or hate that drove me down that road? My life seemed out of my own control. I was driven by a determination to cling to Daniel, for better or worse, to keep him as I had not been able to keep the fruit of my womb.

But if he was my weakness, I was also his. He did love me, I'm sure of it. He had not expected to have a second chance, but that's what I was offering, and he was grateful for it. When I said I must have my own key to his house he handed over the spare without a murmur, and I knew then that no new woman would be able to dislodge me from his life, no matter what.

—

MY GRANDMOTHER DIED that month, leaving me an inheritance which promised to change my life. Instead of the tiny flat I would have to scrimp and save to afford, I could look at houses. By great good fortune the house next door to Daniel's—the end of the terrace—was up for sale. I made an offer straightaway and had it accepted. The mortgage would mean large monthly payments, but it would be worth it to live so close to Daniel. I imagined how someday we would knock down walls to make our two houses one from within, just as our apparently separate lives were joined already.

While I waited for the survey and search to be completed, I divided my time between Saskia's flat and Daniel's house. We were still working out the boundaries of our new relationship; I knew I had to be careful not to push him too far, too fast, but to give him plenty of space. Things were a bit awkward with Saskia, too. Living together in her tiny flat had put a strain on our friendship. I sensed, too, that she disapproved of my clinging to Daniel after he'd treated me so badly, although she couldn't point the finger, having fallen for yet another inappropriate, unavailable man. By unspoken agreement, we didn't discuss our relationships. Sometimes, by prior arrangement, I spent the night at Daniel's when he was out with his new girlfriend, so Saskia and I could both have a break.

Daniel and I got together about twice a week. Usually, we would have a meal together, maybe go on to the pub, and I'd spend the night. We'd resumed a sexual relationship, although it was not as I would have liked. Frustratingly for me, Daniel found normal intercourse impossible. The thought of my missing womb, the idea that I was 'not whole', killed his sexual desire. He went limp every time. But I could usually arouse him with my mouth, so oral sex became usual for us.

One day as I was going 'home' to Saskia's flat—the exchange of contracts still hovering mysteriously just out of reach—I took a detour to search out a corner shop and came back a different way. Usually I approached Saskia's flat, which was on the second story of an old house, from the front, but this time my detour brought me out on the street immediately behind hers, and when I glanced up at the trees, which were just beginning to bud, I glimpsed through them a pale, translucent shimmering which was immediately and horrifyingly familiar to me.

Praying I was wrong, I began to dodge and shift about, desperate for a better view.

I saw it plain: a growth, like the puffed throat of a frog, projected from the back wall of Saskia's house. I knew at once what it meant, and only wondered how I could have been blind for so long. Daniel's nameless 'other' was Saskia, and Saskia's guilty secret was Daniel.

She didn't try to deny it when I confronted her; she actually felt relieved. 'He made me promise that I wouldn't hurt you by telling—I never wanted to hurt you! And I guess I kind of thought—well, it's so obvious that he loves you more than he cares about me, so I thought, what's the point of putting you through hell for a little sexual fling. He'd only find someone else—he's that sort, you know.'

'Yes, yes,' I said impatiently. 'I knew he had a girlfriend—I just didn't know it was you. I feel such a fool—'

'Oh, no, Bess, you mustn't! I'm sorry, I really am. I do love Daniel—I can't help how I feel—but you're my dearest friend; you're more important to me than he is. If you want me to, I'll break it off with him. I'll never see him again. All you have to do is ask.'

I hoped she was lying. I didn't like the idea that her feelings for him were so shallowly rooted. I shook my head, staring into her eyes. 'Of course not. You can't break it off with him now. You're carrying his child.'

———

SASKIA KNEW NOTHING about it, and didn't believe me. She'd had her period only a week before, and besides… Yes, I knew about the single ovary, and the tipped cervix. But I had my own experience to go on, and I knew what I'd seen.

'Did Daniel tell you I was p.g.? He's got such a thing about wombs, and conception, and "proper" sex with simultaneous orgasms. He fantasises…' She was concerned about me; I'd gone very pale because I'd just realised what

I'd done with my thoughtless outburst. Saskia didn't know, and she mustn't know; not, at least, until I'd been able to make some plans.

'Bess, what is it? You're so pale. Is this all too horrible for you? I'm so sorry. But I'm not pregnant, I'm sure I'm not—you certainly don't have to worry that I'll take Daniel away. I'm not a very likely candidate to bear him a child…'

'No, I know that,' I said, thinking of her cyst. 'I got a bit hysterical, that's all. It was when I suddenly realised that you and Daniel… But now that I've had a chance to think about it, I'm glad it's you, Saskia, I really am.'

'I'll never take Daniel away from you, Bess. You do know that?'

'Yes. I do know that.'

I TOLD DANIEL the next day, and warned him to be careful. 'She's not like me. She trusts her doctor; she'll go for surgery at the first sign. You've got to act as soon as she tells you, or we'll lose it.'

'How? What can I do? I can't talk to her about alchemy. You're too right, she's not like you. Oh, Bess, this was a mistake, I should never have let it happen.'

His defeatism infuriated me. 'The past is past. Stop moaning about it. We've got another chance now, both of us, through her.'

'But how? She'll want to be rid of it as soon as she knows.'

'I thought the coal cellar. Yours, at a pinch, but mine would be better, if I get possession in time. It wouldn't be so hard to soundproof, we wouldn't have to worry about neighbours.'

Luckily, I was able to exchange contracts only a week later, with vacant possession following the week after that. I was able to invest a full month in getting my house ready before Saskia came to see me with her news.

She'd decided to tell me, but not Daniel.

'It's another cyst, and this one could be the big C. I just can't cope with Daniel's reactions. I'll have to tell him afterward, of course. I know it'll be the end of us—he was so weird about your operation, and he really loved you. I know he doesn't really love me, not for myself. He's got such strange ideas about women's bodies! After the operation…'

Although I didn't expect to be successful, I had to try to talk her out of what she planned to do. 'Maybe you won't have to have an operation. Maybe, if you tell your doctor how important it is for you to be able to bear a child, he might suggest some alternative treatments first. You don't know it's malignant.'

'He's ahead of you on that,' Saskia said. 'He's done a biopsy *in situ*, and then, if it proves to be benign, we could leave it, while I tried to get pregnant: probably take some fertility drug, then *in vitro* fertilisation, followed by a heavily monitored pregnancy—I could spend up to five or six months in the hospital, you know, even before the Caesarean. *Then* they'd do the hysterectomy. All that stuff just to make my body produce a baby. And I'm not even sure that I want one.'

'What? Of course you do!'

She shook her head.

'Come on, Saskia, I can remember when you were trying to get pregnant.'

'That was long ago, and in another country, and besides, the wench is dead. Look, once upon a time I wanted to have a baby with a particular man. I don't want to have a baby with Daniel.'

'If you're worried about taking him away from me…'

She almost laughed. 'Oh, Bess, I know you love him, but he's not for me. I can see that now. I certainly don't want his baby.'

'Have you thought about what *he* might want?'

'Bess, I'm not pregnant, you know. And all this is hypothetical, dependent on the tumour being benign. If it's not…' She made a little cutting motion across her stomach, and I felt sick.

'What about Daniel?'

'Daniel's history. I thought you'd be pleased—I've finally come to my senses. I don't love him. I think probably I never did. All the time what I felt for him wasn't love, it was a kind of desperation. I was desperate to make him love me, value me for myself, and he just couldn't. That's my pathology, you know, to be hooked on men who are incapable of loving me, for whatever reason. Or at least it used to be. But now that I know…now I *am* sick, I'm going to get it cut out of me, the whole mess.'

'Let me make you a cup of tea,' I said.

She commented on the taste—it was very sweet—and I told her that it was a special herbal mixture with extra honey to help build up her immune system.

She smiled gratefully. 'Thanks, Bess. You're with me in this? I mean, I don't expect you to come to the hospital—'

'I'm with you all the way.'

THE SEDATIVE TOOK effect quickly, and I called Daniel to come over and help me carry her down to the cellar, afraid that I might do her an injury if I tried to haul her down on my own.

I'd decorated the low, windowless cellar to look as cosy and cheerful and as much to Saskia's taste as possible, although I knew she'd be bound to see it as a prison. It was just too bad that she didn't love Daniel, or me, enough to see things from our point of view.

I'll pass over the next months quickly. It should have been a happy time, and, of course, Daniel was anticipating the birth with joy, but Saskia couldn't. She was angry and fearful at first, and after the pain began, it was even worse.

My own pains began around the same time, about three months after the beginning of Saskia's confinement: strong, sickening pains deep in my stomach. I remembered what I'd read about the *couvade*, the sympathetic pregnancy suffered by men in some primitive societies. It occurred to me that since I no longer had a womb, this might be my way of sharing Saskia's mystical pregnancy.

Then I began to have trouble swallowing. What with one thing and another it became harder to function, to go out to work, even to take care of Saskia. I longed to give up and quit, to crawl into my bed and sleep, but I could not forget my responsibilities.

I received notice of an appointment with my oncologist. Normally I would have tossed the letter in the bin, but I wasn't feeling normal. I decided to go. It would mean a day off work and a chance to talk to someone who might be more sympathetic to my pain than either Daniel or Saskia.

I got more than sympathy. I learned that there were tumours growing in my throat and stomach.

What I was experiencing was not *couvade* but the real thing.

The cancer had spread so fast and so far that surgery wasn't an option. The doctor spoke hesitantly about radiation and chemotherapy, but I was firmly against.

'You can't kill them,' I said, and he agreed, not understanding that I was stating my firm objection to any attempt to try to kill what I welcomed. If I shook, it was not from fear, but with ecstatic joy. I couldn't wait to get home and share the news with Daniel.

According to the doctor, I have about two months, maybe three, before the end. I am not afraid. The end of this bodily life will be a new beginning, a great and previously unknown transformation. Out of our bodies will come treasures which will have made our lives worthwhile.

LISA TUTTLE HAS been writing strange, weird stories nearly all her life, making her first professional sale in 1971. She is a past winner of the John W. Campbell Award, the British Science Fiction Award, and the International Horror Guild Award. Her first novel, *Windhaven*, written in collaboration with George R.R. Martin and originally published in 1981, is still in print, and has been translated into many languages. Her other novels include *Lost Futures*, *The Mysteries*, *The Silver Bough* and two tales of Victorian detection and supernatural suspense, *The Curious Affair of the Somnambulist and the Psychic Thief* and *The Curious Affair of the Witch at Wayside Cross*, featuring her occult investigators 'Jeperson and Lane'. Tuttle's short stories have been widely published and collected in *A Nest of Nightmares*, *Ghosts & Other Lovers*, *Stranger in the House* and *Objects in Dreams*, and she has edited the anthologies *Skin of the Soul* and *Crossing the Border: Tales of Erotic Ambiguity*. 'My first idea for this story came while I was travelling through London by train,' recalls the author, 'looking out the window at those little moments in unknown people's lives that you'd never see otherwise— glimpses into the windows and back-gardens of the houses we rattled past, houses that from behind present a very different appearance from the streets they face. I imagined how it would be to go past a place you knew very well, your own house or your lover's, and see something shockingly out of place clinging to the back wall: "It was a pale, whitish blister, a sort of bubble or a cocoon the size of a small room. I sensed it was organic, something which had grown rather than been added on. It was as if Daniel's house was a living organism…" I had to write a story to try to find out what my imagined vision might mean. My second idea (one is rarely enough to make a story) was something else that used to intrigue me when I lived in London—how often you will encounter someone with what seems like an eccentric hobby, only to discover they are not unique, but belong to an entire sub-culture that revolves around

the same obsession. London is a city full of weird stories waiting to be written. And the bit of dialogue that opens the story and gives it its title was my memory of a conversation back in the 1980s, with a close friend about our unsatisfactory romantic entanglements at the time. So there were the ingredients: an unhappy love affair, an impossible tumour, and alchemy.'

//

AT HOME IN THE PUBS
OF OLD LONDON

Christopher Fowler

The Museum Tavern, Museum Street, Bloomsbury

DESPITE ITS LOCATION diagonally opposite the British Museum, its steady turnover of listless Australian bar staff and its passing appraisal by tourists on quests for the British pub experience (comprising two sips from half a pint of bitter and one Salt 'n' Vinegar flavoured crisp, nibbled and returned to its packet in horror), this drinking establishment retains the authentically seedy bookishness of Bloomsbury because its corners are usually occupied by half-cut proofreaders from nearby publishing houses. I love pubs like this one because so much about them remains constant in a sliding world: the smell of hops, the ebb of background conversation, muted light through coloured glass, china tap handles, mirrored walls, bars of oak and brass. Even the pieces of fake Victoriana, modelled on increasingly obsolete pub ornaments, become objects of curiosity in themselves.

At this time I was working in a comic shop, vending tales of fantastic kingdoms to whey-faced net-heads who were incapable of saving a sandwich in a serviette, let alone an alien planet, and it was in this pub that I met Lesley. She was sitting with a group of glum-looking Gothic *Gormenghast* off-cuts who were on their way to a book launch at the new-age smells 'n' bells shop around the corner, and she was clearly unenchanted with the idea of joining them for a session of warm Liebfraumilch and crystal-gazing, because as each member of the group drifted off she found an excuse to stay on, and we ended up sitting together by ourselves. As she refolded her jacket a rhinestone pin dropped from the lapel, and I picked it up for her. The badge formed her initials—LL—which made me think of Superman, because he had a history of falling for women with those initials, but I reminded myself that I was no superman, just a man who liked making friends in pubs. I asked her if she'd had a good Christmas, she said no, I said I hadn't either and we just chatted from there. I told Lesley that I was something of an artist and would love to sketch her, and she tentatively agreed to sit for me at some point in the future.

The World's End, High Street, Camden Town

IT'S A FUNNY pub, this one, because the interior brickwork makes it look sort of inside out, and there's a steady through-traffic of punters wherever you stand, so you're always in the way. It's not my kind of place, more a network of bars and clubs than a proper boozer. It used to be called the Mother Red Cap, after a witch who lived in Camden. There are still a few of her pals inhabiting the place if black eyeliner, purple lipstick and pointed boots make you a likely candidate for cauldron-stirring. A white stone statue of Britannia protrudes from the first floor of the building opposite, above a shoe shop, but I don't think anyone notices it, just as they don't know about the witch. Yet if you step inside the foyer of the Black Cap, a few doors further down, you can see the witch herself, painted on a tiled wall. It's funny how people miss so much of what's going on around them. I was beginning to think Sophie wouldn't show up, then I became convinced she had, and I had missed her.

Anyway, she finally appeared and we hit it off beautifully. She had tied back her long auburn hair so that it was out of her eyes, and I couldn't stop

looking at her. It's never difficult to find new models; women are flattered by the thought of someone admiring their features. She half-smiled all the time, which was disconcerting at first, but after a while I enjoyed it because she looked like she was in on a secret that no one else shared. I had met her two days earlier in the coffee shop in Bermondsey where she was working, and she had suggested going for a drink, describing our meeting place to me as 'that pub in Camden near the shoe shop'. The one thing Camden has, more than any other place in London, is shoe shops, hundreds of the bastards, so you can understand why I was worried.

It was quite crowded and we had to stand, but after a while Sophie felt tired and wanted to sit down, so we found a corner and wedged ourselves in behind a pile of coats. The relentless music was giving me a headache, so I was eventually forced to take my leave.

The King's Head, Upper Street, Islington

THE BACK OF this pub operates a tiny theatre, so the bar suddenly fills up with the gin-and-tonic brigade at seven each evening, but the front room is very nice in a battered, nicotine-scoured way. It continued to operate on the old monetary system of pounds, shillings and pence for years, long after they brought in decimal currency. I'm sure the management just did it to confuse non-regulars who weren't in the habit of being asked to stump up nineteen and eleven pence half-penny for a libation. Emma was late, having been forced to stay behind at her office, a property company in Essex Road. The choice of territory was mine. Although it was within walking distance of her office, she hadn't been here before, and loved hearing this mad trilling coming from a door at the back of the pub. I'd forgotten to explain about the theatre. They were staging a revival of a twenties musical, and there were a lot of songs about croquet and how ghastly foreigners were. I remember Emma as being very pale and thin, with cropped blonde hair; she could easily have passed for a jazz-age flapper. I told her she should have auditioned for the show, but she explained that she was far too fond of a drink to ever remember

anything as complicated as a dance step. At the intermission, a girl dressed as a giant sequinned jellyfish popped out to order a gin and French; apparently she had a big number in the second act. We taxed the barman's patience by getting him to make up strange cocktails, and spent most of the evening laughing so loudly they probably heard us on stage. Emma agreed to sit for me at some point in the future, and although there was never a suggestion that our session would develop into anything more, I could tell that it probably would. I was about to kiss her when she suddenly thought something had bitten her, and I was forced to explain that my coat had picked up several fleas from my cat. She went off me after this, and grew silent, so I left.

The Pineapple, Leverton Street, Kentish Town

THIS TUCKED-AWAY pub can't have changed much in a hundred years, apart from the removal of the wooden partitions that separated the snug from the saloon. A mild spring morning, the Sunday papers spread out before us, an ancient smelly Labrador flatulating in front of the fire, a couple of pints of decent bitter and two packets of pork scratchings. Sarah kept reading out snippets from the *News of the World*, and I did the same with the *Observer*; but mine were more worthy than hers, and therefore not as funny. There was a strange man with an enormous nose sitting near the Gents' toilet who kept telling people that they looked Russian. Perhaps he was, too, and needed to find someone from his own country. It's that kind of pub; it makes you think of home.

I noticed that one of Sarah's little habits was rubbing her wrists together when she was thinking. Every woman has some kind of private signature like this. Such a gesture marks her out to a lover, or an old friend. I watched her closely scanning the pages—she had forgotten her glasses—and felt a great inner calm. Only once did she disturb the peace between us by asking if I had been out with many women. I lied, of course, as you do, but the question remained in the back of my head, picking and scratching at my brain, right up until I said goodbye to her. It was warm in the pub and she had grown sleepy; she actually fell asleep at one point, so I decided to quietly leave.

The Anchor, Park Street, Southwark

IT'S PLEASANT HERE on rainy days. In the summer, tourists visiting the nearby Globe fill up the bars and pack the riverside tables. Did you know that pub signs were originally provided so that the illiterate could locate them? The Anchor was built after the Southwark fire, which in 1676 razed the South Bank just as the Great Fire had attacked the North side ten years earlier. As I entered the pub, I noticed that the tide was unusually high, and the Thames was so dense and pinguid that it looked like a setting jelly. It wasn't a good start to the evening.

I had several pints of strong bitter and grew more talkative as our session progressed. We ate Toad-in-the-Hole, smothered in elastic gravy. I was excited about the idea of Carol and I going out together. I think she was, too, although she warned me that she had some loose ends to tie up, a former boyfriend to get out of her system, and suggested that perhaps we shouldn't rush at things. Out of the blue, she told me to stop watching her so much, as if she was frightened that she couldn't take the scrutiny. But she can. I love seeing the familiar gestures of women, the half smiles, the rubbing together of their hands, the sudden light in their eyes when they remember something they have to tell you. I can't remember what they say, only how they look. I would never take pictures of them, like some men I've read about. I never look back, you understand. It's too upsetting. Far more important to concentrate on who you're with, and making them happy. I'd like to think I made Carol feel special. She told me she'd never had much luck with men, and I believe it's true that some women just attract the wrong sort. We sat side by side watching the rain on the water, and I felt her head lower gently onto my shoulder, where it remained until I moved—a special moment, and one that I shall always remember.

The Lamb & Flag, Rose Street, Covent Garden

YOU COULD TELL summer was coming because people were drinking on the street, searching for spaces on the windowsills of the pub to balance their beer glasses. This building looks like an old coaching inn, and stands beside an arch over an alleyway, like the Pillars of Hercules in Greek Street. It's very old, with lots of knotted wood, and I don't suppose there's a straight angle in the place. The smoky bar is awkward to negotiate when you're carrying a drink in either hand—as I so often am!

This evening Kathy asked why I had not invited her to meet any of my friends. I could tell by the look on her face that she was wondering if I thought she wasn't good enough, and so I was forced to admit that I didn't really have any friends to whom I could introduce her. She was more reticent than most of the girls I had met until then, more private. She acted as though there was something on her mind that she didn't want to share with me. When I asked her to specify the problem, she either wouldn't or couldn't. To be honest, I think the problem was me, and that was why it didn't work out between us. Something about my behaviour made her uneasy, right from the start. There was no trust between us, which in itself was unusual, because most women are quick to confide in me. They sense my innate decency, my underlying respect for them. I look at the other drinkers standing around me, and witness the contempt they hold for women. My God, a blind man could feel their disdain. That's probably why I have no mates—I don't like my own sex. I'm ashamed of the whole alpha male syndrome. It only leads to trouble.

I made the effort of asking Kathy if she would sit for me, but knew in advance what the answer would be. She said she would prefer it if we didn't meet again, and yelped in alarm when I brushed against her hip, so I had to beat a hasty retreat.

The King William IV, High Street, Hampstead

PAULA CHOSE THIS rather paradoxical pub. It's in the middle of Hampstead, therefore traditional and okay, with a beer garden that was packed on a hot summer night, yet the place caters to a raucous gay clientele. Apparently, Paula's sister brought her here once before, an attractive girl, judging from the photograph Paula showed me, and such a waste, I feel, when she could be making a man happy. I wondered if, after finishing with Paula, I should give her sister a call, but decided that it would be playing a little too close to home.

We sat in the garden on plastic chairs, beside sickly flowerbeds of nursery-forced plants, but it was pleasant, and the pub had given me an idea. I resolved to try someone of the same gender next time, just to see what a difference it made. I picked up one of the gay newspapers lying in stacks at the back of the pub, and made a note of other venues in central London. I explained my interest in the newspaper by saying that I wanted to learn more about the lifestyles of others. Paula squeezed my hand and said how much she enjoyed being with someone who had a liberal outlook. I told her that my policy was live and let live, which is a laugh for a start. I am often shocked by the wide-eyed belief I inspire in women, and wonder what they see in me that makes them so trusting. When I pressed myself close against her she didn't flinch once under my gaze, and remained staring into my eyes while I drained my beer glass. A special girl, a special evening, for both of us.

The Admiral Duncan, Old Compton Street, Soho

FORMERLY DECORATED AS a cabin aboard an old naval vessel, with lead-light bay windows and a curved wood ceiling, this venue was revamped to suit the street's new status as a home to the city's homosexuals, and painted a garish purple. It was restored again following the nail-bomb blast that killed and maimed so many of its customers. Owing to the tunnel-like shape of the bar, the explosive force had nowhere to escape but through the glass front, and caused horrific injuries. A monument to the tragedy is inset into the ceiling of the pub, but no atmosphere of tragedy lingers, for the patrons, it seems, have bravely moved on in their lives.

In here I met Graham, a small-boned young man with a gentle West Country burr that seemed at odds with his spiky haircut. We became instant drinking pals, buying each other rounds in order to escape the evening heat of the mobbed street beyond. After what had occurred in the pub I found

it astonishing that someone could be so incautious as to befriend a total stranger such as myself, but that is the beauty of the English boozer; once you cross the threshold, barriers of race, class and gender can be dropped. Oh, it doesn't happen everywhere, I know, but you're more likely to make a friend in this city than in most others. That's why I find it so useful in fulfilling my needs. However, the experiment with Graham was not a success. Boys don't work for me, no matter how youthful or attractive they appear to be. We were standing in a corner, raising our voices over the incessant thump of the jukebox, when I realised it wasn't working. Graham had drunk so much that he was starting to slide down the wall, but there were several others in the vicinity who were one step away from being paralytic, so he didn't stick out, and I could leave unnoticed.

The Black Friar, Queen Victoria Street, Blackfriars

THIS STRANGE LITTLE pub, stranded alone by the roundabout on the north side of the river at Blackfriars, has an Arts and Crafts-style interior, complete with friezes, bas-reliefs and mottos running over its arches. Polished black monks traipse about the room, punctuating the place with moral messages. It stands as a memorial to a vanished London, a world of brown Trilbys and woollen overcoats, of rooms suffused with pipe smoke and the tang of brilliantine. In the snug bar at the rear I met Danielle, a solidly built Belgian au pair who looked so lonely, lumpen and forlorn that I could not help but offer her a drink, and she was soon pouring out her troubles in broken English. Her employers wanted her to leave because she was pregnant, and she couldn't afford to go back to Antwerp.

To be honest, I wasn't listening to everything she was saying, because someone else had caught my eye. Seated a few stools away was a ginger-haired man who appeared to be following our conversation intently. He was uncomfortably overweight, and undergoing some kind of perspiration crisis. The pub was virtually deserted, most of the customers drinking outside on the pavement, and Danielle was talking loudly, so it was possible that she

might have been overheard. I began to wonder if she was lying to me about her problems; if, perhaps they were more serious than she made them sound, serious enough for someone to be following her. I know it was selfish, but I didn't want to spend any more time with a girl who was in that kind of trouble, so I told her I needed to use the toilet, then slipped out across the back of the bar.

The Angel, Rotherhithe

ANOTHER OLD RIVERSIDE inn—I seem to be drawn to them, anxious to trace the city's sluggish artery site by site, as though marking a pathway to the heart. The interesting thing about places like The Angel is how little they change across the decades, because they retain the same bleary swell of customers through all economic climates. Workmen and stockbrokers, estate agents, secretaries, van-drivers and tarts, they just rub along together with flirtatious smiles, laughs, belches and the odd sour word. The best feature of this pub is reached by the side entrance, an old wooden balcony built out over the shoreline, where mudlarks once rooted in the filth for treasure trove, and where you can sit and watch the sun settling between the pillars of Tower Bridge.

As the light faded we became aware of the sky brushing the water, making chilly ripples. Further along the terrace I thought I saw the red-haired man watching, but when I looked again, he had gone. Growing cold, we pulled our coats tighter, then moved inside. Stella was Greek, delicate and attractive, rather too young for me, but I found her so easy to be with that we remained together for the whole evening. Shortly before closing time she told me she should be going home soon because her brother was expecting her. I was just massaging some warmth back into her arms—we were seated by an open window and it had suddenly turned nippy—when she said she felt sick, and went off to the Ladies. After she failed to reappear I went to check on her, just to make sure she was all right. I found her in one of the cubicles, passed out.

The Ship, Greenwich

THE DINGY INTERIOR of this pub is unremarkable, with bare-board floors and tables cut from blackened barrels, but the exterior is another matter entirely. I can imagine the building, or one very like it, existing on the same site for centuries, at a reach of the river where it is possible to see for miles in either direction. I am moving out towards the mouth of the Thames, being taken by the tide to ever-widening spaces in my search for absolution. There was something grotesquely Victorian about the weeds thrusting out of ancient brickwork, tumbledown fences and the stink of the mud. It was unusually mild for the time of year and we sat on the wall with our legs dangling over the water, beers propped at our crotches.

Melanie was loud and common, coarse-featured and thick-legged. She took up room in the world, and didn't mind who knew it. She wore a lot of make-up, and had frothed her hair into a mad dry nest, but I was intrigued by the shape of her mouth, the crimson wetness of her lips, her cynical laugh, her seen-it-all-before eyes. She touched me as though expecting me to walk out on her at any moment, digging nails in my arm, nudging an elbow in my ribs, running fingers up my thigh. Still, I wondered if she would present a challenge, because I felt sure that my offer to sketch her would be rebuffed. She clearly had no interest in art, so I appealed to her earthier side and suggested something of a less salubrious nature.

To my surprise she quoted me a price list, which ruined everything. I swore at her, and pushed her away, disgusted. She, in turn, began calling me every filthy name under the sun, which attracted unwanted attention to both of us. It was then that I saw the ginger-headed man again, standing to the left of me, speaking into his chubby fist.

The Trafalgar Tavern, Greenwich

I RAN. TORE myself free of her and ran off along the towpath, through the corrugated iron alley beside the scrap yard and past the defunct factory

smoke-stacks, keeping the river to my right. On past The Yacht, too low-ceil-inged and cosy to lose myself inside, to the doors of The Trafalgar, a huge gloomy building of polished brown interiors, as depressing as a church. Inside, the windows of the connecting rooms were dominated by the gleam-ing grey waters beyond. Nobody moved. Even the bar staff were still. It felt like a funeral parlour. I pushed between elderly drinkers whose movements were as slow as the shifting of tectonic plates, and slipped behind a table where I could turn my seat to face the river. I thought that if I didn't move, I could remain unnoticed. In the left pocket of my jacket I still had my sketchbook. I knew it would be best to get rid of it, but didn't have the heart to throw it away, not after all the work I had done.

When I heard the muttered command behind me, I knew that my sanc-tuary had been invaded and that it was the beginning of the end. I sat very still as I watched the red-headed man approaching from the corner of my eye, and caught the crackle of radio headsets echoing each other around the room. I slowly raised my head and for the first time saw how different it all was now. A bare saloon bar filled with tourists, no warmth, no familiarity, no comfort.

When I was young I sat on the step—every pub seemed to have a step—with a bag of crisps and a lemonade, and sometimes I was allowed to sit inside with my dad, sipping his bitter and listening to his beery laughter, the demands for fresh drinks, the dirty jokes, the outraged giggles of the girls at his table. They would tousle my hair, pinch my skinny arms and tell me that I was adorable. Different pubs, different women, night after night, that was my real home, the home I remember. Different pubs but always the same warmth, the same smells, the same songs, the same women. Everything about them was filled with smoky mysteries and hidden pleasures, even their names, The World Turned Upside Down, The Queen's Head and Artichoke, The Rose and Crown, The Greyhound, The White Hart, all of them had secret meanings.

People go to clubs for a night out now, chrome and steel, neon lights, bottled beers, drum and bass, bouncers with headsets. The bars sport names like The Lounge and The Living Room, hoping to evoke a sense of belonging,

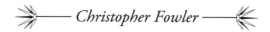

but they cater to an alienated world, squandering noise and light on people so blinded by work that their leisure-time must be spent in aggression, screaming at each other, shovelling drugs, pushing for fights. As the red-haired man moved closer, I told myself that all I wanted to do was make people feel at home. Is that so very wrong? My real home was nothing, the memory of a damp council flat with a stinking disconnected fridge and dog-shit on the floor. It's the old pubs of London that hold my childhood; the smells, the sounds, the company. There is a moment before the last bell is called when it seems it could all go on forever. It is that moment I try to capture and hold in my palm. I suppose you could call it the land before Time.

The Load Of Hay, Havistock Hill, Belsize Park

THE RED-HAIRED officer wiped at his pink brow with a Kleenex until the tissue started to come apart. Another winter was approaching, and the night air was bitter. His wife used to make him wear a scarf when he was working late, and it always started him sweating. She had eventually divorced him. He dressed alone now and ate takeaway food in a tiny flat. But he wore the scarf out of habit. He looked in through the window of the pub at the laughing drinkers at the bar, and the girl sitting alone beside the slot-machine. Several of his men were in there celebrating a colleague's birthday, but he didn't feel like facing them tonight.

How the hell had they let him get away? He had drifted from them like bonfire smoke in changing wind. The Trafalgar had too many places where you could hide, he saw that now. His men had been overconfident and undertrained. They hadn't been taught how to handle anyone so devious, or if they had, they had forgotten what they had learned.

He kept one of the clear plastic ampoules in his pocket, just to remind himself of what he had faced that night. New technology had created new hospital injection techniques. You could scratch yourself with the micro-needle and barely feel a thing, if the person wielding it knew how to avoid any major nerve-endings. Then it was simply a matter of squeezing the

little bulb, and any liquid contained in the ampoule was delivered through a coat, a dress, a shirt, into the flesh. Most of his victims were drunk at the time, so he had been able to connect into their blood-streams without them noticing more than a pinprick. A deadly mixture of RoHypnol, Zimovane and some kind of coca-derivative. It numbed and relaxed them, then sent them to sleep.

But the sleep deepened and stilled their hearts, as a dreamless caul slipped over their brains, shutting the senses one by one until there was nothing left alive inside.

No motives, no links, just dead strangers in the most public places in the city, watched by roving cameras, filled with witnesses. That was the trouble; you expected to see people getting legless in pubs.

His attention was drawn back to the girl sitting alone. What was she doing there? Didn't she realise the danger? No one heeded the warnings they issued. There were too many other things to worry about.

He had been on the loose for a year now, and had probably moved on to another city, where he could continue his work without harassment. He would stop as suddenly as he had begun. He'd dropped a sketchbook, but it was filled with hazy pencil drawings of pub interiors all exactly the same, and had told them nothing. The only people who would ever really know him were the victims—and perhaps even they couldn't see behind their killer's eyes. As the urban landscape grew crazier, people's motives were harder to discern. An uprooted population, on the make and on the move. Fast, faster, fastest.

And for the briefest of moments he held the answer in his hand. He saw a glimmer of the truth—a constancy shining like a shaft through all the change, the woman alone in the smoky saloon, smiling and interested, her attention caught by just one man; this intimacy unfolding against a background warmth, the pulling of pints, the blanket of conversation, the huddle of friendship—but then it was gone, all gone, and the terrible sense of unbelonging filled his heart once more.

CHRISTOPHER FOWLER IS the award-winning author of a number of short story collections and more than thirty novels, including the popular 'Bryant & May' series of mysteries. He has fulfilled several schoolboy fantasies—releasing a terrible Christmas pop single, becoming a male model, posing as the villain in a *Batman* graphic novel, running a night club, appearing in *The Pan Books of Horror Stories*, and standing in for James Bond. His work divides into black comedy, horror, mystery, and tales unclassifiable enough to have publishers tearing their hair out. His autobiography, *Paperboy*, was about growing up in London in the 1950s and '60s, while *The Book of Forgotten Authors*, featuring insightful mini-essays on ninety-nine forgotten authors and their forgotten books, was based on a series of columns he wrote for the *Independent on Sunday* newspaper. "'At Home in the Pubs of Old London' follows my continuing fascination with obsessives,' explains Fowler, 'coupled with the realisation that London pubs are in some strange way a constant feature in a fast-changing world. It's odd how pubs largely keep their clientele through all kinds of social upheavals. I particularly recall the interior of a local pub where I grew up in Greenwich, and went back recently to find that although the furnishings had changed, it held the exact same atmosphere as it had when I was seventeen. In terms of psychic geography, pubs hold key positions, and they're vanishing fast (something like five a week in London) so to my lead character they represent something special.'

///

BARKING SANDS

Richard Christian Matheson

ON VACATION.

Hawaii. Where fat, brown people treat flowers like Jesus.

All us.

Mommy. Daddy. Grampa Don.

My brother who came out of Mommy with less brain than a cat.

He smiles at everything. I call him Kitty. Daddy thinks it's funny.

Kitty can only open his mouth and stare and shake. Like there's a maraca inside him.

We rented a Toyota Tercel.

'Cheapest car worth dog-fuck.'

That's Grampa Don talking. Mommy hates it when he says dirty stuff. But he's always drinking beer. Loses track of where his tongue is pointing and just says it. Grampa Don's always making trouble.

We're on our way to Barking Sands.

It's a beach on the southern tip of Kauai. The sand barks there. Big, bald-headed dunes of it chirping and growling like someone is poking it while it sleeps. The wind does it; like a ventriloquist using the grains of sand as its dummy. It's a very sacred place. They say the ancient tribes are still living on the cliffs way above Barking Sands. I say that inside the Tercel while it bounces over the muddy road. The mud is red and splashes the car so it looks like it has scrapes that are bleeding. Like when Kitty falls down and cries and I just stand and watch him and hope he bleeds to death.

'There's no tribes still living,' says Mommy, eating an ice cream cone I couldn't finish, making sure it doesn't drip on the upholstery.

Her tongue moves around it like a red bus going up a twisty road. Daddy breathes in the air and says it hasn't smelled like this in Los Angeles since cave men went to work in three-piece fur suits.

Grampa Don spits out the window, and the car hops and rocks, having a spaz attack. The Kauai roads feel like the moon. There's no one going out to Barking Sands but us. It's getting late and the road is lonely.

It is the moon. Just on Earth.

The sky will be dead soon. I feel a little afraid but for no reason.

Kitty looks at me and smiles but sees my face and starts to cry. If I had a knife I'd slash his throat. I imagine his dead body lying face-up, in the casket, suddenly awake. Screaming and trying to get out but making no sound. Muted by the birth defect that gave him a busted speaker. I feel bad for him down there, trapped forever under the earth, stuck in his box, screaming. But he'll never do anything with his life anyway.

Maybe it's better to know where he is.

Grampa Don just cut one and all four windows are cranked down. A sweet and sour old-man cloud is sucked out. The blue ocean is starting to seem like a choking face. We're far from the hotel where we're staying and I hate Hawaii. Being here with them.

Last night we went to a Luau and I stared at the pig on the long table. He looked alive. But his eyes didn't move and as I tried to figure out what he was thinking, a big smiling man, in a white apron, cut into the pig with a shiny knife and slid a section of the pig's body right out, like one of those wooden ball puzzles that's made of different sections of wood.

He dropped it on my plate and the pig kept staring forward, unable to fight back. The man motioned me to move on with his bloody knife, and began to cut the pig into more pieces, erasing him.

I looked down at the piece of the pig and felt like throwing up. Later I brought the piece back and tried to put it where it had been on his body; reattaching his flesh. But by then, he was just bones and a head. The eyes were still facing forward and I pet him a little, seeing my own value as no higher than his, and hating people for what they'd done to him.

Then, Daddy came and dragged me through a bunch of tourists with greasy mouths, lining up to watch the torches and grass skirts. I looked back to see the pig being taken away, its bones passing above the crowd, on a tray, like some terrible crown.

'Barking Sands.' Mommy is pointing.

Grampa Don is already out of the car and looking for a place to dump garbage. But there isn't one and he tosses it on the ground saying it will just rot and become a hotel lobby, over time, with enough rain and 'fucking tourist money'.

He says all the dinosaur bones grew into roads and rental cars after millions of years. He's had four cans of beer since we left the Coco Palms Hotel, where we're staying, and he's unzipped and hosing down a tree trunk.

His ancient nozzle sprays Corona on everything like some poison Daddy uses back in Los Angeles, to make snails' heads explode.

Kitty points to a sign that says this is a holy burial ground. He likes words; their shape, worming together to form meaning he doesn't understand. Grampa reads the sign and keeps sprinkling snail napalm like a punctured can.

'This place is too fucking humid.' Grampa Don is wiping his head, like those guys at the 76 station chiselling bugs off the windshield.

Daddy takes pictures even though the sign says no photography 'cause it's a holy place and I guess that's bad. Daddy doesn't care. Mommy smiles and poses under the big cliffs that go up and up and up. Her dress looks like it belongs in a vase. Kitty is crawling on the sand, chasing our footprints like a rabid bloodhound that needs to be shot in the head. I wish I could get away from them all.

It's very windy and sand blows, sticking us with pins you can't see. I cover my eyes and we all lean into the wind. Mommy says we look like arctic explorers going up a snow slope. She wants a happy family. But we aren't.

I hate these trips. Being together.

Grampa Don takes Kitty's hand. Daddy takes Mommy's. A storm fills the sky with black sponges.

Grampa Don lags behind and we all get to the Toyota. It's starting to rain. Daddy starts the car and the mud is turning into dirty, orange glue that grabs our wheels. They spin.

'Zzzzzzzzzzz.' Kitty sounds like a trapped tire.

The car is a mad dog chained to a tree. Thunder shakes us. Lightning cuts up the sky. Something is wrong. The sky is not happy or pretty anymore. The air smells like dead things and angry wind makes all the plants and flowers look like they're bending over to get sick.

There is warm fog. I can't see the ocean anymore. It crashes, attacking.

'What's the fuckin' problem?' yells Grampa Don.

Mommy tells him not to talk like that and he curses at her. Daddy tells him to leave her alone. They start to argue.

I hate their guts.

Grampa Don rolls down his window to look at the tyres. I notice something moving through the high sugarcane. He says he hates it here and yells at the mud and the sky and the big sand dunes that bark like wild dogs surrounding helpless animals.

The car tries harder to move. Grampa Don is getting all wet. Mommy tells him to close the window and suddenly he makes a weird noise. An arrow with red feathers is sticking through his neck, sideways. He turns and I see the sharp tip dripping blood on his tank-top. There is mud and blood on his face. He can't breathe. There are wet bubbles in his neck.

Mommy screams.

I see feathers moving through sugarcane. Blue ones. Yellow ones. I see brown skin. Hands, eyes.

Grampa Don tries to scream and blood comes out of his mouth and sprays on everything. Kitty thinks Grampa Don is being funny and laughs, but makes no sound. Daddy screams at him to shut up and Kitty starts to cry. His face turns bright red.

Feathers.

We did something wrong. Something bad.

I am scared as they hide in the sugarcane. I know I'll be dead in another minute. I know I can't escape in this mud and rain. I look at my family. Mommy tries to help Grampa Don and Daddy keeps flooring the gas, too stupid to realise it doesn't help. I say nothing as they ask me to help. I do nothing.

I hate them.

An old man and two people who just argue all the time. A retard brother someone should've cut into little pieces a long time ago.

The car is stuck. No matter what Daddy does. More arrows break the glass. We are bloody. We are dying. Rain is pounding harder, pinning us to the mud, and the tyres bury us deeper, spinning.

Digging us a grave.

As my family screams, I close my eyes and listen to the sand.

RICHARD CHRISTIAN MATHESON is an acclaimed author and screenwriter/producer for television and film. He has worked with Steven Spielberg, Bryan Singer, Richard Donner, Ivan Reitman, Stephen King, Roger Corman and many others and created, written and produced acclaimed television series, movies and mini-series, including his adaptation of King's 'Battleground' for TNT's *Nightmares & Dreamscapes*, which won two Emmy Awards. His suspense novel, *Created By*, was a Bram Stoker Nominee, and his short fiction has been collected in *Scars And Other Distinguishing Marks*, *Dystopia* and *Zoopraxis*. A surreal Hollywood novella, *The Ritual of Illusion*, was issued by PS Publishing. About his story in this volume, Matheson says: 'There are places untied from time. Ghostly cities, ancient cathedrals. Places in serene recess, where centuries drift unnoticed. And there are places more precious; rarest of all. Places that bear no sign of man's signature, existing within their own exquisite privacy. When I first saw Barking Sands beach I was overcome by its beauty: endless, unearthly dunes, misted by miles of primordial waves; somehow dream-like. It was said the dunes barked; an anomaly of wind which allowed voice. I found it spiritual, oddly troubling. I walked the vastness, listening carefully, imagining what the sand might be saying; if it were invitation or warning. As with all things seductive, there were two answers.'

THE ABORTIONIST'S HORSE
(A NIGHTMARE)

Tanith Lee

NAINE BOUGHT THE house in the country because she thought it would be perfect for her future life.

At this time, her future was the core upon and about which she placed everything. She supposed that was instinctive.

The house was not huge, but interesting. Downstairs there was a large stone kitchen recently modernised, packed with units, drawers, cupboards and a double sink, with room for a washing machine, and incorporating a tall slender fridge and an electric cooker with a copper hood. The kitchen led into a small breakfast room with a bay window view of the back garden, a riot of roses, with one tall oak dominating the small lawn. At the front of the house there was also a narrow room that Naine christened the parlour. Opposite this, oddly, was the bathroom, again very modern, with a turquoise suite she would never have chosen but quite liked. Up the narrow stair there were a big linen cupboard, and three rooms, the largest of which was to be Naine's bedroom, with white curtains blowing in fresh summer winds. The two smaller rooms were of almost equal size. One would be her library and workroom.

The third room also would come to have a use. It, like the larger bedroom and the parlour, faced to the front, over the lane. But there was never much, if any, traffic on the lane, which no longer led down into the village.

A housing estate had closed the lane thirty years before, but it was half a mile from the house. The village was one mile away. Now you reached it by walking a shady path that ran away behind the garden and down through the fields. A hedgerow-bordered walk, nice in any season.

The light struck Naine, spring light first, and almost summer light now, and the smells of honeysuckle and cow parsley from the lane, the garden roses, the occasional faint hint of hay and herbivorous manure blowing up the fields.

You could just hear the now and then soft rush of cars on the main road that bypassed the village. And church bells all day Sunday, sounding drowned like the ones in sunken Lyonesse.

Her Uncle Robert's death had given Naine the means for this venture. She had only slightly known him, a stiff memory of a red-brown August man handing her a lolly when she was five, or sitting on a train with the rest of the family when she was about thirteen, staring out of the window, looking sad at a bereavement.

The money was a surprise. Evidently he had had no one else he wanted to give it to.

The night of the day when she learned about her legacy there was a party to launch the book Naine had been illustrating. She had not meant to go, but, keyed up by such sudden fortune, had after all put on a red dress, and taken a taxi to the wine bar. She was high before she even entered, and five white wines completed her elevation. So, in that way, Uncle Robert's bequest was also responsible for what happened next.

At twenty-seven, Naine had slept with only two men. One had been her boyfriend at twenty-one, taken her virginity, stayed her lover for two years. The second was a relationship she had formed in Sweden for one month. In fact, they had slept together more regularly, almost every night, where with the first man she had only gone to bed with him once or twice a week, so reticent had been their competing schedules. In neither case had Naine felt very much, beyond a slight embarrassment and desire for the act to be satisfactorily over, like a test. She had read enough to pretend, she thought adequately, although her first lover had sadly said, as he left her for ever to go to Leeds, 'You're such a cool one.' The Swede had apparently believed her sobs and cries. She knew, but only from masturbation, that orgasm existed. She had a strange, infallible fantasy which always worked for her when alone, although never when with a man. She imagined lying in a darkened room, her eyes shut, and that some presence stole towards her. She never knew what it was, but as it came closer and closer, so did she, until, at the expected first touch, climax swept through her end to end.

At the party was a handsome brash young man, who wanted to take Naine to dinner. Drunk, elevated, she accepted. They ended up at his flat in Fulham, and here she allowed him to have sex with her, rewarding his varied and enthusiastic scenario with the usual false sobs and low cries. Perhaps he did not believe in them, or was only a creature of one night, for she never heard from him or saw him again. This was no loss.

However, six weeks later, she decided she had better see a doctor. In the past her methods of contraception had been irregular, and nothing had ever occurred. It seemed to her, nonsensically but instinctively, that her lack of participation in the act removed any chance of pregnancy. This time, though, the spell had not worked.

Abortions were just legally coming into regular use. For a moment Naine considered having one. But, while believing solidly in any woman's right to have an unwanted foetus removed from her womb, Naine found she did not like the idea when applied to her own body.

Gradually, over the next month, she discovered that she began to think intensely about what was inside her, not as a thing, but as a child. She found herself speaking to it, silently, or even aloud. Sometimes she was even tempted to sing it songs and rhymes, especially those she had liked when small—'Here We Go Round the Mulberry Bush', and 'Ride a Cockhorse to Banbury Cross'. Absurd. Innocent. She was amused and tolerant of herself.

Presently she was sure that the new life belonged to her, or at least that she was its sponsor. With this in mind, she set about finding a house in the country where the child might be brought up away from the raucous city of its conception. The house by the lane looked so pretty at once, the cow parsley and docks standing high, the sunlight drifting on a pink rose classically at the door. When she learned there was the new hospital only two miles away in Spaleby, and besides, a telephone point in the bedroom for the pre-ordained four-in-the-morning call for an ambulance, Naine took the house. And as she stepped, its owner, in over the threshold, a wave of delight enveloped her, like the clear, spotted sunshine through the leaves.

AS NAINE WALKED up to the bus-stop by the main road, she was thinking about what a friend had said to her over the phone, the previous night. 'You talk as if it didn't have a father.' This had come to Naine only hours afterwards. That is, its import. For it was true. Biology aside, the child was solely hers, and already Naine had begun to speak of it as feminine.

She realised friends had called her less and less, during the fortnight she had been here. In the beginning their main interest had seemed to be if she was feeling 'horribly' ill—she never was. Also how she had 'covered' herself. Naine had put on her dead mother's wedding ring, which was a little loose, and given the impression she and a husband were separated. Once the friends knew she was neither constantly spewing nor being witch-hunted as a wanton, they drew off. Really, were they her friends anyway? She had always tended to be solitary, and in London had gone out perhaps one night in thirty, and that probably reluctantly. She enjoyed her work, music, reading, even simply sitting in front of the TV, thinking about other things.

The bus-stop had so far been deserted when Naine twice came to it about 3:00, for the 3:15 bus to Spaleby. Today, in time for the 1:15 bus, she saw a woman was already waiting there. She was quite an ordinary woman, bundled in a shabby coat, maybe sixty, cheerful and nosy. She turned at once to Naine.

'Hello, dear. You've timed it just right.'

Naine smiled. She wondered if the woman could see the child, faintly curved under the loose cotton dress. The bulge was very small. 'You're in Number 23, aren't you?' asked the woman.

'Oh…yes I am.'

'Thought so. Yes. I saw you the other day, hanging your washing out, as I were going down the lane.'

Naine had a vague recollection of occasional travellers using the lane, on foot, between the stands of juicy plants and overhanging trees. Either they were going to the estate, or climbing over the stile, making off across the land in the opposite direction, where there were three farms, and what was still locally termed the Big House, a small, derelict and woebegone manor.

'Miss your hubby, I expect,' said the woman.

Naine smiled once more. Of course she did, normal woman that she was; yes.

'Never mind. Like a lot of the women when I was a girl. The men, had to go to Spaleby, didn't come back except on the Sunday. There was houses all up the lane then. Twenty-seven in all, there was. Knocked down. There's the pity. Just Number 23 left. And then modernised. My, I can remember when there wasn't even running water at 23. But you'll have all the mod cons now, I expect.'

'Yes, thank you.'

'I expect you've done a thing or two to the house. I shouldn't wonder if you have.'

Naine sensed distinctly the nosy cheerful woman would love to come in and look at Number 23, and she, Naine, would now have to be on guard when the doorbell rang.

'I haven't done much.'

'Just wait till hubby gets home. Shelves and I don't know what-all.'

Naine smiled, smiled, and wished the bus would arrive. But she would anticipate Naine would sit with her, no doubt. Some excuse would have to be found. Or the guts to be rude and simply choose another seat.

Two cars went by, going too fast, were gone.

'Now the lane used to go right through to the village, in them days. There wasn't no high road here, neither. You used to hear the girls mornings, going out at four on the dot, to get to the Big House. Those that didn't live in. But the Missus didn't encourage it. She was that strict. Had to be. Then, there was always old Alice Barterlowe.' The woman gave a sharp, sniggering laugh. It was an awful laugh, somehow obscene. And her eyes glittered with malice. Did Naine imagine it—she tried to decide afterwards—those eyes glittering on her belly as the laugh died down. At the time Naine felt compelled to say, 'Alice Barterlowe? Who was that?' It was less the cowardly compulsion to be polite than a desire to clear the laugh from the air.

'Who was *she*? Well that's funny, dear. She was a real character hereabouts. When I was a nipper that were. A real character, old Alice.'

'Really?'

'Oh my. She kep' herself to herself, did old Alice. But everyone knew her. Dressed like a man; an old labouring man, and rode astride. But no one said a word. You could hear her, coming down that lane, always at midnight. That was her hour. The hoofs on the lane, and you didn't look out. There goes Alice, my sister said once, when we'd been woke up, and then she put her hand over her mouth, like she shouldn't have said it. Nor she shouldn't. No one was meant to know, you see. But handy for some.'

This sinister and illogical dialogue ended. The woman closed her mouth as tight as if zipped. And, before Naine could question her further—or not, perhaps—the green bus came chugging along the road.

'OLD ALICE BARTERLOWE. Oh my goodness yes. I can remember my gran telling me about her. If it was true.'

It was five days later, and the chatty girl in the village shop was helping Naine load her bag with one loaf, one cabbage, four apples and a pound of sausages.

'Who was she?'

'Oh, an old les. But open about it as you like. She had a lady-friend lived with her. But she died. Alice used to dress up just like the men, and she rode this old mare. Couldn't miss her, gran said, but then you didn't often see her. You *heard* her go by.'

'At midnight.'

'Midnight, that's it.'

'Why? Where was she going?'

'To see to the girls.'

'I'm sorry?'

'Girls up the duff like.'

'You mean...you mean pregnant?'

'She was an abortionist, was Alice.'

Naine had only felt sick once, a week after she had moved in. Sitting with her feet up for half an hour had taken it right off. Now she felt as if someone was trying to push her stomach up through her mouth. She retched silently, as the chatty girl, missing it, rummaged through her till.

I will *not* be sick.

I *won't*.

The nausea sank down like an angry sea, leaving her pale as the now hideous, unforgivable slab of cheese on the counter.

'Here you are. Three pound change. Yes, old Alice, and that old horse. Half-dead it looked, said my gran, but went on for years. And old les Alice was filthy. And this dirty old bag slung on the saddle. But she kept her hands clean as a whistle. And her stuff. There wasn't one girl she seen to come to harm.'

'You mean—it didn't work?'

'Oh it *worked*. It worked all right. They all got rid of them as wanted to, that Alice saw to. She was reliable. And not one of them got sick. A clean healthy miscarriage. Though my gran said, not one ever got in the family way after. Not even if she could by then. Not once Alice had seen to her.'

On the homeward shady path between the hedges and fields, Naine went to the side and threw up easily and quickly amongst the clover. It was the sausages, she thought, and getting in, threw them away, dousing the bin after with TCP.

——

RIDE A COCK-HORSE to Banbury Cross,

To see a fine lady upon a white horse—

The rhyme went round in Naine's head as she lay sleepily waking at five in the summer morning. The light had come, and patched beautifully through her beautiful butterfly-white curtains. On a white horse, on a white horse—

And something sour was sitting waiting, invisible, unknowable, not really there.

Old Alice Barterlowe.

Well, she had done some good, surely. Poor little village girls in the days before the Pill, led on by men who wouldn't marry them, and the poor scullery maids seduced at the Big House by some snobby male relative of the strict Missus'. What choice did they have but those clean strong probing fingers, the shrill hot-cold pain, the flush of blood—

Naine sat up. Don't think of it.

Ride a cock-horse, clip clop. Clip clop.

And poor old Alice, laughed at and feared, an ugly old lesbian whose lover had died. Poor old Alice, whose abortions always worked. Riding astride her ruinous old mare. Down the lane. Midnight. Clip clop. Clip clop.

Stop it.

'I'll get up, and we'll have some tea,' said Naine aloud to her daughter, curled soft and safe within her.

But in the end she could not drink the tea and threw it away. A black cloud hung over the fields, and rain fell like galloping.

WHEN NAINE PHONED her friends now, they could never stay very long. One had a complex dinner on and guests coming. One had to meet a boyfriend. One had an ear infection and talking on the phone made her dizzy. They all said Naine sounded tired. Was there a sort of glee in their voices? Serve her right. Not like them. If she *wanted* to get pregnant and make herself ill and mess up her life—

Naine sat in the rocker, rocking gently, talking and singing to her child. As she did so she ran her hands over and over along the hard small swelling. I feel like a smooth, ripening melon.

'There's a hole in my bucket, dear daughter, dear daughter...'

Naine, dozing. The sun so warm. The smell of honeysuckle. Sounds of bees. The funny nursery rhyme tapping at the brain's back, clip *clop,* clip *clop.*

———

NAINE WAS DREAMING. She was on the Tube in London, and it was terribly hot, and the train kept stopping, there in the dark tunnels. Everyone complained, and a man with a newspaper kept saying, 'It's a fly. A fly's got in.'

Naine knew she was going to be terribly late, although she was not sure for what, and this made it much worse. If only the train would come into the station, then she might have time to recollect.

'I tell you there's a fly!' the man shouted in her face. 'Then do it up,' said Naine, arrogantly.

She woke, her heart racing, sweat streaming down her, soaking her cotton nightdress.

Thank God it was over, and she was here, and everything was all right. Naine sat up, and pushed her pillows into a mound she could lean against.

Through the cool white curtains, a white half-moon was silkily shining. A soft rustle came from the trees as the lightest of calm night breezes passed over and over, visiting the leaves.

Naine reflected, as one sometimes does, on the power of the silliest dreams to cause panic. On its Freudian symbols—tunnels, trains, *flies.*

She stroked her belly. 'Did I disturb you, darling? It's all right now.' She drank some water, and softly sang, without thinking, what was tapping there in her brain, 'Clip *clop,* clip *clop.* Clip *clop,* clip *clop.* Here comes the abortionist's *horse.*' Then she was rigid. 'Oh Christ.' She got out of bed and stood in the middle of the floor. 'Christ, Christ.'

And then she was turning her head. It was midnight. She could see the clock. She had woken at just the proper hour. Alice Barterlowe's hour.

Clip *clop,* clip *clop...*

The lane, but for the breeze, was utterly silent. Up on the main road, came a gasp of speed as one of the rare nocturnal cars spun by. Across the fields, sometimes, an owl might call. But not tonight. Tonight there was no true sound at all. And certainly not—*that* sound.

All she had to do now, like a scared child, was to be brave enough to go to the window, pull back the curtain a little, and look out. There would be nothing there. Nothing at all.

It took her some minutes to be brave enough. Then, as she pulled back the curtain, she felt a hot-cold stinging pass all through her, like an electric shock. But it was only her stupid and irrational night-fear. Nothing at all was in the lane, as she had known nothing at all would be. Only the fronds of growing things, ragged and prehistoric under the moon, and the tall trees clung with shadows.

Past all the houses Alice had ridden on the slow old wreck of the horse, down the lane, and through the village. To a particular cottage, to a hidden room. In the dark, the relentless hands, the muffled cries, the sobs. And later, the black gushing away that had been a life.

Why did she do it? To get back at men? Was it only her compassion for her own beleaguered sex, in those days when women were more inferior than, supposedly, during the days of Naine?

Go away, Alice. Your time is over.

It was so silent, in the lane.

Clip *clop,* clip *clop,* clip *clop,* clip *clop.*

Here comes...

Naine went downstairs to the bathroom. She felt better after she had been sick. She took a jug of water and her portable radio back upstairs. A night station played her the Beatles, Pink Floyd, and even an aria by Puccini, until she fell asleep, curled tight, holding her child to her, hard, against the filmy night.

THE DOCTOR IN Spaleby was pleased with Naine. He told her she was doing wonderfully, but seemed a bit tired. She must remember not to do too much. When they were seated again, he said, sympathetically, 'I suppose there isn't any chance of that husband of yours turning up?'

Naine realised with a slight jolt she had been convincing enough to convince even the doctor.

'No. I don't think so.'

'Some men,' he said. He looked exasperated. Then he cheered up. 'Never mind. You've got the best thing there.'

When she was walking to the town bus-stop, Naine felt weary and heavy, for the first time. The heat seemed oppressive, and the seat for the stop was tormentingly arranged in clear burning yellow light. Two fat women already sat there, and made way for her grudgingly. She was always afraid at this point of meeting the awful, cheery, nosy woman. Because of the awful woman, Naine no longer pegged out washing, and had kept the postman waiting on her doorstep twice while she peered at him from an upstairs room, to be sure.

Somehow, to see the awful woman again would be just too much. She might start talking about Alice Barterlowe. Naine was sure that her child, in its fifth month, was generally visible by now. That would set the awful woman off, probably. *No use for old Alice, then.* No. *No.*

When the bus came, the journey seemed to last for a year, although it took less than half an hour. All the stops, and at every stop, some woman with a bag. And these women, though not the awful woman, might still sit beside her, might say, Oh, you're at Number 23 in the lane. The lane where the abortionist rode by at midnight on her nag.

Exhausted, Naine walked down from the main road. She made herself a jug of barley water and sipped a glass on the shady side of her garden. The grass had gone wild, was full of daisies, dandelions, nettles, purple sage and butterflies.

'I'm so happy here. It's so perfect. It's what we want. I mustn't be so silly, must I?' But neither must she ever speak her fear aloud to her child. Of all the things she could tell the child—not this, never this.

And round and round in her head, the idiotic rhyme, compounded of others that had gone wrong...

Clip *clop,* clip *clop.*

She must have been courageous. Alice. To live as she did, and do what she did. Especially then. It took courage *now.* Naine could recall the two girls caught kissing at school, and the ridiculous to-do there had been. Did they *know* what they were *doing?* Dirty, nasty. They had been shunned, and only forgiven when one confessed to pretending the other was a boy. They were *practising* for men. For their proper female function and role.

Naine, of course, was properly fulfilling both. Naine must like men, obviously. Look at her condition. It was her husband who was in the wrong. She had been faithful, loving, admiring, aroused, orgasmic, conceptive, productive. But *he* had run off. Oh yes, Naine was absolutely fine.

She did not want any dinner, or supper. She would have to economise, stop buying all this food she repeatedly had to throw away.

But then, she had to eat, for the sake of the child. 'I will, tomorrow, darling. Your mother won't be so silly tomorrow.'

She had told the doctor she could not sleep, made the mistake of saying 'I keep listening—' But he was ahead of her, thank God. 'The pressure on the stomach and lungs can be a nuisance, I'm afraid. Ask Nurse to give you a leaflet. And you've only moved out here recently. I know, these noisy country nights. Foxes, badgers rustling about. Whoever said the country was quiet was mad. It took me six months to get used to it.' He added that sleeping pills were not really what he would advise. Try cutting down on tea and coffee after 5:00 p.m., some herbal infusion maybe, and honey. And so on.

After the non-event of dinner, Naine watched her black-and-white eighteen-inch TV until the closedown. Then she went into the next room and had a bath.

She had never been quite happy with the bathroom downstairs. It could be grim later, when she was even heavier, lumbering up and down with bladder pressure, to pee. Maybe when things were settled anyway, she could move the bathroom upstairs, put the workroom here.

The child's room, the room the child would have; she had been going to paint that, and she ought to do so. Blue and pink were irrelevant. A sort of buttermilk colour would be ideal. Pale curtains like her own. And both rooms facing on to the lane. It would not matter about the lane, then. By then, Naine would laugh at it, but not the way the awful woman had laughed.

Clip *clop.* Clip *clop.*

After the bath, bed. Sitting up. Reading a novel, the same line over and over, or half a page, which was like reading something in ancient Greek. And the silence. The silence waiting for the sound.

Clip *clop.*

Turn on the radio. Bad reception sometimes. Crackling. Love songs. Songs of loss. All the lovely normal women weeping for lost men, and wanting them back at any cost.

At last, eyes burning, lying down. We'll go to sleep now.

But not. The silence, between the notes of the radio. A car. A fox. The owl. The wind. Waiting…

Clip *clop,* clip *clop.*

It was the horse she couldn't bear. It was the horse she saw. Not old Alice in her dirty labourer's clothes, with her scrubbed hands and white nails. The horse. The horse whose hoofs were the sound that said, *Here comes Alice, Alice on her horse.*

Old horse. Try to feel sorry for the poor old horse, as try to feel proud of courageous Alice. But no, the horse's face was long and haggard, with rusty drooping eyes, yellow, broken, blunt teeth, dribbling, unkempt. Not a sad face. An evil face. The pale horse of death.

'I'm sorry I can't sleep, baby. You sleep. You sleep and I'll sing you a lullaby. Hush-a-bye, hush-a-bye.'

But the words are wrong. The words are about the white pale horse. The night-mare. The nag with the fine lady, the old lesbian. Clippity-clop—

Clip *clop* clip *clop*

Clip *clop* clip *clop*

It was coming up in her, up from her stomach, her throat, like sick. She couldn't hold it in.

'Clip clop clip clop clip clop clip clop here comes the abortionist's horse!'

And then she laughed the evil laugh, and she knew how it had trundled and limped down the lane, its hoofs clipping and clicking, carrying death to the unborn through the mid of night.

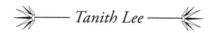

'IT'S MY WORK that's the problem. I didn't realise it would be so awkward.' She was explaining to the estate agent, who sat looking at her as if trying to fathom the secret. 'I'll just have to sell up and get back to London. It really is a nuisance.'

'Well, Mrs Robert…well, we'll see what we can do.'

As Naine again sat on the hot seat waiting for the bus, she thought of the train journey to London, of having nowhere to go. She had tried her friends, tentatively, to see if she could bivouac a day or two. One had not answered at all. One cut her short with a tale of personal problems. You could never intrude. One said she was so sorry, but she had decorators in. This last sounded like a lie, but probably was true. In any case, it would have to be a hotel, and the furniture would have to be stored. And then, flat-hunting five months gone, in the deep, smoky city heat. The house had been affordable down here. But London prices would allow her little scope.

It doesn't matter. I can find somewhere better after you're born. But for now. For now.

She knew she was a fool, had perhaps gone a bit crazy, as they said women did during pregnancy and the menopause. Even the kind doctor, when she had vaguely confessed to irrational anxieties, said jokingly, 'I'm afraid that can be par for the course. Hormones.'

To leave the house—*her* house—how she had loved it. But now. Not now.

No one came to look at the house, however. When she phoned the agents, they were evasive. It was a long way out unless you liked walking or had a car. And there had been a threat of the bus service being cut.

Day by day.

Night by night.

Over and over.

Its face.

The horse.

SHE WAS DREAMING again, but even unconscious, she recognised the dream. It was delicious. So long since she had felt this tingling. This promise of pleasure. Her sexual fantasy.

She was in the darkened room. Everything was still. Yet someone approached, unseen.

They glided, behind dim floating curtains. The faint whisper of movement. And at every sound, her anticipation was increasing. In the heart of her loins, a building marvellous tension. Yes, yes. Oh come to me.

Naine, sleeping, sensed the drawing close. And now her groin thrummed, drum-taut. Waiting…

The shadow was there. It leaned towards her.

As her pulses escalated to their final pitch, she heard its ill-shod metal feet on the floor. A leaden midnight fell through her body and her blood was cold.

Its long horse face, primal, pathetic and cruel. The broken teeth. The rusty, rust-dripping half-blind eyes. It hung over her like a cloud, and she smelled its smell, hay and manure, stone and iron, old rain, ruinous silence, crying and sobbing, and the stink of pain and blame and bones.

The horse. It was here. It breathed into her face.

Naine woke, and the night was empty, noiseless, and then she felt the trapped and stifled pleasure, which had become a knot of spikes, and stumbling, half-falling down the stairs, to the inconvenient lower bathroom, she left a trail of blood.

Here, under the harsh electric light, vomiting in the bath, heaving out to the lavatory between her thighs the reason the light the life of her life, in foam and agony and a gush of scarlet, Naine wept and giggled, choking on her horror. And all the while knowing, she had nothing to dread, would heal very well, as all Alice's girls did. Knowing, like all Alice's girls, she would never again conceive a child.

TANITH LEE NEVER learned to read—she was dyslectic—until almost age eight, and then only because her father taught her. This opened the world of books to her, and by the following year she was writing stories. She worked in various jobs, including shop assistant, waitress, librarian and clerk, before Donald A. Wollheim's DAW Books issued her novel *The Birthgrave* in 1975. After that, she published more than one hundred novels and collections, including *Death's Master*, *The Silver Metal Lover*, *Red as Blood* and the Arkham House volume *Dreams of Dark and Light*. She also scripted two episodes of the BBC series *Blakes 7*, and her story 'Nunc Dimittis' was adapted as an episode of the TV series *The Hunger*. She was a winner the World Fantasy Award and the British Fantasy Award, and she received Life Achievement Awards from the World Horror Convention, the World Fantasy Convention and the Horror Writers Association. 'John Kaiine, my husband, came up with the title,' she explained about the preceding story. 'Both he and I tend to get titles out of thin air, frequently without a story attached. (And anyone who's seen much of my work lately will realise that he has also given me many ideas and plot-lines for stories—which, with my own stream of ideas, makes sure I am a seven-day-a-week writing factory.) The title is so threateningly pictorial that, of course, the story itself arrived swiftly on its heels—or hoofs.'

DESTROYER OF WORLDS

Gwyneth Jones

I'M TRYING TO create in my mind the image of a little boy. He's four years old, his hair is brown and not clipped short; it's long enough to curl in the nape of his neck like a duck's tail. He is wearing a blue jacket with green facings, green lining to the hood. Red mittens dangle on a woollen cord from the cuffs of his sleeves, his little hands are bare. I remember him clearly, but it isn't enough. I want to *see* him. I'm walking around the park, called Delauney's Park, though who Delauney was no one has any idea. There's a playground with squishy asphalt so the children won't break their heads. There's a gravel football pitch, there's a shelter with toilets (always locked), and a space of turf, greenery, shrubberies, trees. The park is small, tired, urban. It was all the world to us. We used to come here, not every day but very often, right from the beginning. I remember playing hide and seek. It was a winter's day, the winter before he started school, the rose hips bright red vase-shapes on the bare bushes. I saw him walk out from behind the shelter, having failed to find me, those little mittens hanging pitifully. Head down, so utterly lost and bereft, oh dear sweet child. I was hiding behind a tree.

I walk around and around, a woman alone, staring at toddlers. I'm not trying to control myself, I know that the expression on my face looks frightening but I have licence. I don't have to make that slight constant effort we all make in public, maintain the barrier, don't let your emotions leak out. Tell any one of these mothers-with-small-children, and even fathers-with-small-children, what has happened to me, and whatever I do, they will accept. If I lie down and kick my legs and scream and mash my face into the ground that will be fine. As if I was three years old.

He never did that. He was a sweet child.

And out of the tail of my eye I see him. He's there, *there he is.* I turn my head, very very slowly. I can hold him in place, *I can see him*, the little boy standing by the corner of the shelter, looking to and fro, looking for me. I don't have to concentrate, he's there independently, no effort, *I am really seeing him*… It lasts only a fraction of a second, like the existence of a rare, fragile element in a scientific experiment. Then I'm fighting the whole weight of reality again. He's there still but it's an effort to hold the image, quivering like a stilled frame on a TV screen, and that's no good. It was my imagination.

Up in the back of the park, furtherest from the road and the playground, there's a certain bend in the path, a corner that is always in the shadow of tall laurel bushes. A place you think dogs wouldn't pass, they'd crouch with hackles raised and back away. He was afraid of that spot. We used to tell each other maybe it was haunted. He liked to be frightened, children do like to be frightened, *just a little.* Really it was the deep shade he didn't like, I'm sure; but a child's uneasiness is convincing. You think they must know something they haven't the words to tell. I'm walking around and around, mad woman staring. I come to the murky corner because I must, and I see him again. The little boy is there, completely without my volition.

I WENT HOME. My husband was curled in a foetal position on the couch in the living room, daytime TV on the screen. My mother had left the day before. She'd been wonderful, bearing up with a brave face, cooking meals for us and so on. I think we were both relieved to be alone again, although there is no relief when a thing like this has happened. But her departure means we have moved into the next phase. We've brought the baby home from the hospital, we've had the few days' buffer state of importance and fuss, we've reached the point when we are on our own and the task opens up, limitless, this time our baby is his death. I'm trying to recapture this little boy: putting him to bed, his bath-time, his sweet little body, he's giggling, running all wet and rosy from the towel that's trying to catch him, minuscule little erection. I want him here, I want to see him here. 'I saw him,' I said. 'In the playground. Eric, listen. I saw him. I really did.'

My husband said, 'What's the use in that? You didn't lose him anywhere near the park.'

I sat down on the armchair, the old one with the leaf-pattern in black and white on the upholstery, the leaves he used to trace very seriously with baby fingers.

'You think I'm mad.'

'I think in your state of mind you can easily force yourself to see a ghost. I just don't understand why you're doing it.'

'I want to know what happened to him. I want to see it.'

'That's disgusting,' he said.

My child, called Christopher after his grandfather, went out with me to the shops. In the Post Office I looked around and he was gone. I ran out into the street. He was nowhere. And when I was sure he was gone, you can imagine. You can imagine how I ran up and down, calling his name, how I flung myself at passers-by, how I was shaking from head to foot, how terror possessed me. We always called him Fery, it was his own name for himself. He's gone to the fairies, he's gone. It's eight days. He's dead.

In cases like this, suspicion always falls on the family, especially on the man. The police were going to be suspicious of us as a matter of course. I think we made it worse for ourselves by being certain, straight away, that he was dead. I think I made it worse for us by my terror. But how could we believe anything else? The child is gone for an hour, for three hours, he's been missing for a day and a night. How are we supposed to unknow what everyone else in the world knows about what happens to a child snatched away like that…just because it is our child, this time, not a story on the news?

They told us not to give up hope. Children have funny whims, he might have wandered off, taken a bus, decided to run away from home. Paedophiles often are not violent, he might turn up safe in some sad bastard's miserable bed-sit. Fools. We can't give up hope, we will hope forever: but we know he's dead. I think of him when we had the builders in before he was two years old. My baby goes up to the foreman and takes hold of the man's big, plaster-in-grained hand, wants to show him a Lego house. It's potty-training summer, the little boy is dressed merely in a blue T-shirt that leaves his round middle and his little bum bare. 'You'll have to watch him,' says the builder-man to me, very seriously. 'He's too friendly.'

A child must not be friendly, that's provocation. A child must not smile, must not take an adult's hand, that's flirtatious. I shake with fury. They're saying it was his fault. They're saying he brought it on himself. I try to imagine him here, giggling and wriggling among the cushions, very small. But all I see is something like a great sky folding into itself from horizon to horizon, bellying and billowing into a vast ochre mushroom cloud that rises and fills the universe. A million megatons of death, nothing can be saved, destroyer of worlds.

'I'm going to go back to work,' said Eric. 'Do you want your sister down?'

By work, he means that he'll return to his office at the back of our house, the room that overlooks the garden; where he tele-works on his computer. Projects, consultancies. I have no more idea of what he does, in detail, than if I was the child myself. He makes good money. I don't have a job, which means I have nowhere to go. My sister has offered to take unpaid leave, desert her family, come and be with me. I don't want her.

'No,' I said. 'I'll be fine.'

A POLICEWOMAN COMES to visit the house, with a uniformed constable, also a woman. They ask me if they can have a look around. Would I mind? They want to search our house, and I'm supposed to say well of course, please, step this way. My face serene, a little polite smile, as if they've come to read the gas meter. I am not supposed to resist, or question. I am not supposed to say, *you think my husband killed our son*. It's such an insane charade, dealing with the police. The WPC in uniform sits there holding her mug of tea, (I offered: they accepted). She has her face arranged in a solemn look of sympathy. I think she's really sorry, how could she not be sorry, but it's like tissue paper. Any move I make, anything I say will tear it and reveal the police agenda. Any sign that I've ever read a tabloid report on a child's disappearance, or watched the news, or seen a TV mystery drama where *it was the father, of course it was the father, you can see the solution a mile off... It was the mother, you can see she's disturbed...*will be an admission of guilt. The superior officer searched the house. The WPC sat with me. Strange, I'd have thought it would be the other way round. Eric stayed in his office. When she came back the superior officer started to ask me a few questions.

I said, 'How can you think my husband had anything to do with this? He's desperate. He's sitting up there out of his mind with grief. He doesn't eat, he doesn't sleep—'

'Mrs Connors,' she said. 'Hazel... I'm still hoping Christopher will be found. Believe me, it does happen. Children are found, more often than not. But don't you think a man who had killed his seven-year-old son would be distraught?'

It was as if she'd hit me. Seven years old. My image in the park was wrong, completely wrong. He doesn't look like that any more. His ghost can't look like that. Three years. I'd forgotten a whole three years. This is what happens to you when the Destroyer of Worlds has filled your mind. Your whole memory unravels, crumbles, you can't hold it together. I stared at her, and the mug of tea in my hands dissolved. I couldn't feel it any more, it fell to the floor and cooling tea spilled all over my feet.

She looked at the mess. I didn't. I was thinking of how much work I had to do, getting him to appear to me not as a four-year-old but as he was the day I lost him. That's the only way I'll find out what happened. She took my hand, and I let her do that.

'Hazel, why wasn't Christopher in school that day?'

'He had a cold. I kept him at home, but he seemed well enough to come out with me.'

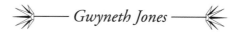

'But your husband was at home?'

'He works at home. He does his share of looking after Fery, but he works office hours. Am I getting points for answering the same questions in the same words fifty times over?'

A pause, a look of reproof. I'm tearing the tissue paper.

'Christopher's seven years old. Did you ever think of having other children?'

'No,' I said. 'I'm planning to go back to work. But it wouldn't make sense, at the moment. Wouldn't have made sense. When Eric isn't working at home, he has to travel. He's away often. I would have gone back to work, when Fery was old enough to be home alone.'

What the superior officer is really asking about is our sex life. No children? Why? Don't you sleep together? So, what does your husband do instead? I won't tell her anything.

WHEN FERY WAS two, he buried a wooden train in the sandpit at Delauney's Park. It was red and blue, it had yellow wheels, it was called Thomas. He didn't tell me that Thomas was missing until we were about to go home; and it was winter and getting dark. I searched, as well as I could. I couldn't find that little train at all. I didn't have a chance, the sandpit was too big and Fery could not tell me where I should dig. We went back the next day, and we still couldn't find Thomas. We never found him. But all that year, and longer, Fery went on looking. Stranger than that: wherever we were, including when we were on holiday in Italy, if we passed a playground he must go in. If there was a sandpit, he must dig. He was looking for Thomas. Long afterwards, he still remembered. I'd be in Delauney's Park, the mothers sitting together the way we do, on the edge of the sandpit: I'd see my four-year-old casually get hold of a shovel and start turning over the cool, dirty, lollipop-stick infested sand. I'd know he was looking for Thomas, but he didn't want anyone to know because he knew it was silly. And I'd want to help him. As if any day could be that winter's day, and we could tear the tissue paper and step back, undo the wrong we did, catch up the dropped stitch, make the little red and blue train appear.

I walk down to the row of shops. The pharmacist, the bakery, the bank on the corner. The greengrocers. They will vanish soon. The only shops in the world will be inside shopping malls, nothing but TO LET signs blossoming on the High Street. The mothers-with-children, and the occasional fathers-with-children, queue up in the Post Office with the foreign students and the pensioners. I look inside. I am trying to make him appear, there by the carousel of cheap greeting cards. He's looking at the cards, investigating the dirty jokes, lingering with tender emotion over sugary cartoon animals. He's at an age where the attraction is equal, either way. This is the way I'll find him. Not by running and sobbing, not by marching in a line across waste ground, searching the back alleys, pulling up floorboards. Not by looking up the paedophile register. I will walk along this row of shops, pushing the doors and glancing in. This is where he was lost, this is where he will be found. Where else could he be? Lost Thomas logic. I'll take his hand, I'll say *there you are*, exasperated: and we'll go home together. Years from now, as long as the same shops are still here, as long as I can find anywhere little shops that remind me of these, it could happen.

What was he wearing? A boy, his body no longer blurred by the chubby disproportion of babyhood, not even a small child any more. A boy nothing like the sweet baby with the red mittens, in Delauney's Park. I need a different ghost. (I need all the ghosts.) He was wearing trainers and track-suit trousers, black with white stripes. He was wearing red boxer shorts and a green T-shirt, and grey socks. He was wearing a grey hooded sweater with some sporting logo on the front, and a black quilted jacket. He was carrying nothing. He was too old to be visible in mothers-with-children world. He was not holding my hand. We've asked and asked, the police have asked and asked. No one saw him that morning. No one remembers me except as the mad woman, running up and down, distraught, flying up to the counter at the bank, demanding wildly *have you seen a little boy?* I don't remember him myself.

That day was scheduled to be like a thousand other lost days, all its millions of precious images discarded, mislaid, never filed. Even now, I have forgotten most of it.

I'm trying desperately hard, and then suddenly I let go. I can't help myself, it's like a muscle failure. I turn away, defeated; and there he is. Glimpsed, corner of my eye. I turn my head slowly, slowly, inching it round… He's there, crystal clear, no effort. He is standing by the greeting cards, sideways to me, the soft curve of his cheek, his eyes intent and a little furtive.

and then what happened, I beg of him.

Fery looks around. He isn't looking at me. He's looking at something that isn't in my memory, no matter how I struggle to recover it. I want to look where he's looking, towards the opening door of the Post Office, but wanting will do me no good, because surely I did not look that way. I never saw whoever it was, whatever, the monster, the horror that took my child. I try to turn my head anyway, but there's an awful barrier, and suddenly I'm on the floor, thank god I'm wearing trousers, retain some dignity sprawled there, sobbing, fighting off hands that try to raise me up. The shock was physical, the shock of knowing I saw him. I really saw him. I have forced myself to see a ghost.

When I found he wasn't with me, and he wasn't in the street, I hurried home. He wasn't there. Eric wasn't in, either. I called Fery's best friend's mother: no reply. Another friend's mother, no reply. I went to Delauney's Park, no sign. That part lasted about an hour. The running up and down and sobbing—that lasted I don't know how long. I called my husband on his mobile, I left a message. I called the police. I ran up and down again, by this time meeting everywhere the concern of the street, it was an incident room already. The man in the Post Office, the young girl with the stringy hair in the bakery, the cashier at the bank. If this was a soap opera I would have known their names but I didn't. We knew each other viscerally, like animals using the same pathways in some natural environment, we didn't need names to get along. That's all changed. I'm a celebrity now.

The man behind the Post Office counter called Eric. He came and took me home.

I told him that I'd seen a ghost again. He said, 'Would you like to go away? Far away? If the police will let us? I think that might be the best thing.'

'No,' I said. 'You don't understand. I forced myself to see a ghost, but the ghost is real.'

THE HUSBAND GETS interviewed at the police station. He hasn't been arrested, he's nowhere near being arrested, but he's in an interview room. The interviewing officer has a chaperone on hand, like a male doctor about to examine a woman patient's intimate parts; everything is being recorded on video. I know about this interview because Eric told me.

They asked him about our sex life.

'Would you say you and your wife had a good physical relationship?' asked the policeman.

Let it be recorded. 'Off and on, satisfactory. I mean, fine,' said Mr Connors. 'Sometimes good, sometimes not so good. Like most people. We've been married ten years you know.'

'Was she ever maybe a bit too much for you? Too demanding?'

'I wouldn't have said that was a problem.'

He was trying to guess what I might have answered, and hoping our two stories would agree. That's the charade the police force on you, with their insistence that it's up to you whether you answer or not. With their tissue-paper sympathy and their watchful eyes.

'D'you ever stray, I mean, have you ever had an affair?'

'No.'

'What about your wife?'

'Not that I know of.'

'She was your first girlfriend, wasn't she. You've never looked at another woman?'

'Looked? I don't know about looked. I'm happy with the relationship we have—'

They have investigated our lives. They have found among our books and videos adult movies, arthouse movies that they construe as pornographic. They have invented a sour, twilight existence for the woman who stays at home although her son is seven years old, and the man who works at home except when he goes on mysterious trips away. The man who finds the adult workplace and his adult wife too demanding. Everything looks bad in their light.

'Don't you see what they're doing,' I yelled at him. 'They're setting you up as some kind of pervert, and you can't stop them. Damned if you answer, damned if you don't.'

'They won't find any evidence,' said my husband, shrugging, 'will they?'

We looked at each other for a long, long moment, until I could see nothing but the mushroom cloud, boiling and silently thundering up into the sky. What can happen? What does it matter? It doesn't matter if they call Eric a pervert, it doesn't matter if I scream in the Post Office. Nothing can be worse than this.

Destroyer of Worlds.

'I'm going to follow him,' I said, 'I want to know everything. I don't care how bad it is.'

NOTHING HURTS. YOU could saw my leg off, I'd feel nothing. Being 'hounded by journalists' is not a torture, being interviewed by the police is not a torture, making appeals on the TV is not a torture. Don't pity the families in these cases, pursued by the greedy, prurient media. We feel nothing. I've felt more outrage over an unwanted piece of junk mail, long ago, than over a tabloid reporter on the doorstep, or the sting of a camera flash in my eyes. I couldn't care less. I walk out. I go and stand in the street. I lean against the wall of the bus shelter, waiting.

I see a boy in a black quilted jacket and black trousers coming out of the Post Office. I know why nobody saw him, he is totally anonymous. There is no sign of the baby's body I loved, no sign of the sweetness of his smile. When he was five he once confided in me *I keep getting stiffies...* Where on earth had he picked up that expression? In the classroom, obviously, other children have older brothers. Had he any idea what he was saying? I don't think so. Once, I lost him for ten minutes in our public library. When I found him he said he'd gone to the toilet for a wee. He'd gone into the Gents alone because he thought he couldn't go in the Ladies without me. Very proud, very independent. There was a man in there, he said. Who looked at me, and I was scared. The Gents at the Public Library is unsafe for little boys. Thinking like this is a disgrace, but what is to be done? My blood ran cold. I said, don't go there again.

But I can't keep on going in the Ladies, he said. Not all my life. So what will I do?

I'm following my ghost down the street. There must be someone with him, taking him away, but I only see my child. He's walking aimlessly, oh how I love to see him when he doesn't know I'm watching. To see him look into a shop window, to see him bend down over a piece of litter, studying it, hope springing eternal, has he won a million pounds? He walks on, carrying this old crisp packet, his companion: little boys need to have something to hold. A stone, a ball, a pencil, an elastic band; a boiled sweet furred in pocket-grime. Of course I won't tell him but of course I know…this affection is easy to read. I am not repelled. When he gets older I will remember these days and I will understand a young man's obsession with his favourite toy, his faithful companion, his treasure. Having a son will explain the whole sex to me, at long last. The boy on the street stops and half turns: a stilled frame, quivering. He's looking back, seems to look at me with an expression of intense malignity, eyes narrowed, inhuman rage—

He has read my thoughts.

He will never be a young man. He is dead.

I saw him again at the railway bridge. He was up there, crossing the line. I still could not see who was with him. I was in the car park, all the suburban commuters' cars in rows. Everyone has their place, I imagine. Eric doesn't like to drive, he walks when he comes to take the train. The boy on the bridge looked back at me, with incredible hatred.

I followed him, we climbed over the fence and into the waste-ground beside the line. Brambles, unkempt winter grass, weedy sycamores, naked straggling buddleia thickets with dead flower spikes. Rusting cans, rotted litter, slugs and snails, blackened ballast, the view from a train window. A path like a grey snail's trail, a little boys' path. Is it true that he came this way, or is the ghost lying to me?

Who brought him here? What happened?

There's a hut by the track, the roof of tar-paper, the slatted walls obliterated by crusted grime. It's a den, a hideout, it's somewhere things can happen out of sight. My path is heading towards it. No ghost now...but then suddenly there he is. I don't understand what I see, then I realise he's naked. A flash of pitiful white arms and legs, a face blank oval, and in the quivering frozen frame he's running, brambles whipping his little ribs, rusty cans bruising his bare feet, I can't hear him but I know he's crying, terrified and shamed. He's running and running, crying for help, but there's someone catching him—

How do you kill a little boy? By accident, is my best hope. You want him to stop screaming, you're afraid someone will come. You took him to a lonely place but it had to be somewhere nearby and now it isn't lonely enough. Big adult hands, squeezing the child's throat, or throwing him down, and his fragile temple crashing against stone. Something like that, in a moment. He was fighting for his life and he didn't know he was going to lose until he'd lost. He didn't die helpless, he didn't die smothered, pinned, held down, knowing the whole world had betrayed him—

I found myself crouched by the snail path, fists in my pockets, head bent, dizzy and nauseous. The vision had gone, but I was seeing in my mind's eye my baby's skin darkly marked, printed with the pattern of that black jacket, clear as frost flowers. I'll tell the police, I thought. They won't believe me, but they'll come here and search. They'll leave no stone unturned. I listened to the distant hum of traffic, and looked at my watch. The ghost had led me where I wanted to be led. I knew that, really. I stood up and went on down to the track.

I was beside the railway line, walking up and down, looking at my watch, shivering, oh god, how long between these suburban trains, when Eric arrived. I saw him coming, I didn't try to get away. 'Come home,' he said. 'Hazel, come on home.'

'How do people kill themselves? I don't know how to do it. But I'll find a way.'

He nodded, and took my arm. I didn't resist. He ought to say please don't leave me or all we've got left is each other, or someday we'll make a new life. But ideas like those don't come. There is nothing left, no human need, regret, affection nor pity. Destroyer of Worlds.

'You know how I felt about Fery,' I said.

'I know,' said my husband, leading me away. He has never reproached me, he has never said it was your fault, you lost him. How could you. Ideas like that don't come either. Not yet.

'I loved him too much.'

'Yes. You loved him too much.'

What a cruel thing to say.

———

I HAVE COMMITTED a grave crime. I have given birth to a child, and made him my whole world, in a society where children are not safe, where little boys can be taken from the street and never seen again. Now there's another turn of the screw, they are taking away from me my last memories. They are saying he was already lost, before I ever went out to the shops that morning. They are saying he never walked beside me, he never peeped at the greetings cards in the Post Office with that furtive, tender attention which I remember so clearly. No, they destroy that world. He was lost already, he was long gone. Where did I lose him, and when?

In Delauney's Park the mothers-with-children, and occasional fathers-with-children, are in possession until school is over. They talk to each other, they play with their toddlers, they nurse their babies. They sit like cows in the grass, silently ruminating over the weariness of broken nights. Then the schoolchildren appear, first from the nursery then from the primary school classrooms. They yell, they run around, they play with dolls or footballs, they pose and swagger and compare the prices of their trainers; they are cruel to each other. But the light changes and the shadows grow. The mothers-with-buggies all go home, except maybe for one lost soul, smoking a cigarette, naked ankles, skirt too short, her baby grizzling vaguely.

When the light has changed the park has a different clientele. Bloodstained needles, used condoms, teenagers and derelicts: all of them no more than decayed and broken-down kids themselves, that's why the

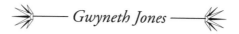

after-dusk playground is their home. They sell illegal drugs, and they bandy words with the schoolchildren, the bold, inquisitive ones who have lingered. Fery was one of those. Always ready to run, he promised me, at the first sign of trouble. Did he stay out too late one evening and I didn't notice? Did he fail to come home, and my husband was so wrapped up in his work he didn't know? Eric tells me they are going to search the park again, because of something I said or something someone remembered. The police will walk through the shrubberies in a line, working like a single machine, picking up every scrap of detritus. They will reach into the dark by that bend in the path, where the laurel bushes make their permanent shade, and they'll find...I don't know what. Maybe they'll find out why it has always felt bad. If a ghost can exist after death then why not before? My son and I used to be sure that spot was haunted.

I won't watch the search. I think I'll stay here, in his bedroom, with the soft toys that he'll never consign to oblivion, the pictures of cartoon animals, the battered childish things that he would have abandoned. I'm lying on his bed, where we used to cuddle together, bedtime, story-time, I'm saying now I have to go and he's saying, no, stay, stay with me not with daddy; just for once. He doesn't know what he's saying, soft arms holding onto me. He's only a baby. I don't have to be in the park, this is the foul place, the place that dogs wouldn't pass. This is where I lost him. This is where he destroyed all the worlds.

GWYNETH JONES IS the author of many fantasy, horror novels and thrillers for teenagers under the name 'Ann Halam', and several highly regarded science fiction and fantasy novels for adults. She's won the James Tiptree Award, two World Fantasy Awards, the Arthur C. Clarke Award (for *Bold as Love*), the Children of the Night Award, the Pilgrim Award for SF criticism, and the Philip K. Dick Award, amongst other honours. Of 'Destroyer of Worlds', the author reveals: 'This was inspired by a newspaper report I read, about a little boy killed in the same way as suggested in the story. The details stuck in my mind as a parent's worst nightmare, and showed me that none of the horrors of being haunted by a ghost need necessarily be supernatural.'

PELICAN CAY

David Case

PROLOGUE

THEY LEFT ANOTHER load of supplies down on the rocks this morning. I haven't bothered to pick them up yet, although I blinked out a message thanking them and letting them know I was still *all right.* There were three men in the boat. I think they were the same three as last time but they still appeared terrified. They kept looking up here and their faces were so white it seemed as if I'd turned the beam of the lamp onto them. They dropped the crates off—heaved them out, really—without ever touching the boat to shore. You'd think they'd know, by now, that I'm not infected. Still, I'm thankful for the supplies…they could just as well leave me, like the others.

I've been here two weeks now, in the lighthouse, and I'm getting much better at signalling with the big lamp and at receiving messages from the ships. They sent too fast, at first. But thank God for the light, there would be no way to communicate without it and it feels better to be in touch with the world, even if only by lamp—even if they won't believe me.

I wonder if my paper knows I'm here; if they've tried to contact me? What a story! And how absurd to think of it that way, now…as a newspaperman

instead of...what I am. I wonder, too, what they'll do about me when the others are all dead? I don't think that will be too long now. I've been observing them through the glasses and they seem less furious, slower, weaker. They're all very thin. I saw three of them eating a dead one, earlier. I don't know if they killed him or not and I don't know if they are beginning to regain human instincts...like feeding. But they didn't seem ravenous or even very determined about it, they were just pulling ribbons of flesh off his bones and chewing them in a desultory manner, as if it were something they dimly recalled doing in the past.

A few of them are gathered on the docks now, not too near the water. They're terrified of water. They seem to be looking out at the patrolling ships or maybe beyond, to the dim line of the Keys. I can see the Keys quite clearly from the tower. It really is a remarkable vista, the lone line of islands spanned by the bridges. It was just over two weeks ago that I drove along those linked islands. A long time. I think about it often, too, for I have a great deal of time to think and, terrible as it was, it is better than thinking of the future...

I

UNITED STATES HIGHWAY One begins in Fort Kent, Maine, at the borders of icy Canada, and ribbons all the way down the Eastern Seaboard, spanning the islands in the tropical Gulf like concrete cartilage linking the spine of some coral sea beast. I'd followed that road from New York, spent the night in Miami and, in the early morning, with the bay on one hand and the straits on the other and the dew still sparkling on the tropical flowers, I motored slowly over the bridges. I had plenty of time and was enjoying the drive. I'd not been in the Keys for years and noticed the highway had developed in terms of human progress—at night, I feared, a neon holocaust threatened—but the morning mood was changeless. Like feathered boomerangs behind a screen of palm trees, the pelicans were banking and sliding sideways into the blue waters of the Straits of Florida. Behind the planing birds the sun climbed from the Atlantic and began its arc towards the Dry

Tortugas and Mexico. A few early anglers were fishing from the bridges, not as efficiently as the pelicans; a shrimp boat paralleled my passage, high pronged masts distinctive, draped with net; a young couple wearing scuba gear basked on thrusting black rocks, drinking wine from the bottle and laughing with white teeth. It was a pleasant trip on a pleasant morning. I figured my stay would be pleasant, too. If I got a story out of it, that was fine and, if I didn't, that was fine, too. There are worse things than an expense account assignment in Florida, I thought.

And how wrong I was.

───

THE MANGROVE INN was built out over the water, the outdoor platform at the back raised on wooden stilts. A tourist was on the platform, having his picture taken beside a hanging shark. The shark looked mildly embarrassed. I parked the car and went into the bar. It was air-conditioned and traditional, with fishnets on the walls and starfish ashtrays. I was a bit early and didn't think my contact was there yet, but as I moved to the bar the girl stood up from a dark corner booth and raised her eyebrows.

'Mister Harland?'

I nodded and she walked towards me, a pretty girl, blonde, wearing a light cotton dress. She had nice eyes and a nice smile. She said, 'I'm Mary Carlyle,' and held her hand out. 'Dr Elston asked me to meet you.'

'I'd expected him.'

'Yes. He was…well, busy, I suppose. Anyhow, I had to cross over and he thought perhaps I could bring you back to Pelican in my boat.'

'Yes, all right,' I said. Then: 'What's Pelican?'

She looked mildly surprised. 'You don't know?'

'No. Elston wrote me. He asked me to meet him here. He asked me not to write or phone—in fact, he made rather a point of that—just to be here, today.' I made a gesture, manifesting my presence. 'My paper seemed to think he was newsworthy—eminent biochemist and all that—and I wasn't inclined to pass up a trip to the Keys. I'm a bit intrigued by all the secrecy, I must say.'

'Oh, that. It's very secret on Pelican,' she said, smiling.

I had an idea that she didn't really feel like smiling when she said that. It was a shadowed smile…or, perhaps, a smile that foreshadowed something.

'It must be…since I have no idea what it is.'

'Pelican Cay. It's an island.'

'And that's where Elston is?'

'Um hum.'

The bartender came wandering down the bar, flicking at the polished surface with a towel. I asked Mary if she would like a drink and she said, 'Of course.' I liked her immediately. I also thought it could do no harm to talk to her. I had no idea how much she knew about why Elston had summoned me, but if it was anything at all, it was more than I knew. I was completely in the dark and curious about the things that—that no one should ever have to know. We got a couple of tall rum punches and went back to the booth. I sat opposite with a starfish ashtray between us, both of us in cool shadows.

'Are you his assistant?'

'Oh, no,' she said, laughing. 'Do I look like a biochemist?'

'Not really.'

'I'm relieved. Actually, I live on Pelican. I'm one of the few natives, a real Conch. I was born there and never saw much reason to leave. Until recently…' she added.

I waited but she didn't follow that up.

I said, 'Have you any idea what it's about?'

She shrugged and sipped her drink, gazing at me across the rim of the glass.

'Or why Elston chose me?'

'Ummm,' she said.

'I don't know if you're familiar with my sort of work…'

'Don't be modest.'

'… but I don't write scientific papers and it seems…well…strange that Elston wanted to talk to me. Intriguing, in point of fact. A biochemist contacting a scandalmonger…'

Mary was laughing again. She said, 'Dr Elston chose you because of your well-known discretion.'

'Hardly.'

'Oh, yes. When you refused to reveal your sources to the investigating committee after you broke the Warden scandal, and risked going to jail... well, he feels he can trust you.'

'It's like that, is it?'

'Like that,' she said, suddenly serious.

Well, she obviously knew something. But she was fencing. I thought I might engage her at an oblique angle. I said, 'You know, Mary, I don't like being an investigative reporter.' She blinked, surprised. I managed a sheepish grin. 'I've always wanted to write a novel,' I told her, and that was true enough, but to my purpose. 'I've tried. Not recently. Platitudes have bested me...and time...and following the course of least resistance. I make investigations and I write about them. I've acquired a certain reputation. And yet...the media deform truth. And that, in itself, is a truth. A fact, given to the masses, becomes malleable, as if the printed page were a distorted looking-glass, casting anamorphic reflections. The most blatant lie acquires an aura of truth, truth, in turn, is shadowed and pigeonholed and compartmented to fit the reader's mind.' I shrugged, not looking at her. I was turning the starfish ashtray on the table between us.

'Strange talk from a newspaperman,' she said.

'Not so very strange. I'm no Diogenes, holding up a lantern. And yet...I do write the truth, be that as it may. And I want people to be truthful with me.' I looked up. 'Mary?' I said.

She flushed slightly.

She leaned closer; said, 'Look, I'd better level with you, Mister Harland...'

'Jack,' I said. 'And yes, you had.'

'All right. Jack. It was my idea to write to you. I sort of talked Dr Elston into it, with the help of a few drinks and a little flirting. Oh, he wanted to. I didn't force the idea on him. But he would never have done it, on his own. What I'm saying is...you may have come down here for nothing. Elston may not go through with it. But I figured it was worth a chance.'

'Then you do know what it's about?'

'No, I don't.' Now she was playing with the ashtray, turning it back and forth like the pointers in a game of chance. 'He wouldn't tell me. But I do know he's doing something, some sort of work, that he doesn't want to do. He let me know that much, no more. He was…disturbed. More than disturbed. I got the impression that he's in deeper than he intended, that his work is being applied in a manner of which he does not approve.' She had a way of gesturing when she spoke, as if punctuating her words and making her statements profound—but it didn't seem intentional or mannered. She was just a lively girl who got things done…who had got me to the Keys. 'Dr Elston is a timid man, the classic scientist who knows little of humanity. He can be manipulated just as he manipulates his chemicals—just as I manipulated him into writing you. He was afraid to meet you today, Jack…afraid someone would find out.' My eyebrows went up. 'Oh, no, he's not being restricted in any way, nothing like that. But he's afraid. Afraid of his employers, afraid of his work. He trusts me, probably because I have no connection with those employers…or perhaps because he needs to trust someone. But he's given me no details.'

'So you're just a catalyst, causing reactions.'

'That's about it.'

'Who are these employers?'

'The government. A government agency.'

'Which agency?'

'I don't know.'

I looked at her. She said, 'Really…I don't.'

'It's getting interesting.'

'It can get more than interesting, I think. This agency has taken over a large portion of Pelican…fenced it off in a compound, posted guards all around it… ruined the island. And this happened just after the ban on germ warfare.'

She gazed thoughtfully at me.

'Is that it? Germ warfare?'

'Not that, I think. But something…that should be stopped. Elston wants it stopped. I suggested you. He'd heard of you, vaguely; he's not the sort to read newspapers. I told him about the Warden thing and convinced him that you could let the world know what's being done here, and thereby halt it, without implicating Elston. So that's the story, so far. I can't guarantee that he will talk to you, after all. As I said, he's a timid man; he may well back out. He looked a bit sick after telling me as much as he did, in fact. But I think he will and I hope he does.' She smiled. 'I have an interest in this, you see. I bitterly resent them ruining Pelican. It was a paradise, now it's like a prison. Why, they even fenced off my favourite beach!' Then, serious again, she said, 'Whatever they're doing there, it's really very secret. Since the agency took over, we can't even get an open telephone line out; have to channel all calls through a switchboard within the compound. That island is my home, Jack; you can imagine how I— and the other residents—feel about it. Jack, I work for the Coast Guard. Just a part-time thing. There's a supply depot there and a lighthouse just off shore and…well, even the Coast Guard has to go through the switchboard, even the lighthouse is only connected to Pelican by a cable. No radio. One of my duties, in fact, is to talk to the lighthouse keeper. Sam Jasper. He's very talkative.'

'A talkative lighthouse keeper?'

'Yep. Phones in all the time. You think maybe he's in the wrong line of work?'

'Well, talking to you is…interesting.'

'I hope it pays off,' she said.

I nodded. Our drinks were finished. I would have liked another and she was looking at her glass, but she had piqued my interest; I figured this might be a bigger story than I'd planned on. I said, 'Shall we go, then?' and we went.

II

IN THE LAUNCH, which she handled expertly, she told me a bit about Pelican Cay. I took my shirt off and leaned against the gunwale, enjoying the spray and listening to her. Pelican, she told me, was a small island with one town looping in a crescent around a natural harbour. It had a colourful history. The first inhabitants had been wreckers, salvaging cargo from ships that had gone aground on the unmarked reefs—and were often lured onto those reefs by the wreckers. I raised an eyebrow at that; she shrugged; that was how it had been. Construction of the lighthouse had finished the wrecking industry in the mid-nineteenth century, however, and the locals had turned their bloodstained hands to cigar-making, salt refining and, of course, fishing. It had been as populous and important as most of the Keys, for a while, but had declined after the Overseas Highway was completed in 1938, when the linked islands became more accessible and convenient. Mary was pleased by that; she liked Pelican as it was—as it had been before the agency moved in.

'Of course, that's exactly why they did move in,' she said. 'It's an easy place to guard, to keep isolated and secure—and any stranger who showed up would be instantly noticed. Oh, the odd tourist makes the crossing…not enough to spoil things, though—they add to the local colour by contrast, bring in some money and, most important, give the locals an audience to which to play. We Conches are all born actors.' She turned to smile at me. I recalled the way she gestured when she spoke. 'Shrimpers, fishermen, Cuban refugees, retired smugglers…but they all play up to their images.'

She made Pelican sound pleasant and I could well understand why she resented the intruders.

'What about accommodation?' I asked.

'There's an inn. It functions mostly as a bar these days, but they'll give you a room. The Red Walls.'

'What?'

'That's the name of the place. The Red Walls. Red as in blood, don't you know? The walls awash with blood. Used to be a smugglers' den and the shrimpers drink there now…quite a history to the place, probably a story in itself. The locals will be pleased to give you all the gory details…embellished, no doubt; they're rather proud of the reputation, they cherish infamy. Anyhow, you can check in there and I'll let Dr Elston know where you are and try to get him to contact you, all right?'

I agreed.

'And maybe…' a spray of salt water slanted from her cheek; she paused; then: 'Maybe you'd better not tell anyone who you are…why you're here, I mean. Just pretend to be a tourist. I don't expect they'd like it, if they knew Elston was talking to you…and he will feel better about it, anyway.'

'Oh, I'll use my famous discretion,' I said.

'I don't know if they'd...' she hesitated, then shrugged. She didn't continue. A moment later she pointed. 'There's the lighthouse.'

I saw the grey tower rising up, mild surf breaking at the base. I could make out the low outline of the island. The launch was quick and the island came up fast. I saw a stretch of water between the island and the lighthouse and, anticipating my query, Mary said, 'The lighthouse is off shore...sort of. About a hundred yards out, but there's a rock reef connecting the two so that you can walk out at low tide, if you're nimble. A reef and...' she smiled...'a cable, connecting Sam Jasper to me. He'll be getting twitchy by now, with no one to talk to all morning.'

'Well, you are nice to talk to.'

She looked at me, tilting an eyebrow.

'The sheriff thinks so, too,' she said. 'He's my boyfriend.'

I said, 'So much for that.'

PELICAN CAY CAME up.

White as bleached bones in the sunlight, it dazzled; the glare made the shadows solid slabs of blackness so that, adjacent, they did not relate. Light and shade did not flow together through grey transition, they existed in separate dimensions...just as the island could be perceived on two levels—a pleasant, sun-washed isle...and the base whence wreckers had lured ships to destruction. Now, physically divided by the fenced compound, the dichotomy was truer than insight, more solid than a mood. Seagulls screamed as they dived at the water and the timeless cry could have been the wail of doomed sailors drowning in the surf. The heat was so great it seemed to obey gravity, heavy on my shoulders and, in that glaring heat, I felt a chill...

THEN WE WERE moving into the harbour, gliding past shrimp boats and a few cabin cruisers and some naked kids who were jumping off the dock. I noticed at least three waterfront bars. The screaming of the gulls faded; there was nothing sinister in the happy cries of the children. My mood passed.

Mary brought the launch into the Coast Guard slot and jumped nimbly out. I figured she would have no trouble crossing over the reef to the lighthouse. I tossed my overnight bag onto the dock and stepped out with seemly caution. Since she was the sheriff's girl there was little sense in risking a soaking by feigning nimbleness. She tied the boat to the iron stanchion with a deft, intricate loop that looked, to me, like a Gordian knot. We walked up the wooden planking and I paused to put my shirt on. I had already started to burn. The docks were fenced off and there was a customs shed, but the gates were open and no one stopped us as we passed into the street. A pair of shore patrolmen sauntered past, all dazzling white. They looked into one of the bars. They appeared more wistful than dutiful. The dark interior was inviting, textured shadows unlike those black umbrae that had so strangely chilled me as we sailed in. But Mary said she would walk me to the inn and we set off along the curved waterfront. Most of the town's business fronted on the harbour and we walked past a turtle kraal, a ship's chandler, a Cuban cigar-maker busy in his window and a couple more bars. Then we came to the jail and the sheriff came out.

He was a tall, fair-haired man with dark aviator glasses and a chin as big and square as a boot. He had a big, white Stetson in his hand and, when he saw Mary he put the hat on, so that he could take it off again as he greeted her. He gave her a big smile and then looked suspiciously at me—not official suspicion.

'Jerry, this is Jack Harland. Jack, Jerry Muldoon, Pelican's only lawman.'

The suspicion left his face. He stuck his hand out and we shook. His hand was as big and square as his chin and I was surprised at how pleasant his smile was—one of those natural, easy smiles.

Mary said, 'Jerry knows why you're here.'

'Good thing, too,' he said. 'I saw the two of you a-walkin' together, took it to mind that he was bent on courtin' you.'

'Oh, no!' I said, hastily. 'I'm not even nimble.'

'Ummm. What I mean is, it's a good thing you're here, not that I knew why you were here.'

'Well, it's a nice change to be welcomed by the law,' I told him. I meant it, too. I had been advised to get out of town by sundown a few times. I said, 'I take it you resent this…agency, too?'

'Sure do. Damn usurpers.'

'What?'

'Usurpers,' he said.

He put his hat on again and pulled the brim down to the top of his dark glasses, so that he had to tilt his head back to look at me.

'That's what they done, they done usurped my authority,' he told me. 'I was the only law on this here island and I admired to have it thataway, oh-yuh.' His jaw worked as if he were chewing tobacco, but he wasn't. Then he grinned and Mary giggled and I saw he was joking—playing his role. But joking on the square, I thought.

'Where are you staying?' he asked, dropping the accent.

'I was taking Jack to the Red Walls.'

Jerry laughed. 'You'll get your ear bent there, Jack. All those old boys that can't forget the old days—nor remember them with any accuracy, either. They get them a landlubber, they plumb wear his earholes out.' He slipped in and out of his rednecked accent and grace. 'It was quite a place, though, going back a few years, from what I hear. Had the plumbers in there, year or two back, they were fitting a new toilet. Had to rip the plaster out; found eighteen wallets that had been slipped down a hole in the wall, where the whores and pickpockets slung them after they took the money out. Shootin's, stabbin's...you name it. Not the same now, though; tamed down. Or so I hear. Couldn't say for sure, 'cause there's no way I'm gonna walk into that place on my own.'

'You'll scare Jack,' Mary chided him, embarrassing me and making me wish I had deboated more nimbly.

'Naw,' Jerry said. 'What I hear, Mr Harland is used to playing with the big boys. He won't scare. Although, come to think of it, I ain't so sure that these ain't the real big boys he come to play with here.'

He looked thoughtful, rubbing that incredible jaw.

'Might be sort of scary, at that,' he said.

Jerry Muldoon looked like he wouldn't be scared of a grizzly bear, and his point was well taken...

III

THE RED WALLS was a solid mahogany structure built to withstand hurricanes, which it had. My room was adequate and had an air-conditioning unit in the window. The bathroom was down the hall, but that was no inconvenience, for I was the only guest. I hadn't been asked to register. I took a cold shower, changed my clothing and went down to the bar to wait. Mary had to get in touch with Dr Elston in person, not trusting the telephone, and I had nothing to do but wait. The barroom was impressive, a huge chamber that would have made a passable cathedral, with arches and beams across the ceiling. The walls, disappointingly, weren't red. They were white. And they were slatted like Venetian blinds, so that they could be opened to take advantage of the sea breeze. They were open when I came down, laying bars of sunlight across the floor in a grid. I took a wicker stool at the bar and the barman was pleased to have a customer—the shrimpers and fishermen who made up the steady clientele were plying their trade at that hour. I ordered a tall rum punch and the barman waited across the counter, fidgeting, obviously feeling obligated to entertain me with tales of the notorious Red Walls. I didn't feel much like talking. I was thinking about Elston and speculating on what he would, I hoped, tell me. But the bartender looked so hopeful that I figured it was only common decency to give him an opening.

'Sort of quiet here today,' I said.

He beamed.

'The place'll get livelier, later on,' he assured me. 'When the boats come in. Not as lively as it used to be, mind you. I could tell you a tale or two…'

'Which you no doubt will…'

'…about this place that'd curl your toes. Yessir. This here place was known far and wide. Why, I remember…'

He talked. It was quite interesting, really, and I listened and made proper responses and drank a second rum. He was still talking when Elston came in…

'...SO, LIKE I say, there was thirteen shrimpers standing at the bar here. This is going back ten, fifteen years. They was standing here, elbows on the bar, drinking away and minding their business, when what should happen but this jigaboo walks in. He's got him a gun. In he walks, bold as brass, says, "This is a stick-up!" Now, these thirteen shrimpers are all facing the bar, they don't pay him no mind. He waves the gun about. He's waving it, he says, "I say, this is a stick-up!" Well, sir, these thirteen shrimpers looks at one another and shakes their heads. Then they all turn around, nice and easy, all at the same time. There's thirteen of 'em, mind. And twelve of them got guns!' He chuckled. 'So there this jigaboo stands, he's got one gun and twelve shrimpers are all pointing guns at him. What's he do? Why, he puts his gun away and he says, "I guess I done robbed the wrong bar!" And he ups and buys a drink for the house. Yessir! Things was plenty lively in them days...'

The barman was chuckling merrily and preparing to launch into another story, but I shoved my glass out for a refill in order to distract him.

Elston was standing just inside the door.

I knew right away that it was Elston from Mary Carlyle's description of the man...timid. He had stepped to the side of the entrance, into the shadows, and his eyes shifted furtively around the big room. I raised my hand, casually, and he nodded with a quick, jerky movement. He looked out the door, then came across the room with a crab-like, sidewinder gait.

'Harland?' he whispered.

'Yeah. Shall we go up to my room?'

He hesitated; then: 'Better stay here, just as if we had met socially, at the bar...as one does.'

He didn't strike me as the type to meet socially at a bar, but I nodded. The bartender, looking grieved that I had found another conversationalist, slid my drink across the counter. He looked at Elston, but Elston didn't notice and didn't order a drink. His eyes still flitted about.

'Let's go down to the end of the bar,' I suggested.

I took another seat there. Elston stood. The bartender, glowering, began washing glasses.

'What's it all about?' I asked.

'You won't mention my name?'

'If you don't want me to.'

'You swear you won't bring me into it?'

'Boy Scout's oath and all that.'

'This isn't funny, Harland, not at all funny.'

'Sorry.'

He nodded. He said, 'I'm not so sure this is a good idea. I let Mary talk me into this. But...' He took a deep breath, as if about to submerge under water, then very quickly he said, 'I want you to expose what is being done here before it goes any further. It must contravene the ban on germ warfare or something, some treaty or agreement...I know nothing of such matters, but I'm sure that public outrage...'

'I'm no scientist, so if this is technical...'

'Technical? Well, of course it's technical...my work, I mean. But...gruesome, that's what it is. Gruesome. It was bad enough with the animals, but now that they have determined to use human volunteers—' He shuddered and rolled his eyes. His whisper was a rasping thing in that great, vaulted chamber. It was eerie.

'Dr Elston...if all you want is to prevent this research, or whatever it is, why don't you simply resign? Refuse?'

'It's too late for that!' he snapped. He had spoken loudly, and he shot a startled glance down the bar, but the bartender was taking no interest in our talk. In a lower tone, he said, 'It's done, God help me. My assistants could carry on without me, at this point...assistants provided by them. And I'm not sure—' with his eyes flitting about '—that they'd let me resign. I'm afraid of them, Harland.'

'Who are they?'

'A branch of the government...nameless. The navy provides ships and guards, but I'm not concerned with them, it's the others...the civilians...the ones who represent...ruthless men, Harland. If you had seen what I have seen...'

He seemed to be seeing those things now, looking through me. He was a shaken man, and frightened. I didn't like him, but I felt a touch of pity; perhaps some sympathetic vibration of his fear.

'You'll tell me?'

'Yes, yes. I will give you the details and you must reveal them to the world, without implicating me. Surely that will be enough, this fiendish thing will be stopped once it has come to light.'

I nodded. I took out my notepad and pen. Elston chewed his lip. He placed one hand flat on the counter and, not looking at me, he said, 'It began...it was pure research, my goal was to treat madness...not to create it.' He glanced at me and I moved my pen, just scribbling; waiting for details. He was grimacing as he continued, 'My research was in chemical lobotomy...not a pleasant thing in itself, but in certain cases...it is sometimes necessary to make the incurables...obedient. I trust you will understand that?' He looked at me doubtfully, the sort of man who must always preface an opinion by a justification. I sort of nodded. That he was taking such pains—and they were pains, they registered physically on his countenance—to excuse his involvement removed any lingering doubts I might have had, about this being a hoax, at any rate.

'I meant only good,' he went on, still staring at me, gauging my reaction or looking for scepticism. I kept my face blank. I had written one word: Lobotomy. A Pandora's Box of a word, opening up dark implications just as the lobotomist opened up a skull.

'Go on,' I said, unwilling to express the vindication he sought as he searched my face.

'My work came to their attention. This agency of the government. They saw possibilities that had never occurred to me—nor ever would have. I was not...given all the facts. I was given a government grant and brought to this place, provided with all the facilities to continue my research, assigned eager—too eager—assistants. I worked. That is what I have always done. I have few friends and little social life. I work. Naïvely, I still believed I was in control of my research, that I was working towards my own goals.' His lips tightened in a bitter smile. 'Well, gradually, I came to see what they intended.' He paused, twitching his cheek up several times, as if chewing and tasting his words. He did not relish the flavour of those syllables. 'If only I had renounced them then. I was still important to the project, it was still mine and without me...but I did not renounce them and there's no sense speaking of what has not been.'

He dropped his head. With his face still twitching, it seemed he was gnawing through his breast.

'They did not threaten me—but the threat was there; they spoke of the Russian menace—they were menacing. And then there were...volunteers...' My pen moved on the paper. I wrote: *Volunteers*. There were two words on the paper that should not have been linked and an icy sensation climbed up my spine.

'Volunteers,' he repeated. 'Say, rather, men to whom the alternative was worse. Well, who thought it worse, not knowing...' His head snapped up abruptly. He had to look directly at me as he said the next words. 'There are chemicals, Harland...chemicals that warp the fabric of the soul, that alter the structure of the mind as surely as the scalpel. This treatment...'

He stopped.

Loudly, he said, 'So I don't get much time for fishing, but I understand it's good here... I'm sure you'll enjoy yourself, Mister...I didn't get your name...'

I blinked in surprise; Elston was very white.

'Well, it was pleasant meeting you,' he said, and he looked wildly about for a reason to be there. He snatched up my drink and gulped at it, then clutched it possessively, leaving *me* no reason for being there. Then he nodded curtly and brushed past me. Bewildered, I turned, getting an elbow on the bar and I saw the man who had just come in—the man Elston had seen a moment sooner.

He wore a dark suit and necktie in that blistering heat and he wasn't sweating. He had steel-framed spectacles and his hair was close-cropped and he looked about ten pounds underweight—but it was underweight the way an athlete in training is underweight. He was heading for the bar, not looking at us. The open walls had laid a grid of sunlight across the floor and he moved through that grid as if describing an arc or a graph, not so much a man as—a statistic.

Elston crossed in front of him, nodding *en passant*.

The man nodded back.

Elston took two more steps, then turned jerkily back.

'Oh, hello, Larsen,' he said, as if he'd just identified the newcomer.

'Doctor,' said Larsen.

'I just stopped in for a drink, you know,' Elston said.

'Uh-huh,' said Larsen.

'Well…back to the grind,' Elston said and he walked to the door with his shoulders squared, like a man anticipating a bullet in the back. He went out. For a moment, framed in the doorway, he looked two-dimensional, a flat shadow of himself. Then he was gone and Larsen was standing at the bar.

I put my notebook away.

'Nice day,' I said.

'They're always nice here.'

'Hot, though. You must be boiling in that suit.'

'Not really.'

The barman came down and Larsen ordered a beer. The barman served it without a word, the same barman who had talked non-stop to me. Larsen didn't touch the glass.

'Tourist, are you?'

'That's right. For the fishing.'

'Um. Staying long?'

'Just a day or two.'

'Uh-huh,' he said.

He picked up the glass and turned to face me. His eyes were like lenses. I felt I was being filmed and filed away behind those steel-rimmed sockets. They drew me like a vacuum. He sipped his beer and I drank the last of my rum and all the while he watched me with his eyes glinting behind his spectacles.

IV

LARSEN HAD THE one beer and left.

I felt he was taking a part of me with him, that he had dragged some intangible segment from my spirit, unravelled a thread of my soul and wound it up again inside his skull, where he would dissect it at his leisure. I was sweating heavily and it had nothing to do with the heat now. It was the sweat of anxiety and Larsen had pulled it from my pores.

The bartender nodded at the door.

'One of them geezers from the compound, we don't care to have their trade. Damn liberty, it is, them comin' here. That guy you was talkin' to...he was really filling your ear, eh? He come from the compound?'

'I don't know him,' I said.

'That a fact? Why, the way he was gibbering away, I figured you was old friends. Some folks is like that, though...they'll bend anyone's ear, even a total stranger's.'

He proceeded to manifest that fact while I considered Elston and Larsen...what Elston had managed to tell me and how Larsen had affected me. I was truly interested now...and disturbed. The big room with the open walls had been cheerful: now it was atrabilious, Larsen had left gloom in his wake. The bright grid of sunlight remained, yet now those lines did not illuminate the cathedral distances—they segmented the room in a sequence of cramped oblongs, like crypts in a graveyard.

I wondered if Elston had been frightened off for good or if he would contact me again? Perhaps through Mary Carlyle, certainly not by telephone.

Then, thinking about the telephone and realising I might have to stay on Pelican longer than I'd expected, I asked the bartender to put me through to the Mangrove Inn. He did so, grumbling about the delay as the call went through the switchboard and, taking the phone, I felt sure that my call was being monitored. But that was all right. I told the owner of the Mangrove that I'd decided to spend a day or two on Pelican and asked if my car would be all right in his parking lot. He assured me it would and assumed I would be fishing. I didn't disabuse him—or the monitor—of that. The bartender had been listening as well, and after I hung up he spent some time telling me where to get the best value in hiring a boat. I told him I'd surely take his advice. I supposed that I should, too, to validate my cover story, but I didn't want to go fishing and cursed Elston for throwing that at me in his panic. I was no fisherman and my inept attempts would be a dead giveaway. But then, rationalising nicely, I figured that the average fisherman spends more time drinking than fishing and it would look odd were I to follow an aberrant routine. It would look...fishy. So I had another drink, quite in line with my cover—and needed it, after being in the line of Larsen's gaze...

IN MY ROOM I stretched out on the bed and glanced at the meagre notes I'd taken. There wasn't much there, certainly nothing concrete, but the words were chilling. Lobotomy is a harsh word, not softened when prefaced by *chemical...* no more on the page than in the wreckage of a mind. I read the words, aware that my lips were moving as I mouthed the unsavoury syllables, then I tore the page out, and the two pages beneath where an impression might have been indented, and I burned them in the ashtray and flushed the ashes down the toilet in the hallway. I was taking this seriously now, absolutely. Larsen's ominous appearance had impressed me more than Elston's aborted statement. There was something cold and dangerous about Larsen. Not a viciousness so much as a void of compassion, a man to whom charity would be alien. He had the eye of a serpent and I'd fluttered like a bird, mesmerised by his gaze. I felt that, had he moved towards me, I would not have been able to retreat; that he'd pinned me with his eyes like a moth on a display board whilst he studied the texture of my spirit, traced the veins of my instincts and laid bare the articulation of my bones.

I was still sweating from the encounter.

I moved to the window and gazed out. A middle-aged man slowly and methodically pedalled past on a bicycle. He had a terrycloth sweatband around his high-domed, glabrous brow. His Adidas shoes went up and down on the pedals. His bony back was bent deeply over the dropped handlebars. The bike was a ten-speed, on an island devoid of hills where those multiple gearings were as useless as the fashion that compelled him to have them. Man had spent the long aeons rising from the slime: he had learned to walk upright: now racing handlebars were pushing his face once more, unseeing, into the mud. I was feeling distinctly uncharitable towards the human race—a legacy, no doubt, of Larsen's gaze. I mourned Darwin. The industrial revolution had put paid to evolution; now giant, pea-brained athletes may outlast the dinosaurs and wizened accountants survive to breed; millions of joggers jarring their spines will fall in love over Perrier water and produce little joggers to trot through a world where trend has superseded evolution.

And men like Larsen existed.

ELSTON COULD WELL have been a bleeding heart, panicking for slight reason, but Larsen—there was a good reason for him to be there. I lay on the bed, waiting. I didn't expect Elston to contact me again so soon, probably not until Mary Carlyle inspired him once more, but I waited, anyhow, and after a while I slept and when I woke up I thought, for a moment, that the walls were vibrating or grating—as if all the violence that had taken place in this building in the past had somehow seeped into the fabric of the walls. I sat up. The vibrating slowed. It had been the drumming of my heart. Yet I had not been dreaming. I took a deep breath and smiled at my fanciful sensation. This strange island, with its sordid past, and its great panorama of pretence, was affecting me. But whatever was going on here, it was not supernatural.

Unnatural, perhaps.

My heartbeat was regular now.

I was hungry and decided to try the diner I'd noticed across the street...

V

THE FISHERMAN'S CAFÉ, a long, narrow building much ravaged by time, was diagonally across the street from the Red Walls. It wasn't elegant but it was handy. I went in, squinting from the dazzling sun, and took a seat at the chipped Formica counter. The Cuban counterman agreed to make a sandwich and served good coffee in a cracked mug. There was one other customer, an old fellow at the end of the counter. He had one eye, a greasy cap and leathery skin. After a while he walked down and stood beside me.

'I see you just come outta the Bloodbath.'

'I beg your pardon? What?'

He pointed across the street, his finger like a gnarled rope, his hand mangled from long years on the shrimp boats.

'Place there. See you come out.'

'Oh, the Red Walls? I did.'

'Yeah, that place. Bloodbath is what we calls it.'

I smiled at the idea that the Red Walls was too euphemistic for this old sailor.

'Ain't no place now like that was then. My oh my, that was a place. That surely was a place.'

'So I've heard.'

He squinted at me. Strangely enough, he squinted with the empty socket, not the eye.

'You'll be no Conch, then?'

'No.'

'Didn't think you was a Conch.'

'Coffee?'

'Wouldn't say no.'

He sat on the stool beside me. The Cuban slid a mug across and the old man enfolded it in his remarkable hand.

'Lost an eye in there,' he said.

He was peering down into his coffee mug and, for a moment, I thought that his eye had dropped in like a lump of sugar and he was wondering if he should stir it.

'In the Bloodbath,' he said. 'What you call the Red Walls. That's where I lost my eye. You notice I only got the one eye? That's 'cause I lost it in there. Fightin'.'

'Oh,' I said.

'Cuban fella and me, had to get at it. Over a woman, you know. Quite the woman. No better'n she ought to be, but a good old gal. Old Jenny what they called the Wolfgirl, on accounts how she used to howl. Howlin' fool, she was. Dead now, Jenny. Forget how she died. This big Cuban and me, we got down to it with fish-knives. Not like you see in the moving pictures, no sir. We was sword fightin', up and down the bar. Hunks of flesh and bone flying all over the place. I flipped a big chunk of shoulder right off of him. That's how I lost my eye. Knife got wedged in his tendons, see, so that I had to sort of lever it out like haulin' in on an anchor. That's when he got my eye, while I was liftin' his shoulder off. Figured we was even. Neither of us relished fightin' much after that. Worse on him, really. Big, strappin' fella, worked on the docks, weren't much use there after he lost that big chunk of shoulder. Hanged hisself, in the end.'

He turned the mug around in his hand like the memories unwinding in his mind.

'That was in the Bloodbath, too, come to think of it. Nothin' to do with me, though, unless maybe he was broodin' and mopin' about his shoulder. Yep. Got to feelin' morose, the way some of these Cuban fellas get to feelin', got him a rope and walked in the bar, just plain announced he was aimin' to hang hisself. Plenty of fellas in there, friends of his, they tell him he hadn't ought to do that, but he says his mind is plumb made up. Don't even care if he has to go to Hell 'cause of it. Throws the rope over one of them big beams up to the ceiling, puts the noose around his neck and commences to haul away. Well, it was plain as day he was never gonna hang hisself that way. Plain as the nose on your face.' He squinted at me, the empty socket closing like an envelope. 'Say, I ain't borin' you, am I?'

'Not at all,' I told him.

He nodded and went on, 'We all got to feelin' sorry for him. He looked so danged foolish, tuggin' away with his eyes poppin' out, standin' on his tip-toes. One of his friends asked if he wanted some help. So he sort of nodded, looked like he nodded…hard to tell, his head in the noose and all. So three or four of his buddies got the end of the rope and give him a hand; hauled him off the floor and tied the end of the rope to the bar rail. Brass, it was. The bar rail. He kicked around awhile and we had some drinks. Then we got to thinkin' as he might of changed his mind and we cut him down but it was too late, if he did change his mind, 'cause he was already hanged. Be a bitch, he did change his mind.'

He giggled with fond memories, a man whose history was carved upon his body in runic scars and wrinkles and who added to his substance by subtracting an eye.

He saw I was fascinated.

'Say, can I get some rum in this coffee?'

'All right.'

The Cuban pulled an unlabelled bottle out and sloshed a healthy portion in his mug. The old man took a big gulp. He had a more interesting delivery than the bartender and I wanted to hear more. I said, 'Things like that don't happen so much these days, huh?'

'Not so much, not at the Bloodbath.' He gave me another eyeless squint. 'Strange things happen, though. Maybe even stranger than what usedta be. Not so natural, maybe.' Now he was squinting at his cup, with his good eye. I nodded to the Cuban, who poured some more rum in. There was more rum than coffee now, and the old man stared into the amber fluid as if seeking inspiration reflected in the surface. He looked vaguely uncomfortable.

'Things like fightin' and hangin', they is natural enough. Thing what I saw the other mornin', now…that was strange. Happen it's the strangest thing I ever see…'

His voice trailed off. I felt he wanted encouragement—a proud man who wished to pay for his rum with words—and said, 'What was that?' but he didn't seem to hear me. He was thinking, either choosing his words or gathering his recollections. Then he looked up and said, 'Say, now…you wouldn't be connected with this government thing here, would you?'

'No. I'm just…' I hesitated. I had been about to tell him that I was just a tourist, but somehow I couldn't bring myself to lie to this old man. 'No, I'm not.'

'Didn't figure you was. You don't look like most of them government Johnnies. Thought as I'd ask, though. On account of…they got lots of security up to the compound,' he added. I realised that he was actually debating whether to continue; it didn't seem in character. For some reason he was wary. But then his basic nature won out and he began to speak.

———

'I GOT A boat,' he said. 'Used to be I did a bit of free trading, you take my point. Well, now, other side of the island there is this little cove, place you can land and nobody sees you. 'Cept you can't land there no more, they told me to bugger off. But they don't give a hoot what's on my boat, nothin' to do with customs duty, just don't want me there. Well, I tell you this 'cause it was around there I saw this strange thing. Maybe three weeks ago, it was after they told me not to land there no more, but I had to go sneakin' back. I'd left some crates there, things what I didn't want found. Nothin' bad, nothin' like dope or stuff, just some duty-free stuff from the islands. Anyhow, I sneaked back there, took the dinghy so I wouldn't make no noise and got to the cove all right; got ashore and dug up these crates. Then, just 'cause I was there, I went on up to the fence—this big fence they has built around the compound—just to have me a look. It was dawn. Just before dawn, sky sort of pearl-coloured and plenty of shadow for me to stand in. Well, that's when I see this strange thing.'

I was well and truly interested now. I nodded to the Cuban and got some rum in my own coffee.

'Happen you won't believe this I'm saying,' he went on. 'Tell you. My name's Tate. John Tate, although of late they's taken to callin' me One-Eye Tate. That don't matter. What I mean is, you can ask anyone about John Tate, they'll tell you he's an honest fella; might say he talks a piece too much but that what he says is straight. You can ask. Thing is, this I'm tellin' you, I don't believe it myself. I mean, I saw it, but I don't believe it, you follow me.'

I nodded. I had taken but a single bite from my sandwich. The Cuban was washing plates at the far end of the counter. Tate pulled a crumpled pack of cigarettes from his pocket and extracted one. It was wrinkled and a fine dust of dry tobacco spilled from the end.

'Well, while I'm standin' there in the shadows, just without the fence, a group of these Johnnies comes down from the big building. Laboratory, I guess it is. I was just about to light a cigarette, just stopped from strikin' the match in time; they'd of see me, I hit the match.' Now he lighted the crinkled cigarette, as if he'd been waiting to use it as evidence as he gave witness. Dry smoke writhed up around the grotto of his empty eye socket. 'So down they come, there's half a dozen of 'em, two of 'em got white coats like doctors or scientists and three of 'em are wearing dark suits. You see these dark suits guys around town, time to time. Don't like the weave of 'em, myself. But it's the other guy, the sixth guy, that takes my interest. He's wearin' a white thing, not like the doctors, more like a patient wears in hospital. And he looks…unnatural. Looks like a robot, maybe. Or like one of them zombies what you get down to Haiti and Jamaica, them living dead Johnnies, you see it? Face all blank, eyes all rolled back white, he's to droolin' down his chin somewhat. Walks stiff. Knees and elbows ain't got much bend to 'em. Well, sir, I figure he's a pretty sick fella, and naturally I wonder why they's walkin' him down to the beach at dawn.'

He shifted on his stool. He had the mug in one hand and the wrinkled cigarette in the other and it appeared he couldn't decide which to lift to his mouth. And it seemed a monumental decision; he looked nervous and jumpy.

'I hunker down to have me a observation,' he said, speaking more slowly now. 'Down they come. They stop and then I see this big slab of concrete. It's real big, big square block with an iron ring set in the top. Thing must of weighed, I don't know…must of weighed plenty more'n a ton. Well, they gather around it. One of the dark suits takes the ring, gives it a pretty hard tug. Them dark suits is sort of skinny, but they looks to be strong enough. Slab of concrete don't budge at all. Too heavy.'

Now Tate raised the coffee mug to his lips, very slowly, as if that, too, were too heavy. He sipped. Big veins stood out in his forearm and his hand was shaking slightly.

'Dark suit fella nods; he's satisfied.'

Tate nodded himself, not with satisfaction. He lowered the mug and raised the cigarette, both movements distinct, as if his arms were connected by a system of levers across his sunken chest. One went down and one went up. He moved by clockwork, timing his tale.

'Then one of the doctors says to the sick fella, "Lift it." No hemmin' nor hawin', just tells him to lift it. Now, I can see it ain't possible for a man to lift it. Anyone can see that. 'Ceptin' this sick-lookin' Johnny. What's he to do but step right up and take the iron ring in his right hand and commence to lift. Matter-of-fact, like it was a pillow. Don't set his feet, don't take no deep breath, nothin'. Just commences to lift. It was awful funny. Strange funny, I mean. Got some ground mist rising around them, sky all grey, they look strange standin' around that concrete slab, like maybe they was worshippers at a tomb. And this guy is lifting!'

Tate lifted the mug, lowered it, lifted again; his leathery face was strained with the imagined effort.

'I mean, his face don't change none, it's blank, got no expression to it, but he is liftin' so hard I can hear his joints creak. He really thinks he can lift that slab!

'Now, ain't no man what could lift it, it's plain too heavy, but he don't know that. Ain't no big guy, neither. The others are all watchin' him and he's liftin' hard as he can and the slab ain't shiftin' at all, don't move an inch. The doctor says, "Lift it," again, but the guy is trying as hard as he can.

'Then the real strange thing happens.'

He put the mug down on the counter with a solid clunk, as if he wanted no further part of it. The Cuban looked up. His hands made slippery sounds in the soapy water.

'What I don't believe, 'ceptin' I see it. I've been a fisherman in my time, I've fought the big fish for hours, game as any man. I know when even the strongest guy has got to give in. But this guy don't know that. And all of a sudden there is this snap, just like a tree splitting in a hurricane. A loud crack...' the onomatopoeia of the word struck him: he repeated it, 'Crack,' relishing the word...but not the image behind it.

'And the guy has broke his own arm!'

Tate grimaced and gave a little shudder. 'Well, the bones are stickin' out from the elbow, where it has snapped.' He touched the inside of his own elbow. 'Blood is spoutin' out on the slab. And the guy is still liftin'. With his arm ruined, broke near in half and the bones all sticking out splintered, he is still trying to lift that concrete slab!'

He shook his head and peered at me. He looked down. I suddenly realised that I was gripping my own arm, rubbing it. It ached, tingling with some sympathetic vibration. I saw that concrete slab like a sacrificial altar, running with blood. My hand seemed to be stuck to my arm; it was hard to pull it away. When I did, the effort registered in my spine...my backbone seemed to be raising as if, set with rings, it was a handle by which his tale was hoisting me.

'I don't blame you, you don't believe it, but that is what I saw. Guy still had no expression, you could tell he was to feelin' no pain, he's heavin' with that bust flipper... Made me sort of sick. Ain't told no one about it before, 'count of I hadn't ought to be there and 'cause I maybe didn't have it all straight in my mind. But that's what happened. No, I don't blame you, you doubt it. Don't believe it, myself.

'But I saw it, though; that is the thing.'

I said, 'I believe you, Tate.'

'You do?' He looked pleased.

I said, 'Listen, could you take me to that place?'

Then he looked uncomfortable. He drained his cup and I nodded for a refill. The Cuban came down, his forearms lathered with soapsuds. He poured some rum. It didn't make Tate look any more comfortable.

Tate said, 'I don't believe I fancy going to there again.'

I didn't press him. I paid the tab and left without finishing the sandwich. Elston didn't contact me, I turned in early and had unquiet dreams...

There had been wreckers.

This island had been founded and prospered upon wreckage, they had drawn innocent ships onto the reefs with false lights and butchered the sailors as they foundered in the surf. They had not been sadistic men, those wreckers, nor cruel for the sake of cruelty. It was simply what they did, a way of life.

And there was wreckage now—the broken spar of a shattered arm, the breeched hull of a mind...drawn by the false light of science beamed from such as Larsen's eyes...

Unquiet dreams...

VI

THE SUN, TOO hot to be contained, spread in a pale curtain across the sky. It was ten in the morning and I was walking the pebbled beach south of the town with some vague idea of having a look at the compound, or at least the surrounding fence. Elston hadn't been in touch and I didn't fancy spending the day waiting for a contact that might not come. The bartender at the Red Walls, drawing with his index finger in some spilled beer, had given me a rough idea of how the compound was fenced off and I knew I should come to that barrier soon. I would have liked to have a look at the cove on the far side of the island, and that immovable concrete slab, but knew that was only possible by boat. Nor would there be anything to see now. Just a slab of concrete. But the image that John Tate had stamped into my mind was graphic. He knew how to deliver a tale and I could visualise those men standing around the slab; could hear, in my mind, the terrible sound of shattering bones. I remembered Elston's whispering, rasping voice, as well, and thought of the connection between the two…and of Larsen, with his eyes magnified in the lenses of his spectacles, glinting at me.

I scrambled over some layered limestone and at the highest point of the island, which was not very high, paused to fill my pipe and gaze out over the sea. The water was very clear. I could see the sandy bottom some eight feet below and, further out, the water bubbled green over a coral reef. The lighthouse, from there, seemed to be on the island, a fold of the landscape hiding the stretch of water between. Seagulls looped around the grey tower and the beacon flashed with regularity, almost invisible in the glaring sunlight. I wondered why Sam Jasper left the light on in the daytime—if it was normal procedure, or if he had simply forgotten? Sitting on the limestone shelf I smoked contemplatively for a while. But it was too hot to enjoy the tobacco. I tapped the pipe out and walked on and, in a short time, came upon the tall, metal-meshed fence. It ran down to the edge of the water and I could go no further. Beyond, I knew, was the beach that Mary liked and which was now barred to her.

Then, suddenly, I laughed.

There was a hole in the fence.

With all that supposedly tight security and the monitored telephones and the secrecy, it struck me as very funny that the fence should be breached. Several strands of wire had been snapped off and bent back. The gap was large enough for a man to slip through and, for a moment, I was sorely tempted to do so—to enter that secret compound and see what I could see. I had actually moved up to the fence before I thought better of it. I would not be able to get into the buildings and would no doubt be apprehended before I'd gone very far and it was hardly worth compromising myself for the sake of a stroll through the grounds. I still thought it amusing that the security had been breached and wondered if someone, like Mary, resenting the barrier, had cut through to get to the further beach—or simply to aggravate the intruders.

I pulled a strand of the wire out and inspected the end. It hadn't been cut, it had been broken or twisted apart. It was heavy-gauge, hard to bend, and on one jagged end I noticed a dark stain. It looked like blood.

Then I heard voices.

I couldn't make out the words, but they sounded excited and they weren't far away. I looked around, thinking to secrete myself and eavesdrop, but there was no place to hide near the fence. I didn't care to be found there, by the break. Innocent of it, I nevertheless felt guilty. I turned away and went back over the limestone shelf and sat down on the far side. I felt excited, as if I were the quarry in a chase. The voices were yet closer and I risked a glance over the rocks.

Two men in naval whites were coming along the fence on the far side, following the line. As I looked, they came to the break. One of them cursed and both looked disturbed. They were armed and the flaps on their holsters were unsnapped. They looked around, standing back to back and whispering together over their shoulders. One shrugged. They were nervous and I caught a few snatches of their talk—enough to discern that they were arguing over who should remain guarding the break and who should report it. I wasn't sure which duty was the less desirable one. But then one, the one who had cursed, said, 'Well, what's the point? He's already got through, he won't be coming back this way.' They whispered some more, then both of them started back the way they'd come, heads turning as they looked around. I waited until they were out of sight. Then I slid down the limestone shelf and headed back to town.

The guards hadn't thought the break in the fence was funny at all.

Neither did I now.

━━

WALKING BACK, I passed close to the lighthouse.

The rock-bridge leading out was just emerging from the water, like a fossilised spine excavated by the tide. At the end of that spine the lighthouse reared up and wailed its mournful warning and the regular, pale beat of the beacon flashed like a charm in a hypnotist's hand. I paused and gazed at that tall pharos rising from the sea. How like a symbol for man's conceit, I thought. The grey tower aspires to the heavens, yet is rooted in the rocks… and man, considering the stars, disturbs the grass. What did man do, atop his shining towers, up there in those cloistered domains? Had he climbed there to a purpose, or was he no more than those swooping gulls who, having dined on filth, rise above the clouds?

I went on; I had decided to call on Mary Carlyle.

VII

THE COAST GUARD Depot was a small white building with green shutters on the windows and a step before the door. It looked more like a country cottage than anything else. The door was open and I looked in. There was an office at the front and a storeroom at the back. Mary Carlyle was sitting behind a desk with some papers spread out in front of her and Jerry Muldoon was balanced on the corner of the desk, one leg swinging back and forth, hands clasped over his knee. Mary gave me a bright smile. Jerry might possibly have looked a little annoyed at my entrance, but nothing serious. I supposed they had been flirting.

'I see you survived the night,' Jerry said.

'Neither stabbed nor shot, although I was well regaled with tales of stabbing and shooting.'

'Mostly true, probably.'

'Didn't you arrest a man there once, Jerry?' Mary put in, shifting some papers without looking at them.

'Why, yes. More than one, but only one that was serious. Shrimper that killed his wife, then got carried away and killed his wife's sister and carved his own brother up a mite. Had to point my gun at him.'

He said that as if it distressed him. He shook his head once and his jaw was so heavy that it acted as a counterweight, so that his head swung a couple more times by inertia. 'I locked this fella up in the jail and he couldn't understand why. He kept asking me why in hell he had to get locked up. He was serious. I said, "For crissake, you just killed two women and wounded a guy," and he looked at me, sort of puzzled; said, "But that was family." And he meant it. Didn't think the law had any business interfering in a family matter. They're like that, shrimpers. He looked so puzzled that I felt sorry for him; for what he thought was unjust. Funny. Guy kills two women and I feel sorry for him.'

'You're all heart, Jerry.'

'Why...yes,' he said.

I said, 'I don't expect you've heard from Elston?'

'Didn't he see you? He promised...'

'He stopped at the inn yesterday. But just as he was starting to talk, a man came in...man called Larsen...' I saw that they both knew the man, or the name...'and scared Elston off. Not, I hope, for good.'

'Oh. Damn,' she said. 'It's no wonder. Larsen is head of security. Nasty sort, I should think. Did he suspect anything?'

'I don't know. He's the sort of man that always looks suspicious. But Elston acted so damn flustered that he could have given it away.'

She gnawed at her lower lip.

'I'll talk to him...' she began, and then the phone rang. She smiled. 'But first I'll have to talk to Sam Jasper, I see. That's the direct line to the lighthouse.'

She reached for the phone. Jerry started to say something to me, then stopped. His teeth snapped shut. Mary's face had recoiled from the receiver as the shout came out. Jerry and I looked at each other. We had heard the words clearly enough. 'Help! For crissake, get some help out here...' Mary, looking startled, held the phone out and the sheriff took it. The cry for help came again, 'He's trying to get into the lamproom! He's trying to claw through the damn floor! Get me some help out here, Mary...fast!'

Jerry said, 'Hold on! This is Muldoon. What in hell are you yelling about, Sam?'

'Muldoon? Thank God. A berserker, Jerry. Tried to damn well kill me... after I went and saved his damn life, too...tell you he's trying to claw through

the floor...he'd of killed me, he hadn't been full of water...' His voice was disjointed and terrified. 'Listen! You hear him clawing? Can't you hear it?'

'Hold on, old fella. I'll be right out.'

Jerry hung up the phone with Sam Jasper still shouting over the cable. The last words I heard were, '...bastard bit me!'

Jerry looked at Mary.

'Think he's slipped a cog?'

'No,' she said, definitely.

'Ummm. Fella that lives in a lighthouse... Well, I'd best get out there.' He looked at his wristwatch. 'How's the tide?'

'It's out,' she said. 'But wait. Take the launch from here, that'll be faster.'

He nodded. I touched his arm.

'Mind if I come with you?'

He hesitated. 'Can't do no harm,' he said. Then he said, 'You got some idea on this?' I shrugged. Mary was looking at me, her face clouded and worried, and she wasn't worried for Sam Jasper's sanity.

JERRY STRODE ACROSS the water from the dock to the launch and I jumped in right behind him, nimble as hell. Mary was pulling at the painter to cast us off as Jerry started the engines. She slipped on the wet dock and banged her knee against the iron staunchion. The skin split. It looked painful. She freed the line and tossed it to Jerry. 'Get that gash fixed,' he said. 'You get coral dust in that, it'll be nasty.' She nodded quickly and stepped back. A trickle of blood ran down her skin. She gave us a nervous sort of half-wave and then Jerry was taking the boat out of the harbour fast. A couple of red-sailed Sunfish were gliding across the roadstead and then bobbled perilously in our wash, one of the sailors shaking a fist at us. We turned towards the lighthouse. It thrust up beyond the slope of the island, then slid away as the angle changed. I could see the line of black rocks extending from the island to the larger rock on which the lighthouse rested. The sea was lashing around the rocks, white and foamy. They were slippery with seaweed. I was just as glad we had taken the boat; that rocky bridge was not to my liking. Jerry was

watching the rocks carefully, coming in parallel with them on the shortest course to the lighthouse.

We both saw the figure at the same time.

'What the hell...?' Jerry said.

The man was on the rocks, coming from the lighthouse, leaping and bounding as if unconcerned about the treacherous footing—or so terrified that panic dictated his movements. He wore a long white coat, the tails flapping behind him like broken wings, and his face was...terrible. His eyes were rolled back white and hollow and white foam sprayed from his lips like an echo of the foam breaking at his feet. He sprang to a rock, hunkered down for an instant, then bounded to the next; slipped but leaped forwards before he could fall. His mouth was open, lips squared back from his teeth, a grimace of torment.

'Is that Sam?' I asked.

'Not Sam,' Jerry said.

The launch had headed for the rocks as Jerry stared at the bounding figure. He corrected, swinging the prow back out. I could sense his indecision, whether to turn the boat after the fleeing figure. But then he looked at the lighthouse.

'We'd best see to Sam first,' he said.

He hadn't drawn his gun, either, and I liked him for his priorities.

JERRY WENT UP the winding staircase first and I followed close behind. The staircase ended at a trap door which led up to the lamproom. The trap door was steel...and it was smeared with lines of blood and tracks of gore. Pieces of flesh and fingernail were pasted, by blood, to the steel...as if the man who had clawed at that door had been buried alive and was clawing at his crypt in final desperation. I tilted my head back, gaping upwards, and as I did so a shard of flesh dropped from the door and fell sluggishly past my face. I thought of John Tate's description of the man who had broken his arm against the unliftable weight. But it was not right...the figure on the rocks had been more vigorous and his attack upon the trap door a thing of fury.

Jerry was shaking his head, looking at those gory tracks.

'Sam! It's Muldoon!' he called. There was no response. 'It's Jerry, Sam!'

'Jerry? You get him?' Sam called from above, his voice distorted through the floor between us, drawn out and quivering as if his words were elastic.

'He's gone. I saw him on the rocks.'

There was another pause while Sam considered this; then; 'You got a gun, Jerry?'

'Yeah, I got a gun. Open up.'

The bolt rasped slowly from the socket and the trap door lifted a few inches. Sam Jasper peered out, balanced at the edge, ready to slam the door closed again. He was an old man with wild white hair and darting fear in his eyes. Jerry stepped back to let Sam see him. Sam gave a little whine of relief and let the heavy door drop back with a clang. He was sitting on the floor. The big lamp was flashing behind him.

'He bit me, Jerry,' Sam said, quite calmly.

Then he began to rave...

VIII

DR WINSTON WAS a middle-aged, likeable fellow, who ran the local clinic. There was no hospital on the island and Winston was the only resi-dent doctor—bar those, an unknown number, within the compound. He was not a native, but he had come there years before, simply because Pelican Cay needed a doctor and he needed nothing more than to practise his craft. Muldoon told me these things while we brought Sam Jasper back from the lighthouse, and I liked Winston the moment I saw him. He was fat; his belly hung over his belt and was obviously never subjected to exercise. He chain-smoked with nicotine-stained fingers and was short of breath. A certain colour to his cheeks and configuration of his nose hinted at a fondness for the vat. I figured straight off that this was a man one could trust.

When Jerry and I helped Sam Jasper into the clinic, Winston didn't seem surprised; seemed the sort that was seldom surprised by anything. Sam was between us, stumbling and twitching. He'd been in shock and mostly incoherent since we found him in the lamproom. Winston asked no questions. He looked at Sam's eyes and told us to get him onto a bed. Sam stretched out obediently, almost as if going to sleep, then sat up abruptly and looked around the room fearfully, turning his whole head while his eyes remained fixed in their sockets. Jerry kept a hand on his bony shoulder and Winston summoned his nurse; instructing her to administer a sedative. He examined Sam, his eyes darting about. Sam had a gash on his forearm and a slighter gash on the back of his hand, nothing that looked serious.

'Human?' Winston asked Jerry.

'What?'

'Those bites. Human, are they?'

'That's right.'

'Thought so. Seen a few of those.'

He spoke to the nurse again, telling her to give Sam an anti-tetanus shot and antibiotics. She bustled efficiently about, a matronly, grey-haired woman with kindly eyes, and Winston started to question Jerry about how it had happened.

Then Sam, sedated and calmer now, sat bolt upright.

'It was a hell of a thing,' he said.

'I'll get him, Sam,' Jerry said, but Sam didn't hear.

'Hell of a thing, I say,' he repeated.

'You ever see him before?'

'What? See him? Naw, not before I pulled him out of the water. He was from up there.'

'Up where?' Jerry asked.

Winston hovered near, hands clasped behind his back, ready to halt the questioning if Sam began to get agitated. I hoped that didn't happen, I wanted to hear what Sam Jasper had to say—to fit his story in with John Tate's and Elston's and—the break in the fence.

'Why, up the compound,' Jasper said.

'Now, Sam, how do you know that?'

'He was wearing one of them white kimonos, as sick people wear in hospitals, is how. Hell of a thing.'

'You say you saved him…pulled him out of the water?'

Jasper nodded. The nurse was standing beside the bed with a hypodermic. She looked at Dr Winston and Winston looked at Jerry. Jerry stepped back a pace, waiting for her to put the needle in before he continued his questioning, but Jasper was talking now and didn't stop. He said, 'First I saw of him, he was clinging to the rocks. On the seaward side, see, as if he's hiding from someone on the island. I see him from behind, see that white coat. Figured him for a drunk, but for that white coat. The water's lapping at his feet and he keeps shifting from one foot to the other, like he don't want to get his shoes wet. I called out to him but he didn't hear me, least he paid me no mind. A couple of seagulls started diving at him, flying around his head, he slapped at them like they was flies.' The nurse slipped the needle into his arm and pressed the plunger. Jasper glanced at her as if the process interested him, but he kept speaking to Jerry, from the side of his mouth. 'Well, then he slips off the rocks and falls into the water. Don't guess he could swim. He was clinging to the rocks with both hands and he's screaming, but he's screaming without making no noise, if you follow me. Screaming silent, mouth wide open but no sound coming out. Well, I didn't much fancy chancing my feet on them rocks, so I got out the rowboat. Time I rowed out he was still clinging to the rocks. Like a limpet, he was. I got the idea that he was too scared to pull himself out…scared of the water, see… like in a dream when you can't run away from what scares you. Must have been powerful strong, the way he was thrashing about you'd have thought he'd break his own grip. I got the boat up aside him, wedged up against the reef, and reached down to give him a hand. He looked up at me. Make you shudder, his face would. His mouth was wide open like his jaw was bust, I could see all his cavities and that little doodad what hangs down in your throat, but I couldn't see naught but white in his eyes, they was all rolled back like a horse in a fire. I pulled him into the boat. Wasn't a big man, nor heavy, but he was strong. Took a grip on my arm like a vice. But he never seemed to see me, he just sat in the boat all dumb. I figured it was best to row back to the lighthouse and phone in for help than to row to the island and have to walk the guy into town, and that's what I did. Had a job getting

332

him out of the boat; had to pull the boat right up on the shore before he would step out. He could walk, all right, but he was wobbling, figured as he'd gulped down plenty of water. Soon as I get him into the lighthouse I take to pumping him out, got him coughing and spitting. All of a sudden he shakes himself like a wet dog.' Jasper shook himself as he said this, perhaps demonstrating what the other man had done—or perhaps shuddering involuntarily. 'Then he turns on me. Like a wild animal, all teeth and nails, and he's strong. I tried to hold him but he just throws me aside and bites me in the arm. Well, this puts a fright to me. He's crazy and he's plenty strong— it's a good thing he's still wobbly. I get away and run up the stairs with this guy snatching at my heels. Got into the lamproom and bolted the trap. Just in time, too. And what's he to do but try to claw right through the trap. I mean, it's steel, even a crazy fella ought to see that, but he claws away at it. I was so shook up I got to thinking he might claw through, at that. That's when I phoned in…'

'I think that's enough for now, Jerry,' Dr Winston said. 'I have to clean that wound and get some stitches into it.'

Jasper said, 'Terrible thing. That white coat, like that you see on a sick man…that was the worst of it, maybe—that and the silent…screaming…'

'Take it easy now,' Jerry said.

He looked puzzled. Jasper lay back obediently and Winston started cleaning his torn arm. I followed Jerry into the office.

'What do you think of that?' he said.

Well, I was thinking of that. The man had tried to claw through solid steel…and John Tate had seen a man—a man in a white coat try to lift an immovable object. Yet that man had broken his arm and the man who had attacked Sam Jasper had not had a broken arm; Tate's man had been obedient and devoid of emotion and Jasper's man had been ferocious. But both had been silent and immured to pain. Elston spoke of the chemicals that warp the fabric of the mind…and someone had torn through that heavy gauge fence. Chunks of the story that fitted together, not in a flat plane like a jigsaw puzzle but in a three-dimensional tableau—fitted together only roughly, but with contours that would dovetail once further knowledge had smoothed

the rough edges. My thoughts flitted around through what I knew and wondered how much I should tell Jerry. I liked and trusted him, and he was the sheriff, but I had an idea that this thing was far beyond his jurisdiction.

I turned to him, intending to speak.

But Jerry was on the phone.

'YEAH, YEAH,' JERRY said. 'Yeah. Security, I guess.'

He waited impatiently, eyebrows raised. The phone made electric noises. Jerry started to say something to me, then paused and listened into the receiver.

'Yeah, got a problem here,' he said. 'Larsen? Yeah, this is Muldoon. Yeah, a guy run amuck, wearing a white coat…you be inclined to know anything about that? You do, huh? What? Naw, I don't need any assistance…it's only one guy. What the hell. I can handle it, just wanted to let you know. Sure, I know you got the authority, damn it. But I got a say in the matter, right? Damn right. I'll hold him for you but I ain't about to sit on my thumbs while he runs around loose. Forget it. Yeah, yeah, I know.' Jerry sighed. 'Okay, I'll expect a couple of your people. But in the meanwhile I'm gonna be looking. What? What?' he shouted. 'He's only one man, how in hell do I arrest him if I don't get close to him? Are you crazy?' Jerry set his jaw and glared at the phone. Then he slammed it down in the cradle.

He was angry.

He started to walk out without a word, then stopped and turned to me. He looked bewildered.

'Shoot him,' he said.

'What?'

'That's what Larsen told me to do. He said not to try to take the man alive, to shoot him. What the hell is happening on this island? He's only one man!'

Then he walked out.

I hadn't had a chance to tell him what I knew, but I didn't suppose it mattered. I figured it was time that I tried to use the telephone myself…

IX

'SORRY, SIR...I REALLY can't say,' the electronic voice chanted. The operator was nervous. Her words crackled with an electricity of their own. It was as exasperating as conversing with a recording.

'But surely you have some idea?'

'Sorry, sir...a difficulty with the lines.'

I said, 'Oh, hell,' and hung up. It was frustrating to have a story and be unable to phone the paper; it built up explosively inside me. Oh, it wasn't much of a story, really—not yet; not the important exposé I'd hoped to get from Elston. But it was certainly worth a phone call. There was something particularly gruesome about the affair, the isolation of a lighthouse, the old keeper trembling in the tower while a madman raged below. It would—I grimaced despite myself—sell newspapers. And that, for better or worse, was what my job was, what any newspaperman's job was, first and foremost—to sell papers. Whether one did this by revealing truth or popularising culture, by wallowing in scandal or spreading gossip or drawing comic strips, the job was the same. I was feeling cynical. Or maybe just honest with myself, knowing that my real success had come not because my exposé had put a halt to the Warden misappropriations, but because readers, thirsting for the blemished wine of scandal, had bought newspapers. Whatever good had come of it had been no more than a side effect and the public funds that had been saved had been saved for a public that preferred the vicarious thrill of being exploited. And mine was a respectable paper, at that.

Someday, I would write my novel.

Now I was going to write about what was happening on Pelican Cay. But what *was* happening? I had to find the hinge before I could open this mysterious box. I had uncovered graves of mouldering graft and unsealed Pandoran abuses in the past, but whatever I was looking for here did not deal with self-interest and the profit motive; it was deeper than greed, and more evil. Greed is a trait of living things, an integral slice of the will to survive and evolve, unpleasant, but part of the natural order. Whatever was being wrought behind those high fences had no place in nature.

———

THERE WAS NO Western Union office on Pelican, but I thought maybe Mary Carlyle could help me. Surely the Coast Guard had communications not dependent on the switchboard and perhaps she could manage to patch me through to New York. With that in mind, I took leave of Dr Winston and headed down the waterfront.

It was then I became aware of how seriously the powers within the compound were taking the hunt for the escaped madman. Uniformed shore patrolmen were all over the place, walking in threes, and I spotted half a dozen civilians strolling about like tourists but with an intent they could not hide…lean, fit, hard-faced men like Larsen. My nerves began to flash like beacons and my flesh crawled like the tide, carrying the flotsam of foreshadowed fear. I told myself this was a newspaperman's reaction to a story about to break, but in my heart I knew it was more than that…I was scared.

———

'JACK!'

It was Mary, coming towards me. I noticed that she had a bandage on her knee, where she'd struck it against the stanchion. I said, 'I was just coming to see you,' and she said, 'I was just going to see Jerry. Is Sam all right?'

I told her, briefly and without the gory details, what had happened. She watched my face as I spoke. I added that Jerry wasn't likely to be in his office for a while and she looked around, as if she expected to see him.

'Poor Sam,' she said. 'I'm glad he's all right.'

'Listen, Mary… Is there any way you can connect me to the mainland from the Coast Guard depot? The telephone lines seem to be out.'

She nodded. 'I know. And I could, although we aren't supposed to use the radio now…except that I'm out, too.'

'What?'

'I've been given the day off. Dismissed, and quite curtly. Something very hush-hush is going on. I left the depot sort of flustered and forgot my handbag. When I went back for it there was a guard on the door. He wouldn't let me in. They sent the bag out to me, but for some reason they don't want anyone in there. The radio, I suppose. It figures, what with the telephones not working…or being worked…' She looked around again, looking for Jerry or, perhaps, determination. She said, 'Look, I have nothing to do now, Jack; I can run you over to the Keys in the launch, if you like. You can phone from there.'

I considered it. I have regretted my decision since, but at the time it seemed premature to leave Pelican before the madman had been captured… to rush off with the first half of a story only to be gone when the conclusion occurred. If I had…but perhaps, even then, they would not have let us go. At any rate, I said, 'Well…let me buy you a drink, Mary; I may take you up on your offer later.'

Now Mary seemed indecisive, fidgeting with her handbag and looking around.

She said, 'Do you think there's any connection?' I knew exactly what she meant, but she added, 'Between Elston and the attack on Sam Jasper?'

'Yes; I do.'

'So do I.'

'I must talk to him again.'

'It's more than a story, isn't it? I mean…something grotesque is going on here.' She gestured in that way she had, turning a hand over. 'Something that will affect us all.' It had already affected her; I saw the effect registered in her face, troubled and concerned. Two shore patrolmen walked past us with angular strides. A third came up behind, quickly hurrying to catch up. Mary glanced at them. Then she smiled slightly and said, 'I'll take that drink, Jack. I've nothing to do. Nothing I *can* do,' she added.

I could tell she didn't feel like making any decisions, even in selecting a place to have a drink. I took her arm and guided her towards the nearest bar.

———

'HOW'S YOUR KNEE?' I asked.

'Ummm? Oh, it's okay. You have to be careful if you get any sort of break in the skin here. The coral dust is liable to get in it…keeps it from healing.'

She touched her thigh, just above the bandage. 'Silly of me; I was in such a hurry to cast you off. I like Sam Jasper.'

'Well, he's all right, it wasn't serious; just scared him.'

I believed that to be true.

We were sitting in a pleasant dockside tavern. The bar was fashioned out of the side of a rowboat and we were sitting at the gunwales. A gun port had been cut out of the side of the boat in the middle and the snout of an old iron cannon thrust out. It made for a nice decor and I wondered if, in the wild days, loaded with grapeshot, it had ever been tilted to clear the premises of rowdies? The bartender wore a head-rag and eye-patch and addressed the customers as landlubbers, but he seemed to enjoy his role so hugely that it didn't seem phoney. A few locals were drinking rum at round wooden tables and a drunk slept, undisturbed, at the stern of the bar. Mary and I, by tacit agreement, were not talking about what we both were thinking and it made the conversation somewhat disjointed. She was a very pretty girl, but I didn't think about that, either. Then, by some strange alchemy, we knew that something had happened.

It came to us, and to the other customers, as if by a vibration sensed below the level of sound, just flirting with awareness. Drinking men looked up from their drinks, puzzled; Mary and I exchanged a glance. One does not explain these things. A moment later a young bait-cutter rushed in with the news that Sam Jasper's attacker had been captured. A sigh—silent but definite—passed through the drinkers, not so much because they hated or feared the madman, but because, independent men, they resented having the wharfs and streets crawling with shore patrol. The bait-cutter knew no details, he had only got the news a moment before, but no one doubted it.

I said, 'Let's go see Jerry. I'd like to get some details. Then you can run me across to the Keys, if you will.'

Mary agreed.

We finished our drinks and walked down the waterfront to the police station through crowded streets that hummed with excitement.

338

THE POLICE STATION was a small, concrete building with Jerry's office in the front and a single cell at the back. Jerry was sitting on the edge of his desk, the door to the cell was open and the cell was empty. Jerry looked bemused. He smiled when he saw Mary, but it was a serious sort of smile.

'We heard...' Mary started.

'You get that knee fixed up?' he asked.

'Yes. We heard...'

'Yeah, we got him.'

I glanced towards the cell again.

'Naw, he ain't here. They got him.' He slid from the desk and moved to the door, closing it for no apparent reason—just something to do. He said, 'I found him but I let them take him. I don't know. Something about the way Larsen talked on the phone...I don't like the guy, don't like men like him, but he impressed me...maybe that ain't the word I mean, but anyhow...' He reached up to his head, as if intending to adjust his hat-brim, but he wasn't wearing a hat. His hand hovered before his face and he looked embarrassed; he scratched his cheek, just as he'd closed the door—for something to do. Then he looked directly at us and said, 'I guess maybe I mean he scared me.' Then, wanting no comments on that admission, he went on, 'I found him hiding in a jumble of crates down on Third Wharf. Not hiding, exactly... just sort of sitting there. I was going to arrest him, I found him, Larsen be damned, but it was the damnedest thing...'

He hesitated. Mary and I said nothing, knowing he was wondering if he should continue. Then his jaw set. A look of distaste contorted his handsome countenance.

'He was eating a dead dog,' he said.

———

MARY GAVE A little gasp and her face twisted up. I felt faintly sick. Jerry said, 'A little brown dog. Just a stray. Don't know if he killed it or found it dead, but he was squatting there beside the crates just sort of picking at it... not really eating as if he were hungry, but just pulling a piece off from time

to time and chewing it, sort of like he couldn't decide if it was to his taste…
more curious than hungry. Just a little brown stray…'

'Eating a dog!' Mary rasped. 'The poor man!'

'Poor dog, the way I see it,' Jerry said.

'Oh my God…'

'Chemicals that warp the fabric of the mind…' I whispered, but they
didn't hear me.

Jerry said, Well, I saw that…I didn't try to make the arrest. I called
Larsen and then I just stayed back and watched the guy. I see what Sam
meant about that white coat, it was sort of eerie…worse if he'd been naked,
you know? Coat was all spattered with blood by then and the tails were dragging on the wharf. He'd tug at it from time to time, as if he would have liked
to take it off but didn't know how. Then the damnedest thing happened…
they sent a truck down from the compound. Like a dog-catcher's van, it was,
with a cage in the back. And must of been a dozen guys with it. Not shore
patrol. Some of them were Larsen's crew, dark suits and all, and some were…
well, doctors, I guess. They were all plenty scared. Even them hard-faced
guys, they were scared. The guys in suits had rifles. And…listen to this! The
doctors had nets!'

'Nets?' I said, stupidly.

'Nets. Goddamn nets. Just like they was butterfly collectors…just like in
the cartoons, when the warders snag a crazy guy with butterfly nets. But the
nets weren't like in cartoons, really…they weren't on the end of poles, I mean.
Just big nets with ropes on 'em, sort of like the gladiators, some of them, use
in Hollywood films…or in old Rome, far as I know. They ignored me and
I didn't say a word. The guys with the nets whispered together, then began
to move in on him from all sides—three sides, there was a big crate on one
side.' I had the impression that Jerry was trying to be absolutely accurate in
his description, as if he didn't think we would believe him—or didn't believe
it, himself. 'The guys from Larsen's crew kept their rifles trained on him, the
way they looked, all tense and tight jawed, I knew they would of shot him
the moment he made a move. Just the one guy, but they would of shot him. I
never had call to shoot a guy, myself,' he said irrelevantly; then, to the point:

'Seeing them that way, what did I do but draw my own gun. Didn't mean to. Just sort of had it in my hand before I knew it. Well…they moved in and tossed the nets over him. He was preoccupied, he didn't seem to notice. They got about six nets onto him from all angles. Then, holding the ropes, they started to pull him towards the van. The minute he felt them tugging, he went berserk. He began to thrash about, he was rolling in the dead dog and tearing at the nets…foaming at the mouth…but he didn't make no sound. Lord, that fella was strong. He got to his feet, even though all six of the doctors were hauling to keep him off balance, and he sort of staggered in one direction while the men on that side backed off and those on the other side tried to hold him and got dragged along. He had one hand out from the nets, all hooked up like a talon, reaching for them. Made my flesh crawl. Few strands of the net parted and I could see they had wire inside the rope, no way he could break the nets, but he sure tried.' Jerry paused for breath. He was sweating. 'Finally they got him to the van, more by coaxing him that way than hauling him, and they prodded him with long poles until he tumbled inside, into the cage. They tossed the ropes in and slammed the doors and bolted them. He was hammering on the inside of the van and the metal was bulging out when he hit it. Then they drove off. Nobody said a word to me and I didn't ask.'

Jerry shrugged.

'He must have some terrible contagious disease,' Mary said.

'I guess. But nets? Not a very dignified way to treat a man, even a madman…'

Very quietly, I said, 'He bit Sam Jasper.'

'Oh, Christ!' Jerry said, we looked at each other, sharing an icy thrill of horror and, at that moment, Larsen burst in…

———

LARSEN CAME THROUGH the door and his hard, cold face was vibrant with emotion now, his whole, lean body taut and quivering. Ignoring Mary and I, he confronted Jerry.

'Why in hell didn't you tell me someone was attacked!' he shouted.

'Take it easy,' Jerry said, thrusting his big jaw out.

'Who was attacked? You said he didn't get into the room with Jasper...'

'Well, now, is that what I said? Well, I guess I said it because it's true.' Jerry spoke with controlled fury; he didn't like Larsen and he didn't like the man's approach. Larsen was slightly taken aback.

Calmer, now, he said, 'I heard that the lighthouse keeper had been attacked.'

'Yeah. Well. That was before he bolted himself into the lamproom, right? He got hurt a bit before that.'

'Jesus! You should have told me, Muldoon!'

'That a fact? Well now, how was I supposed to know that? You never told me a thing. A guy gets attacked, he ain't hurt bad, I get him to the clinic... what's the problem?'

'The clinic? He there now?'

'Last I saw him.'

'How long ago was that?' Larsen snapped. Then he said, 'Think really carefully, Muldoon. Please.'

Jerry looked at his watch, then at me.

I said, 'About three hours.'

Larsen turned to me; said, 'Who the hell are you?'

Jerry said, 'Yeah, it was just on three hours.'

'Oh, Christ,' Larsen said. He was white-faced and his eyes, magnified by the spectacles, seemed huge. He turned, stiffly, as if his spine were fixed in the floor and he was rotating his body around it.

Then he rushed out.

Jerry leaned back against his desk, as if his energy had suddenly been vent. Then he grabbed his hat, slammed it on and started in pursuit of Larsen. Mary and I exchanged a glance and we started after Jerry. Mary called for him to wait and he stopped, waiting for us and watching Larsen. Larsen was running and he ran like a sprinter. I doubted that Jerry could have overtaken him. But Jerry didn't try, he was content to follow at a fast walk, with Mary and I at his heels. It was only a short distance and when we got there Larsen was standing in the doorway. He hadn't gone in. And he had a revolver in his hand...

'NOW, THAT'S A strange way to call on a sick man,' Jerry grunted. He wasn't being funny. We stepped up behind Larsen and looked past him—looked where he was looking. The matronly nurse was sitting on a bunk. Her uniform was open and there was a bandage on her neck. She was staring at the gun in Larsen's hand, looking bewildered. Then she saw Jerry move up behind him and figured everything was in hand. She remembered herself and modestly drew her uniform closed.

'No need for that, young man,' she said, nodding at Larsen's gun. She switched her gaze to Jerry. 'Didn't you see the doctor?'

'What happened?' Larsen asked.

'I have no idea who you are,' she said. 'Didn't the doctor tell you, Jerry?'

'I...haven't seen him.'

'Oh...I thought...well, it's certainly not a matter for firearms...'

Larsen put his gun away. He wore it in a holster on his hip. He left his coat unbuttoned. Jerry started to move past him, but he blocked the doorway, not going in. He said, 'What happened?' again and when the nurse looked at Jerry, the sheriff nodded.

She said, 'Well, it was an awful thing. Sam Jasper...he seems to have lost his mind. He was sleeping and I looked in on him just as he started having convulsions. Seemed to be in terrible pain. I called the doctor and went over to comfort Sam and all of a sudden he...he bit me. He sat right up in bed and bit me. Didn't know what he was doing, of course. He must have been allergic to one of the shots I gave him.' She fingered the bandage on her neck. 'It isn't serious, he just sort of snapped at me. Then he ran out.'

'Where's the doctor?'

'Why, he went looking for Sam. He looked at my neck and saw it wasn't bad, saw I could take care of it myself, so he set out to bring Sam back before he hurts himself.'

'How long ago was this...when he bit you?' Larsen said, speaking each word distinctly.

'Why...not more than ten, fifteen minutes. I figured you'd run into the doctor, is that why you came along, Jerry?'

Larsen relaxed visibly. I could see his shoulders roll as they untensed. He stepped on into the room then. 'Was the doctor hurt…wounded…too?' he asked.

'Why, no. He was in his lab. I'm not really hurt, either…it's just a scratch. Sam meant no harm.'

'He broke the skin, though?'

'Well, yes. Who is this man, Jerry?'

'I ain't sure, ma'am,' Jerry said, looking at Larsen. Larsen had moved to the desk. He lifted the phone. The nurse said, 'Phone isn't working, young man; could have told you that had you asked permission to use it.' Larsen ignored her. He snapped something into the phone, a number or code. The phone squawked. A moment later Larsen was speaking.

———

THEY CAME FOR the nurse in an ambulance, three attendants and two of Larsen's men. She protested. 'Nothing wrong with me,' she said, 'and if there were the doctor could take care of it. I'm a trained nurse, I know when…'

'Please don't be difficult,' Larsen said. 'This is for your own good. You… you may have contracted a rare disease… Well, it's best that we examine you, that's all.'

'Jerry?' she asked.

Jerry looked embarrassed. He said, 'Well, maybe you had ought to let them have a look, Julia.'

'Well…if you say so. Lot of nonsense, you ask me. But I don't need the stretcher, I'm not in shock.'

'Please get on the stretcher,' Larsen said. He nodded and one of the attendants took her by the arm. She bristled. Jerry said, 'Now, see here, Larsen… this woman is a civilian, you have no authority to order her around. She said she'd come and—'

Larsen wheeled on Jerry. I thought he was going to shout. But when he spoke, his voice was soft, almost pleading. He said, 'Muldoon, don't interfere in this. Please. There are things you don't understand.' Jerry's big jaw was sliding out like an avalanche, but something in Larsen's tone stopped his

anger. He said, 'I guess you'd better do what he says, Julia. I'm sorry. I don't know what the hell's going on.'

The nurse made a huffing sound. She shook off the attendant's hand and climbed onto the stretcher as if mounting an inflated horse in the water, trying to be dignified about it. She lay back and the attendants pulled the straps around her, with her arms against her flanks. 'Ow! Not so tight,' she said. 'This is absurd. You don't need those…'

'Use 'em,' Larsen said. The nurse looked at Jerry and Jerry looked at Larsen. Jerry didn't like anything about this, but he was past protesting. His shoulders drooped. They carried the nurse out and loaded her into the back of the ambulance, still strapped tightly to the stretcher.

Larsen watched them drive off. Then he looked at his watch, lowered his arm and immediately raised it again, as if the time hadn't registered on the first look. His lips moved slightly, counting to himself…counting the minutes since or the minutes until…what?

LARSEN WENT OUT of the door, buttoning his jacket. On the doorstep he turned back and said, 'Muldoon, you want to help, see if you can find the doctor. Keep him away from Sam Jasper. We'll find Jasper ourselves. I hope.' Without awaiting a reply, he moved off. Little eddies of dust swirled at his heels. As soon as he was out of sight I lifted the telephone, wanting desperately to get through to Elston. The switchboard that had just made contact for Larsen grated the same, 'I'm sorry, sir, the lines are out of order.' Winking at Jerry, I said, 'This is Larsen.'

There was a pause.

Then the voice, sounding human for the first time, said, 'You're not Larsen. Who is this?'

I slammed the phone down.

'Well, it was worth a try,' I said, feeling silly. Jerry grinned, but not much. He was lost in thought…thinking about things that, as Larsen had said, he did not understand. It was a hell of a position for a sheriff to be in. It wasn't so good for a newspaperman, either.

'Mary,' I said, 'I think maybe you'd better run me over to the Keys…'

X

MARY AND I walked down the cobbled street and turned into the docks. Mary looked at me, frowning, her step faltering. The gates were closed and locked and there was an armed guard on the other side of the wire. She raised her eyebrows and I shrugged. We walked on to the gate and the navy guard came to polite attention. 'Sorry, ma'am…sir…no one is permitted through until further notice.' I was going to speak, but Mary had her bag open; showed him her Coast Guard ID card. His eyes skimmed it. 'I have to use the launch,' she said. He was a young fellow and not too sure of himself. He said, 'Just a moment, please,' and went back to the guardhouse. Through the window we could see him talking on the telephone. He came back out, slightly flushed, as if he'd just been given a rocket. 'Sorry, no one is…' He broke off the rote statement and grinned sheepishly. 'They said you couldn't go through,' he told us. 'Sorry.'

'You mean no one is allowed off the island?' I said.

'Well, I wouldn't know about that, sir. No one is allowed through this gate, is all I know.'

'What the hell is it all about?' I tried to sound formidable and authoritative. 'Some sort of quarantine?'

'Dunno, sir. Heard it was smallpox, or something.'

'Well, so much for that,' I said. Mary was still holding her ID card out in front of her. She tightened her fist, crumpling it. I nodded to the guard and he saluted and Mary and I walked back from the harbour.

I said, 'Well, whatever they're afraid of, they sure as hell can't keep it a secret now. Closing the island off…that will have to be explained…'

'Which means that they're more afraid than secretive,' she said. 'That it's more important to keep…something…contained on Pelican, than it is to keep it secret…'

'I wonder how long?'

'I guess you'll get your story,' she said, smiling a little. 'I didn't get you down here for nothing, Jack. You'll have an exclusive…if they ever let you write it.'

That disturbed me. We came out onto the waterfront. Quite a few men were standing about, shrimpers and fishermen and local shopkeepers, discussing the

situation. No one seemed to know what it was all about, but they all thought it an unwarranted liberty. They were angry and surly and they glared at the shore patrolmen, who looked as confused as everyone else. Someone, loudly, said, 'I don't give a damn what they say, I'm taking my boat out in the morning and ain't nobody about to stop me.' Several other voices joined in, agreeing.

'… burn the damn place down…'

'Didn't want 'em here, the first place…'

They weren't a mob yet, they stood in individual clusters, but they were plenty angry. I said, 'Someone had better give them an explanation pretty damn soon or things could get ugly.'

'I'm going back to Jerry's; if they have decided to bring things out in the open they ought to let him know first. Coming?'

I hesitated. 'No, I think I'll go back to the Red Walls. I'd like to get my notes written up as much as I can…have them ready as soon as the phones are working or I can get a boat.'

Mary walked off. I turned in the opposite direction. I had to pass several groups of men, but no one glared at me, they hadn't mistaken me for the enemy. Maybe they knew just who I was, as far as that went…I hadn't been very subtle. Things had just moved too fast to even think about building a cover story. Well, I wasn't worried about that, now. Worried, yes. But not about that…

XI

WHAT WERE THEY playing at, those government bastards: what was Jerry Muldoon thinking of, letting them take Nurse Jeffries away? It was different with a crazy guy that ate dead dogs…he was one of them and, anyhow, what harm could you do to a guy that already ate dead dogs? But Nurse Jeffries was a local; they were fiercely possessive. That was the thread that ran, embellished by rare obscenities, through the pattern of the talk in the bar of the Red Walls. The crowd was feasting on their resentment, a smorgasbord of rancour; indignation gurgled like a percolator and invective was chewed and

savoured in lumps, like a fat sausage. 'Ain't the point. Maybe they has got proper doctors up to there, ain't the point; they didn't take her 'cause it was best for her, they took her 'cause Jerry let 'em!'

THEY WERE IN an ugly mood, although it probably wasn't particularly ugly for such a gathering. I had intended to go straight to my room, avoiding the bar, but I heard the loud conversation from the doorway and it intrigued me. I figured I would be able to get some good background material from the outraged locals. I went past the stairs, but in the doorway of the bar, I hesitated. I wasn't sure I wanted to go in there, or that I should. The bar seemed to have become an informal sort of town hall for shrimpers and fishermen, a place where mobs are born and lynchings launched. This was as rough a group of men as I'd ever encountered. I'd heard talk of the old days, when things were rougher, but they were plenty rough for me, with their Buck knives and bill hooks in their belts and their leather skin all seamed with veins. Not sure of my welcome, I looked in from the doorway. A dozen men were strung out along the bar and one woman, with net stockings and a black eye, had hiked herself up on the counter.

A beefy, bearded man was saying, 'Like telling us we can't go to our boats. What the hell! They're our boats!'

'Like saying we can't fetch a little rum, a little Havana, up from the islands.'

'That's different. That's agin the law. It ain't right, but it ain't lawful.'

'Politicians!' said a thin man with long black hair drawn back in a ponytail and a scar down his cheek. 'Politicians, see, they got to be crooked by their nature. See it? They weren't crooked, they would never of riz in politics. Figures, don't it? But you or I do something what they ain't told us to do, they pass a law what makes us crooked.'

'These guys ain't politicians, though.'

'They're bastards, though…'

THE BARTENDER NODDED in agreement with the piratical philosopher and, nodding, spotted me in the doorway. He sensed my uncertainty and waved

me in. Everyone else, seeing his gesture, turned to look at me. They stopped talking and stared at me, grim and hard-eyed. I knew how the misguided stick-up man must have felt when they turned on him, aborting his crime. They didn't look hostile, exactly, but they looked infinitely capable of hostility.

I walked up to the bar and the bartender moved down to meet me, two ships joining on a charted course. I knew he was doing this to make me feel welcome and that embarrassed me. I was damned if I would act nervous and, instead of stopping at the end of the bar nearest the door, I walked right down the bar to the far end, running the gauntlet of their attention. The woman, laughing, swung a playful leg at me. The bartender passed me, going in the opposite direction, and now he had to retreat, paralleling my course along his own side of the bar. This struck me as funny and I laughed. The bartender laughed too, although he probably didn't know why. Greeting me by name, he asked if I wanted my usual and that broke the tension. The locals relaxed. One by one, they nodded, not so much to me as to the realisation that I was a neutral. I knew how a Swiss must feel. The bearded fellow nodded first, then the man beside him, then the pirate, and the nod ran down the line, heads rippling in sequence, like falling dominoes. Then they ignored me.

I STOOD AT the end of the bar, by the stairs, listening to the talk and wondering if I should buy a round for the house, or if that would compromise my neutrality? I had a second drink. The bartender, my ally, kept looking down to make sure my glass was filled. The woman gave me a shy look that, with her black eye and coarse demeanour, was rather endearing. A gradual change altered the mood of the drinkers. They were men of abrupt rage never long sustained.

'Listen!' said one. He slapped his hand on the bar like a gavel. 'Listen, what if that dog-eater had walked in here?'

'Hey, that would of been something.'

'We'd of showed him what we does to dog-eaters, eh?'

'It would of been just like the old days!' cried an ancient mariner, gleefully.

This was rare good humour to them and everyone was laughing and drinking and taking turns in making lewd suggestions to the woman. Her

replies outdid them. They had actually slipped from outrage to gaiety as abruptly as if they'd stepped from shadow into light and their levity depressed me far more than their resentment had. I finished my second drink and shook off the eager bartender. I didn't run the gauntlet again; I went up the back stairs to my room.

***

THESE WERE THE descendants of the wreckers.

I could still hear the undulation of their mingled voices from my room. Laughter came in sudden bursts, punctuating the steady drone. They were speculating on how they would deal with a man who ate dead dogs and they spoke of that unfortunate man without the slightest sympathy, just as, I knew, a wrecker from the past would have joked with his peers, mocking the way some pitiful victim had squirmed and pleaded under his cudgel— and then, without the faintest feeling of wrongdoing, dutifully fetch his loot home to his adoring wife and happy children.

I felt a timeless despair.

XII

I DOZED IN depression and awoke to find the walls vibrating again. They seemed to pulse in and out like plastered lungs, billowing around me. It was not my heartbeat. A distant shouting sounded. I sat up, frightened, filmed by a pyrexia of dread. Then I realised the commotion came from below, running like fluids up the timbers of the building. There was a cry of anger…a crash…another cry that rose to a scream. It appeared that the ephemeral good humour of the crowd had turned surly again: autophagous anger devouring itself with ravenous rage. They had few tools, those rough men; they saw every frustration as a nail to be hammered by violence.

Then, of a sudden, the noise ceased.

There was no transition, no gradual ebbing of the uproar—there was bedlam and then there was a silence so absolute that it was sound in itself…a

cosmic boom. That void of sound roared in my ears. Fights do not end in such abrupt silence, unless…

I went downstairs…

FROM THE BALCONY, gripping the banister, I looked into the barroom. The men were standing in a circle, looking inwards and down. The bartender was standing back, a broken truncheon in his hand. The woman was leaning against the counter, one hand at her throat. No one moved. I waited, scarcely breathing, knowing that there was some terrible centrepiece to that silent circle. I wanted to bear no witness to this scene: my impulse was to creep back up the stairs but I could not move. My legs seemed to grow from the floor, my hand was glued to the railing.

The big, bearded man moved. Something flashed silver in his hand—flashed silver and, turning, flashed red. His hand went to his pocket, he stepped aside. Another man moved. One by one they broke from that ring, cast off by the centrifugal force of shock; they went to the doors. I saw the body around which that motionless orbit had described its silent arc. Blood had spread out like melted wax; in that blood, the body was like a fossil, preserved forever in red amber.

It was Sam Jasper, and he was dead.

The woman walked out, stumbling, still holding her throat. Only the bartender remained. He still gripped the broken truncheon, like driftwood that kept him afloat in reality; his face was as bloodless as if he, too, had spilled his veins onto the floor.

I was able to move then—I had to move, for my trembling legs threatened to collapse. I went down the final steps into the room. The bartender turned towards me.

'I don't know,' he said.

He had anticipated my words; already launched from my throat, they came out, anyway: 'What happened?'

'I don't know,' he said, again.

I was trying not to look at Sam. I looked at the telephone and the bartender followed my gaze. He moved towards the phone and I stepped forwards. Then he came back towards me and I stopped. It was like some ritual dance choreographed in Hell. He moved the broken club like a baton, leading the silent music of our gavotte. Then he broke the pattern, leaning against the bar, his head lowered. He began to speak.

———

'JASPER,' HE SAID. 'But not like Jasper. He came in the door. Someone asked him how he was, but he didn't answer. His mouth was open but not making any noise and…drooling. He came at us. Not fast, he had a strange, deliberate step…not like he was weak, like he was just remembering how to walk…' The barman's throat worked convulsively, disgorging his words as if vomiting up poisoned food. '… His fingernails…teeth…like an animal… Nobody did anything at first, we all knew old Sam…' He looked at me as if he wanted confirmation. I nodded. I could imagine those men, confronted by the unknown, unable to react…unable to identify the nail that had to be hammered. 'But then he grabbed Sally. She'd jumped up on top of the bar. Sometimes she used to dance on the bar,' he said, as if that were miraculous. 'Sam got her by the ankle…pulled her off. Her back hit the edge of the bar and she screamed…then everyone got hold of him…it was because of Sally… if she hadn't of moved…that's when Sam went for her, when she jumped up on the bar…' He stared at me. He was justifying it. An attack on a woman had played the catalyst to their stunned immobility, it was a thing to which they could react in their fashion. I nodded my understanding.

'But he was too strong,' he said, wonderingly.

'Just an old man everybody knew…too strong. He was throwing men aside, snapping his teeth…I thought he was going to kill Sally. I came over the bar and hit him…with this—' he held up the truncheon '—and he didn't even feel it. It snapped over his shoulder… Old Sam, but too strong…'

He let the broken club roll from his hand onto the counter; his voice was hollow. 'Then there was a knife,' he said. 'I don't know who started it… someone…then they all had knives and hooks out, they were stabbing into

Sam like they couldn't stop, like they was all crazy, like sharks when they get frenzied…or like they was too scared to stop. And Sam didn't seem to know he was being stabbed. It went on and on. Then Sam was down on the floor, he must of been dead. All his blood has poured out, he's dead, and everyone steps back from him…and Sam sits up!'

I flinched. The bartender's voice went into me as those knives had gone into Sam Jasper; I was bleeding sweat, congealed fear seeped from my pores The bartender gripped my arm; said, 'He sat up and his jaw dropped open; then he fell over again…but all his blood was out and…he moved after he was dead…'

He was trembling. His hand shook on my arm and the trembling passed on into me. What terrible determination had caused Sam Jasper to move, to defy mortality with a final convulsion?

Locked together by the coupling of his hand, we shuddered face to face. Then he looked away.

'They left,' he said, as if aware for the first time that we were alone in the room. 'They all left.'

I understood that. Murder had been done and these were not men to plead self-defence or to stand trial…nor to go, as Nurse Jeffries had, to the compound.

'It wasn't like the old days,' he said.

His hand dropped away from me. He went down the bar and hesitated by the telephone. Then he turned and went out the door. I waited for a few minutes. Then I went down to the phone. The switchboard said, 'Sorry, sir, the lines are still out of order…' and I said, 'You'd better listen to me.' Ten minutes later Larsen arrived.

XIII

EVEN HAD THE phone been working, it would never have occurred to me to call Jerry Muldoon, although, legally, Jasper's death should have been his concern. And I wasn't thinking of getting a story, either. I was lost in an emotional wilderness. I only hoped that Larsen would know what to do—that there was something that could be done. Waiting for him, I prayed that Mary Carlyle would not walk in, bearing some news for me. Mary had liked Sam Jasper. And that was not Sam on the floor, that sticky mould of red aspic…nor, worse, had it been Sam in the moments before he died. I could never tell Mary what had happened here. But I could tell Larsen—in his way, he too was a dead man.

I went behind the bar and poured myself a huge brandy.

I was halfway through it when Larsen arrived. He came in with half a dozen men and, while they inspected the body—gingerly, at first—he came directly over to me.

He said, 'You were right to call me, Harland.'

'I thought I might be. Have a drink?'

His cold eyes flickered.

'The bartender left too,' I said.

'I'm going to need your help, Harland.'

I poured Larsen a drink. He didn't refuse it. When I'd first seen him, he'd sipped very slowly at a beer; things were changed. They were taking Sam Jasper out on a rubber sheet and, as they stepped, their heels made squishing sounds in the congealing blood.

'How can I help?'

'The men he fought with…who killed him. I want you to identify them.'

'I didn't see the fight. I told you, I—'

'The men who were in the bar earlier,' he said.

'I don't know if I can.'

'I guess you'll co-operate. You phoned me.'

'No, I don't mean I won't…I'm not sure I can. I didn't know any of them by name or—'

He nodded crisply; said, 'Understand this. You can't protect anyone. I'm not talking about a criminal charge here, this isn't crime and punishment. These locals are…independent types. They won't come in voluntarily, we'll have to find them. All of them. And they'll be hiding, thinking they are guilty of murder or—'

'Guilty? It strikes me that if anyone on this island is guilty of anything—'

'Don't be antagonistic,' he said. Then he took his spectacles off and rubbed his eyes. He looked at me, for the first time, without the lenses between us. He seemed more human. He said, 'Guilt? I know about guilt. I think every one of us, working on this thing, feels guilty. Sometimes, Harland...sometimes I feel guilt so heavy that it's like a shroud draped over me. I have to stop whatever I'm doing and take a deep breath. And doing that, I only manage to inhale the guilt, it gets in my lungs, inside me. I'm not a robot, Harland. I thought I was a patriot...but a guilty patriot. Now...well, now we do what we can.' He put the spectacles back on, as if hiding behind them. He took a slug of brandy. He was waiting for me to speak.

I said, 'I only know what the bartender told me...'

Larsen nodded impatiently.

'He... Sam Jasper...was inhumanly strong. He was insane, of course, but when the knives went into him he scarcely seemed to notice, he—'

'I know,' Larsen snapped. 'I don't need an account of the affair, I know what...they...can do.'

'They?'

He ignored that.

He said, 'Do you know if any of them were...wounded?'

'No. But Sam was fighting with them...and he had attacked a woman... so I think we can assume he inflicted some damage.'

Larsen sighed, nodded; said, 'I want you to describe every one of the men who were in this room, as best you can. Then I'll want you to identify them as we bring them in. We have to find them, and we have to do it in the next couple hours.'

'Is that possible?'

'Probably not.'

'And if you don't?'

'I'm not at liberty to discuss that. Just in case we do. If we don't...why, then, you'll know about it, just like everyone else. You won't like it.'

'This...disease, this madness. It's infectious, right?'

'Of course it's infectious, goddamn it! You've seen what happens.'

'And you have to find these men in time to treat them, to give them an antidote or inoculate them or whatever…'

'Whatever! You're wasting time.'

'I have to be sure just what I'm doing, just why I'm helping you, Larsen.'

'I told you, there will be no criminal charges. Isn't that enough?' He was looking at his watch. 'Please, Harland,' he said, quite softly.

'All right. I'll do the best I can.'

He nodded. 'We'll go up to the compound. You can dictate the descriptions in the car. I'm already having my men round up all the known regulars from this place, shrimpers, fishermen…it's just possible…'

One of the others came up to him, awaiting orders.

Larsen said, 'Get that blood up. All of it. We don't need… Then seal the place.' The man nodded. The blood, too? I thought. Larsen turned back to me. 'Well, come on, then.'

I finished my drink and followed him towards the door.

Larsen grabbed my arm and maybe he said it to impress the urgency on me, or to frighten me, or maybe he just felt like saying it. He said: 'None of us may get out of this, Harland…we may never leave this island. And, believe me, it won't be a tropical paradise then…'

XIV

DRINKING BLACK COFFEE from a white mug, I sat behind a table in a small whitewashed room feeling depressed and sick and tired. I had described the men—and the woman—as best I could and, although the descriptions seemed pitifully inadequate to me, Larsen seemed satisfied. I expect he had a file on everyone who lived on Pelican. From time to time he nodded, as if in recognition. There was something almost intimate in our relationship as I confided in him in the back seat of the car. When I mentioned the woman, he said, 'That'll be Sally…salad girl on the shrimp boats…ship's whore, to speak plainly,' and he also put names to the bearded man and the long-haired philosopher…several others—I paid little heed; perhaps I did not want these men to have names, to label those I was betraying and thereby make them individuals. My information was slight. My memory for details had been blurred, knocked out of focus, yet Larsen drew from me more than I thought I knew in the shadowed intimacy of that moving car. I had exhausted my recollections by the time we entered the compound.

We drove up to the main building, a single-storey affair with wings on either side, and Larsen escorted me to the whitewashed room. His men had not been idle. They started bringing the locals in as soon as I had taken my seat. Larsen stood beside me, behind the table. There was a gooseneck lamp there and he kept his hand on the flexible shaft, tilting it up and down. The bulb was very bright, very white against the wall. Larsen leaned forward; his face sprang out with an albedo to shame the moon, lips drawn back, clenched teeth geometrical. Dark veins in his neck defied the lurid glare. Then he leaned back into darkness and his face receded.

They brought the locals in one by one, two guards to each man and another guard on the door. They were angry, bewildered men, roused from bed or rousted from bars without explanation. The Cuban counter-man from the Fisherman's Café was one of the first; he looked sullen and dejected. Others who had heard the news looked sly and cunning. They all stared directly at me and I felt the lowest form of traitor, but I neither flinched nor looked away, convinced that I was doing what had to be done, despite these secret police tactics. I recognised several of the locals, but not from the Red Walls. I spoke to no one and they just glared at me, their faces distorted by elongated shadows thrown up from the lamp. Perhaps they could not identify me as they looked into that glare. I shook my head each time and Larsen sighed. Knowing I had to identify the men who had been involved, I nevertheless felt satisfaction each time I was able to negate one.

Then they brought in an old man and my memory snatched his face from the crowd at the bar, moulding it to the frightened countenance that stood before me in this silent inquisition. It was the old man who had spoken fondly of the old days. I hesitated. I felt Larsen stiffen beside me. The old man was squinting in the direct beam of the lamp and I didn't know if he could

see my features, but I knew he could see my head, at least in outline; that he would know if I nodded.

Larsen sensed my hesitation; he tilted the lamp higher and the old man's shadow sprang up the wall, crooked and distorted. The shadow seemed to have more substance than the man who cast it; there was a reality too dark to be illuminated in this room.

At last, I nodded.

The old man went rigid and Larsen's head snapped around towards me. I nodded again. Larsen flicked a glance at the guards. They took the old man by the arms and led him out. He was protesting in a high-pitched whine. I felt truly treacherous now and Larsen must have known this, for he placed his hand on my shoulder reassuringly and, as if to certify the humanity behind the gesture, he took his spectacles off for a moment.

Then they brought the next man in.

TWICE MORE, I nodded.

I must have confronted forty or fifty men and only three of them had been in the bar. The bearded man had not been found, nor the long-haired fellow with the political views. The woman had not been brought in, nor had the bartender, but in those cases the identification was definite and they may have found them without bringing them before me in my stark chamber. Then the steady stream of—what? Suspects? Victims? Carriers?...whatever, the stream of unfortunates brought there to stand before their tortured shadows began to taper off. In the first stormtrooper round-up Larsen's men had gathered up the unsuspecting and the innocent, but those who had been involved had already gone into hiding with, from their point of view, good reason—a man had been killed, one old, unarmed man had been stabbed to death by a mob and they had no desire to stand trial on that count. They were terrified by the bizarre aspects of the thing and, even discounting the murder, they knew that Nurse Jeffries had, under somewhat similar circumstances, been forced to go to the mysterious compound. They were not inclined to listen to the reasoning of authority and, even if they had, the time element

was against that approach. I couldn't blame them for going into hiding. But while they hid, the disease was incubating.

———

'HOW LONG DOES it take?' I asked.

Larsen and I were alone behind the table. The guard on the door had his back to us, hands clasped, looking down the corridor. No one had been brought in for the last ten minutes.

'What?'

'For the disease to take effect?'

'That's not...' He paused, leaning towards me so that his face came into the light as if he now were being identified, waiting for my dreaded nod. 'Oh, hell, it's a bit late in the game to play classified information, isn't it? I appreciate your help, Harland. The time...it varies according to the subject's weight and metabolism and, to a lesser degree, the body area where the...infection... was transferred. Say an average of...three hours.'

'That soon?'

'That soon,' he said, playing with the lamp, manipulating the shadows, twisting the flexible neck from side to side in his strong hands. I felt the same need to do something with my own hands. I got my pipe out and began to fill it carefully. He twisted the lamp and I stuffed tobacco in the bowl and lit it. A great cloud of smoke billowed out and hung over us. I remembered how Larsen had spoken of the cloud of guilt that often enveloped him. The drifting smoke made filigreed shadows up the wall. The shadows moved; they were not as enduring as guilt.

He was fairly strangling the lamp.

'It must be very virulent,' I said.

'Of course. Harland, it's a disease such as the world has never known. A disease that never should have been known...and we created it here.'

'What is it? Viral?'

'Chemical.'

Chemicals that warp the fabric of the mind... I said, 'Chemical? But how can that be contagious?'

Larsen dropped his head, twisting his own neck just as he'd twisted the lamp. He said, 'I don't know. But it is.' The light, reflecting from his taut face, seemed to come from within his skull. 'It's directly infectious, by contact. It's not...well, it's not the Black Death, say. It won't sweep across the world and decimate the population. Thank God for that. And yet, in its way it's far more horrible. It's so—' he sought the word '—so personal! Yes, that's it, exactly. Personal.' The word itself seemed anathema to this bureaucratic man. 'It goes beyond disease, Harland; it reaches into the realm of superstition and snatches up the stuff of legend, the dark fears that evolved with man. Werewolves, Harland...and vampires...' His face rose and fell as if under heavy blows. He looked sick. He said, 'These men...the men who contract this thing...officially, in the reports, they are termed subjects of Chemically Modified Behaviour. Informally...' he looked at me. 'We call them ghouls.'

I winced.

He said, 'An ugly word, and not just terminology. Yet when you've seen them...it is a word that caught on quite easily, amongst the guards and attendants, at first...until even the doctors use it. I use it. You...' He looked at me with a hint of a smile. 'You, no doubt, will use it in your story...'

'You know who I am, then?'

'... if you ever get to write it.'

No threat was intended in his words—no threat from him. I puffed and smoke flowed laterally across the table, crossing the lamp like clouds shredding before the face of the moon.

I said, 'How soon must the antidote be administered?'

Larsen looked as if he didn't understand the question. His thin lips drew back from his teeth and he snapped the light off. From the sudden shadows, he said, 'Not my field... I only know we have to have them before the damned thing takes effect. And...' he looked at his watch. 'I don't guess we're going to do it.'

He stood up and moved around the end of the table.

'I have things to arrange,' he told me. 'Will you wait here? They may bring a few more in before it's too late.'

'Of course,' I said.

He nodded and walked out. The guard saluted. I heard his footsteps drum hollow down the corridor and I didn't envy him his task...the arrangements he must make.

———

MY PIPE HAD gone out.

I struck a match and re-lit it and, as if that flare had been a signal, the guard on the door turned and stepped into the room. I had supposed he was there to make sure I didn't leave but, with proper deference, he said, 'What's going to happen next, sir?'

I gaped at him and he blushed. He was quite young.

'Oh, I realise I'm not cleared for classified information, sir, but...you know how it is...a man can't work in a place like this without getting a pretty good idea of what's going on. And my wife will be worried, I haven't been able to call her...I just wanted some idea of how long we'd be quarantined...'

I realised that Larsen and I had come in with such a flurry of haste that he had not explained the situation to the guard—or perhaps disdained informing a subordinate of anything. The young man obviously thought I was one of them. It was a natural enough mistake. Larsen and I had been collaborating as equals and he had even deferred to me on deciding which of the men brought in had been infected. The guard probably thought me an expert in detecting symptoms of the disease before they became apparent to others. It was too good a chance to pass up.

I said, 'I can't tell you that,' trying to sound just curt enough to be authoritative without discouraging him.

'I'm sorry sir.'

He started to turn away.

'A bad business,' I said.

'Yes, sir. Very bad.'

'I just arrived...from the other laboratory...' I said. He showed no signs of disbelief. 'I've been in such a rush, I haven't had time to get the details. How did the first...subject...escape, do you know? The one who broke through the fence?' I held my breath. He didn't doubt me at all.

'Oh, Jefferson,' he said. 'Why, he broke the restraining straps. He'd been taken to the laboratory for an examination or something and someone slipped up; didn't use the reinforced straps, I guess.'

'Damned inefficiency.'

He blinked at me; said, 'Worse than inefficiency, if you'll pardon my saying so, sir. I guess maybe you don't know about Duncan?' I shook my head. 'Johnny Duncan. Friend of mind. Hell of a nice guy, Duncan. He was on the door, tried to stop the ghoul. Jefferson, I mean, sir. Only it's hard to call one of them by their name...by the name they had when they were human, you know? Makes it seem worse, somehow. Anyway, Duncan tried to stop him and the...and Jefferson tore his arm damn near off. It was just hanging there by a few ropes of tendon. Right arm, it was. Poor Duncan, he was right-handed; had to use his left hand when he shot himself...'

'Shot himself?'

'Left-handed.'

He seemed to think this sinistral suicide more deplorable than had it been dextral; thus had morality been compromised and mutated in this place.

'Funny, you know...I was there by that time; I felt as if I ought to stop him from shooting himself, but he just looked at me and I couldn't do a thing. Even if it meant I got in trouble over it...couldn't do a thing. He put the gun to his head. He was in terrible pain, what with his arm torn off like that, but it wasn't the pain...it was knowing he was gonna turn ghoul. Hell of a guy. He said goodbye to me; made me feel awful. Then he blew his brains out. Wasn't married, Duncan; that's one thing.'

'But...the antidote...'

'Oh, you don't have to tell me that, sir.' He looked shy...maybe sly. He said, 'I know there's no antidote.'

I looked down at my glowing pipe and pretended that the alarm passing over my face was due to a congested stem. Slowly, I said, 'These subjects...the ones I was able to identify, and the nurse...how are they being...treated?'

'Oh, it's painless, sir. No need to worry about that. One of the docs gives 'em an injection, it's over in a few seconds.' He smiled at me. He was really quite young, his cheeks fuzzy, an innocent young man assuring me that murder was done efficiently and painlessly.

He said, 'That's what you meant when you said, antidote, huh? Funny how you scientists always use words that mean less than they ought. Meaning no offence, sir. Euphemism, is it? Well, anyhow, I guess that Duncan figured a bullet was just as painless as a shot in the arm, and a whole lot quicker. Or maybe he was afraid they wouldn't give him the shot, come to think of it; that they'd let him turn ghoul and study him in place of Jefferson...'

'Yes,' I said. I felt a band of sickness tighten across my diaphragm. I had just condemned, with a nod, three men to death. And yet, if I hadn't...it was mercy killing, benevolent condemnation, I could justify it...and yet—

The guard was saying, 'Maybe they would of, too, far as that goes. Of course, that was before all these other guys got infected. Got more ghouls than they know what to do with, now; can't study all of them. I don't know about the other lab...the one you come from...fact is, I didn't even know there was another one. But we only got three cells here strong enough to hold 'em and you can't put 'em in together or they'll eat each other. Guess they never reckoned on having more than three at once. So the only humane thing to do...but you know about that, sir.'

On abrupt impulse, I stood up. Yes, I knew about that...now; the knowledge was stalking around like a footpad in my soul.

'It seems to me that you know a good deal more than you're cleared for,' I said, jaws tight.

The guard looked frightened.

'I'm sorry, sir,' he said, blanching.

I pointed at him with my pipe-stem, paused, then sighed.

'Where is Elston now?' I asked.

'He's in his lab, sir. It's just down the hall, third door on the right,' he said quickly, hoping that other matters would intervene between us. I gave him a crisp nod and brushed past. He saluted. I walked down the corridor with my heels drumming just like Larsen's.

XV

ELSTON WAS IN his laboratory, but he was not working; he was seated on a high stool, all sunk up in himself. I had the impression of a dunce at a blackboard. I closed the door and he looked up. 'You,' he said, without surprise. He was beyond surprise. I walked over to him and knocked my pipe out against the edge of a shelf. Test tubes rattled in its rack and arcane fluids sloshed about in beakers.

'You should have contacted me sooner,' I said.

'I wish to God I had.'

'Will you tell me about this…thing?'

'It's too late.'

'It could prevent a recurrence elsewhere.'

'I doubt…' he said, and paused, as if his doubt were a categorical statement. His eyes turned about, looking for some object deserving of that doubt. 'I doubt that even the government would attempt such a thing again. I am not a brave man, Harland…but there does not exist a torture that would ever again induce me to co-operate.'

'But you never intended this.'

'My God, no! I…never…' His voice trailed off. He lifted a murky beaker and looked into it, as if he expected to find resolution there, or mirage; reading the runes of science. He moved the beaker and the fluid sloshed about; peering at it, he seemed to be contemplating a rare vintage, a distillate of evil. I felt that the fluid should be roiling and giving off vapours; had he suddenly drained it on a compulsive whim, I would not have been surprised.

Abruptly he began to speak, driven to explain and exonerate himself.

'In my research into chemical lobotomy, I discovered a process by which to make men mindless. I had not sought this result, it was a side effect, accidental. These…subjects…were totally obedient and docile, but they were immensely powerful, for they no longer had inhibitions of any sort. They no longer knew the limitations of self-preservation; were no longer confined by human instinct. They could, upon command, perform tasks that amazed me…'

'The man who broke his arm lifting against an unliftable weight?'

'You know of that? Yes, that is an example. No normal man could exert enough pressure to break his own skeleton. But, feeling no pain and totally uninhibited, a man treated by this process became a superman.'

'But to what purpose?'

'To my purpose, to my intentions, it was merely a side effect. I sought to make the incurable manageable, that was all. The purpose put to this by the agency, however…the dark vision of those fiends…they foresaw an army of living robots…'

'Of course. Men without fear, unable to feel pain, totally obedient…'

'That was the idea. An army that would walk through enemy fire, keep on walking even though they had been shot several times, had limbs blown off…even crawling, legless, to carry out the attack…only an absolutely mortal wound could stop them; even dead they could move for a few moments. It is shock that stops a wounded man, but only death itself could stop these poor creatures. But there was a flaw. Nearly mindless, they could make no decisions, could not discriminate between friend and foe; nor were they belligerent. They were unstoppable but they were useless. I believed that we had come to a dead end, and I was glad. But the devious minds that controlled me…those minds must be as warped as those of my creations, their thoughts twisted through hideous configurations which bleed out humanity and distil pure evil…' He looked directly at me. 'The next stage…I balked at this, they threatened…well, no matter; I am a coward; I did as they wished.'

Elston shook his head from side to side.

'Harland, I took the obedience out. I made these creatures savage and bestial, instilling bloodlust and ferocity…the very factors that my original research had been designed to quell. It was not a difficult thing, merely a matter of finding the proper chemical balance. And again we seemed to have reached a dead end. Again I was glad. In taking the obedience from them, I made them unmanageable.'

'Then you were back where you started…'

'Not quite. In one day, these men that controlled me, in one day those minds had realised a use for this…monstrosity.'

'I can see none.'

'Nor did I. But we are not like them. By this time, other scientists, scientists who thought like them, were working with me. They had access to all my material. It was one of those men who discovered that this state of mindless bloodlust could be transmitted from man to man, from host to victim. The chemicals that transfigured the mind ran rampant through the body. They infected the blood, the saliva…and could be transmitted, like any disease…like leprosy, like plague…but far, far more terrible. It was communicable madness.'

He put his hands to his face, dragging his fingers down his cheeks.

'I still don't see…'

'No, you wouldn't. I…again I protested. But by this time the work could have continued without me—or so I told myself, to justify what I did. And it was hideous. The first man we treated tore his eyes out. Obviously not a trait desirable in a soldier. We corrected that. We tested their aggression by putting them in a cage together.' He closed his eyes, remembering what he had seen in those cages. 'To find the proper balance, you see. They did not want these…ghouls, they call them…they did not want them to be so ferocious that they killed. That would have defeated their purpose…'

'And that purpose was?'

Elston ignored me. He continued, 'Like rabid dogs…that was the desirable condition…wounding and then leaving the victim alive, so that he, in turn, would become…one of them. The madness would spread by geometrical progression. I say madness, I might say bestiality…there is no term for them, really. Ghouls—they call them ghouls—they caused them to be created and then call them that. They are not cannibals, yet they would eat human flesh as any other…nor necrophagics, although they would devour a corpse…quite casually, these mindless things would devour…themselves.' He paused for a few moments, head cocked as though listening for the echo of his words from amongst the vials and beakers. 'But this is no more than a side effect of their condition. They might just as well eat nothing and starve to death. A side effect, just as their fear of water. I could have removed that inhibition, of course. It was deemed wise to let it remain a way to control them, surrounding them by water, confining them; useful on this island and later, in other places…'

'What places, Doctor?'

Again he ignored me. 'Well, it was done. I had regulated their fury to the proper degree. That fury was contagious. In the initial instance, when the disease is induced by injection, the time period between treatment and the onset of the violence can be regulated—that is, knowing the subject's weight and metabolism, I can regulate the dosage, leaving the disease like a slow fuse within him. But when it is transmitted directly from man to man, with the disease at full virulence in the host, it will take effect within hours in the victim. This was just as they wished it; it suited their scheme.'

'But what was that scheme?' I asked.

He looked at me, his fingers still dragging at his cheeks, drawing the flesh down.

'Their plan, Harland,' he said. 'Their plan was…to infect enemy prisoners of war!'

I saw it then. My flesh crawled.

'They would be treated to go berserk in, say, a month's time. Then allowed to escape, or be dealt in an exchange of prisoners, with the abomination smouldering in them. You can imagine the results. They laughed, those men…my masters…they laughed, thinking of a plague of ghouls behind the enemy lines. It would be most effective. The carriers would no doubt be killed, but not before inflicting wounds which would, in turn, create a second wave of monsters.'

'My God,' I whispered. 'The cold calculation…'

'Think of the panic, the confusion, the horror, when the enemy troops… and then the civilians…began to go berserk in ever-increasing numbers. By the time they realised what was causing it, if they ever did, it would be too late. The enemy army would be demoralised, if not destroyed. Perhaps the nation, itself…destroyed as surely as the minds of the infected. Then it would be a simple matter of quarantining the enemy country or holding the battle lines firm and waiting for the self-destruction. Such was their plan. They were greatly pleased with it…'

'It could escalate…to what proportions? Where would it stop?'

'We had to predict that. The…ghouls…would not survive for long. They cannot take care of themselves, they neglect the normal bodily needs.

Those not killed outright would die, in due course, of accident, starvation, dehydration. But to say how long it would take…' He shrugged.

I heard a gun go off from somewhere without the compound.

'I guess we'll find that out now,' I said.

Elston said, 'What?' and then he understood and said, 'Why, yes; so we shall…' Incredibly, there was a spark of scientific interest in his eyes…interest detached from guilt and regret. I turned and walked away and I don't think he even noticed. His motives in summoning me had been laudable, but he was yet a scientist interested in his work. The horror of it all…well, as Elston might have put it: that was a side effect, no more. He had talked into me, as if I were a recording device and now, to him, I was switched off. I think, of the two, I respected Larsen more.

——

I WANDERED THE corridors for awhile. There was a great deal of activity, both naval and civilian types rushing about; no one paid me any notice. From time to time I heard gunfire. Presently I returned to the whitewashed room. The guard was no longer on the door. I went in and sat down behind the table. A few minutes later Larsen came in.

'Where in hell have you been?' he asked.

'I took a walk. I don't suppose there was anything wrong in that, was there? Or am I under restraint?'

'What's eating you, Harland?'

'There is no antidote.'

'Oh. How did you…oh, it doesn't matter. Yes, we're killing them. What else can we do? We have no facilities to lock up so many, even if we wanted to. Can't lock them up together, you know. Anyhow, it's best for them. Wouldn't you wish to be killed, if the alternative was becoming one of them?'

He was right, I supposed; or less wrong. I nodded, or shrugged. Right and wrong could not be taken in chunks, demarcated like the light and shadow of that room.

He said, 'We're shooting them as we find them; it's too late for anything else.'

'Are you finding many?'

'Too many.'

He leaned out into the corridor and said something. Then he stepped aside and two uniformed guards came in with a stretcher. There was a body on the stretcher, covered with a sheet; not moving. They slid the stretcher on the table and Larsen pulled the sheet down. I looked at a dead man's face.

'Recognise him? Was he in the Red Walls?'

I studied the face very carefully. In death, the man looked normal enough. But I had never seen him before.

'No,' I said.

'Are you sure?'

'Positive.'

'You know what that means?'

'Of course. The second stage has begun.'

'So we no longer need your help, Harland. It was worth a try. I never really expected…'

'How fast will it escalate?'

'God knows. If every one of the men Jasper infected—except for the three we got in time—if they infect even two more…I can't say. I suppose it's a matter of mathematics.' He turned to the guards. 'Take that away,' he said, and they jumped forwards and lifted the stretcher. 'Got to burn the bodies,' he said, to me. 'It can spread from a corpse. If a dog or a rat got at one of the bodies…the dead flesh still carries the change, you see. We learned that in the early experiments, before we were using human…volunteers. The catalyst, being chemical, doesn't need a living host. It can lurk in dead tissue and be ingested…got to burn them. I wouldn't even trust them to the worms.' The strain was showing on Larsen. He looked even thinner than before, his eyes were bigger behind his spectacles and his close-cropped hair stuck up in clumps.

'The worst part will be the women,' he said.

I didn't get that, for a moment; said, 'There was only the one woman, the salad girl…' but Larsen shook his head.

'No, the others. These men have wives, girlfriends…no bond of love will save them, if they are together when…' He paled suddenly. 'No, the worst part won't be the women,' he said.

'What, then?'

'The children,' Larsen said.

And horror ran, like malaria, in my veins…

XVI

LIKE DEMONS IN Hell, the guards stood around the rim of the smouldering pit. They had dug the pit behind the laboratory, not far from the fence, and they were burning the corpses. The lab was equipped with an incinerator, but it was not large enough for the grisly task. As they had not anticipated needing cells for more than three at one time, so they had not figured on having to burn so many. The stench was appalling. I stood in the open back door of the building, staring out and smoking my pipe; fearful and wondering.

Black smoke, shot through with red flashes, billowed up from the pit. The sky was pale in the east, making the smoke seem blacker and thicker as it coiled up in ebony ropes and plumes, a Stygian cable anchored in the pit. I watched as two guards carried a corpse to the rim. They looked as if they stood at the doors to Hell, washed with the red glow. They threw the body into the inferno. A wave of increased heat struck me; sparks spun from the incandescent crater and threads of orange weaved through the writhing black funnel. One of the guards slapped at his thigh. A spark had struck him. And then they brushed their hands together, gazing down into the fiery pit for a moment before stepping away, workmen with a task well done. They might have been advertising beer on television…a hard job done and now it's time to relax with an ice cold…

Larsen stepped up beside me, his thin nostrils twitching.

'Jesus,' he said.

Then he grinned and said, 'That pipe of yours sure does stink.'

I blinked at him, astounded, and then, suddenly, we were both laughing at his joke. It wasn't forced laughter, we were honestly convulsed by his wit. He wrinkled his nose. Laughing, I said, 'If we get a midget ghoul, you

can stuff him in my briar,' and Larsen howled with glee. I puffed away and the deep bowl of my pipe glowed and billowed in feeble imitation of the fiery pit.

Then, abruptly, we were not laughing.

It had been a strange impulse and only dimly grasped, yet I doubt I have ever laughed with such good humour as I did that night by the smouldering pit...

'HOW MANY?' I asked.

'Nine,' he told me. 'Not counting the nurse.'

He rubbed his lean jaw. One side of his face seemed to have ignited in the seething glow; the other was as dark as the smoke, the muscles in his cheek twisting in turbulent coils—a stormy face in a volcanic dawn. I knew that my own face reflected the same disunion, cleft by the chiaroscuro of the flames. Like carnal mirrors, we reflected one another.

'I don't know if we should be encouraged or discouraged by the numbers,' he said. 'Don't know what they signify. The more we get might mean the fewer left...or it might mean we are simply drawing from a larger pool...'

'I know. We don't know how many men Jasper actually wounded, but even if only three or four got away...three could become nine...or twelve... even with minimal numbers...' Even as I spoke, I was aware that I was thinking strictly of numbers as a statistic; not of the men they represented. And that I had to. And then, the third stage... 'Thank God we're on an island with a limited population.'

'I may decide to evacuate,' he said. He looked at me as if he wanted my advice. 'If we can't control the spread...but we'll have to make damned sure none of the evacuees is infected. Some system of quarantine before boarding the boat. I'm not sure I want that responsibility, that decision... Well, it may be a moot point. They may not let us leave.'

'If you do...we do...what about them? The...ghouls?' The word had a bitter taste; I was appalled that I'd used it. 'Will you just abandon them here?'

He looked at me with fire running down his profile.

'That decision will come from higher up…and I'm just as glad of that.'
He rubbed his neck; his splayed fingers cast slender shadows and his hand
glowed red; the heat rose and fell as if some terrible bellows pulsed in the pit.

'It's the ones who stayed in town that are hard to flush out…and have
more opportunity to infect others,' he said. His lips twisted the words out.
'Most of the ones we got had come to the beach or inland. We've started a
house-to-house search but the damnedest part is that we can't tell who is
infected and who isn't until it takes effect.'

'Are there no symptoms that show before?'

'I asked Elston about that, a few minutes ago. None that he knows of.
He's…a dedicated man. He begged me not to burn all the corpses…to save
a few for him to dissect.'

'Maybe he hopes to find an antidote.'

'That's a charitable supposition,' Larsen said.

He looked very human then, with his face inhumanly blazing in the
glow. I wondered if he knew that Elston had written me. He knew who I
was and maybe he'd known all along; maybe he, too, had wanted it stopped,
wanting it helplessly from within the cage of his duty, the bureaucratic web
that trapped his life. I felt the absolute helplessness of the man, the frustration; his life and his volition had been frozen in the ice of obedience, trapped
as surely as a heart within a ribcage, mind within a skull. I thought I might
ask him—we had become friends, I think, in some twisted fashion—but as
I was about to speak gunfire sounded off to the side.

We both looked.

A man—a ghoul…the word asserted its rights in my mind…was running along the outside of the fence—not running as if frightened, for they
knew no fear, but running as if he had started to run by pure chance and
was too mindless to halt; running by inertia, as the planets run around
the stars.

Three navy men in white uniforms were running after him, pausing to
fire from time to time. They were hitting him. I saw blood spray out twice
and once the impact of a bullet drove him to his knees, but he bounded up
immediately and ran on. Immune to shock, he would run until the bullets

broke his legs—and then he would crawl—until a shot pierced his heart or brain; he moved by descriptive law.

The fence took an outward turn just behind the pit. The ghoul ran into it. The three pursuers slowed and one went to his knees to take aim. Then the ghoul clenched his fist through the mesh of the fence and tore it open. I could hear the heavy metal snap. Beside me, Larsen snorted. The ghoul slid through the broken fence and bounded into the compound. The guards scattered back from the pit, darting silhouettes against the red glare and red-rimmed shadows against the smoke. The ghoul loped towards the inferno. He didn't see the pit, or he disregarded it. He ran right up to the rim and past it—not falling, but running into the flames. A moment later he came up from the other side, clothing ablaze and flesh melting from his bones. He was climbing out. He slipped and slid back, then came crawling out again. His hair was burning. The three navy men were through the broken fence now and, standing side by side, like a firing squad, they shot into his body. They backed off, shooting. Blood sizzled like fat in a frying pan. Slowly the creature slipped back into the pit and did not emerge again.

One of the guards laughed.

'Saves carrying that bugger,' he said.

***

I PASSED A hand across my eyes. I understood his jest, his coarse and callous attitude. God help me, I understood. It had been the same as laughing with Larsen at my pipe and I, too, had started to think of them as ghouls, to reason with the mentality of the Inquisition and to loathe them with instinctive fear and hatred that obscured all pity. This was primordial fear, a horror that should have been left behind when man evolved from the slime…and now rose up again to brutalise and numb the emotions, as contagious as any disease.

The fire flared and crackled merrily as it fed on this new kindling. I was sickened. I felt I could stay there no longer. I turned to Larsen. His face was like a stone idol with living eyes. Sparks swirled and darted through the night; he looked on his fiery celebration as helplessly as any worshipped god.

'I'll go back to town,' I said.

Larsen looked at me; for a moment he didn't seem to know who I was or why I was there.

'If I may?'

'You're no prisoner, Harland. No more than are we all. But you'll be safer here.'

'No, I'll go.'

'As you like. I can't spare an escort.'

I hadn't thought of that. Numbed by the horror, I had forgotten the danger. Or it was danger too grim to register on the mind.

Larsen said, 'I'll check out a rifle for you, if you like.'

He must have thought I might have qualms about that, for he added, 'It will be safer for you if you're carrying a gun. My men are scared. They might not be too hesitant about shooting a stranger walking alone. The rifle will be like a safe conduct, I guess.'

He stared directly at me.

The rifle was offered as a talisman, not a weapon.

'Thank you,' I said, not for the rifle.

I had never shot a man. I didn't know if I could. But it would be comfortable to have the option.

XVII

'JACK! THANK GOD you're all right!'

The front door of the jail had been locked and when Jerry opened it he stepped quickly back. He had a gun in his hand. I looked at his gun and he regarded my rifle. Mary spoke from behind him and, a bit sheepish, Jerry holstered the gun. Just a bit sheepish, like a thin veneer laid over grim determination. He said, 'I had a look for you at the Red Walls; place was swarming with…patrols, I guess. But they wouldn't tell me anything.'

'They don't know much.'

Jerry was locking the door again; said, 'Do you?'

'Yes; most of it.'

I leaned the rifle against the wall. I was drained with the tension of that solitary walk back from the compound, my nerves like vibrant webs under my skin. Jerry was waiting for me to tell him what I had discovered. Mary did not look so eager to hear it. I gazed out the window at the dawn through which I'd passed. It was a glorious morning, with sunrise ringing golden blows against the shield of dusk. A fan of pale light spread out in the eastern sky, opening slowly, as if reluctant to reveal the day. These things were better wrapped in darkness.

'You've seen Elston?' Mary asked.

'I saw him. And Larsen. I've been in the compound; I saw some other things that...I'd rather not have known.'

'What in hell is going on?' Jerry asked. He was fingering the bolt on the door. 'They've had vans down here with loudspeakers, telling everyone to stay inside and keep the doors locked.' He slid the bolt back and forth, as if playing a game of chance with the lock. 'I got a special visit from one of Larsen's men...polite sort of guy...but he sort of told me to stay right here and keep out of it. Whatever it is.'

'And he heard shooting,' Mary put in.

'There's nothing you can do, Jerry,' I told him. 'It's better to stay here. And keep Mary here. This thing...well, it's a highly contagious disease...of a sort...'

'Of a sort?'

And then, with Jerry swearing from time to time and Mary's eyes growing huge and frightened, I told them what I'd found out and what I'd seen. I was grabbing words in clumps and throwing them out, glad to be rid of them; but they left hollow impressions behind. When I finished we stood silent for a time. I could feel the pattern of my nerves tingling; felt as if the schematics of my nervous system were visible, glowing through my flesh.

Jerry twisted his hat brim. 'I wonder if they really would have done that?' he mused. 'If they really would have used it as a weapon?'

I said, 'Probably not. The people who develop these things aren't the ones who have the say on using them.'

He nodded, holding his hat so that his head dipped from it, exposing a wrinkled brow. He said, 'I was in the army. Didn't mind the idea of fighting. Never would of wanted to do a thing like that, though; ain't no enemy deserves a thing like that.'

'If only Elston had been more...courageous,' Mary said.

'A strange man, Elston. I'm not sure...'

'Well, I reckon we'd best get Mary off the island,' said the sheriff. He had slipped into his redneck accent; I wasn't sure if it was deliberate.

'I doubt they'll let anyone leave until...'

'Hell, they can't tell me not to go to the police cruiser. I'm still the law here...outside the compound, leastwise.'

'They wouldn't let me use the Coast Guard boat,' Mary said. 'Different thing, that is.'

'We could try,' I said.

'Why, sure. Anyone tries to stop us, I'll arrest him.' He gave us a grim smile. 'I'll run you two over to the Keys. Guess I ought to come back, myself...although I can't say I'm too damned keen on the idea.'

'There's no reason to; nothing you can do.'

'That's not the point, so much. Just that the sheriff hadn't ought to run out on a thing like this.' He was still mangling his Stetson; it was on the back of his head now, battered and twisted. His dedication was twisted, too; his sense of duty and obligation. I knew how he felt. Some insane part of my mind was telling me that I should stay on Pelican and see this out. It was more than getting a story, far more than a dedication to my work, but the turnings of such a resolve were too devious to follow, too sigmoidal to trace through the mind. I wanted to go.

Jerry said, 'There's no antidote at all, eh?'

'They've not found one.'

'And no one knows how long it will take for this thing to run its course?'

'No.'

He shook his head. 'Hell of a thing to do to a nice little island like this. Nice people. Well, let's go down to the boat, let's just see if we can...'

'Jerry...if they let us leave...I don't want you to come back here,' Mary said.

'Aw...we'll talk about that later.'

He moved to the door, drew the bolt and hesitated; then he threw the door open and stood back, with his gun ready. The street was empty. From the doorway we could look across the waterfront and out into the harbour. A large swordfish was hanging on a scale on the dock, hoisted up to be weighed and measured. Flecks of blue and green glinted in the drying skin. It would never be weighed now, never mounted. It seemed a shame. It was a big one; it had been caught at the wrong time, a death so vain it did not even bolster a fisherman's vanity. The harbour was jammed with bobbling boats and there were navy boats crossing back and forth across the approaches. Jerry stepped into the street and looked both ways. A patrol was moving down the front, going away from us. There was no one else in sight. Mary and I moved out behind Jerry. I had forgotten the rifle; I went back for it. I followed Mary out and, as I did so, a loudhailer boomed from a naval gunboat.

'Turn back! This island is under quarantine! Turn back at once!' We saw the gunboat but we couldn't see the reason for the command. Then, as we watched, a fishing boat slid into view, coming from the south. Jerry squinted at it. He said, 'Why, that's John Tate's boat. What's he doing out there?'

I said, 'Tate? He told me he often ties up at one of the coves to the south, instead of using the harbour.'

'He still does that? Old Tate! Used to do some free trading. Never very much; little rum or Havana. Hasn't run a thing in ten years but he still clings to the image.'

Tate's boat continued on its course.

I could see him on the bridge, a spindly old man with one eye and plenty of memories. The gunboat had veered towards him, intersecting his course, a white bow wave breaking from the grey prow. Tate spun the wheel and his wooden boat cut sharply to starboard. I had only met him the one time, but he'd left an impression. I could imagine him grinning with ferocious glee as he pitted his seamanship against the power of authority once again. He had run contraband past customs before and it was just like the old days—except he must have thought it a game, now, when he was doing nothing he thought illegal and could toy with them without fear of punishment or confiscated cargo. His small boat seemed to stand up on its stern as it changed course. The gunboat cut back, ponderous by comparison, and massive. The two vessels were dangerously close. The loudhailer sounded again. I couldn't make out the words. Beside me, Jerry cursed violently. 'They're gonna ram him!' he shouted.

'Oh my God!' Mary cried.

I saw Tate raise his fist, shaking it vehemently at the man on the ridge of the gunboat. He didn't believe they were serious, I thought; he believed that some inexperienced navy captain was misjudging his approach and playing the game too close. Tate waved his gnarled fist, scolding the gunboat. The nimble wooden boat ducked down into a tough and the bow of the grey gunboat reared up. Tate's fist came down; he still thought it was a mistake, but he realised it was a serious mistake. Then the gunboat rammed him.

———

TATE'S FISHING BOAT went down within minutes.

The gunboat had taken the stern right off and veered away, like a bull hooking into a matador. I couldn't see Tate. He must have been knocked down by the impact. Fragments of wood and rope dragged back from the gunboat, festooning the high prow and the bows of Tate's boat pointed up to the sky and slid back and under. The water sighed as it closed.

The gunboat continued on.

Sailors looked back from the rails, but the boat never stopped. Jerry's head was thrust forwards, the cords in his thick neck standing out like dark ropes, his throat rigged by rage.

He said, 'They aren't going to pick him up.'

'No,' I said softly. 'They wouldn't take him aboard…that wasn't the idea.'

We looked, shading our eyes, but Tate never surfaced. Then looked at one another.

'So much for that idea,' Jerry said.

We went back to the jail.

———

MARY HAD BEGUN to sob hysterically. The sheriff put his hand on her shoulder and she clasped her own hand over his, her body vibrating. The tremors ran down Jerry's forearm.

'John Tate,' she whispered. 'Old pirate. He would have loved to live through this, wouldn't he? It would have made such a fine story…better than how he lost his eye…how he eluded the navy gunboat…' She smiled sadly.

'Or how he helped hang a man in the Red Walls,' I said, not knowing why I said it; it seemed such an insignificant thing, viewed against the backdrop of his own death.

Jerry began to pace the room, like a prisoner in his own jail. 'We're safe enough here,' he said. 'We'll just have to wait it out.'

'But how long?' Mary sobbed.

We had no answer to that.

Jerry said, 'I guess it could be…days…maybe weeks, even.' He looked at me for confirmation. I didn't know. He said, 'We could always lock ourselves in the cell; they couldn't get at us there.'

'Weeks…' I said. 'What about food? Supplies?'

'Lord! I never thought of that. We'll have to get some stuff in here.' The thought of preparing for a siege was not appealing.

'They may decide to evacuate…'

'Yeah, and they may not. We'd better not take a chance…that chance. There's a shop just down the front.'

'I think, if we're going out again, we'd better do it now. This is likely to get worse before it gets better…liable to spread until…well, I'll go with you.'

'No, you stay here with Mary.'

'Nothing I'd like better than not going out there again. But Mary will be safe enough here, with the door barred, and the two of us can carry a lot more. There's no sense in making more than one forage. And…we can watch each other's backs.'

'He's right, Jerry. I'll be okay here. Just…don't be very long.'

'You sure?'

'Yes,' she whispered. Jerry regarded her for a moment, then he nodded.

'Let's go,' he said, and we went.

XVIII

I STEPPED DELIBERATELY, as if my footfalls were ticking off the moments, punctuating the passage of time. Jerry preceded me through the deserted streets. The low sun blocked sharp patterns on the buildings, as clearly defined as the light in the whitewashed room, but my own shadow dragged reluctantly at my heels, as if cast from a different source—thrown from me by the glow of my fear. A low fog was clinging against the walls and a heavier fog came rolling out from a side-street, curling like a cat across Jerry's boots. He stumbled, as if he'd tripped on the mist. He held his gun at his side, pointing down. I quickened my pace to catch him up and we moved on together. The walk was a hundred yards, no more. It seemed eternal. We met no one.

MENDOZA'S MARKET WAS a dusty storeroom with shelves and glass-fronted counters stocked with tins of almost everything. The door wasn't locked. Jerry stood just inside the entrance and shouted for Mendoza, who lived above. There was no response. We looked around the gloomy room.

Jerry said, 'We should of made us up a shopping list. Well, grab one of these boxes and fill 'er up with whatever takes your fancy; might as well dine to our taste.'

He began plucking tins from the shelves. I crossed to the other side of the room and began raiding the shelves myself, paying little attention to what I took, just tossing things into a big cardboard box. I didn't expect we'd have much appetite. The box was quite heavy when it was full; I had to tuck the rifle under my arm and use both hands to lift it. Jerry had filled his box before I finished; he held it easily under one arm. We moved back through the cluttered room, the tins rattling in the boxes. At the door, I paused.

'How about tobacco?'

'Why, yes…we might feel the urge to do some smoking, at that. I think Mendoza keeps the tobacco in the counter at the back. Might grab a couple bottles of rum from back there, too; can't do any harm to have some rum. Might help, even.'

'I'll get it,' I said.

I lowered my box to the dusty floor and stepped to the back of the room. I saw a variety of tobacco, in all forms, in a glass display case. The rum bottles were on a shelf behind. I filled my pockets with tobacco and stepped around the end of the counter…and a white face loomed up from the shadows!

I TRIED TO scream.

My vocal chords rebelled; they stiffened like frozen iron in my throat and only a strangled gasp came from me. I recoiled. The butt of the rifle struck the glass case, shattering it. I distinctly heard each splinter of glass fall out, the tinkling sounds echoed by the rattle of tins as Jerry shifted the box. He was shouting something from the door, and I think I was shouting then, too; I know my mouth was open and a rushing filled my ears. I swung the rifle up before me, not aimed as weapon but crossed against my breast like a crucifix against a vampire.

Jerry shouted again.

'Move!' He was advancing towards me along the shelves.

But then I slumped against the broken case, my vitality sucked from me in the deflation of sudden terror. Jerry was behind me, one hand on my shoulder; the other thrust the pistol past me. I could feel the big man tremble. I shook my head. It took great concentration, my skull was heavy, my neck limp. By then I'd realised there was no danger…horror, yes, but no danger. The face had not moved towards me; I had inclined my head towards it as I reached for the rum and the white face had seemed to rise, thrown from the dark shadows as if buoyant from a heavy sea.

The man was dead, spread-eagled behind the counter as if nailed there by his final convulsions.

Jerry let his breath out slowly.

I was hollow. My energy, my life force, my very bones seemed to have been sucked from me into the vacuum of fear. I was still shaking my head—an act of inertia. I had thought the man alive, reaching for me—and I had been unable to flee, had never thought to use the rifle…had waited for his touch…

'Mendoza,' Jerry said.

The hand that had been trembling on my shoulder was firm now, solid as a stone, but the hand that gripped the gun had begun to shake as he lowered it.

He moved me aside and leaned over the corpse. He did not touch it. 'Looks like he might of died of natural causes,' he said. 'Heart attack, maybe...he wasn't young...'

'Yes, it looks that way.'

Jerry looked at me, face as white as Mendoza's.

'Isn't it remarkable?' he said. 'Here and now...a man dying of natural causes...it makes you see that life goes on.'

He paused, wondering if his statement had been absurd...or profound.

'I never killed anyone,' he said. Nor had he yet. But the gun was in his hand...he would have; he might have to. He was peering into my face. He said, 'Harland, do you think these...things...will go to Heaven?'

I gaped dumbly at him and he flushed; the question had been genuine.

'Yes,' I said. I held no brief for the hereafter, but I said, 'Yes.'

And he said, 'I'd like to think so...'

WALKING BACK DOWN the front with the heavy boxes, we met a patrol coming from the other direction. When they saw us they spread out and their rifles came up. They looked terrified—as terrified as we must have looked.

'Take it easy,' Jerry snapped.

'Don't come too close. Just move on.'

'Listen,' I said. 'There's a dead man in Mendoza's. We don't know he's one of...them...but you'd better send someone to get the body.'

He didn't look as if he understood.

'To burn it,' I said.

'Oh. Yeah. You just move on.'

We moved on. The patrol turned, watching us. Then they went on in the other direction. When we had come to the jail, I looked back. The patrol had moved on down the street, past Mendoza's and, as I looked, they turned to the right, inland...towards the compound. I hoped they wouldn't forget to send a van for Mendoza's body. I looked out at the harbour. There was some wood floating about, timber and planks, and an oily slick spreading slowly through the water. The swordfish still hung, neglected forever now, on the scales. The grey gunboats passed to and fro across the mouth of the harbour. How long? I wondered. How long would it be?

XIX

MARY WAS LOOKING out the window as we approached.

Framed in the window, her face seemed to be disintegrating, dissolving with fear. Her cheeks were pinched in and her eyes were huge and staring. Jerry waved but she didn't acknowledge the gesture. She turned, looking back into the room. Her profile spread like a pale wash against the glass. Then we had passed the window and I heard the bolt rasp free. Mary opened the door and stepped out. Jerry's shoulders twitched as, instinctively, he tried to comfort her in his arms, but found the laden box between them. Mary was crying.

'Hey, now…it's okay,' the sheriff said.

'It's not okay; nothing is okay.'

'We'll be all right. Just a question of—'

'Doctor Winston is here,' she said.

'Hey, that's great,' Jerry said. He went through the door. Winston was standing in the corner, smoking a cigar, hands clasped behind his back. He looked as if he were thoughtfully considering a diagnosis.

'Glad you made it,' Jerry said. He put the box on the desk. 'That you thought to come here.'

'Mary doesn't seem to think it such a good idea,' Winston said. He was calm enough, but he'd been chewing on the cigar; the wrapper had started to uncurl.

Jerry looked at the girl, blinking.

'Doctor Winston has been…wounded,' she said.

Jerry started, all his big body going taut.

'He hasn't touched me,' Mary added, quickly. 'He came to the door. I let him in. I was glad to see him…I didn't know he had been hurt…'

'How'd it happen, Doc?'

'Why, it was one of these lunatics that seem to be about. That's why I came down here…to see if you had any idea what is going on here? Something to do with the research in the compound, is it? I tried to phone there but couldn't get past the switchboard and, by the way, I've heard nothing from my nurse…'

'How long, Doc?'

'What? Well, I phoned there at—'

'How long is it since you were attacked?'

'Well, what does…or *does* it?' Comprehension came into the doctor's face. He took the cigar from his teeth. 'It does matter, eh? Apparently you know more about this than I. What is it, some sort of germ warfare?'

'Doc…how long?'

Winston winced at Jerry's tone. They were friends; he didn't understand it. He had paled slightly under his normal flush and Jerry's jaws were tight with great bands of muscle.

Winston said, 'Better part of an hour,' and he was watching the sheriff carefully, gauging his reaction. Winston was a big, heavy man; he looked to have a slow metabolism. I relaxed somewhat but, in relaxing, went icy cold. 'What is it, Jerry? What sort of thing is it? Am I liable to contaminate you by being here?' Jerry didn't know what to say.

I said, 'Let's have a drink.'

I think I'd managed to keep my voice normal. Jerry shot me a grateful glance. I opened a bottle of Mendoza's rum and Jerry fetched glasses. We weren't going to share the bottle with Winston. He was standing behind the desk and we stood opposite. Winston took a large swallow and licked his lips.

'Excellent,' he said. Then: 'Well? Is it terminal?'

'Not terminal,' I said.

I had taken this upon myself and Jerry was glad enough to waive his authority. I sipped some rum. Winston watched me. I wasn't sure if I should deceive him or not. Every man has his own way of facing death and a right to face it that way and if this had been a natural disease, no matter how lethal or painful, I would have told him the truth. But it was not natural. This was a thing that created its own values and judgements.

I said, 'They have an antidote, at the compound.'

Jerry gave me a sharp look and I could tell he was thinking the same as me. Then he narrowed his eyes and looked down at his boots.

'That's why your nurse was taken to the compound,' I went on. 'We'll have to take you there, or bring the antidote here. That's all.'

'Well, that's a relief,' Winston said. 'The way you were all acting, I thought I was a goner. But what is it, anyway? The way these lunatics are running around...some new strain of rabies?'

'I believe it's something of that nature.'

'They shouldn't have been fooling around with that.'

'They know that...now.'

I refilled our glasses. I didn't flinch as I leaned across the desk to pour into the doctor's glass. Mary's glass was still full; she said, 'Is it wise to be drinking? I mean...hadn't we better keep our wits about us?'

'I think it's better if we have a few drinks,' Jerry said.

Mary knew what we were going to do, then. She said, 'Oh, yes. I'll have a drink as well.' Then she realised that she already had a full glass in her hand. She sipped. Tears streaked her cheeks, but she was no longer sobbing. We drank slowly and steadily. Doctor Winston seemed to be actually relishing the rum. Jerry and I needed it. We watched the doctor carefully, wondering what the first signs would be; whether it would be a sudden rage or a gradual transition? Unblinking, he gazed back over the rim of his glass. I started to pour some more rum.

'Hadn't we better see about this antidote, then?' Winston said. 'I suppose it should be administered as soon as possible. I'll prescribe a good healthy dosage of rum for all of us afterwards.'

He spoke slowly, as if deliberating each word. I wondered if he were getting drunk or if the process was starting to affect his ability to form the words. But he looked at us with clear, alert eyes. He looked almost amused. I had a terrible idea that we hadn't deceived him, after all, that he was playing the game with us, protecting our feelings as we tried to protect him from the truth.

Jerry snorted and slammed his glass down on the desk.

'I'll take the doc up to the compound now,' he said. 'You stay here with Mary. We won't be long.'

I said, 'I'll go with him, if you like.'

Jerry stared at me. He appreciated my offer and he knew the doctor a lot better than I did. I think he was tempted to let me do it. But maybe he didn't trust my nerve; he had seen me cringe from dead Mendoza, never even attempting to use the rifle.

'No, it's better if I go,' he said.

Winston was looking back and forth between us.

'I don't suppose I could go on my own?' he said.

Again I saw that look in his eyes. Jerry saw it, too.

'Come on, doc,' he said.

———

MARY WAS SITTING with her face in her hands. She looked up at me once or twice, then lowered her face again immediately. We were not drinking now. I was taut as a tuning fork, waiting to vibrate to the sound of the gun... but no shot sounded.

Then Jerry came back in, his face a mask of anguish.

'Goddamn me!' he cried.

He slammed the door; across the room, the bars rattled.

I looked at Jerry, puzzled. I have never seen such torment on a face. He walked to the bars and gripped them, a prisoner outside the cell...inside a black despair.

'He knew,' Jerry said. 'He walked on ahead of me...never looked back once. I guess he knew. I followed him. But I walked slower and slower...and he just kept on at the same pace, so I was dropping behind...and when he turned off towards the compound, I stopped and came back. I let him go. I couldn't do it! Goddamn me to Hell!' he screamed, cursing himself...for not killing his friend.

For a long while, no one spoke...

XX

AFTER A WHILE Mary made a meal which none of us even pretended to eat. No shots had sounded for a long time. I looked out the window every few minutes but there was nothing to see. It was like a ghost town. A newspaper tumbled down the waterfront, starting to shred. A sea breeze had come up; it whined through the empty streets. From a wharf further down the front a door or shutter banged with a determined rhythm. The swordfish still hung from the scales, dry now; it looked like *papier mâché*. I felt sorry for the swordfish. It helped a bit to spread my sympathies. The others were looking out too, from time to time. We never looked out together, just took it in haphazard turns.

Jerry said, 'There's nobody...nobody at all. Maybe it's tapering off. No patrols, either...funny...' He came back from the window.

A little later, Mary looked out.

She saw the shore patrolman first...

HE WAS ALONE and looked relaxed.

He was standing down by the dock, looking out towards the patrol gunboats, not even watching his back. I breathed a sigh of relief. It must be over...at least this particular patrolman believed it to be over, for he showed no signs of alertness or fear. He seemed interested in the boats, as if he were waiting for them to do something, perhaps for the blockade to disperse. Jerry opened the door and stepped out. He called to the man. The man didn't seem to hear. Jerry called again, louder. The patrolman heard then. He seemed to shake himself around inside his crisp white uniform, like a dog shaking off water. Then he turned to face us.

Jerry's breath went out in a rush.

I couldn't breathe at all.

The ghoul in the white uniform made no move towards us; he stood, relaxed, watching us as he had watched the boats, with those blank, white eyes.

We went back in and barred the door.

We didn't look out for a while.

When we did, later, he was gone...

387

XXI

AFTER THAT, WE avoided the window. We did not look out, not wanting to see what was in the streets, and we did not look at it, not wanting to see what might…be looking in. From time to time we heard things…shuffling past the building; once something banged against the wall. But there was no real effort to get in. We sat at the desk in the centre of the room and looked at our hands. We drank a little rum. At one point, Mary raised the question that had been troubling me—and perhaps Jerry, as well.

'What shall we do if someone…normal…wants to join us?'

She didn't wait for a reply; said, 'I mean, when Doctor Winston knocked on the door, I let him in as a matter of course…and then I found out…I mean, how will we know?' She spoke the last word in a strained voice that rose towards hysteria. I had no answer. She said, 'We can't refuse to let someone in, if there's a chance they might be all right…' She gestured with both hands, vehemently, as if we were arguing with her…'We can't leave them out there…'

Jerry said, 'I guess what we'd do—will do, it happens—is lock 'em up in the cell. Keep 'em at gunpoint and explain that we're sorry but can't take any chances and get 'em in the cell. If they're still all right after…oh, say five hours, to be on the safe side…then we can let them out.'

Mary nodded. 'I hadn't thought of that.'

'There is a flaw, Jerry,' I said, shaking my head. When they both looked at me, I said, 'It's a good plan if only one person comes, but suppose two or three show up here? If they come separately—locking them up…would be like locking a man up with a time bomb, which might or might not explode… or a tiger, which might or might not be hungry. It would be torture.'

'Hell,' he said.

'Elston told me they had tested the ferocity of the subjects locking them up together,' I added. 'It was not a pretty sight, although no doubt, of great scientific interest,' I said, bitterly.

'Well…if one of us kept a constant watch…the moment one of them showed any signs of going berserk, we could kill him before the other was attacked…'

'Could we?' I asked.

Jerry dropped his head. He had not been able to kill Doctor Winston and I had not even aimed my rifle at Mendoza and Mary...yet, who knows what one can do? 'We might manage that,' I said.

'What else can we do?'

'There's one thing.' I hesitated, wishing that Mary had been sleeping; not wanting to disturb her even more. But she was listening carefully; she had an interest in the matter, after all. I said, 'We might need the cell for ourselves.'

'How do you mean?' Jerry asked.

'They're inhumanly strong. They could break in here, if they wanted in... no, not wanted to, they're too mindless for that...but if the urge takes them. I thought...well, if they do try to break in, we can lock ourselves in the cell.'

Jerry grimaced. He said, 'I don't like that idea at all...locked in there, cowering back from the bars...with things maybe reaching in, trying to get at us...' His great torso rippled; he shuddered like an earth tremor. 'I'd rather be mobile...run...shoot if we have to... Yeah, I can shoot them...and hell, we don't know how long we have to stay here.'

I hadn't relished the thought myself; it was an option I thought I should mention. I said, 'It may be a moot point. Maybe no one, normal otherwise, will come. Let's wait and see.'

And maybe it was a moot point.

But I was to be reminded, in a terrible way, of our agonising dilemma... the problem was not unique to us...

We spoke no more, with nothing to say. Time moved ponderously. And very slowly the light changed at the window.

The long night had begun...

XXII

WE SAT IN the lighted cube of our sanctuary and things moved in the darkness without. The sounds they made were soft, as if they caressed the walls lovingly, longingly, yearning to enter. They sensed we were within; they

gently stroked the walls around us. We knew we should turn the light out…
that it was drawing them to the jail like a beacon…but knowing is one thing;
we could not cherish darkness—by dawn we would have been inhuman.

LIKE A PRISONER marking his passing sentence, Jerry drove his fist into his
palm, not hard but as regular as a metronome; he winced with each soft blow,
as if stung. Beside him, Mary sat with her face buried in her hands. From time
to time she would shudder and look up, tearing her face from its shelter by
main force…from the hooks of her hands came her tormented countenance,
haggard, white, ghastly, the flesh drawn from her fingers. I looked past them, at
the bars and, beyond, the shadow of the bars on the wall of the cell. My backbone was like a bar, riveting me to my chair…multiple bars, split by currents of
fear and spreading like splintered bamboo through my torso—casting shadows
on my soul. I was breathing heavily. We all were. And then something else was
breathing heavily, at the door. Jerry looked up. His gun was on the table, but he
did not touch it. The breath from without seemed to billow into the door; the
door was solid, yet I felt as if it were fluttering like a sail, about to float open. A
hand stroked the contours of the door, seeking, testing. Then it moved away;
moving on, it drew with it shreds of my sanity…

SUDDENLY, I WAS back in Mendoza's.

My mind out of time, I had just broken the glass case and the sound
shattered in my ears. Mary's face was writing; Jerry was vibrating; my mind
snapped back and I knew I had heard glass break behind me. There was
glass in the window. I remembered seeing Mary at the window, through the
pane…drawn against my will, I turned…

Sally the salad girl was reaching in…

Her face was framed in the window and her arm groped towards me,
dripping blood where the glass had cut her. She was far more terrible than
the men—somehow, she was still feminine and sensual, her painted lips
drawn back as if smiling with lewd desire, her eyes rolling as if with passion,

a mockery of what she had been; reaching out, it seemed she wished to fold me lovingly to her breast. I could not look away. Then she yielded, like a prostitute rejected; I did not go to her—she drifted away.

On the floor, shards of broken glass glinted in the light.

Within my body, my senses were shattered like the glass, cold splinters piercing my heart, sharp edges filing at the rim of my mind, jagged pieces rasping at my soul. I could almost hear fear grinding away at my guts. It was too much. The grinding horror wore away my humanity and polished my awareness to a smooth lump; I slipped into obfuscation. I did not move, I scarcely blinked. Things groped at the window and fondled the walls. And then the bars had double shadows. Dawn was at the window.

———

MARY SHIVERED INTO reality, as if coming into focus from distortion or changing dimensions by some time warp. Jerry stood up, stiffly. I found I could move. I could think once more. The night had ended.

XXIII

FROM THE WINDOW, we saw a destroyer standing off beyond the harbour. My first thought, such was my state of mind, was that the navy intended to shell the town. But that was foolish and I smiled—although grimly—at myself. I did wonder what they planned, however. A destroyer was hardly necessary to quarantine fishing boats and motor cruisers. Some decision had probably been reached—been forced upon them once the first member of the patrols had been infected. Maybe it was only the one—the one we had seen—but we had no way of knowing, nor, I suppose, did they. It had taken that option from them. The search-and-destroy mission had automatically failed the moment a single member of the patrols became one of the enemy… to continue the patrols was to risk spreading the horror into the compound itself. They weren't likely to chance that. And it explained why the patrols had been withdrawn. But not what they intended to do.

SOMETIME LATER A helicopter came in.

It was a big one and it passed over us, heading towards the compound. It didn't stay long. It vanished towards the west and then, half an hour later, a second 'copter came in—or the first one returned. It followed the same pattern, landing within the compound and flying off a short time afterwards. I wondered if reinforcements were being brought in, or if the compound was evacuating? Jerry, wondering the same thing, tried to phone through to the compound, but even the switchboard failed to answer now. The phone rang hollow and dead, a forlorn sound, as if the telephone itself knew it was not to be answered and sounded its despair.

Jerry slammed it down, cursing.

A few seconds later, it rang.

The sound startled us and we gaped stupidly at each other. Then Jerry snatched it up. 'That's right,' he said, and at the same time I heard a loud-speaker blaring from somewhere in the streets behind us. Jerry said, 'That's right. Three of us. Right, we'll be there at ten exactly. Well, sure...but look... how do we tell if they're...all right? If we do find any others...is there some way to tell?' He listened, tight-lipped. 'All right,' he said. He put the phone down.

'They're evacuating us from the navy pier,' he said.

'Thank God,' Mary whispered.

'We're to be there at ten o'clock, on the dot...and they won't wait long.' Then, anticipating my question, he said, 'They didn't say how we could tell... said that everyone would be checked by a doctor, at the pier.'

'Then they have found a way!' I said. 'Maybe Elston's damned autopsies proved fruitful.'

Jerry nodded doubtfully.

A van moved down the waterfront, going fast and not stopping. The loudspeaker sounded the message, the same message we had received over the telephone. I wondered if they were phoning every number in the town; I had an eerie echo of telephones ringing, unanswered, in empty houses; ringing in sequence up and down the streets, forlorn and futile. The van passed and

I saw armed men holding their weapons ready at the windows; it turned up the cobbled streets and we heard the message repeated again and again as it wound through the town, making an effort to get through to anyone hiding there…anyone who could understand. The message was given in Spanish on every third broadcast. I was cheered greatly by this, by the knowledge that something had been determined, something was being done, authority was taking measures. I suppose, without actually admitting it, I had feared that the compound had been overrun and that we were on our own. The authorities were responsible for this horror we were in, yet it was still reassuring to know they continued to function.

I said, 'Well, thank Heaven.'

But Jerry said, 'It might not be so easy.'

He was at the window, looking out.

He said, 'Christ, they're all over the place!'

I felt my throat constrict. I joined him at the window and the hair came up stiff on my neck. The loudspeaker seemed to have attracted the ghouls, to have played the catalyst that brought them out of lethargy, summoning them from their various places and bringing them to the waterfront. There must have been twenty of them. They came filtering out of the side-streets and from the warehouses, moving in the wake of the van…some Pied Piper syndrome which Elston would have termed a side effect, bringing them together. I recognised the bearded man from the Red Walls and, I think, two or three others from the initial infection. There were several women; one clutched a baby to her breast in a mockery of the maternal instinct. The baby was dead. They moved after the van and then, when it had vanished, milled about mindlessly. They did not attack one another. From time to time two or three of them, following their own paths, would come into contact—would bump or brush together—and then they would snap and slash at each other in a momentary bestial rage, but it was fleeting ferocity. An instant later they would wander apart again. They did not kill each other. Elston could be proud of the nicety with which he had regulated their instincts…

AT NINE O'CLOCK a landing craft came wallowing into the harbour and dropped its ramp alongside the navy pier. The pier was some distance down the front and it was hard to see just what was happening, but we saw men in blue uniforms splashing through the shallow water and others running along the pier. They all carried automatic weapons. They deployed in a crescent around the pier. Several men in white coats detached themselves from the crescent and moved forward. They were all on the seaward side of the link fence. A group of men in khaki came through the defensive lines, carrying strange, bulky objects. They moved quickly and, within minutes, those objects had been transformed into a tent-like affair of poles and canvas. It looked like the shield they put around a broken-legged racehorse on the track, before they shoot it—letting the animal linger longer in agony so the spectators will not have their delicate sensibilities offended. This structure was erected near the fence, on the perimeter of the armed crescent. As soon as it was up, the men in khaki hurried back to the dock. The men in white vanished behind the canvas.

It was 9:30.

The navy pier was only ten minutes away—walking.

We were ready to go—waiting.

While this activity was going on, the ghouls were still wandering along the docks. They showed little interest in the proceedings at the pier. They didn't even look dangerous, somehow; demented, tormented, with the madness transfiguring their features, but not dangerous.

Jerry said, 'You know…it's funny…you'd think it would be more horrible with that whole load of things out there, but it don't seem as bad as it did with one—when Sally looked in the window. One thing, alone…' He was looking out, squinting, tight lines drawn around his mouth. 'Well, it ain't like snakes, is what I mean,' he said.

Mary and I looked at him.

I realised what he was doing—that he was just saying the first thing that came into his head, to hold our attention; to keep us from considering the gauntlet we soon must run.

He said, 'Now, you take your snakes. One snake, on his own…he ain't so scary. But you get a whole pit of snakes, all squirming together and wriggling

about, that scares anybody. Now, you'd think that whole load of ghouls would be the same. But it ain't.' He paused. I thought he'd run dry, but he was just getting his words in order. He said, 'I guess they're more on the line of rats in a sack.'

Mary and I looked at each other, then at Jerry. But he knew what he was saying.

He said, 'Knew a fella once, used to make his living plucking rats out of a burlap bag. That's right. He'd go around the bars toting this big bag full of rats. He wasn't welcomed in restaurants, but he'd go in bars. He'd have fifteen, twenty rats in there. Well, he'd let everyone look in the sack, they'd see all them rats squirming around, they'd get pretty edgy. Then this fella, he'd wager he could reach down in that sack with his bare hand and pluck a rat out. Well, nobody would believe him. He'd get plenty of takers on his bet. Then, sure enough, he'd reach in and grab him a rat and pluck it right out, all wriggling and squealing. Saw him do it a dozen times. Never the once did he get bit.' Jerry looked at his hand, as if amazed that it had not been bitten. 'So one time I'm having a drink with him, I ask him what the secret is. He'd had some drink, he tells me there's no secret to it at all; he don't know why they don't bite him, they just don't. But here's the thing. He said that when he first started rat-plucking, he tried it with just one rat in the bag. Well, he got bit every time. But as long as there was more than one rat in there, he never got chawed. Now, that was the secret, although he didn't see it as a secret. When there was a whole squirming mass of rats, they just didn't bite. He could pluck them out one by one, fifteen, twenty in a row, never got nipped—but as soon as there was just one rat left in the sack, it bit him every time. Just something in the nature of rats in a sack. Well, you see what I mean...'

He had spoken slowly and thoughtfully.

It was 9:35.

THE CANVAS SHELTER on the pier was billowing like a sail and the men who'd gone in there wearing white coats came out looking like astronauts or deep sea divers. They were bundled into thick, protective clothing, heavy

leather gauntlets and helmets with black glass visors. The visors were lifted and their faces showed white in the openings. These were obviously the men who would examine prospective evacuees—who would, I hoped, examine us.

It was 9:40 and we were discussing whether we should walk steadily down the front, carefully avoiding the ghouls, or try to make it in one quick rush. We had already determined that we must make our approach down the waterfront, even though it was swarming with ghouls. The alternative was to sneak through the back streets and with narrow roads turning and intersecting that was too dangerous—we would have no warning if one of the things were lurking around a turning, in a doorway, in an alley. On the front we could, at least, see the danger.

But to run or walk…

Mary summed that up.

She said, 'I don't think I could walk,' and we knew what she meant. We decided to run. It might not be the safest policy, for quick movement might well draw their attention, just as the loudspeaker in the van had attracted them to it, but we doubted our nerve—doubted we could walk through that terrible throng. I felt my heart might explode if I denied my impulse to run… to maintain a moderate pace while my heart and brain screamed for the primordial solution, the flight that instinct demanded.

———

AT 9:45 A van roared down to the gates.

The back opened and men jumped out, some in uniform and some in civilian clothing. The men in protective clothing opened the gates and the men from the van rushed through. The driver moved the van some ten yards down the barrier, then jumped out and ran back to the gates. A second van arrived, then a third. The occupants all passed through the gates and rushed directly out to the landing craft. There was no examination and I figured that must have already been done, at the laboratory. Examination at the pier was for us and any others who had remained in the town. I watched carefully but saw neither Elston nor Larsen. I figured they had left in the helicopters.

Then it was time for us to leave.

———

WE WENT OUT the door fast, Jerry first and Mary next and I brought up the rear, shamefully close upon her heels. We went straight across the front to the fence, wanting that barrier on one side of our course. We passed within six feet of a ghoul. He turned stiffly, watching us, but did not offer pursuit. Two others took tentative steps towards us but, in doing so, they brushed against one another. They snarled in silence and snapped. Then we were running along the line of the fence and, for all our fear, it was easy. We made it to the gates with no more trouble than our labouring lungs and jangling nerves could claim.

We were not the first there.

Half a dozen others had come from the nearer streets of the town, joining at the fence, warily regarding one another. The gate was closed again and the men in protective suits had their visors down. Sunlight reflected from the black glass, glinting like stars in the void. They were faceless behind the glass, alien and inhuman. We drew up, panting, beside the others. Jerry spoke to a man he recognised. Three or four others came dashing from the streets, running hard. One was a woman, sobbing hysterically.

From behind his visor, one of the examiners said, 'All right. You'll come through one at a time. Go behind the canvas and take your clothing off. Take everything off.' He paused at the gate. 'The rest step back. Move it!'

Someone pushed the hysterical woman forward.

The visored man opened the gate and let her through. The men in blue uniforms had their automatic weapons trained on the rest of us. Two of them, standing apart from the line, held their guns on the woman. The visored man closed the gates again and the woman went behind the canvas. Two men in protective clothing followed her in.

Suddenly I felt like laughing…laughing wildly.

I realised that the canvas had not been erected to house some delicate instrument that could detect the latent disease but simply for the sake of modesty…so that we could undress in privacy! Modesty in the face of this horror! So was authority bound within their dimensions.

Then a darker realisation followed.

I knew we had hoped for too much from these saviours. They had found no way to detect the disease, they simply intended to examine us, naked, looking for any recent wound or break in the skin through which the disease might have got into our bodies.

I didn't, at first and with my mind jumping madly, see how this would affect us.

The woman emerged from behind the canvas and was directed to the pier. She moved on, stumbling and sobbing. She looked back once. The gate opened again and a man passed through. Jerry took a step forward and the guns all trained on him.

He stopped dead, raising his hands to shoulder-height.

'There's another woman here,' he said. 'For crissake let her go through next!'

The man at the gate nodded. Sunlight ran like black fire up his helmet.

None of the ghouls had come any distance towards us, they were still milling about back by the jail.

Jerry took Mary gently by the shoulder and pushed her towards the gates, then stepped back. She looked at him over her shoulder, trying to smile, as she moved forwards. The faceless man had his hand on the gate, ready to open it the moment the preceding man had been cleared behind the canvas.

Abruptly, he stiffened.

The instant he stiffened, I saw the reason…and tumultuous horror spun through my guts.

He had seen the bandage on her leg.

'Remove that,' he said.

Mary looked puzzled and Jerry hadn't yet understood. He still had his hands raised.

Mary said, 'What do you mean?' and the visored man said, 'The bandage.'

'What? Oh…no, that's all right. I cut myself the other day, it's not… what you think…' She had started speaking easily, as if confident the explanation would suffice, but her words trailed off weakly. The man with the black glass face was rigid. I knew that his features, behind the visor, would be as hard and as cold as the glass itself.

Mary bent down and pulled the bandage from her leg. The cut was red and ugly-looking. The man stared at her.

'I'm sorry,' he said.

'What the hell?' Jerry shouted.

The guns were trained on him from behind the fence and his hands were still raised, as if he'd thrown them up in amazement.

'They...won't...' I whispered.

'I'm sorry,' the faceless man said. 'There's no point in examining you further, miss. No one with an open wound can leave.'

'It isn't that!' Mary screamed.

Her cry drew the attention of the guns. They shifted from Jerry to her. The faceless man was shaking his head, perhaps in negation, strengthening his words with the gesture—or perhaps in pity. The second man had come out from behind the canvas and headed for the landing craft. The others were pressing forward, clamouring to get through the gate.

One of the visored men by the canvas called, 'What's the hold-up, Jim? Get them through here!'

Jim said, 'Please step back. You're holding things up...I don't want to have to...' He turned his helmeted head to the side, indicating the line of armed guards. They were quite ready to shoot.

Mary gasped and moved back from the gates.

Jerry stepped forward, past her. He faced the faceless man. Jerry's visage was like brittle glass itself. Had the visored man possessed a human countenance, Jerry might have argued with him, but they just looked at each other. Jerry had lowered his hands. I could tell what he was thinking as clearly as if my mind had been linked to his and the thought pulsing between us. He wanted to draw his gun and kill the faceless man who stood between Mary and safety. But he knew it would do no good—less than good, for he would be shot down in turn and Mary would still be on this side of the fence...without him.

After a long moment he turned back to us.

His face had shattered...just like glass.

XXIV

MARY WAS CALM, remarkably calm. We stood back from the gates, watching the others go through one by one. None of them were turned back. Mary said, 'It's the same decision we faced…talked about facing…in the jail. If someone should come…'

'It's not the same,' Jerry rasped. But it was.

Then everyone else had gone through and the faceless man was looking at us.

Mary said, 'Jerry…please go through.'

'Well, I'm just likely to do that, ain't I?' he said.

Mary gave a little whimpering sigh. It was impossible to tell if it expressed relief or frustration; emotions were blurred in all of us now, our senses confused by anomie. It was worse for Mary, if anything, with an edge of guilt on her disorientation—without her, we could have gone through the gates.

The visored man said, 'Anyone else?' His voice was soft; he didn't like what he had to do.

'Jack…no sense in you staying,' Jerry said.

I wanted to go. My muscles actually lurched in the direction of the gates and I had to restrain my body. I could feel my bones distinctly within my flesh, the scaffold of my skeleton fixing me in place. I shook my head, refusing my own instincts rather than Jerry's suggestion.

'Please go,' Mary said. 'It will be easier for me…'

And Jerry said, 'Our supplies will last longer with just the two of us, Jack…'

It was so tempting I feared my honour would prove weak.

'No one else!' I called.

The visored man regarded us. Then he nodded and turned away. The line of men in uniform began to retreat, keeping formation and closing the crescent in around the pier. They moved as if executing a formal manoeuvre on the parade grounds, functioning exactly in a world gone mad. They had left the canvas shelter where it was; it snapped in the breeze, like a tent abandoned on a holiday in Hell.

Jerry's big hand closed on my shoulder in gentle gratitude.

'If it had been your girl...' he said.

Maybe, I thought.

One by one the guards were filtering out of the line and boarding the landing craft. The men in protective clothing were already aboard.

The three of us stood there by the gates and a line of faces gazed at us from the boat. It looked like a row of disembodied heads posted around a stockade. The last uniformed man had started up the ramp when a ghoul came loping out of a side-street and flung himself onto the fence...

———

LIKE A DEMENTED monkey, the ghoul began to scale the barrier. He was moving with purpose and I was reminded of Jerry's tale of the solitary rat in the bag. His groping hand reached the top and clamped over the barbed wire. Blood ran down his arm. He jerked himself up. The other ghouls watched him, as if impressed by a virtuoso performance and envious of his agility.

The last guard was halfway up the boarding ramp when he looked back and saw the ghoul. His face set. The others, on board, were calling for him to hurry, but he turned back and sighted his weapon. He took aim as stolidly as if he'd been on the shooting range. I understood it. It was not a human target upon which he sighted. There was no need to kill the ghoul, the guard could have boarded in plenty of time, but he was guided by some instinct older than reason and deeper than logic. He squeezed off a burst from his automatic weapon. Cartridges spun over his shoulder, glinting in the sunlight. Splinters of bone and gore cascaded from the ghoul. Blood hung in a thin mist around him. He jerked; his body heaved up, then dropped back. He hung suspended from the top of the fence, his hand impaled on the barbed wire. Thick drops of blood fell from him and he swayed like some carnal fruit, bursting with red ripeness.

The guard grimaced—with satisfaction.

He turned back up the ramp. Spent cartridges were scattered at his feet and he looked down at them for a moment, as if they were runes which he had cast. Then he kicked at them. They spun off the ramp and dropped into the water. The guard went on up the ramp and then the ramp drew up and the three of us were alone.

⸻

MARY BURIED HER face in Jerry's chest, clinging there, as if using his body as a shield against the sight of the dead ghoul. He stroked her hair.

'We'd better get back to the jail,' he said.

'Again?' The word was muffled against his chest, carved into his body. 'Go through them again?'

'It's the safest place.'

I said, 'Jerry...when we left...I didn't close the door. I didn't think...they might be in there now.'

He winced.

'What about one of the vans?' Mary said.

'They seem attracted to them...' I said.

'Still, if we drive around without stopping,' Jerry said.

Mary said, 'I meant to drive back to the jail...'

'Jack left the door open, goddamn it!' Jerry snapped. Then: 'Why shouldn't he have left the door open? How did he know we'd be going back?'

He spoke as if it were an exercise in logics. He was looking around, standing with his back to the fence. Further down the fence, towards the jail, the dead ghoul was still hanging by his spiked hand...as if, like the swordfish, he had been suspended there to be weighed and measured and mounted. Blood still dripped from his erupted body, not spraying out—his heart no longer pumped—but falling in heavy globs obedient to gravity. The living ghouls still milled aimlessly about.

Jerry said, 'If we drive around they won't be able to catch us...as long as the gas holds out. But after that...those vans aren't as strong as the jail. They could break into a van and we'd be confined, unable to manoeuvre... Damn! If only we knew how long we have to hold out here...how long we'll be isolated before they...before they do whatever they're going to do about the island. We have to get to some place we can defend.'

'What about the compound?' Mary said. 'Take the van to the compound? The telephone is probably working from there, at least we could be in touch with...the world.'

Jerry considered that.

He was bareheaded now. He had lost his hat somewhere along the line. The sea breeze ruffled his fair hair.

'What's it like in the compound, Jack? Defensible?'

But I couldn't remember what the compound was like. I could remember only that small whitewashed room…and the stinking pit. Black smoke rose from that pit, a tower of smoke like…

'The lighthouse!' I cried.

'Why…yes. That's right!'

Mary was nodding enthusiastically. 'There'll even be supplies there. Sam Jasper's things. We won't have to go back to the jail…'

'The tide?' I asked.

'We'll take a boat,' Jerry said, then paused, glancing out at the harbour, where John Tate had been rammed. The destroyer stood at the approaches, attended by gunboats. It would not be wise to take a boat.

Mary thought for a moment; said, 'We can cross by the reef in half an hour.'

'And so can they,' said Jerry.

'But only one at a time…we can shoot them down one by one, if we have to…if they come… If they come in daylight.'

'Oh, Christ…I don't know.'

'But wait!' Jerry said. 'They won't cross water, right? They won't go into water. That reef is none too solid. There must be a tyre iron or something in one of the vans…if we could lever a couple of rocks out of place, make a break in the line…it should work.'

'I think it's our best bet,' I said. 'I'd rather be there than here. And someone might be more inclined to rescue us from there…in a day or two they must realise we aren't infected…a boat or helicopter…'

'Mary?' the sheriff said.

'I…yes. Anything rather than staying here or going back to the jail… waiting for them to break in. Yes. The lighthouse.'

I think we all felt greatly cheered at having reached a decision. At least we were still in control of our own options. We moved to the nearest van.

THE KEYS WERE in it.

We all got in the front, Jerry at the wheel and Mary between us.

Jerry waited a few moments before he switched on the ignition but, once he did so, he started the van moving immediately. We drove towards the ghouls.

The ghouls watched us come.

Jerry drove at them in first gear, steadily, and they made no attempt to get out of the way. They seemed fascinated by the van, by a large moving object…something of a magnitude to register on their dimmed perceptions. As we closed on the crowd, I saw Jerry's hand lift from the wheel and hover for a moment over the horn. It was a reaction from habit and he grinned grimly as he realised he had been about to sound the hooter.

'No way through them,' he muttered.

'We'll have to force our way through…'

Mary, tight-lipped and rigid between us, said, 'Can't you drive faster?'

She yearned for the sanctuary of the lighthouse.

Jerry said, 'Afraid to ram them too hard…don't want a fender jammed into a tyre or to bend the radiator back into the fan…just try to brush them aside…'

More ghouls were moving towards us. One was hanging on the fence, swinging by one hand, as if he'd discovered a new pleasure. I saw one come out of the open door of the jail and gaze up at the sun. He didn't blink. I wondered if they would soon be blind? I wondered if that would matter?

Jerry was saying, 'Why, there's Joe Wallace…used to play cards with him…Tim Carver…Ike Stanton… Hell, I know these people! Used to know them when they were people…There's Mrs Jones. Aw, hell…there's the Carpenter kid…he's only seven years old…'

I looked where he was looking and saw the child, its face preternaturally aged by drooling madness. I couldn't tell if it was a boy or a girl.

Larsen had been right about that…the kids were the worst. I guessed there were about forty of them on the waterfront, men, women and children.

I had no idea how many were in the town or how many had been killed…nor how long they would survive.

They were still individuals.

They shared the same mindless countenance, but they moved in different ways, not following a pattern, each affected differently. Some hopped and leaped like frogs, some crept along, some stood upright while others were hunched over, faces downcast as if ashamed of their condition. Most of them seemed to be injured in some way. I saw one youth whose arm had been torn off at the shoulder; perhaps he had torn it off himself, for he held the severed limb in his other hand. A woman had torn her hair out; her glabrous skull was dotted with hundreds of pinpoints of blood. One had no lower jaw. Two were naked. I stared at them in terrible fascination.

'Why, there's my hat!' Jerry said, and he brought his hand to his bare head.

The white Stetson was lying in the street just outside the jail. I thought, for a second, that Jerry was going to halt the van and retrieve it. But he drove steadily on, into them. The ghouls didn't move out of the way, but they allowed themselves to be brushed aside. They seemed quite passive and docile. I began to hope that the initial frenzy had worn off, that it had been a temporary rage that had burned itself out. That hope burned like acid in my heart.

Then they attacked the van.

━━━

A GHOULISH FACE loomed up at my window.

Mary screamed. There was a loud banging on the side of the van, shaking it. Another bang came from the roof. Someone was hammering and pounding at the panels and the windscreen suddenly shattered in a jagged star.

Jerry cursed. He stepped on the accelerator and the tyres skidded and squealed. For a moment the van did not move; someone was holding the rear bumper. Then there was a screech of metal and the bumper peeled free from the van. We surged forward with a jolt…and the engine stalled.

Jerry snapped the ignition and it rasped. The engine didn't catch. I feared it was flooded. I think I was shouting at Jerry, and Mary was screaming over and over. But then the engine caught and we were moving again. As the van lurched forward the door on the driver's side was jerked completely off. A ghoul held it by the handle and he fell back as the door came free. The door sailed up like a steel kite, floating. Then we were through them and going fast. I looked back. The ghouls were coming, following after us. Jerry was hunched over the wheel and Mary and I were shouting for him to drive faster. He grunted and touched his forehead again. I figured he regretted losing his hat.

The lighthouse rose up like surging hope.

It was an ugly grey tower upon which gargoyles might have perched, but it looked beautiful to me. Jerry brought the van to a skidding halt, slewing sideways in the sand, just where the reef began. The tide was going out and the black rocks broke through the surface all the way to the lighthouse. For a moment we just sat there. Time was precious, but we had to sit for an instant as the void of our drained emotions filled.

Jerry reached into the toolbox behind the seat and came up with a tyre iron. He said, 'This should do it.'

I was looking out the back, but we had gone beyond the sweep of the island. If the ghouls were still coming, I couldn't see them. I knew that their span of attention was too feeble to keep them going in pursuit of a vanished prey...but feared that, once headed in our direction, inertia would keep them moving.

Jerry jumped out from his doorless side and stood, looking back. He had his gun in one hand and the tyre iron in the other. 'No sign of them,' he said. 'I reckon we made it.'

Then a hand reached down from the top of the van.

I remembered the bang I'd heard on the roof and my mouth sprang open. I shouted, leaning past Mary. The hand hovered, tilting at the wrist, delicately groping at the air. Then it descended onto Jerry's shoulder.

Jerry didn't react.

He had heard me shout and must have supposed it was my hand, seeking his attention. He was still looking back along our trail. Mary screamed and the sheriff looked towards us and then he looked up, just as the hand tightened on his shoulder. His face exploded with frenzy; he dropped the tyre iron and started to lift the gun; then the ghoul heaved his big body up and hauled him onto the roof of the van.

I saw the polished toe of his boot kicking wildly.

I threw open my door and rolled out, bringing the rifle up, seeming to move in slow motion. On the top of the van they were pressed together like lovers in a terrible embrace. The ghoul loomed over Jerry; Jerry was struggling, trying to throw the creature off. I didn't fire. In my horror, I did nothing. Jerry pressed his big revolver into the ghoul's midriff and, as I gaped at them, he began to fire into the thing. The ghoul's body jerked as the heavy-calibre slugs went into him. Jerry was cocking and firing the gun with terrible deliberation, fast but steady, and I saw the ghoul's spine unpeel from his back, the bony articulation coming out from his flesh like the backbone of a fish. The spine snapped in the middle and the bloody ends twanged apart. The ghoul's arms and legs went limp.

Jerry heaved him away and rolled from the van. The ghoul spread out across the roof, one hand hanging down on either side. His face was turned to me. He was still alive and, broken in half, trying to move.

I crossed behind the van. Jerry was sitting in the sand, panting. He was looking at his left arm. I moved towards him and we both looked at his arm and, as we did so, a red line appeared. His flesh was white, numbed by the ghoul's inhuman grip, and on that pale background a thin thread unravelled, as if slipping from a tapestry—and a trickle of blood oozed from the broken skin.

'Aw, hell,' he said, very softly. 'Aw, hell…'

And he looked at the lighthouse, so close now and so unobtainably far.

Grey and bleak, it rose up beyond him.

XXV

MARY CLUNG TO him.

She was gasping and sobbing and heaving violently at him, almost attacking him in her despair. Jerry was trying not to touch her. He held his left arm out to the side.

He said, 'I'll go back.'

She was crying. 'Jerry! Jerry! No!'

He said, 'I'll hold them for a while…stop as many as I can.' He looked down at Mary, then at me. I understood. I took her by the shoulders and dragged her from him. She struggled against me, babbling incoherently, her mouth forming words that had no meaning…sounds that arose from depths far beyond language, from feelings far more ancient than speech. She struck at me. I had to change my grip. Jerry was reloading his revolver, tucking the shells into the open chamber with amazing delicacy. He snapped the cylinder closed and began fingering the bullets remaining in his belt. His lips moved; he was counting. He wanted no mistakes in that enumeration. He would have a use for the final bullet.

'Jerry,' I said. Words were absurdly inadequate. I said, 'I'm sorry, Jerry. I…I'm glad I knew you.'

Mary was reaching for him, clawing for him.

And he couldn't even kiss her goodbye.

He said, 'Mary,' and his voice broke. His eyes were glazed over. He shook his massive body and turned. He didn't look back. He walked back the way we'd come with his shoulders square and I saw him raise his hand to his forehead. I knew he wished he had his Stetson as he walked back through the sunlight…

———

'MARY, PLEASE…GO TO the lighthouse!'

She ignored me.

She didn't even hear me. She stood on the rocks and looked back. Jerry had turned past the rim of the island. We couldn't see him. Mary had tried to go after him and three times I'd had to stop levering at the reef and drag her back to the rocks. I handed her the rifle and she took it, holding it by the barrel, not knowing what it was. Crazed with grief and horror, her mind had slipped out of focus. Keeping one eye on her, I attacked the reef again. It was a harder job than I'd thought. The rocks didn't roll off separately but splintered and came apart, spongy veins separating hard layers.

Jerry's gun sounded.

It went off six times and Mary's body jerked at every shot, just as if those bullets were slamming into her. I wondered if the sixth bullet had been for himself? But then he was firing again. He had reloaded, giving us all the time he could. He fired four more times. Then there was silence.

Mary sank down on a rock. One foot trailed in the water. I pried a black slice off and stepped back, wondering if the gap was wide enough. It wasn't. I knelt on the slippery reef and tried to lift a huge segment of stone. It was too heavy for me I wished that Jerry had stayed to help break the reef. I heaved with all my might and the rock would not move.

Then the ghouls were coming.

—

LOPING, BOUNDING, SKULKING...IN their various fashions, they came for us. One was dragging a disembodied forearm at his side. I didn't want to know whose arm it had been. I heaved. The rock was far too heavy for me to lift, it was impossible that I should raise it and yet, ponderously, that great slab shifted. Fear had granted me strength as surely as mindless inhibition granted it to the ghouls. I rose up with the stone clasped to my breast; let it slide away, sideways, into the water. The water bubbled light green as the rock sank.

Mary screamed.

The first ghoul was on the reef, bounding from rock to rock. Blood streamed from an empty eye-socket. The other eye was fixed upon us. I backed away, reaching out for the gun, but Mary was too petrified to hand it to me; didn't even know she had it. She was so terrified that she took a step forwards, towards the ghoul.

I snatched the rifle from her, throwing us both off balance. Mary slipped forwards and I fell back. The ghoul sprang up from the rocks, he seemed to soar over the break as I fired from my knees, awkwardly, and the recoil shoved me over the slippery stone. Flailing wildly, I dropped backwards into the warm sea.

I surfaced, kicking and gasping. I had lost the rifle. I took one automatic stroke towards the rocks, then recoiled, pushing away. The ghoul's leap had fallen short...the gap had proved wide enough and the creature was in the water. His gory head bobbed up and down, water streaming from the open

mouth, blood streaming from the open eye-socket, the other eye white and wild with terror. He was reaching for the rocks.

Mary stood there, staring down at the monster, frozen fast by her horror. 'Go back!' I cried.

Water swirled into my mouth, choking me.

The ghoul's hand slapped down on the rock, shifted…and clamped on Mary's ankle.

She never made a sound as the creature dragged her down into the sea. The water bubbled around them. She was trying to swim and the frenzied thing tore at her. Three or four other ghouls had come up to the break in the reef; they stood there, staring down at the ghoul in the water—and the woman. I stroked to the rocks beyond the gap and hauled myself out, gasping. I looked into the gap from my side of the break and the ghouls looked in from their side and in the water between there was blood.

Mary's face turned to me.

She pleaded with her eyes, silently.

She reached out towards me and my hand went out to her, but she was too far away. She was closer to the other side. The ghoul had gone under now and Mary was alone in the turbulent gap. She twisted violently, trying to kick off from the rocks, but she had drifted too close. The ghouls reached down.

She still made no sound, even as their hands closed over her and they drew her up onto the rocks. I would have shot her, of course…but I had lost the rifle. Mary was on the flat rock. She kicked spasmodically with one leg. The ghouls bent over her, slowly, solicitously, as if they had rescued her from drowning…bent to her, as if to give the kiss of life…

EPILOGUE

I THOUGHT I saw Mary amongst them today.

I was watching through the binoculars, a group of them were milling about by the rotting swordfish and one looked rather like Mary. But I

stopped watching. I didn't want to know. I only want to know how much longer it will be, how many days or weeks I must sit here in my grey tower, rooted in the sea and rising towards the heavens. Not much longer, perhaps. They don't seem as frenzied now, they don't even fight amongst themselves when they make contact. I wonder if the madness is wearing off…if they are recovering some human instinct…or simply wasting away, weakening and dying? I hope it was not Mary I saw. When I looked later, most of them had gone. One was dead—lifeless, at least. The body had burst open and a length of intestine had uncoiled. I saw a seagull land on the ghoul's shoulder and dip its sharp beak into the gruesome cavity.

The gull's head came up and it seemed to shudder, as did I. Larsen's words came back to me. If a dog or a rat got at one of the bodies… Again the gull's beak dipped; the plumed throat pulsed. Above the patrol boats the sky was clear and blue. The seagull was sated. It poised, wings lifted, then bore itself away.

DAVID F. CASE was born in upstate New York, but since the early 1960s he lived in London, as well as spending time in Greece and Spain. The author of an estimated 300 books or more under various pseudonyms, he was a regular contributor to the legendary *Pan Book of Horror Stories* during the early 1970s, and his stories were collected in *The Cell: Three Tales of Terror* (aka *The Cell and Other Tales of Horror*), *Fengriffen and Other Stories, Brotherly Love & Other Tales of Faith and Knowledge, Pelican Cay and Other Disquieting Tales, Masters of the Weird Tale: David Case, Fengriffen & Other Gothic Tales* and *The Cell & Transmorphic Tales*. Case's novels include *Beast of Shame* (as 'Don Holliday'), *Wolf Tracks*, and *The Third Grave* from Arkham House. His short stories 'Fengriffin' and 'The Hunter' were filmed as, respectively, —*And Now the Screaming Starts!* (1973) and *Scream of the Wolf* (1974). 'Pelican Cay' was originally going to be published by the late James Turner in an anthology he planned to edit in the mid-1980s for Arkham House entitled *Summoning the Shadows*. When the horror market changed in America, the book was shelved and Case's powerful novella languished in a file for many years until its publication in *Dark Terrors 5*, where it was rewarded with a World Fantasy Award nomination. 'I wrote "Pelican Cay" in a seedy hotel in downtown Chicago,' recalled the author, 'but had lived in the Florida Keys before that, which inspired the atmosphere and setting. The Red Walls, or maybe Doors, was an upmarket place when I was there, but there were plenty of tales from when it was the haunt of shrimpers and salad girls (girls who signed on shrimp boats but didn't necessarily make salads). A fella was drowning his sorrows there once and, morose, said he would commit suicide if he dared. They hanged him from the rafters. My favourite: thirteen shrimpers are standing at the long bar. A guy runs in with a shooter and shouts "This is a stick-up!" The shrimpers turned around and twelve had shooters, the other had a bill-hook. The bandit says, "I guess I've robbed the wrong place". But he bought a round of drinks and they let him go.'

THE RETROSPECTIVE

Ramsey Campbell

TRENT HAD NO idea how long he was unable to think for rage. The guard kept out of sight while she announced the unscheduled stop, and didn't reappear until the trainload of passengers had crowded onto the narrow platform. As the train dragged itself away into a tunnel simulated by elderly trees and the low March afternoon sky that was plastered with layers of darkness, she poked her head out of the rearmost window to announce that the next train should be due in an hour. The resentful mutters of the crowd only aggravated Trent's frustration. He needed a leisurely evening and, if he could manage it for a change, a night's sleep in preparation for a working breakfast. If he'd known the journey would be broken, he could have reread his paperwork instead of contemplating scenery he couldn't even remember. No doubt the next train would already be laden with commuters— he doubted it would give him space to work. His skull was beginning to feel shrivelled and hollow when it occurred to him that if he caught a later train he would both ensure himself a seat and have time to drop in on his parents. When had he last been home to see them? All at once he felt so guilty that he preferred not to look anyone in the face as he excused his slow way to the ticket office.

It was closed—a board lent it the appearance of a frame divested of a photograph—but flanked by a timetable. Stoneby to London, Stoneby to London… There were trains on the hour, like the striking of a clock. He emerged from the short wooden passage into the somewhat less gloomy street, only to falter. Where was the sweet shop whose window used to exhibit dozens of glass-stoppered jars full of colours he could taste? Where was the toyshop fronted by a headlong model train that had never stopped for the travellers paralysed on the platform? What had happened to the bakery displaying tiered white cakes elaborate as Gothic steeples, and the bridal shop next door, where the headless figures in their pale dresses had made him think of Anne Boleyn? Now the street was overrun with the same fast-food eateries and immature clothes shops that surrounded him whenever he left his present apartment, and he couldn't recall how much change he'd seen on his last visit, whenever that had been. He felt suddenly so desperate to be somewhere more like home that he almost didn't wait for twin green men to pipe up and usher him across the road.

The short cut was still there, in a sense. Instead of separating the toyshop from the wedding dresses, it squeezed between a window occupied by a regiment of boots and a hamburger outlet dogged by plastic cartons. Once he was in the alley the clamour of traffic relented, but the narrow passage through featureless discoloured concrete made him feel walled in by the unfamiliar. Then the concrete gave way to russet bricks and released him into a street he knew.

At least, it conformed to his memory until he looked closer. The building opposite, which had begun life as a music hall, had ceased to be a cinema. A pair of letters clung to the whitish border of the rusty iron marquee, two letters N so insecure they were on the way to being Zs. He was striving to remember if the cinema had been shut last time he'd seen it when he noticed that the boards on either side of the lobby contained posters too small for the frames. The neighbouring buildings were boarded up. As he crossed the deserted street, the posters grew legible. MEMORIES OF STONEBY, the amateurish printing said.

The two wide steps beneath the marquee were cracked and chipped and stained. The glass of the ticket booth in the middle of the marble floor was too blackened to see through. Behind the booth the doors into the auditorium stood ajar. Uncertain what the gap was showing him, he ventured to peer in.

At first the dimness yielded up no more than a strip of carpet framed by floorboards just as grubby, and then he thought someone absolutely motionless was watching him from the dark. The watcher was roped off from him—the several indistinct figures were. He assumed they represented elements of local history: there was certainly something familiar about them. That impression, and the blurred faces with their dully glinting eyes, might have transfixed him if he hadn't remembered that he was supposed to be seeing his parents. He left the echo of his footsteps dwindling in the lobby and hurried around the side of the museum.

Where the alley crossed another he turned left along the rear of the building. In the high wall to his right a series of solid wooden gates led to back yards, the third of which belonged to his old house. As a child he'd used the gate as a short cut to the cinema, clutching a coin in his fist, which had smelled of metal whenever he'd raised it to his face in the crowded restless dark. His parents had never bolted the gate until he was home again, but now the only effect of his trying the latch was to rouse a clatter of claws and the snarling of a neighbour's dog that sounded either muzzled or gagged with food, and so he made for the street his old house faced.

The sunless sky was bringing on a twilight murky as an unlit room. He could have taken the street for an aisle between two blocks of dimness so lacking in features they might have been identical. Presumably any children who lived in the terrace were home from school by now, though he couldn't see the flicker of a single television in the windows draped with dusk, while the breadwinners had yet to return. Trent picked his way over the broken upheaved slabs of the pavement, supporting himself on the roof of a lone parked car until it shifted rustily under his hand, to his parents' front gate.

The small plot of a garden was a mass of weeds that had spilled across the short path. He couldn't feel it underfoot as he tramped to the door, which was the colour of the oncoming dark. He was fumbling in his pocket and then with the catches of his briefcase when he realised he would hardly have brought his old keys with him. He rang the doorbell, or at least pressed the askew pallid button that set off a muffled rattle somewhere in the house.

For the duration of more breaths than he could recall taking, there was no response. He was about to revive the noise, though he found it somehow distressing, when he heard footsteps shuffling down the hall. Their slowness made it sound as long as it had seemed in his childhood, so that he had the odd notion that whoever opened the door would tower over him.

It was his mother, and smaller than ever—wrinkled and whitish as a figure composed of dough that had been left to collect dust, a wad of it on top of and behind her head. She wore a tweed coat over a garment he took to be a nightdress, which exposed only her prominent ankles above a pair of unmatched slippers. Her head wavered upwards as the corners of her lips did. Once all these had steadied she murmured 'Is it you, Nigel? Are you back again?'

'I thought it was past time I was.'

'It's always too long.' She shuffled in a tight circle to present her stooped back to him before calling 'Guess who it is, Walter.'

'Hess looking for a place to hide,' Trent's father responded from some depth of the house.

'No, not old red-nosed Rudolph. Someone a bit younger and a bit more English.'

'The Queen come to tea.'

'He'll never change, will he?' Trent's mother muttered and raised what was left of her voice. 'It's the boy. It's Nigel.'

'About time. Let's see what he's managed to make of himself.'

She made a gesture like a desultory grab at something in the air above her left shoulder, apparently to beckon Trent along the hall. 'Be quick with the door, there's a good boy. We don't want the chill roosting in our old bones.'

As soon as the door shut behind him he couldn't distinguish whether the stairs that narrowed the hall by half were carpeted only with dimness. He trudged after his mother past a door that seemed barely sketched on the crawling murk and, more immediately than he expected, another. His mother opened a third, beyond which was the kitchen, he recalled rather than saw. It smelled of damp he hoped was mostly tea. By straining his senses he was just able to discern his father seated in some of the dark. 'Shall we have the light on?' Trent suggested.

'Can't you see? Thought you were supposed to be the young one round here.' After a pause his father said 'Come back for bunny, have you?'

Trent couldn't recall ever having owned a rabbit, toy or otherwise, yet the question seemed capable of reviving some aspect of his childhood. He was feeling surrounded by entirely too much darkness when his mother said 'Now, Walter, don't be teasing' and clicked the switch.

The naked dusty bulb seemed to draw the contents of the room inwards— the blackened stove and stained metal sink, the venerable shelves and cabinets and cupboards Trent's father had built, the glossy pallid walls. The old man was sunk in an armchair, the least appropriate of an assortment of seats surrounding the round table decorated with crumbs and unwashed plates. His pear-shaped variously reddish face appeared to have been given over to producing fat to merge with the rest of him. He used both shaky inflated hands to close the lapels of his faded dressing-gown over his pendulous chest cobwebbed with grey hairs. 'You've got your light,' he said, 'so take your place.'

Lowering himself onto a chair that had once been straight, Trent lost sight of the entrance to the alley—of the impression that it was the only aspect of the yard the window managed to illuminate. 'Will I make you some tea?' his mother said.

She wasn't asking him to predict the future, he reassured himself. 'So long as you're both having some as well.'

'Not much else to do these days.'

'It won't be that bad really, will it?' Trent said, forcing a guilty laugh. 'Aren't you still seeing...'

'What are we seeing?' his father prompted with some force.

'Your friends,' Trent said, having discovered that he couldn't recall a single name. 'They can't all have moved away.'

'Nobody moves any longer.'

Trent didn't know whether to take that as a veiled rebuke. 'So what have you two been doing with yourselves lately?'

'Late's the word.'

'Nigel's here now,' Trent's mother said, perhaps relevantly, over the descending hollow drum-roll of the kettle she was filling from the tap.

More time than was reasonable seemed to have passed since he'd entered the house. He was restraining himself from glancing even surreptitiously at his watch when his father quivered an impatient hand at him. 'So what are you up to now?'

'He means your work.'

'Same as always.'

Trent hoped that would suffice until he was able to reclaim his memory from the darkness that had gathered in his skull, but his parents' stares were as blank as his mind. 'And what's that?' his mother said.

He felt as though her forgetfulness had seized him. Desperate to be reminded what his briefcase contained, he nevertheless used reaching for it as a chance to glimpse his watch. The next train was due in less than half an hour. As Trent scrabbled at the catches of the briefcase, his father said 'New buildings, isn't it? That's what you put up.'

'Plan,' Trent said, clutching the briefcase on his lap. 'I draw them.'

'Of course you do,' said his mother. 'That's what you always wanted.'

It was partly so as not to feel minimised that Trent declared 'I wouldn't want to be responsible for some of the changes in town.'

'Then don't be.'

'You won't see much else changing round here,' Trent's mother said.

'Didn't anyone object?'

'You have to let the world move on,' she said. 'Leave it to the young ones.'

Trent wasn't sure if he was included in that or only wanted to be. 'How long have we had a museum?'

His father's eyes grew so blank Trent could have fancied they weren't in use. 'Since I remember.'

'No, that's not right,' Trent objected as gently as his nerves permitted. 'It was a cinema and before that a theatre. You took me to a show there once.'

'Did we?' A glint surfaced in his mother's eyes. 'We used to like shows, didn't we, Walter? Shows and dancing. Didn't we go on all night sometimes and they wondered where we'd got to?'

Her husband shook his head once slowly, whether to enliven memories or deny their existence Trent couldn't tell. 'The show you took me to,' he insisted, 'I remember someone dancing with a stick. And there was a lady comedian, or maybe not a lady but dressed up.'

Perhaps it was the strain of excavating the recollection that made it seem both lurid and encased in darkness—the outsize figure prancing sluggishly about the stage and turning towards him a sly greasy smile as crimson as a wound, the ponderous slap on the boards of feet that sounded unshod, the onslaughts of laughter that followed comments Trent found so incomprehensible he feared they were about him, the shadow that kept swelling on whatever backdrop the performer had, an effect suggesting that the figure was about to grow yet more gigantic. Surely some or preferably most of that was a childhood nightmare rather than a memory. 'Was there some tea?' Trent blurted.

At first it seemed his mother's eyes were past seeing through their own blankness. 'In the show, do you mean?'

'Here.' When that fell short of her he said more urgently 'Now.'

'Why, you should have reminded me,' she protested and stood up. How long had she been seated opposite him? He was so anxious to remember that he didn't immediately grasp what she was doing. 'Mother, don't,' he nearly screamed, flinging himself off his chair.

'No rush. It isn't anything like ready.' She took her hand out of the kettle on the stove—he wasn't sure if he glimpsed steam trailing from her fingers as she replaced the lid. 'We haven't got much longer, have we?' she said. 'We mustn't keep you from your duties.'

'You won't do that again, will you?'

'What's that, son?'

He was dismayed to think she might already have forgotten. 'You won't put yourself in danger.'

'There's nothing we'd call that round here,' his father said.

'You'll look after each other, won't you? I really ought to catch the next train. I'll be back to see you again soon, I promise, and next time it'll be longer.'

'It will.'

His parents said that not quite in chorus, apparently competing at slowness. 'Till next time, then,' he said and shook his father's hand before hugging his mother. Both felt disconcertingly cold and unyielding, as if the appearance of each had hardened into a carapace. He gripped the handle of his briefcase while he strove to twist the rusty key in the back door. 'I'll go my old way, shall I? It's quicker.'

When nobody answered he hauled open the door, which felt unhinged. Cobwebbed weeds sprawled over the doorstep into the kitchen at once. Weedy mounds of earth or rubble had overwhelmed the yard and the path. He picked his way to the gate and with an effort turned his head, but nobody was following to close the gate: his mother was still at her post by the stove, his father was deep in the armchair. He had to use both hands to wrench the bolt out of its socket, and almost forgot to retrieve his briefcase as he stumbled into the alley. The passage was unwelcomingly dark, not least because the light from the house failed to reach it—no, because the kitchen was unlit. He dragged the gate shut and took time to engage the latch before heading for the rear of the museum.

Damp must be stiffening his limbs. He hoped it was in the air, not in his parents' house. Was it affecting his vision as well? When he slogged to the end of the alley the street appeared to be composed of little but darkness, except for the museum. The doors to the old auditorium were further ajar, and as he crossed the road Trent saw figures miming in the dimness. He hadn't time to identify their faces before panting down the alley where brick was ousted by concrete.

Figures sat in the stark restaurants and modelled clothes in windows. Otherwise the street was deserted except for a man who dashed into the station too fast for Trent to see his face. The man let fly a wordless plea and waved his briefcase as he sprinted through the booking hall. Trent had just begun to precipitate himself across the road when he heard the slam of a carriage door. He staggered ahead of his breath onto the platform in time to see the last light of a train vanish into the trees, which looked more like a tunnel than ever.

His skull felt frail with rage again. Once he regained the ability to move he stumped to glower at the timetable next to the boarded-up office. His fiercest glare was unable to change the wait into less than an hour. He marched up and down a few times, but each end of the platform met him with increasing darkness. He had to keep moving to ward off a chill stiffness. He trudged into the street and frowned about him.

The fast-food outlets didn't appeal to him, neither their impersonal refreshments nor the way all the diners faced the street as though to watch him, not that doing so lent them any animation. He couldn't even see anyone eating. Ignoring the raw red childishly sketched men, he lurched across the road into the alley.

He oughtn't to go to his parents. So instant a return might well confuse them, and just now his own mind felt more than sufficiently unfocused. The only light, however tentative, in the next street came from the museum. He crossed the roadway, which was as lightless as the low sky, and climbed the faint steps.

Was the ticket booth lit? A patch of the blackened glass had been rubbed relatively clear from within. He was fumbling for money to plant on the sill under the gap at the foot of the window when he managed to discern that the figure in the booth was made of wax. While it resembled the middle-aged woman who had occupied the booth when the building was a cinema, it ought to look years—no, decades—older. Its left grey-cardiganed arm was raised to indicate the auditorium. He was unable to judge its expression for the gloom inside the booth. Tramping to the doors, he pushed them wide.

That seemed only to darken the auditorium, but he felt the need to keep on the move before his eyes had quite adjusted. The apparently sourceless twilight put him in mind of the glow doled out by the candle that used to stand in an encrusted saucer on the table by his childhood bed. As he advanced under the enormous unseen roof, he thought he was walking on the same carpet that had led into the cinema and indeed the theatre. He was abreast of the first of the figures on either side of the aisle before he recognised them.

He'd forgotten they were sisters, the two women who had run the bakery and the adjacent bridal shop. Had they really been twins? They were playing bridesmaids in identical white ankle-length dresses—whitish, rather, and trimmed with dust. Presumably it was muslin as well as dust that gloved their hands, which were pointing with all their digits along the aisle. The dull glints of their grimy eyes appeared to spy sidelong on him. He'd taken only a few steps when he stumbled to a halt and peered about him.

The next exhibits were disconcerting enough. No doubt the toyshop owner was meant to be introducing his model railway, but he looked as if he was crouching sideways to grab whatever sought refuge in the miniature tunnel. Opposite him the sweet shop man was enticing children to his counter, which was heaped with sweets powdered grey, by performing on a sugar whistle not entirely distinguishable from his glimmering teeth. Trent hadn't time to ascertain what was odd about the children's wide round eyes, because he was growing aware of the extent of the museum.

Surely it must be a trick of the unreliable illumination, but the more he gazed around him, the farther the dimness populated with unmoving figures seemed to stretch. If it actually extended so far ahead and to both sides, it would encompass at least the whole of the street that contained his parents' house. He wavered forward a couple of paces, which only encouraged figures to solidify out of that part of the murk. He swivelled as quickly as he was able and stalked out of the museum.

The echoes of his footsteps pursued him across the lobby like mocking applause. He could hear no other sound, and couldn't tell whether he was being watched from the ticket booth. He found his way down the marble steps and along the front of the museum. In a few seconds he was sidling crabwise along it in order to differentiate the alley from the unlit façade. He wandered farther than he should have, and made his way back more slowly. Before long he was groping with his free hand at the wall as he ranged back and forth, but it was no use. There was no alley, just unbroken brick.

He was floundering in search of a crossroads, from which there surely had to be a route to his old house, when he realised he might as well be blind. He glanced back, praying wordlessly for any relief from the dark. There was only the glow from the museum lobby. It seemed as feeble as the candle flame had grown in the moment before it guttered into smoke, and so remote he thought his stiff limbs might be past carrying him to it. When he retreated towards it, at first he seemed not to be moving at all.

More time passed than he could grasp before he felt sure the light was closer. Later still he managed to distinguish the outstretched fingertips of his free hand. He clung to his briefcase as though it might be snatched from him. He was abreast of the lobby, and preparing to abandon its glow for the alley that led to the station, when he thought he heard a whisper from inside the museum. 'Are you looking for us?'

It was either a whisper or so distant that it might as well be one. 'We're in here, son,' it said, and its companion added 'You'll have to come to us.'

'Mother?' It was unquestionably her voice, however faint. He almost tripped over the steps as he sent himself into the lobby. For a moment, entangled in the clapping of his footsteps on the marble, he thought he heard a large but muted sound as of the surreptitious arrangement of a crowd. He blundered to the doors and peered into the auditorium.

Under the roof, which might well have been an extension of the low ponderous black sky, the aisle and its guardians were at least as dim as ever. Had things changed, or had he failed to notice details earlier? The bridal sisters were licking their lips, and he wasn't sure if they were dressed as bridesmaids or baked into giant tiered cakes from which they were trying to struggle free. Both of the toyshop owner's hands looked eager to seize the arrested train if it should try to reach the safety of the tunnel, and the bulging eyes of the children crowded around the man with the sugar whistle—were those sweets? Trent might have retreated if his mother's voice hadn't spoken to him. 'That's it, son. Don't leave us this time.'

'Have a thought for us. Don't start us wondering where you are again. We're past coming to find you.'

'Where are you? I can't see.'

'Just carry on straight,' his parents' voices took it in turns to murmur.

He faltered before lurching between the first exhibits. Beyond them matters could hardly be said to improve. He did his best not to see too much of the milkman holding the reins of a horse while a cow followed the cart, but the man's left eye seemed large enough for the horse, the right for the cow. Opposite him stood a rag and bone collector whose trade was apparent from the companion that hung onto his arm, and Trent was almost glad of the flickering dimness. 'How much further?' he cried in a voice that the place shrank almost to nothing.

'No more than you can walk at your age.'

Trent hung onto the impression that his father sounded closer than before and hugged his briefcase while he made his legs carry him past a policeman who'd removed his helmet to reveal a bald ridged head as pointed as a chrysalis, a priest whose smooth face was balanced on a collar of the same paleness and no thicker than a child's wrist, a window cleaner with scrawny legs folded like a grasshopper's, a bus conductor choked by his tie that was caught in his ticket machine while at the front of the otherwise deserted vehicle the driver displayed exactly the same would-be comical strangled face and askew swollen tongue... They were nightmares, Trent told himself: some he remembered having suffered as a child, and the rest he was afraid to remember in case they grew clearer. 'I still can't see you,' he all but wailed.

'Down here, son.'

Did they mean ahead? He hoped he wasn't being told to use any of the side aisles, not least because they seemed capable of demonstrating that the place was even vaster than he feared. The sights they contained were more elaborate too. Off to the right was a brass band, not marching but frozen in the act of tiptoeing towards him: though all the players had lowered their instruments, their mouths were perfectly round. In the dimness to his left, and scarcely more luminous, was a reddish bonfire surrounded by figures that wore charred masks, unless those were their faces, and beyond that was a street party where children sat at trestle tables strewn with food and grimaced in imitation of the distorted versions of their faces borne by deflating balloons they held on strings... Trent twisted his stiff body around in case some form of reassurance was to be found behind him, but the exit to the lobby was so distant he could have mistaken it for the last of a flame. He half-closed his eyes to blot out the sights he had to pass, only to find that made the shadows of the exhibits and the darkness into which the shadows trailed loom closer, as if the dimness was on the point of being finally extinguished. He was suddenly aware that if the building had still been a theatre, the aisle would have brought him to the stage by now. 'Where are you?' he called but was afraid to raise his voice. 'Can't you speak?'

'Right here.'

His eyes sprang so wide they felt fitted into their sockets. His parents weren't just close, they were behind him. He turned with difficulty and saw why he'd strayed past them. His mother was wearing a top hat and tails and had finished twirling a cane that resembled a lengthening of one knobbly finger; his father was bulging out of a shabby flowered dress that failed to conceal several sections of a pinkish bra. They'd dressed up to cure Trent of his nightmare about the theatre performance, he remembered, but they had only brought it into his waking hours. He backed away from it—from their waxen faces greyish with down, their smiles as fixed as their eyes. His legs collided with an object that folded them up, and he tottered sideways to sit helplessly on it. 'That's it, son,' his mother succeeded in murmuring.

'That's your place,' his father said with a last shifting of his lips.

Trent glared downwards and saw he was trapped by a school desk barely large enough to accommodate him. On either side of him sat motionless children as furred with grey as their desks, even their eyes. Between him and his parents a teacher in a gown and mortarboard was standing not quite still and sneering at him. 'Mr Bunnie,' Trent gasped, remembering how the teacher had always responded to being addressed by his name as though it was an insult. Then, in a moment of clarity that felt like a beacon in the dark, he realised he had some defence. 'This isn't me,' he tried to say calmly but firmly. 'This is.'

His fingers were almost too unmanageable to deal with the briefcase. He levered at the rusty metal buttons with his thumbs until at last the catches flew open and the contents spilled across the desk. For a breath, if he had any, Trent couldn't see them in the dimness, and then he made out that they were half a dozen infantile crayon drawings of houses. 'I've done more than that,' he struggled to protest, 'I am more,' but his mouth had finished working. He managed only to raise his head, and never knew which was worse: his paralysis, or his parents' doting smiles, or the sneer that the teacher's face seemed to have widened to encompass—the sneer that had always meant that once a child was inside the school gates, his parents could no longer protect him. It might have been an eternity before the failure of the dimness or of Trent's eyes brought the dark.

RAMSEY CAMPBELL IS described in *The Oxford Companion to English Literature* as 'Britain's most respected living horror writer'. He has been given more awards than any other writer in the field, including the Grand Master Award of the World Horror Convention, the Lifetime Achievement Award of the Horror Writers Association, the Living Legend Award of the International Horror Guild and the World Fantasy Lifetime Achievement Award. In 2015 he was made an Honorary Fellow of Liverpool John Moores University for outstanding services to literature. Among his novels are *The Face That Must Die, Incarnate, Midnight Sun, The Count of Eleven, Silent Children, The Darkest Part of the Woods, The Overnight, Secret Story, The Grin of the Dark, Thieving Fear, Creatures of the Pool, The Seven Days of Cain, Ghosts Know, The Kind Folk, Think Yourself Lucky, Thirteen Days by Sunset Beach, The Wise Friend* and *Somebody's Voice*. He recently brought out his Brichester Mythos trilogy, consisting of *The Searching Dead, Born to the Dark* and *The Way of the Worm*. His collections include *Waking Nightmares, Alone with the Horrors, Ghosts and Grisly Things, Told by the Dead, Just Behind You, Holes for Faces, By the Light of My Skull* and a two-volume retrospective round-up (*Phantasmagorical Stories*). His non-fiction is collected as *Ramsey Campbell, Probably* and *Ramsey's Rambles* (video reviews). *Limericks of the Alarming and Phantasmal* is a history of horror fiction in the form of fifty limericks. His novels *The Nameless, Pact of the Fathers* and *The Influence* have been filmed in Spain, where a television series based on *The Nameless* is in development. He is the President of the Society of Fantastic Films. According to the author, '"The Retrospective" grew from the idea of the museum in an unfamiliar town. It feels to me somewhat like my tribute to Thomas Ligotti.'

///

THE TWO SAMS

Glen Hirshberg

for both of you

WHAT WAKES ME isn't a sound. At first, I have no idea what it is: an earthquake, maybe; a vibration in the ground; a 2:00 a.m. truck shuddering along the switchback road that snakes up from the beach, past the ruins of the Baths, past the Cliff House and the automatons and coin-machines chattering in the Musee Mechanique, past our apartment building until it reaches the flatter stretch of the Great Highway, which will return it to the saner neighbourhoods of San Francisco. I lie still, holding my breath without knowing why. With the moon gone, the watery light rippling over the chipping bas-relief curlicues on our wall and the scuffed, tilted hardwood floor makes the room seem insubstantial, a projected reflection from the camera obscura perched on the cliffs a quarter mile away.

Then I feel it again, and I realise it's in the bed, not the ground. Right beside me. Instantly, I'm smiling. I can't help it. *You're playing on your own, aren't you?* That's what I'm thinking. Our first game. He sticks up a tiny fist,

427

a twitching foot, a butt cheek, pressing against the soft roof and walls of his world, and I lay my palm against him, and he shoots off across the womb, curls in a far corner, waits. Sticks out a foot again.

The game terrified me at first. I kept thinking about signs in aquariums warning against tapping on glass, giving fish heart attacks. But he kept playing. And tonight, the thrum of his life is like magic fingers in the mattress, shooting straight up my spine into my shoulders, settling me, squeezing the terror out. Shifting the sheets softly, wanting Lizzie to sleep, I lean closer, and know, all at once, that this isn't what woke me.

For a split second, I'm frozen. I want to whip my arms around my head, ward them off like mosquitoes or bees, but I can't hear anything, not this time. There's just that creeping damp, the heaviness in the air, like a fogbank forming. Abruptly, I dive forwards, drop my head against the hot, round dome of Lizzie's stomach. Maybe I'm wrong, I think. I could be wrong. I press my ear against her skin, hold my breath, and for one horrible moment, I hear nothing at all, just the sea of silent, amniotic fluid. I'm thinking about that couple, the Super Jews from our Bradley class who started coming when they were already seven months along. They came five straight weeks, and the woman would reach out, sometimes, tug her husband's prayer-curls, and we all smiled, imagining their daughter doing that, and then they weren't there anymore. The woman woke up one day and felt strange, empty, she walked around for hours that way and finally just got in her car and drove to the hospital and had her child, knowing it was dead.

But under my ear, something is moving now. I can hear it inside my wife. Faint, unconcerned, unmistakable. Beat. Beat.

'*Get out Tom's old records…*' I sing, so softly, into Lizzie's skin. It isn't the song I used to use. Before, I mean. It's a new song. We do everything new, now. '*And he'll come dancing 'round.*' It occurs to me that this song might not be the best choice, either. There are lines in it that could come back to haunt me, just the way the others have, the ones I never want to hear again, never even used to notice when I sang that song. They come creeping into my ears now, as though they're playing very quietly in a neighbour's room. '*I dreamed I held you. In my arms. When I awoke, dear. I was mistaken. And so I hung my head and I cried.'* But then, I've found, that's the first great lesson of pregnancy: it all comes back to haunt you.

I haven't thought of this song, though, since the last time, I realise. Maybe they bring it with them.

Amidst the riot of thoughts in my head, a new one spins to the surface. Was it there the very first time? Did I feel the damp then? Hear the song? Because if I did, and I'm wrong...

I can't remember. I remember Lizzie screaming. The bathtub, and Lizzie screaming.

Sliding slowly back, I ease away towards my edge of the bed, then sit up, holding my breath. Lizzie doesn't stir, just lies there like the gutshot creature she is, arms wrapped tight and low around her stomach, as though she could hold this one in, hold herself in, just a few days more. Her chin is tucked tight to her chest, dark hair wild on the pillow, bloated legs clamped around the giant, blue cushion between them. Tip her upright, I think, and she'd look like a little girl on a Hoppity Horse. Then her kindergarten students would laugh at her again, clap and laugh when they saw her, the way they used to. Before.

For the thousandth time in the past few weeks, I have to quash an urge to lift her black-framed, square glasses from around her ears. She has insisted on sleeping with them since March, since the day the life inside her became—in the words of Dr Seger, the woman Lizzie believes will save us—'viable', and the ridge in her nose is red and deep, now, and her eyes, always strangely small, seem to have slipped back in their sockets, as though cringing away from the unaccustomed closeness of the world, its unblurred edges. 'The second I'm awake,' Lizzie tells me, savagely, the way she says everything these days, 'I want to see.'

'Sleep,' I mouth, and it comes out a prayer.

Gingerly, I put my bare feet on the cold ground and stand. Always, it takes just a moment to adjust to the room. Because of the tilt of the floor—caused by the earthquake in '89—and the play of light over the walls and the sound of the surf and, sometimes, the seals out on Seal Rock and the litter of woodscraps and sawdust and half-built toys and menorahs and disembowelled clocks on every table-top, walking through our apartment at night is like floating through a shipwreck.

Where are you? I think to the room, the shadows, turning in multiple directions as though my thoughts were a lighthouse beam. If they are, I need to switch them off. The last thing I want to provide, at this moment, for them, is a lure. Sweat breaks out on my back, my legs, as though I've been wrung. I don't want to breathe, don't want this infected air in my lungs, but I force myself. I'm ready. I have prepared, this time. I'll do what I must, if it's not too late and I get the chance.

'Where are you?' I whisper aloud, and something happens in the hall, in the doorway. Not movement. Not anything I can explain. But I start over there, fast. It's much better if they're out there. 'I'm coming,' I say, and I'm out of the bedroom, pulling the door closed behind me as if that will help, and when I reach the living room, I consider snapping on the light but don't.

On the wall over the square, dark couch—we bought it dark, we were anticipating stains—the Pinocchio clock, first one I ever built, at age fourteen, makes its steady, hollow tock. It's all nose, that clock, which seems like such a bad idea, in retrospect. What was I saying, and to whom? *The hour is a lie. The room is a lie. Time is a lie.* 'Gepetto,' Lizzie used to call me before we were married, then after we were married, for a while, back when I used to show up outside her classroom door to watch her weaving between desks, balancing hamsters and construction paper and graham crackers and half-pint milk cartons in her arms while kindergartners nipped between and around her legs like ducklings.

Gepetto. Who tried so hard to make a living boy.

Tock.

'Stop,' I snap to myself, to the leaning walls. There is less damp here. They're somewhere else.

The first tremble comes as I return to the hall. I clench my knees, my shoulders, willing myself still. As always, the worst thing about the trembling and the sweating is the confusion that causes them. I can never decide if I'm terrified or elated. Even before I realised what was happening, there was a kind of elation.

Five steps down the hall, I stop at the door to what was once our workshop, housing my building area and Lizzie's cut-and-paste table for classroom decorations. It has not been a workshop for almost four years, now. For four years, it has been nothing at all. The knob is just a little wet when I slide my hand around it, the hinges silent as I push open the door.

'Okay,' I half-think, half-say, trembling, sliding into the room and shutting the door behind me. 'It's okay.' Tears leap out of my lashes as though they've been hiding there. It doesn't feel like I actually cried them. I sit down on the bare floor, breathe, and stare around the walls, also bare. One week more. Two weeks, tops. Then, just maybe, the crib, fully assembled, will burst from the closet, the dog-cat carpet will unroll itself like a Torah scroll over the hardwood, and the mobiles Lizzie and I made together will spring from the ceiling like streamers. *Surprise!*

The tears feel cold on my face, uncomfortable, but I don't wipe them. What would be the point? I try to smile. There's a part of me, a small, sad part, that feels like smiling. 'Should I tell you a bedtime story?'

I could tell about the possum. We'd lost just the one, then, and more than a year had gone by, and Lizzie still had moments, seizures, almost, where she ripped her glasses off her face in the middle of dinner and hurled them across the apartment and jammed herself into the kitchen corner behind the stacked washer-dryer unit. I'd stand over her and say, 'Lizzie, no,' and try to fight what I was feeling, because I didn't like that I was feeling it. But the more often this happened, and it happened a lot, the angrier I got. Which made me feel like such a shit.

'Come on,' I'd say, extra-gentle, to compensate, but of course I didn't fool her. That's the thing about Lizzie. I knew it when I married her, even loved it in her: she recognises the worst in people. She can't help it. And she's never wrong about it.

'You don't even care,' she'd hiss, her hands snarled in her twisting brown hair as though she were going to rip it out like weeds.

'Fuck you, of course I care.'

'It doesn't mean anything to you.'

'It means what it means. It means we tried, and it didn't work, and it's awful, and the doctors say it happens all the time, and we need to try again. It's awful but we have to deal with it, we have no choice if we want—'

'It means we lost a child. It means our child died. You asshole.'

Once—one time—I handled that moment right. I looked down at my wife, my playmate since junior high, the perpetually sad person I make happy, sometimes, and who makes everyone around her happy even though she's sad, and I saw her hands twist harder in her hair, and I saw her shoulders cave in towards her knees, and I just blurted it out.

'You look like a lint ball,' I told her.

Her face flew off her chest, and she glared at me. Then she threw her arms out, not smiling, not free of anything, but wanting me with her. Down I came. We were lint balls together.

Every single other time, I blew it. I stalked away. Or I started to cry. Or I fought back.

'Let's say that's true,' I'd say. 'We lost a child. I'll admit it, I can see how one could choose to see it that way. But I don't feel that. By the grace of God, it doesn't quite feel like that to me.'

'That's because it wasn't inside you.'

'That's such…' I'd start, then stop, because I didn't really think it was. And it wasn't what I was trying to say, anyway. 'Lizzie. God. I'm just… I'm trying to do this well. I'm trying to get us to the place where we can try again. Where we can have a child. One that lives. Because that's the point, isn't it? That's the ultimate goal?'

'*Honey, this one just wasn't meant to be,*' Lizzie would sneer, imitating her mom, or maybe my mom, or any one of a dozen people we knew. 'Is that what you want to say next?'

'You know it isn't.'

'How about, "*The body knows. Something just wasn't right. These things do happen for a reason*".'

'Lizzie, stop.'

'Or, "*Years from now, you'll look at your child, your living, breathing, beautiful child, and you'll realise that you wouldn't have had him or her if the first one had survived. There'd be a completely different creature there*". How about that one?'

'Lizzie, Goddamnit. Just shut up. I'm saying none of those things, and you know it. I'm saying I wish this had never happened. And now that it has happened, I want it to be something that happened in the past. Because I still want to have a baby with you.'

Usually, most nights, she'd sit up, then. I'd hand her her glasses, and she'd fix them on her face and blink as the world rushed forwards. Then she'd look at me, not unkindly. More than once, I'd thought she was going to touch my face or my hand.

Instead, what she said was, 'Jake. You have to understand.' Looking through her lenses at those moments was like peering through a storm window, something I would never again get open, and through it I could see the shadows of everything Lizzie carried with her and could not bury and didn't seem to want to. 'Of all the things that have happened to me. All of them. You're probably the best. And this is the worst.'

Then she'd get up, step around me, and go to bed. And I'd go out to walk, past the Cliff House, past the Musee, sometimes all the way down to the ruins of the Baths, where I'd stroll along the crumbling concrete walls which once had framed the largest public bathing pool in the United States and now framed nothing but marsh-grass and drain-water and echo. Sometimes, the fog would roll over me, a long, grey ghost-tide, and I'd float off on it, in it, just another trail of living vapour combing the earth in search of a world we'd all gotten the idea was here somewhere. Where, I wonder, had that idea come from, and how did so many of us get it?

'But that isn't what you want to hear,' I say suddenly to the not-quite-empty workroom, the cribless floor. 'Is it?' For a second, I panic, fight down the urge to leap for my feet and race for Lizzie. If they've gone back in there, then I'm too late anyway. And if they haven't, my leaping about just might scare them in that direction. In my head, I'm casting around for something to say that will hold them while I swing my gaze back and forth, up to the ceiling and down again.

'I was going to tell you about the possum, right? One night, maybe eight months or so after you were...' The word curls on my tongue like a dead caterpillar. I say it anyway. 'Born.' Nothing screams in my face or flies at me, and my voice doesn't break. And I think something might have fluttered across the room from me, something other than the curtains. I have to believe it did. And the damp is still in here.

'It was pretty amazing,' I say fast, staring at where the flutter was, as though I could pin it there. 'Lizzie kicked me and woke me up. "You hear that?" she asked. And of course, I did. Fast, hard scrabbling, click-click-click, from right in here. We came running and saw a tail disappear behind the dresser. There was a dresser, then, I made it myself. The drawers came out sideways and the handles formed kind of a pumpkin-face, just for fun, you know? Anyway, I got down on my hands and knees and found this huge, white possum staring right at me. I didn't even know there were possums here. This one took a single look at me and keeled over with its feet in the air. Playing dead.'

I throw myself on the ground with my feet in the air. It's like a memory, a dream, a memory of a dream, but I half-believe I feel a weight on the soles of my feet, as though something has climbed onto them, for a ride, maybe.

'I got a broom. Your... Lizzie got a trashcan. And for the next, I don't know, three hours, probably, we chased this thing around and around the room. We had the windows wide open. All it had to do was hop up and out. Instead, it hid behind the dresser, playing dead, until I poked it with the broom, and then it would race along the baseboard or into the middle of the room and flip on its back again, as if to say, okay, now I'm really dead, and we couldn't get it to go up and out. We couldn't get it to do anything but die. Over and over and over. And...'

I stop, lower my legs abruptly, sit up. I don't say the rest. How, at 3:45 in the morning, Lizzie dropped the trashcan to the floor, looked at me, and burst out crying. Threw her glasses at the wall and broke one of the lenses and wept while I stood there, so tired, with this possum belly-up at my feet and the sea air flooding the room. I'd loved the laughing. I could hardly stand up for exhaustion, and I'd loved laughing with Lizzie so goddamn much.

'Lizzie,' I'd said. 'I mean, fuck. Not everything has to relate to that. Does it? Does everything we ever think or do, for the rest of our lives...' But of course, it does. I think I even knew that then. And that was after only one.

'Would you like to go for a walk?' I say carefully, clearly. Because this is it. The only thing I can think of, and therefore the only chance we have. How does one get a child to listen, really? I wouldn't know. 'We'll go for a stroll, okay? Get nice and sleepy?' I still can't see anything. Most of the other times, I've caught half a glimpse, at some point, a trail of shadow. Turning, leaving the door cracked open behind me, I head for the living room. I slide my trench coat over my boxers and Green Apple T-shirt, slip my tennis shoes onto my bare feet. My ankles will be freezing. In the pocket of my coat, I feel the matchbook I left there, the single, tiny, silver key. It has been two months, at least, since the last time they came, or at least since they let me know it. But I have stayed ready.

As I step onto our stoop, wait a few seconds, and pull the door closed, I am flooded with sensory memory—it's like being dunked—of the day I first became aware. Over two years ago, now. Over a year after the first one. Halfway to dreaming, all but asleep, I was overcome by an overwhelming urge to put my ear to Lizzie's womb and sing to the new tenant in there. Almost six weeks old, at that point. I imagined seeing through my wife's skin, watching toe and finger-shapes forming in the red, waving wetness like lines on an Etch-A-Sketch.

'*You are my sun*—' I started, and knew, just like that, that something else was with me. There was the damp, for one thing, and an extra sound-lessness in the room, right beside me. I can't explain it. The sound of someone else listening.

I reacted on instinct, shot upright and accidentally yanked all the blankets off Lizzie and shoved out my arms at where the presence seemed to be, and Lizzie blinked awake and narrowed her spectacle-less eyes at the shape of me, the covers twisted on the bed.

'There's something here,' I babbled, pushing with both hands at the empty air.

Lizzie just squinted, coolly. Finally, after a few seconds, she snatched one of my waving hands out of the air and dropped it against her belly. Her skin felt smooth, warm. My forefinger slipped into her bellybutton, felt the familiar knot of it, and I found myself aroused. Terrified, confused, ridiculous, and aroused.

'It's just Sam,' she said, stunning me. It seemed impossible that she was going to let me win that fight. Then she smiled, pressing my hand to the second creature we had created together. 'You and me and Sam.' She pushed harder on my hand, slid it down her belly towards the centre of her.

We made love, held each other, sang to her stomach. Not until long after Lizzie had fallen asleep, just as I was dropping off at last, did it occur to me that she could have been more right than she knew. Maybe it was just us, and Sam. The first Sam—the one we'd lost—returning to greet his successor with us.

Of course, he hadn't come just to listen, or to watch. But how could I have known that, then? And how did I know that that was what the presence was, anyway? I didn't. And when it came back late the next night, with Lizzie this time sound asleep and me less startled, I slid aside to make room for it so we could both hear. Both whisper.

Are both of you with me now, I wonder? I'm standing on my stoop and listening, feeling, as hard as I can. Please, God, let them be with me. Not with Lizzie. Not with the new one. That's the only name we have allowed ourselves this time. The new one.

'Come on,' I say to my own front door, to the filigrees of fog that float forever on the air of Sutro Heights, as though the atmosphere itself has developed bas-relief and gone art-deco. 'Please. I'll tell you a story about the day you were born.'

I start down the warped, wooden steps towards our garage. Inside my pocket, the little silver key darts between my fingers, slippery and cool as a minnow.

In my mouth, I taste the fog and the perpetual garlic smell from the latest building to perch at the jut of the cliffs and call itself the Cliff House—the preceding three all collapsed or burned to the ground—and something else, too. I realise, finally, what it is, and the tears come flooding back.

What I'm remembering, this time, is Washington DC, the grass brown and dying in the blazing August sun as we raced down the Mall from museum to museum in a desperate, headlong hunt for cheese. We were in the ninth day of the ten-day tetracycline programme Dr Seger had prescribed, and Lizzie just seemed tired, but I swear I could feel the walls of my intestines, raw and sharp and scraped clean, the way teeth feel after a particularly vicious visit to the dentist. I craved milk, and got nauseous just thinking about it. Drained of its germs, its soft, comforting skin of use, my body felt skeletal, a shell without me in it.

That was the point, as Dr Seger explained it to us. We'd done our Tay-Sachs, tested for lead, endured endless blood screenings to check on things like prolactin, lupus anticoagulant, TSH. We would have done more tests, but the doctors didn't recommend them, and our insurance wouldn't pay. 'A couple of miscarriages, it's really not worth intensive investigation.' Three different doctors told us that. 'If it happens a couple more times, we'll know something's really wrong.'

Dr Seger had a theory, at least, involving old bacteria lingering in the body for years, decades, tucked up in the fallopian tubes or hidden in the testicles or just adrift in the blood, riding the heart-current in an endless, mindless, circle. 'The mechanism of creation is so delicate,' she told us. 'So efficiently, masterfully created. If anything gets in there that shouldn't be, well, it's like a bird in a jet-engine. Everything just explodes.'

How comforting, I thought but didn't say at that first consultation, because when I glanced at Lizzie, she looked more than comforted. She looked hungry, perched on the edge of her chair with her head half over Dr Seger's desk, so pale, thin, and hard, like a starved pigeon being teased with crumbs. I wanted to grab her hand. I wanted to weep.

As it turns out, Dr Seger may have been right. Or maybe we got lucky this time. Because that's the thing about miscarriage: three thousand years of human medical science, and no one knows any fucking thing at all. It just happens, people say, like a bruise, or a cold. And it does, I suppose. Just happen, I mean. But not like a cold. Like dying. Because that's what it is.

So for ten days, Dr Seger had us drop tetracycline tablets down our throats like depth charges, blasting everything living inside us out. And on that day in DC—we were visiting my cousin, the first time I'd managed to coax Lizzie anywhere near extended family since all this started—we'd gone to the Holocaust Museum, searching for anything strong enough to take our minds off our hunger, our desperate hope that we were scoured, healthy, clean. But it didn't work. So we went to the Smithsonian. And three people from the front of the ticket-line, Lizzie suddenly grabbed my hand, and I looked at her, and it was the old Lizzie, or the ghost of her, eyes flashing under their black rims, smile instantaneous, shockingly bright.

'Dairy,' she said. 'Right this second.'

It took me a breath to adjust. I hadn't seen my wife this way in a long, long while, and as I stared, the smile slipped on her face. With a visible effort, she pinned it back in place. 'Jake. Come on.'

None of the museum cafés had what we wanted. We went racing past sculptures and animal dioramas and parchment documents to the cafés, where we stared at yoghurt in plastic containers—but we didn't dare eat yoghurt—and cups of tapioca that winked, in our fevered state, like the iced-over surfaces of Canadian lakes. But none of it would have served. We needed a cheddar wheel, a lasagne we could scrape free of pasta and tomatoes so we could drape our tongues in strings of crusted mozzarella. What we settled for, finally, was four giant bags of generic cheese puffs from a 7-11. We sat together on the edge of a fountain and stuffed each other's mouths like babies, like lovers.

It wasn't enough. The hunger didn't abate in either of us. Sometimes I think it hasn't since.

God, it was glorious, though. Lizzie's lips around my orange-stained fingers, that soft, gorgeous crunch as each individual puff popped apart in our mouths, dusting our teeth and throats while spray from the fountain brushed our faces and we dreamed separate, still-hopeful dreams of children.

And that, in the end, is why I have to, you see. My two Sams. My lost, loved ones. Because maybe it's true. It doesn't seem like it could be, but maybe it is. Maybe, mostly, it just happens. And then, for most couples, it just stops happening one day. And afterwards—if only because there isn't time—you start to forget. Not what happened. Not what was lost. But what the loss meant, or at least what it felt like. I've come to believe that time alone won't swallow grief or heal a marriage. But perhaps filled time...

In my pocket, my fingers close over the silver key, and I take a deep breath of the damp in the air, which is mostly just Sutro Heights damp now that we're outside. We have always loved it here, Lizzie and I. In spite of everything, we can't bring ourselves to flee. 'Let me show you,' I say, trying not to plead. I've taken too long, I think. They've gotten bored. They'll go back in the house. I lift the ancient, rusted padlock on our garage door, tilt it so I can see the slot in the moonlight, and slide the key home.

It has been months since I've been out here—we use the garage for storage, not for our old Nova—and I've forgotten how heavy the salt-saturated wooden door is. It comes up with a creak, slides over my head and rocks unsteadily in its runners. How, I'm thinking, did I first realise that the presence in my room was my first, unborn child? The smell, I guess, like an unripe lemon, fresh and sour all at once. Lizzie's smell. Or maybe it was the song springing unbidden, over and over, to my lips. '*When I awoke dear. I was mistaken.*' Those things, and the fact that now, these last times, they both seem to be there.

The first thing I see once my eyes adjust is my grandfather glaring out of his portrait at me, his hair thread-thin and wild on his head like a spider-web swinging free, his lips flat, crushed together, his ridiculous lumpy potato of a body under his perpetually half-zipped judges' robes. And there are his eyes, one blue, one green, which he once told me allowed him to see 3-D, before I knew that everyone could. A children's rights activist before there was a name for such things, a three-time candidate for a state bench seat and three-time loser, he'd made an enemy of his daughter, my mother, by wanting a son so badly. And he'd made a disciple out of me by saving Lizzie's life. Turning her father in to the cops, then making sure that he got thrown in jail, then forcing both him and his whole family into counselling, getting him work when he got out, checking in on him every single night, no matter what, for six years, until Lizzie was away and free. Until eight months ago, on the day Dr Seger confirmed that we were pregnant for the third time, his portrait hung beside the Pinocchio clock on the living room wall. Now it lives here. One more casualty.

'Your namesake,' I say to the air, my two ghosts. But I can't take my eyes off my grandfather. Tonight is the end for him, too, I realise. The real end, where the ripples his life created in the world glide silently to stillness. Could you have seen them, I want to ask, with those 3-D eyes that saw so much?

Could you have saved them? Could you have thought of another, better way? Because mine is going to hurt. 'His name was Nathan, really. But he called us "Sam". Your mother and me, we were both "Sam". That's why…'

That's why Lizzie let me win that argument, I realise. Not because she'd let go of the idea that the first one had to have a name, was a specific, living creature, a child of ours. But because she'd rationalised. Sam was to be the name, male or female. So whatever the first child had been, the second would be the other. Would have been. You see, Lizzie, I think to the air, wanting to punch the walls of the garage, scream to the cliffs, break down in tears. *You think I don't know. But I do.*

If we survive this night, and our baby is still with us in the morning, and we get to meet him someday soon, he will not be named Sam. He won't be Nathan, either. My grandfather would have wanted Sam.

'Goodbye, Grandpa,' I whisper, and force myself towards the back of the garage. There's no point in drawing this out, surely. Nothing to be gained. But at the door to the meat freezer, where the game hunter who rented our place before us used to store waxed-paper packets of venison and elk, I suddenly stop.

I can feel them. They're still here. They have not gone back to Lizzie. They are not hunched near her navel, whispering their terrible, soundless whispers. That's how I imagine it happening, only it doesn't feel like imagining. And it isn't all terrible. I swear I heard it happen to the second Sam. The first Sam would wait, watching me, hovering near the new life in Lizzie like a hummingbird near nectar, then darting forwards when I was through singing, or in between breaths, and singing a different sort of song, of a whole other world, parallel to ours, free of terrors or at least this terror, the one that just plain living breeds in everything alive. Maybe that world we're all born dreaming really does exist, but the only way to it is through a trap door in the womb. Maybe it's better where my children are. God, I want it to be better.

'You're by the notebooks,' I say, and I almost smile, and my hand slides volitionlessly from the handle of the freezer door and I stagger towards the boxes stacked up, haphazard, along the back wall. The top one on the nearest stack is open slightly, its cardboard damp and reeking when I peel the flaps all the way back.

There they are. The plain, perfect-bound school-composition notebooks Lizzie bought as diaries, to chronicle the lives of her first two children in the 280 or so days before we were to know them. 'I can't look in those,' I say aloud, but I can't help myself. I lift the top one from the box, place it on my lap, and sit down. It's my imagination, surely, that weight on my knees, as though something else has just slid down against me. Like a child, to look at a photo album. *Tell me, Daddy, about the world without me in it.* Suddenly, I'm embarrassed. I want to explain. That first notebook, the other one, is almost half my writing, not just Lizzie's. But this one... I was away, Sam, on a selling trip, for almost a month. And when I came back... I couldn't. Not right away. I couldn't even watch your mom doing it. And two weeks later...

'The day you were born,' I murmur, as if it were a lullaby, 'we went to the redwoods, with the Giraffes.' Whatever it is, that weight on me, shifts a little. Settles. 'That isn't really their name, Sam. Their name is Girard. Giraffe is what you would have called them, though. They would have made you. They're so tall. So funny. They would have put you on their shoulders to touch EXIT signs and ceiling tiles. They would have dropped you upside down from way up high and made you scream.

'This was December, freezing cold, but the sun was out. We stopped at a gas station on our way to the woods, and I went to get Bugles, because that's what Giraffes eat. The ones we know, anyway. Your mom went to the restroom. She was in there a long time. And when she came out, she just looked at me. And I knew.'

My fingers have pushed open the notebook, pulled apart the pages. They're damp, too. Half of them are ruined, the words in multi-coloured inks like pressed flowers on the pages, smeared out of shape, though their meaning remains clear.

'I waited. I stared at your mother. She stared at me. Joseph—Mr Giraffe—came in to see what was taking so long. Your mom just kept on staring. So I said, "Couldn't find the Bugles." Then I grabbed two bags of them, turned away, and paid. And your mom got in the van beside me, and the Giraffes put on their bouncy, happy, Giraffe music, and we kept going.

'When we got to the woods, we found them practically empty, and there was this smell, even though the trees were dead. It wasn't like spring. You couldn't smell pollen or see buds, there was just the sunlight and bare branches and this mist floating up, catching in the trees and forming shapes like the ghosts of leaves. I tried to hold your mother's hand, and she let me at first. And then she didn't. She disappeared into the mist. The Giraffes had to go find her in the end, when it was time to go home. It was almost dark as we got in the van, and none of us were speaking. I was the last one in. And all I could think, as I took my last breath of that air, was, *Can you see this? Did you see the trees, my sweet son, daughter or son, on your way out of the world?'*

Helpless, now, I drop my head, bury it in the wet air as though there were a child's hair there, and my mouth is moving, chanting the words in the notebook on my lap. I only read them once, on the night Lizzie wrote them, when she finally rolled over, with no tantrum, no more tears, nothing left, closed the book against her chest, and went to sleep. But I remember them, still. There's a sketch, first, what looks like an acorn with a dent in the top. Next to it Lizzie has scrawled, *You. Little rice-bean.* On the day before it died. Then there's the list, like a rosary: *I'm so sorry. I'm so sorry I don't get to know you. I'm so sorry for wishing this was over, now, for wanting the bleeding to stop. I'm so sorry that I will never have the chance to be your mother. I'm so sorry you will never have the chance to be in our family. I'm so sorry that you are gone.*

I recite the next page, too, without even turning to it. The *I-don't-wants: a D & C; a phone call from someone who doesn't know, to ask how I'm feeling; a phone call from someone who does, to ask how I am; to forget this, ever; to forget you.*

And then, at the bottom of the page: *I love fog. I love seals. I love the ghosts of Sutro Heights. I love my mother, even though. I love Jake. I love having known you. I love having known you. I love having known you.*

With one, long shuddering breath, as though I'm trying to slip out from under a sleeping cat, I straighten my legs, lay the notebook to sleep in its box, tuck the flaps around it, and stand. It's time. Not past time, just time. I return to the freezer, flip the heavy white lid.

The thing is, even after I looked in here, the same day I brought my grandfather out and wound up poking around the garage, lifting box-tops, touching old, unused bicycles and cross-country skis, I would never have realised. If she'd done the wrapping in waxed paper, laid it in the bottom of the freezer, I would have assumed it was meat, and I would have left it there. But Lizzie is Lizzie, and instead of waxed paper, she'd used red and blue construction paper from her classroom, folded the paper into perfect squares with perfect corners, and put a single star on each of them. So I lifted them out, just as I'm doing now.

They're so cold cradled against me. The red package. The blue one. So light. The most astounding thing about the wrapping, really, is that she managed it all. How do you get paper and tape around nothing and get it to hold its shape? From another nearby box, I lift a gold and green blanket. I had it on my bottom bunk when I was a kid. The first time Lizzie lay on my bed—without me in it, she was just lying there—she wrapped herself in this. I spread it now on the cold, cement floor, and gently lay the packages down.

In Hebrew, the word for miscarriage translates, literally, as *something dropped*. It's no more accurate a term than any of the others humans have generated for the whole, apparently incomprehensible process of reproduction, right down to *conception*. Is that what we do? Conceive? Do we literally dream our children? Is it possible that miscarriage, finally, is just waking up to the reality of the world a few months too soon?

Gently, with the tip of my thumbnail, I slit the top of the red package, fold it open. It comes apart like origami, so perfect, arching back against the blanket. I slit the blue package, pull back its flaps, widening the opening. One last parody of birth.

How did she do it, I wonder? The first time, we were home, she was in the bathroom. She had me bring Ziploc baggies and ice. *For testing*, she'd said. *They'll need it for testing*. But they'd taken it for testing. How had she gotten it back? And the second one had happened—finished happening—in a gas-station bathroom somewhere between the Golden Gate Bridge and the Muir Woods. And she'd said nothing, asked for nothing.

'Where did she keep you?' I murmur, staring down at the formless red and grey spatters, the bunched-up tissue that might have been tendon one day, skin one day. Sam, one day. In the red package, there is more, a hump of frozen something with strings of red spiralling out from it, sticking to the paper, like the rays of an imploding sun. In the blue package, there are some red dots, a few strands of filament. Virtually nothing.

The song comes, and the tears with them. *You'll never know. Dear. How much I love you. Please don't take. Please don't take.* I think of my wife upstairs in our life, sleeping with her arms around her child. The one that won't be Sam, but just might live.

The matches slide from my pocket. Pulling one out of the little book is like ripping a blade of grass from the ground. I scrape it to life, and its tiny light warms my hand, floods the room, flickering as it sucks the oxygen out of the damp. Will this work? How do I know? For all I know, I am imagining it all. The miscarriages were bad luck, hormone deficiencies, a virus in the blood, and the grief that got in me was at least as awful as what got in Lizzie, it just lay dormant longer. And now it has made me crazy.

But if it is better where you are, my Sams. And if you're here to tell the new one about it, to call him away...

'The other night, dear,' I find myself saying, and then I'm singing it, like a Shabbat blessing, a Hanukkah song, something you offer to the emptiness of a darkened house to keep the dark and emptiness back one more week, one more day. 'As I lay sleeping. I dreamed I held you. In my arms.'

I lower the match to the red paper, then the blue, and as my children melt, become dream once more, I swear I hear them sing to me.

GLEN HIRSHBERG'S NOVELS include *The Snowman's Children*, *The Book of Bunk* and the 'Motherless Child' trilogy—*Motherless Child*, *Good Girls* and *Nothing to Devour*. He is also the author of the widely praised story collections *The Ones Who Are Waving*, *The Janus Tree and Other Stories*, *The Two Sams* (a *Publishers Weekly* Best Book of 2003) and *American Morons*. He received the 2007 Shirley Jackson Award for the novelette, 'The Janus Tree', and is also a three-time International Horror Guild Award-winner. With Peter Atkins and Dennis Etchison, Hirshberg co-founded the Rolling Darkness Revue, a reading/live music/dramatic performance event that toured various cities and featured different guests every year. About 'The Two Sams', the author admits: 'This is probably the most personal story I have put to paper, and therefore, hopefully, the most self-explanatory. Most of my ghost stories were originally conceived to be told to my students, but I have only tried reading this aloud once. Never again...'

//

THE PROSPECT CARDS

Don Tumasonis

Dear Mr Cathcart,

We are happy to provide, enclosed with this letter, our complete description of item no. 839 from our recent catalogue *Twixt Hammam and Minaret: 19th and Some Early 20th Century Travel in the Middle East, Anatolia, Nubia, etc.*, as requested by yourself.

You are lucky in that our former cataloguer, Mr Mokley, had, in what he thought were his spare moments, worked to achieve an extremely full description of this interesting group of what are probably unique items. Certainly no others to whom we have shown these have seen any similar, nor have been able to provide any clew as to their ultimate provenance.

They were purchased by one of our buyers on a trip to Paris, where, unusually-since everyone thinks the *bouqinistes* were mined out long ago-they were found in a stall on the Left Bank. Once having examined his buy later that evening, he determined to return the following day to the vendor in search of any related items. Alas, there were no others, and the grizzled old veteran running the boxes had no memory of when or where he purchased these, saying only that he had them for years, perhaps since the days of Marmier, actually having forgotten their existence until they were unearthed through the diligence of our employee. Given the circumstance of their discovery (covered with dust, stuffed in a sealed envelope tucked away in a far corner of a green tin box clamped onto a quay of the Seine, with volumes of grimy tomes in front concealing their being), we are lucky to have even these.

Bear in mind, that as an old and valued customer, you may have this lot at 10% off the catalogue price, post-free, with insurance additional, if desired.

Remaining, with very best wishes indeed,
Yours most faithfully,

Basil Barnet

BARNET AND KORT,
ANTIQUARIAN TRAVEL BOOKS AND EPHEMERA

No. 839

POSTAL VIEW CARDS, commercially produced, various manufacturers, together with a few photographs mounted on card, comprising a group of 74. Mostly sepia and black-and-white, with a few contemporary tinted, showing scenes from either Balkans, or Near or Middle East, ca. 1920-30. The untranslated captions, when they occur, are bilingual, with one script resembling Kyrillic, but not in Russian or Bulgarian; the other using the Arabic alphabet, in some language perhaps related to Turco-Uighuric.

Unusual views of as yet unidentified places and situations, with public and private buildings, baths, squares, harbours, minarets, markets, etc. Many of the prospects show crowds and individuals in the performance of divers actions and work, sometimes exotic. Several of the cards contain scenes of an erotic or disturbing nature. A number are typical touristic souvenir cards, generic products picturing exhibits from some obscure museum or collection. In spite of much expended effort, we have been unable to identify the locales shown.

Entirely unfranked, and without address, about a third of these have on their verso a holographic ink text, in a fine hand by an unidentified individual, evidently a travel diary or journal (non-continuous, with many evident lacunæ). Expert analysis would seem to indicate 1930 or slightly later as the date of writing.

Those cards with handwriting have been arranged in rough order by us, based on internal evidence, although the chronology is often unclear and the order therefore arbitrary. Only these cards—with a single exception—are described, each with a following transcription of the verso holograph text; the others, about 50 cards blank on verso, show similar scenes and objects. Our hypothetical reconstruction of the original sequence is indicated through lightly pencilled numbers at the upper right verso corner of each card.

Condition: Waterstain across top edges, obscuring all of the few details of date and place of composition. Wear along edges and particularly at corners. A couple of cards rubbed; the others, aside from the faults already noted, mostly quite fresh and untouched.

Very Rare. In our considered opinion, the cards in themselves are likely to be unique, no others having been recorded to now; together with the unusual document they contain, they are certainly so.

Price: £1,650

Card No. 1

Description: A dock, in some Levantine port. A number of men and animals, mostly mules, are congregated around a moored boat with sails, from which

large *tonnes,* evidently containing wine, labelled as such in Greek, are being either loaded or unshipped.

Text: not sculling, but rather rowing, the Regatta of '12, for which his brother coxswained. Those credentials were good enough for Harrison and myself, our credulity seen in retrospect as being somewhat naïve, and ourselves as rather gullible; such, however, is all hindsight. For the time being, we were very happy at having met fellow countrymen—of the right sort, mind you in this godforsaken backwater at a time when our fortunes, bluntly put, had taken a turn for much the worse. When Forsythe, looking to his partner Calquon, asked 'George, we need the extra hands—what say I tell Jack and Charles about our plans?' To that Calquon only raised an eyebrow, as if to say it's your show, go and do as you think fit. Forsythe, taking that as approval, ordered another round, and launched into a little speech, which, when I think back on the events of the past weeks, had perhaps less of an unstudied quality than his seemingly impromptu delivery would have implied. Leaning forward, he drew from his breast pocket a postal view card, and placed it on the table, saying in a lowered voice, as if we were fellow conspirators being drawn in, 'What would you think if I told you, that from here, in less than one day's sail and a following week's march, there is to be found something of such value, which if the knowledge of it became common, would

Card no. 2

Description: A view of a mountain massif, clearly quite high and rugged, seen from below at an angle, with consequent foreshortening. A fair amount of snow is sprinkled over the upper heights. A thick broken line in white, retouch work, coming from behind and around one of several summits, continues downward along and below the ridge-line before disappearing. This evidently indicates a route.

Text: —ania and Zog. Perfidious folk! Perfidious people. Luckily, our packet steamer had arrived and was ready to take us off. A night's sailing, and the better part of the next day took us to our destination, or rather, to the start of our journey. After some difficulty in finding animals and muleteers, we loaded our supplies, hired guides, and after two difficult days, arrived at the foothills of the mountains depicted on the obverse of this card. Our lengthy and laborious route took us ultimately up these, where we followed the *voie normale,* the same as shown by the white hatched line. Although extremely steep and exposed, the slope was not quite sheer and we lost only one mule and no men during the 1500-yard descent. Customs—if such a name can be properly applied to such outright thieves—were rapacious, and confiscated much of what we had, including my diary and notes. Thus the continuation on these cards, which represent the only form of paper allowed for sale to the

Card no. 3

Description: A panorama view of a Levantine or perhaps Balkan town of moderate to large size, ringed about by snow-covered mountains in the distance. Minarets and domes are visible, as is a very large public building with columns, possibly Greco-Roman, modified to accommodate some function other than its original religious one, so that the earlier elements appear draped about with other stylistic intrusions.

Text: vista. With the sun setting, and accommodation for the men and food for the animals arranged, we were able to finally relax momentarily and give justice, if only for a short while, to the magnificence of the setting in which the old city was imbedded, like a pearl in a filigreed ring. I've seen a lot of landscapes, 'round the world, and believe me, this was second to none. The intoxicating beauty of it all made it almost easy to believe the preposterous tales that inspired Calquon, and particularly Forsythe, to persuade us to join them on this tossed-together expedition. I frankly doubt that anything will

come of it except our forcing another chink in the isolation which has kept this fascinating place inviolate to such a degree that few Westerners have penetrated its secrets over the many centuries since the rumoured group of Crusaders forced their

Card no. 4

Description: A costume photograph, half-length, of a young woman in ethnic or tribal costume, veiled. The décolletage is such that her breasts are completely exposed. Some of the embroidery and jewellery would indicate Cypriote or Anatolian influence; it is clear that she is wearing her dowry in the form of coins, filigreed earrings, necklaces, medallions, and rings. Although she is handsome, her expression is very stiff. [Not reproduced in the catalogue]

Text: Evans, who should have stuck to Bosnia and Illyria. I never thought his snake goddesses to be anything other than some Bronze Age fantast's wild dream, if indeed the reconstructions are at all accurate. Harrison, however, has told me that this shocking—i.e. for a white woman (the locals are distinctively Caucasian: red hair, blue eyes and fair skin appearing frequently, together with traces of slight Mediterranean admixture)—deshabille was common throughout the Eastern Ægean and Middle East until a very short while ago, when European mores got the better of the local folk, except, it seems, those here. I first encountered such dress (or *undress)* a week ago, the day after our late evening arrival, when out early to see the market and get my bearings, and totally engaged in examining some trays of spices in front of me, I felt suddenly bare flesh against my exposed arm, stretched out to test the quality of some turmeric. It was a woman at my side who, having come up unnoticed, had bent in front of me to obtain some root or herb. When she straightened, I realised at once that the contact had been with her bare bosom, which, I might add, was quite shapely, with nipples rouged. She was unconcerned; I must have blushed at least as much

Card no. 5

Description: A *naos* or church, on a large stepped platform, in an almost impossible mélange of styles, with elements of a Greek temple of the Corinthian order mixed in with Byzantine features and other heterogeneous effects to combine in an unusual, if not harmonious, whole. The picture, a frontal view, has been taken most probably at early morning light, since the temple steps and surrounding square are devoid of people.

Text: light and darkness, darkness and light' Forsythe said. 'With this form of dualism, and its rejection of the body, paradoxically, until the sacrament is administered, the believers are in fact encouraged to excess of the flesh, which is viewed as essentially evil, and ultimately, an illusion. The thought is that by indulging mightily, disdain is expressed for the ephemeral, thus granting the candidate power over the material, which is seen as standing in his or her way to salvation.' 'What does that have to do with your little trip of this morning?' I remonstrated. We had agreed to meet at ten o'clock to see if we could buy manuscripts in the street of the scribes, for the collection. Paul reddened and replied 'D'you know the large structure on the square between us and the market? I was on my way to meet you, when I happened to pass through there. It seems'—and here he went florid again—'that in an effort to gain sanctity more quickly, parents, as required by the priests, are by law for two years to give over those of their daughters on the verge of womanhood to the temple each day between 10 and noon, in a ploy to quicken the transition to holiness. Any passer-by, during that time, who sees on the steps under the large parasols (set up like tents, there to protect exposed flesh) any maiden suiting his fancy, is urged to drop a coin in the bowls nearest and

Card no. 6

Description: A quite imperfect and puzzling picture, with mist and fog, or perhaps steam, obscuring almost all detail. What is visible are the dim outlines of two rows of faces, some veiled, others bearded.

Text: poured more water on the coals. By now it was quite hot, and I could no longer see Forsythe, but only hear his voice. The lack of visibility made it easier to concentrate on his words, with my eyes no longer focused on <u>details</u> I had found so distracting. 'The incongruity of it all makes my head reel—how could they have maintained all this in the face of the changes around them? After all, a major invasion route of the past three millennia lies two valleys to the west...' Nodding in unseen agreement, my attention was momentarily diverted by the sound of a new arrival entering the room, and seconds later, a smooth leg brushed for a second against mine; I assumed it was a woman, and durst not stir. 'Not that they've rejected the modern at all costs—they've got electric generators and some lighting, a fair amount of modern goods and weaponry find their way in, there's the museum, that Turkish photography shop, the printing press, and—oh, all the rest. But they pick and choose. And that religion of theirs! All the Jews and Muslims and Christians here are cowed completely! Why hasn't a holy war been declared by their neighbours?' With Paul ranting on in the obscuring darkness, I grunted in agreement, and then, shockingly, felt a small foot rub against

Card no. 7

Description: Costumed official, perhaps a religious leader or judge, sitting on the floor facing the camera. He is bearded, greying, with a grim set to his mouth. One hand points gracefully towards a smallish, thick codex held by the other hand. From the man's breast depends a tall rectangular enamelled pendant of simple design, divided vertically into equal fields of black and white.

Text: Sorbonne, three years of which, I suppose, could explain a lot, as for example, his overpowering use of garlic. 'Pseudo-Manicheeism' he continued, 'is solely a weak term used by the uncomprehending for what can only be described as perfection, the last word itself being a watered-out expression merely, for that which cannot be comprehended through the feeble tool of rational and sceptical thinking, which closes all doors it does not understand.

Oh, I know that some of you'—and here he eyed me suspiciously, as if I was running muckin' Cambridge!—'have tried to classify our belief, using the Monophysites as opposed to the Miaphysites of your religion in an analogy that neither comprehends nor grasps the subtlety of our divinely inspired thought! As if It could be explained in Eutychian terms! Our truth is self-evident and is so clear that we allow, with certain inconsequential restrictions and provisos, those of your tribe who wish, to expound their falsehoods in the marketplace, assuming they have survived the rigours of the journey here. You were better to perceive indirectly, thinking of flashing light; the colours green, and gold; the hundred instead of the one; segmentation, instead of smoothness, as metaphors that enable one

Card no. 8

Description: Another museum card, with several large tokens or coins depicted, which in style and shape resemble some of the *dekadrachm* issues of 5th century Syracuse. The motifs of the largest one shown, are, however, previously unrecorded, with a temple (see card 5) on the obverse. The reverse, with a young girl and three men, is quite frankly obscene. [Not reproduced in the catalogue]

Text: tea. I was quite struck with the wholesome appearance and modest demeanour of Mrs Fortesque, who was plainly, if neatly dressed in the style of ten years ago—evidently, they had been out of contact with Society in London since arrival! The Rev Fortesque was holding forth on how they were, as a family, compelled by local circumstance, and frankly, the threat of force, to adhere strictly to the native code of behaviour and mores when out in public, the children not being exempt from the rituals of their fellows of like age. Calquon frowned at this, and asked, 'In every way, Reverend?' to which the missionary sighed, 'Unfortunately, yes—otherwise, we would not be allowed to preach at all.' There was a small silence while we pondered the metaphysical implications of this when a young and angelically beautiful girl

of about twelve entered the room. 'Gentlemen, this is my daughter, Alicia...' smiled Mrs Fortesque proudly, only to be interrupted in the most embarrassing fashion by the sudden sputtering and spraying of Forsythe, whom we thought had choked on his crumpet. Thwacking him on the back, until his redness of face receded and normal breathing resumed, I thought I saw an untoward smirk lightly pass over the face of the young girl. 'What is it, old man?' I solicitously enquired. Paul, after having swallowed several times, with the attention of the others diverted, whispered sotto voce, breathlessly, so that only I could hear 'Yesterday—the temple

Card no. 9

Description: An odd view, taken at mid-distance, of a low-angled pyramidal or cone-shaped pile of stones, most fist-sized or slightly smaller, standing about one to two feet high. A number of grimacing urchins and women, the last in their distinctive public costume, stand gesticulating and grinning to either side, many of them holding stones in their hands. Given the reflection of light on the pool of dark liquid that has seeped from the pile's front, it must be—midday.

Text: brave intervention, with dire consequence. For God's sake, Fortesque, don't...' shouted Forsythe, as I well remember, before his arms were pinned behind him, and with a callused paw like a bear's clamped over his mouth, in much the same situation as myself, was forced helplessly to watch the inexorable and horrific grind of events. Eager hands, unaided by any tool—such is the depth of fanaticism that prevails in these parts—quickly scooped out a deep enough hole from the loose soil of the market square. The man of the cloth, who had persevered in the face of so much pagan indifference and outright hostility for over a decade, was for his troubles and valiant intervention unceremoniously divested of his clothing and dumped in the hole, which was quickly filled—there was no lack of volunteers—immobilising him in the same manner as Harrison, who was buried with his arms and upper breast free. They were just far enough apart so that their fingers could not touch, depriving them in fiendish fashion of that small consolation. I remember the odd detail that Fortesque was half-shaven—he had dropped everything when informed of Harrison's situation. Knowing full well what was in store, he began singing 'Onward, Christian Soldiers' in a manly, booming voice that brought tears to my eyes, whilst Harrison, I am ashamed to say, did

Card no. 10

Description: Group portrait, of nine men. Six stand, wearing bandoliers, pistols with chased and engraved handles protruding from the sashes round their waists, decorative daggers, etc. The edges of their vests are heavily embroidered with metallic thread in arabesque patterns. All are heavily moustachioed. A seventh companion stands, almost ceremoniously, to their right, holding like a circus tent peg driver a wooden mallet with a large head a foot or so off the ground; a position somewhat like that of a croquet player. The eighth man, wearing a long shift or kaftan, is on all fours in the centre foreground, head to the left, but facing the camera like the others. A wooden saddle of primitive type is on his back. A ninth man, dressed like the first seven, is in the saddle, as if riding the victim, who, we see, has protruding from his fundament, although discreetly draped in part by the long shift, a pole the thickness of a muscular man's forearm.

Text: no idea, being sure that all this was misunderstanding, and could easily be cleared up with a liberal application of baksheesh. This was our mistake, as Calquon was led from the judge's compartments, arms bound, to a small square outside, where there was a carved fountain missed by the iconoclasts of long ago (of whom there had been several waves), with crudely sculptured and rather battered lions from whose mouths water streamed into the large circular limestone basin. We followed, of course, vehemently protesting his innocence all the while, and were studiously ignored. Poor Calquon was untied, and forced onto his knees and hands in a most undignified and ludicrous position. A crowd of people had already gathered under the hot midday sun, including many women and children. Hawkers walked through the throng that gathered, offering cold water from tin tanks on their backs, each with a single glass fitted into a decorated silver holder with a handle, tied onto the vessel by a cord. I saw, lying off to the side, on the steps of the fountain, a wooden stake, bark removed from its narrow end, smoothed and sharpened to a nasty point. A fat greasy balding man wearing the red cummerbund of officialdom came out of the crowd, with a bright knife in

Card no. 11

Description: A market with various stalls and their owners. A wandering musician is off to the left, and a perambulating vendor of kebabs, with long brass skewers, is on the right.

Text: painful for everyone concerned, particularly George. A guard in crimson livery, decorated with gold thread, was sitting smoking his hubble-bubble a short distance away from our gloomy group, every now and then looking up from his reverie to make sure things were as they should be. Perhaps it was the smoke from the pipe, or sheer bravado—I have never known, to this day—but Calquon, poor George, asked for a cigarette, which Forsythe immediately rolled and put on his lips, lighting it, since this was impossible for our fellow, whose arms were bound. He took a puff, as cool as if he were walking down Regent Street to Piccadilly, and then, for the first time noticing the women and children seated at his feet, asked us in a parched voice what they might possibly be doing there. I shuffled my feet and looked away, while Paul told him in so many words that they were waiting for his imminent departure, for the same purpose that women in the Middle Ages would gather around criminals about to be executed, in hope of obtaining a good luck charm that was powerful magic, after the fact of summary punishment was accomplished. This, as we were afraid, enraged our unfortunate *en brochette* companion, who became livid as we tried to calm him. Writhing in his stationary upright position, would after all do him no good, given that out of his shoulder (from whence I noticed a tiny tendril of smoke ascending), there was already protruding

Card no. 12

Description: A public square, photo taken from above at a slant angle, from a considerable distance. Some sort of framework or door, detached from any structure, has been set up in one corner. A couple of dark objects, one larger than the other, appear in the middle of that door or frame which faces the viewer, obscuring what is going on behind. A large agitated crowd of men of all ages—from quite young boys to bent, aged patriarchs, all wearing the truncated local version of the fez, are milling around the rear of the upright construction. A number of local police, uniformed, are in the thick of it, evidently to maintain order.

Text: wondering what the commotion was about. I was therefore shocked to see in one tight opening the immobilised head of a young woman of about twenty-five, and in the other her right hand. Instead of the ubiquitous veil, she had some sort of black silk bandage that performed the same function, closely wrapped around her mouth and nose. She was plainly emitting a sullen glare—easily understood, given the circumstance. There was no join or seam; for the life of me, I still do not understand the construction. Every now and then the frame and the woman contained by it would violently shake and judder. The expression under her shock of unruly red hair remained stoic and unperturbed. Walking to the other side *(make sure that Mildred doesn't read this!!)* I saw the crowd of men—there were about 80 to 100, including about twenty or so of the few negro slaves found in these parts—with more pouring into the square—jostling in the attempt to be next: those nearest had partially disrobed, and had taken 'matters' in hand, fondling themselves to arousal, for taking her in the fashion preferred here, which is of that between

men and boys, from behind. Despondent as I was, I had no intention other than to continue, when I was suddenly shoved forward into the midst

Card no. 13

Description: A view down a narrow street, with the high tenements and their overhanging wooden balconies blocking out much of the light. The photographer has done well to obtain as much detail as is shown here. A cupola or dome, and what is perhaps a minaret behind it, are just visible at the end of the lane. Three young (from the look of their figures as revealed by the traditional dress, cf card 2) women in black, each with a necklace from which hangs a single bright large pendant, stand in the middle of the way, at mid-distance. They appear to be approaching the camera. Surprisingly, for all that they are bare-headed, etc., they are wearing veils that conceal their features utterly. There are no others in the street.

Text: said to Forsythe that there was no point to it, that we would have to, at some moment, accept our losses and the futility of going any further. With the others gone, I argued, it was extremely unlikely that we could continue on our own; we should swallow our pride, and admit that we had come greatly unprepared for what we had in mind. It was best, in other words, that we make our run as soon as backs were turned. Forsythe disagreed vehemently, and meant that on the contrary, we were obliged by the sacred memory of our companions to carry on, an odd turn of phrase, considering what we had hoped to accomplish and obtain, by any means. And then he said cryptically, 'It doesn't matter in any case—the deed is done.' I immediately took this as admission that the object of our expedition had been somehow achieved without my knowledge; that was the likely cause of the troubles we had experienced, and the growing agitation of the populace I had uneasily witnessed the past few days. As we discussed our dilemma outside the carpet shop, one of many lining the street, I became aware of a silence, a hush that had descended. People turned to face the wall, in fear, I thought, as I saw three females approaching. These

Card no. 14

Description: A poor reproduction of the second state of plate VII of Piranesi's *Carceri*. In fact, the ascription is given on the verso of the card, the artist's name (G. B. PIRANESI) appearing in Latin capitals inserted amongst the Arabic and Cyrillic letters.

Text: less than the Carceri! What everyone had once thought the malarial fever dreams of a stunted, perverse genius, I saw now only to be honest reporting. I was absolutely astounded, once the dragoman, smelling of garlic and anisette, had removed the blindfold from my eyes. A lump came to my throat, and tears threatened to engulf me, when I thought of the others done away with through treachery, foul ignorance and intolerance. I suppose rumours regarding the disappearance of the sacred entity of the valley had much to do with the situation, too. Controlling my emotions—here, for a man to weep is a sign of weakness, with all the consequences such a perception entails—I saw around me. A number of individuals, male and female, nude or partly so, were being ushered along the spiral staircase wrapped around an enormous stone column down which I myself must have descended only a few minutes before. Natural light played through a number of cleverly placed oculi in the invisible ceiling, concealed by the complex bends and angles of the place. Turning,

Card no. 15

Description: Another crude reproduction of a Piranesi 'Prisons' plate, this number VIII, ascribed as above.

Text: I saw yet another vista of the Italian artist before me, and began to understand, for the first time, that the plan of all his mad, insane engravings was a coherent whole, either taken from the actuality before me, or perhaps *plotted out* from his prints, and converted to reality, by some unsung architectonic genius. The Venetians had been here, I knew, during the mid-1700s,

when things had settled down. Perhaps one of their workmen was given the book, and told to produce, or… With my glance following the staircase from its beginning, flanked by gigantic military trophies, with plumed helmets much larger than any human head, I traced the turn upwards to the left, and saw, between two enormous wooden doors opening on an arch, a large rack. A series of ropes hung down from the supporting wall, and I could see the faint glow of a brazier and hear the distant screams of the poor women and men, white bodies glistening with the sweat of fear, who hung

Card no. 16

Description: Tinted, clearly a display of gemstones, perhaps from a museum of natural history or local geology. One of the larger groups, arranged separately from the others, with green colouring obviously meant to indicate emeralds, appears to be the fragments, longitudinally shattered, of what must have been a single enormous stone.

Text: subincision being the technical expression. As you can imagine, I was wildly straining against my bonds, in fact, you could say I was struggling to the point of extreme violence, to, as it turned out, no avail. In spite of all my agitated effort, I was clamped to some sort of heavy metal framework or stand that immobilised me more or less completely. Naked, helpless, dreading whatever was in store, I saw the same three young women approach into the torchlight from the encircling darkness. Without a word, my gaolers and the others left and I was alone with the unholy trio. As if at a signal, they simultaneously removed their veils and I was momentarily stunned, almost drugged, by the sight of their incredible beauty. Remember, this was the first time I had <u>ever</u> seen one of the local women unmasqued—if these were representative of the rest, it would easily explain any number of puzzling local rituals and customs. In spite of my extreme situation, I could not help myself—the ravishing faces, the fulsome breasts with their shapely crimsoned nipples, the long black glistening hair

Card no. 17

Description: A market place, with many and various stands and displays. An ironmonger, a merchant of brass teapots, a seller of cured leather are all easily discerned. In the centre, arms like a Saint Andrew's cross before his chest, holding a large knife in the one hand, a two-pronged fork in the other, is a seller of grilled and roasted meats. On the small portable gridiron in front of him, a number of sizeable sausages are warming, split neatly length-wise.

Text: darted out with the tip of her tongue, and then slowly extended it again. To my horror, I saw it was no tongue: it was a long razor-sharp dagger or splinter of green glass or stone; a smaragd dirk that was somehow attached or glued to the root of what remained of her tongue. The other two, kneeling close on either side of her, each reverentially held, both with two hands, the one heavy breast nearest them of their chief colleague, as if ritually weighing and supporting these at the same time. This observation was made on the abstract, detachedly, as if I were outside my own body. More mundanely, I was screaming and thrashing—or attempting uselessly to thrash. Praise to the gods that be, I passed out completely, and awoke with the foul deed done, blood running down me and pooling on the cold flagging, and the three dark sisters gone. Looking down, as my original captors re-entered the chamber, I saw that the operation had been carried out, just as had been described to me by the temple priest, and I fainted once more. When

Card no. 18

Description: Not a postal card, but rather a half-length portrait photograph mounted on thick pasteboard, of a family group from about the 1920s. The two parents are quite young, and formally dressed: the father in a dark suit, to which is pinned an unidentified order or medal. He holds a small Bible clasped to his breast. The woman is handsome, in a white lacy blouse

buttoned to the top of her graceful neck, with masses of hair piled high on her head. The young daughter is quite simply beautiful, an angel.

Text: would not have recognised, but for the signal distinctive wedding ring on her finger. 'Mrs Fortesque,' I blurted out, as we stood amongst the milling crowd in the shade of the souk. 'I had no idea—' but stopped when I saw the blush originating from beneath the missionary wife's veil spread to her ample and attractive sun-browned bosom (a pendant black enamelled cross its sole decoration), with the attendant rush of blood turning the aureoles— modestly without cinnabar—to the precise same shade of red so favoured by the local women. I saw, at the same time, the fleshy peaks slowly stiffen and stand, that motion drawing forth a corresponding response on my part, something I hardly had conceived feasible, after the trauma of the operation of four days ago, with the insertion of the papyrus strips to prevent rejoining of the separated parts while the healing occurred. 'I should perhaps explain myself,' she said, regaining her composure. 'The local rules are very strict; were I not, when attending to my public tasks and duties outside the house, to attire myself with what we consider wanton and promiscuous display, it would be here viewed as flagrant immodesty, and punishable, before the crowd, by the

Card no. 19

Description: An ossuary chapel, where the style of the classic Romanesque interior is partly obscured by the encrustation of thousands of skulls and skeletal parts, that form, or cover, the interior architecture. This photograph taken at the crossing, facing the nearby altar, where, instead of a crucifix or a monstrance, an enamelled or painted rectangular metal plaque stands upright, its left side white, its right black.

Text: that the crucifix was now exchanged for a small pendant medallion, half black, half white, the symbol of the local cult. The thought of Mrs

Fortesque having gone, so to speak, over to the other side was shocking, and at the same time extremely piquant and arousing, with my recently acquired knowledge of what *that* fully entailed for the woman involved. Having just come to the rendezvous from my daily session with the local doctor, who was treating me with that disgusting metallic green and gold powder, the source of which I was loath to ponder on, I scarcely thought myself physically capable of what was to follow, given my general and peculiar state. Nonetheless, when the missionary's widow, after furtively glancing about only to find the chapel empty—no surprise, since it was midday and most families were at home, doors shuttered for the day's largest repast—reached for and embraced me, the last thing I had awaited, I found myself responding in a most unexpected fashion. 'But the children—your late husband—' I stammered, as she pushed me back against a column, so the decorative knobs of tibiae and the like bruised my spine, with her bare breasts crushed against my chest and her hot searching lips

Card no. 20

Description: A statue, whose dimensions are given as 13 by 5 by 5 [in, it is assumed], these last representing the base. A female goddess, in flowing robes, very much gravid, standing in a bronze boat formed like the body of a duck, whose head is the prow. Within its open beak it holds a cube.

Text: certain? It's only been a month...' I lingered at these, my own words, astonished at the assertion. 'Of course I am,' she snapped back, then containing herself with difficulty, lowered her tone, and continued, 'I've not been with anyone, before or since,' she said, bitterly smiling. She was very much enceinte, astoundingly so, in a way that would have been impossible had I been responsible for her state. I kept on looking at her in bewilderment. My first thought was 'propulsive force—perhaps; generative principle—never!!' Still holding my hand lightly, she followed up, saying, 'It *does* seem impossible, doesn't it? Not just the time—I mean, given what had happened to you,

in addition. Think, though, was anything odd done to you then, or about that time? I mean...' At that, the thought of the daily calls to the doctor snapped into mind. Once I had found out the disgusting source of the gold and green powders, I had ceased from visiting him again. Had our meeting in the ossuary been before or after the 'treatment's' short course? I could not remember, for the life of

Card no. 21

Description: Another souvenir card assumed to be from the local natural history collection, exhibiting a quite large centipede of unknown type, with several interesting and anomalous features. The scale beside it a quarter-inch stick, since inches would make the creature ridiculously large.

Text: smooth and horrendously distended vulva with a disgusting plop. The three witches—I cannot think of them as being other than that—hurried to the trestle immediately, clicking the emerald daggers they had for tongues excitedly against their teeth. The multitudinous onlookers and priests held their distance. Mrs F seemed to be in a state of shock, but was still breathing with eyes closed. Horrified, I cast a look at Alicia, who stood imperturbed in her youthful nakedness, motionless, still holding the thick black candle cool as you like, as if she were in Westminster Abbey. The bloody caul and afterbirth were snipped at and cut with glassy tongues, and I saw, when the three stepped back, a foul, thick, twitching, segmented thing, snaky, glinting green and gold, thick as a moray eel, writhing between the poor woman's bloody legs. The chief witch nodded to Alicia, who slowly moved forward, setting her candle carefully at her mother's feet. At another signal, she picked up the glistening demonic shape, which unwound itself into a heavy, broad, segmented centipede-like beast of dimensions that left me gasping. Alicia uncoiled the slimy monster, gleaming with ichor, and draped the hellspawn 'round her shoulders, just as if it was a feather boa. Pausing only for a moment, she turned to me with a thin leer, and asked 'Want to hold it? It's *yours* too!'

Revulsed, I turned, while she shrugged and set off on the ceremonial way, the crowd bowing to her and her half-brother, sister, or whatever, the belt of hollow birds' eggs—her only adornment—clicking around her slim hips, brown from hours on the temple steps—as she swayed, during

Card no. 22

Description: A shining centipede probably of gold, coiled upon a dais of ebony, or some other dark wood, this last encrusted with bejewelled precious metal of arabesque form. The central object's size may be inferred from the various items imbedded in it: Roman cameos, Egyptian scarabs, coins from crushed empires and forgotten kingdoms, some thousands of years old, the votive offerings of worshippers over the millennia we infer the sculpture to have existed. The object is fabulous: an utter masterwork of the goldsmith's art rivalled only by the Cellini salt cellar and one or two other pieces. It almost seems alive.

Text: almost worth it. Calquon and Harrison are dead, what has become of Paul, who thought up all this, I have no idea. I have been subjected to the most hideous torture, and seen the most awful sights, that few can have experienced without losing their sanity. It is deeply ironic after all I have been through, that I by chance only yesterday discovered the object, hidden away in my belongings. What remains to be seen is whether I can bring it back to civilisation with myself intact. I cannot trust Alicia, who has clearly let her elevation to high priestess and chief insect-keeper go to her head. During my last interview with her, whilst she dangled her shapely foot provocatively over the arm of her golden throne, I, in a vain effort to play upon her familial bonds and old self, reminded her of her younger brother, who had not been seen for days. At that she casually let drop that he had been sold on to Zanzibar (where there is, I believe, an active slave market) to ultimately disappear into one of the harems of the Arabian peninsula (Philby may be able to inform more fully). 'I never could stand the little pest,' was her remark, so it would be foolish to hope for any sympathy from her quarter. I am being watched quite closely, with great suspicion. Can it be they *know?* If I ever leave here alive, it will be an absolute sensation. Biding my time, I cannot do anything now, but I can at least try to smuggle these surreptitiously scribbled notes out to the French vice-consul in the city where we bought the mules. He is a good fellow, though he drinks to excess at

An additional 52 cards remain (see photo-copies), which although of great interest, bear no hand-written notes, and therefore are not described here, with the following single exception:

Card: not in sequence, i.e. unnumbered by us

Description: A photographic postal card of a large exterior wall of a stone building of enormous size. The impressive dimensions become apparent once one realises that the small specks and dots on the stereobate of the vaguely classical structure are in fact people—some alone, others in groups, these last for the most part sheltered under awnings set up on the steps. What most catches the eye, however, is the magnificent low relief work covering most of the wall, depicting, it would seem, some mythological scene whose iconographic meaning is not apparent. It is in character a harmonious mixture of several ancient traditions: one sees hints of the Hellenistic, Indo-Grecian, and traces even of South-East Asian styles. The contrasts of tone make clear that the bare stone has been brightly painted.

The relief itself: It appears a judgement is being carried out. In the background, solemn ringlet-bearded men draped in graceful robes, all in the same pose, all copies of the other. All hold a square object, somewhat in form like a hand-mirror divided into one field black and one field white, and watch with blank eyes the man before them who is strapped to a plank, while a large fabulous beast, part man, part insect, with elements of the order Scolopendra predominating, tears at him in the fashion of the Promethean

468

eagles, and worse. To the right, a young priestess or goddess, nude but for a chain of beads or eggs around her waist, stands contrapposto, with one arm embraced about an obscene creature, a centipedal monstrosity of roughly her own height, leaning tightly upright against her. She is pointing with her free hand towards the tortured man. The expression on her empty face has affinities with several known Khmer royal portrait sculptures. She faintly smiles, as if in ecstasy.

DON TUMASONIS, AFTER a largely picaresque and misspent youth, settled down, he thought, to a quiet life on the outskirts of a Scandinavian capital, with a charming, if Norwegian wife; lively, if rambunctious cats; and interesting, if space-consuming books. Little did he anticipate the chain of events awaiting, forcing him into the mendicant life of a writer with little more than a bronze parachute to protect him. He has since published stories in *Ghosts & Scholars*, *All Hallows*, *Supernatural Tales*, *Shadows and Tall Trees*, *Shadows and Silence*, *Strange Tales*, *A Walk on the Darkside: Visions of Horror*, *Acquainted with the Night*, *At Ease with the Dead*, *The Year's Best Horror and Fantasy* and *The Mammoth Book of Best New Horror*. As he explains about the preceding, 2003 International Horror Guild Award-winning, story: '"The Prospect Cards" draws its inspiration from many sources: stuffy booksellers' catalogues, volumes of 18th and 19th century Levantine travel, a walk along the Seine, Rider Haggard in his usual more perverse mode, and anthropological literature. Its mood was influenced by the books of George MacDonald Fraser, Glen Baxter and the character of John Cleese. It was meant to be humorous, but seems to have got out of hand.'

///

AFTERWORD

David A. Sutton

THE JONES AND Sutton 'carnival of horror' began many moons ago…
in 1977, when we began co-publishing our award-winning small press
magazine *Fantasy Tales*. Designed unashamedly to look a bit like the pulps,
particularly *Weird Tales*, the magazine included new stories from right across
the genre. Its success in that format led to mass-market paperback editions,
with Nick Robinson our publisher for later volumes.

After that we were hired to revive the flagging *Pan Book of Horror Stories*.
Initially *Dark Voices: The Best from the Pan Book of Horror Stories* came out
from Stephen Jones and former Pan editor Clarence Paget. Kathy Gale, our
genre editor at Pan Books, then allowed us to define a new wave for the series
in the 1990s. Under its revised title, *Dark Voices: The Pan Book of Horror*, we
upped our game in the horror field over a further five volumes, bringing to
readers a whole new variety of authors currently writing contemporary horror.
It was Pan Horror for modern age.

And then came *Dark Terrors: The Gollancz Book of Horror* (1995–2002).
Commissioned at Victor Gollancz by Jo Fletcher, she contracted the series
in both hardcover and paperback, which gave added prestige for an annual
series in the UK. As with its predecessor, this was a non-themed horror

anthology series. We didn't want a thematic 'hook' which the reader could comfortably latch on to. We wanted to fling our readers into the wild, into the screaming pitch of horror, into the psychological, graphic, off-the-wall, or just plainly weird.

From volume 5 the page-count doubled and we could offer much more weird fiction for readers to enjoy. Volume 4 won the British Fantasy Award for Best Anthology in 1999 and, in 2002, volume 6 won The International Horror Guild Award in that same category.

Over the six volumes we published 141 stories. We probably read somewhere near twice that many stories *per volume* in order to make our selections. Some of the authors featured more than once, and it began to feel like we had a little repertory company of writers who could always deliver the goods! Nevertheless, we always tried to bring new writers into the series as well.

In terms of contributors, two tied for the most stories published, with six stories each: Ramsey Campbell and Michael Marshall Smith. Christopher Fowler was represented five times. Six writers had four appearances each: Dennis Etchison, Caitlín R. Kiernan, Graham Masterton, Kim Newman, Nicholas Royle, David J. Schow and Conrad Williams. And with three tales apiece were Terry Lamsley, Joel Lane, Roberta Lannes, Richard Christian Matheson, Jay Russell, Peter Straub and Steve Rasnic Tem.

Sadly, too many of our contributors are now no longer with us: Karl Edward Wagner (1945–1994), Cherry Wilder (1930–2002), Julian Rathbone (1935–2008), C. Bruce Hunter (1944–2009), John Burke (1922–2011), Les Daniels (1943–2011), Ray Bradbury (1920–2012), Basil Copper (1924–2013), Joel Lane (1963–2013), Jay Lake (1964–2014), Tanith Lee (1947–2015), Melanie Tem (1949–2015), David Case (1937–2018), Harlan Ellison* (1934–2018), William R. Trotter (1943–2018), Dennis Etchison (1943–2019), Gahan Wilson (1930–2019) and Storm Constantine (1956-2021).

So, statistics aside, here is *The Best of Dark Terrors*, a compilation of some of the best stories to appear in the course of the series. Some of the authors above are included here, but not all. The method of choosing the most representative stories was a relatively painless task—which ones to add to the line-up in what is, looking back, a very competitive selection of tales. The

AFTERWORD

process was only complicated by the need to represent each volume of the series. This resulted in juggling 'potential' contents listings between each of us as editors until we finally settled on a definitive line-up herein.

If you are a new reader, we hope you are suitably unnerved and inspired by this choice of stories. And you may go back to seek out the original six volumes, where you will doubtless find other gems.

But for now, this is our snapshot, our offering of the dark realm that was *Dark Terrors...*

—David A. Sutton
Birmingham, England

INDEX TO DARK TERRORS:
THE GOLLANCZ BOOK OF HORROR
Volumes #1 – 6 (1995 – 2002)

I: Index by Contributor

BARKER, Clive	'Animal Life'	#2
BARKER, Trey	'Dead Snow'	#6
BAXTER, Stephen	'The Dinosaur Hunter'	#6
	'Family History'	#4
BLYTHE, Gary	Cover	#6
BRADBURY, Ray	'Free Dirt'	#3
BRENCHLEY, Chaz	'Everything, in All the Wrong Order'	#5
BRITE, Poppy Z.	'Entertaining Mr Orton'	#4
	'Self-Made Man'	#3
BROWN, Eric	'Beauregard'	#5
BURKE, John	'A Habit of Hating'	#6
BURLESON, Donald R.	'Tumbleweeds'	#4
CAMPBELL, Ramsey	'The Horror Under Warrendown'	#3
	'Never to Be Heard'	#4
	'No Story in It'	#5
	'Out of the Woods'	#2
	'The Puppets'	#1
	'The Retrospective'	#6

CADIGAN, Pat	'This is Your Life (Repressed Memory Remix)'	#3
CASE, David	'Pelican Cay'	#5
CONSTANTINE, Storm	'Such a Nice Girl'	#3
COPPER, Basil	'There Lies the Danger…'	#6
DANIELS, Les	'Under My Skin'	#6
EDITORS, The	'Introduction'	#2
	'Introduction'	#3
	'Introduction'	#4
	'Introduction'	#5
	'Introduction'	#6
EDWARDS, Les	Cover	#4
EGGLETON, Bob	Cover	#1
	Cover	#2
	Cover	#3
ELLISON®, Harlan	'The Museum on Cyclops Avenue'	#2
ETCHISON, Dennis	'The Dead Cop'	#2
	'Inside the Cackle Factory'	#4
	'The Last Reel'	#3
	'My Present Wife'	#5
FILES, Gemma	'Job 37'	#6
FOWLER, Christopher	'At Home in the Pubs of Old London'	#5
	'The Laundry Imp'	#1
	'Normal Life'	#4
	'Spanky's Back in Town'	#3
	'We're Going Where the Sun Shines Brightly'	#6
FROST, Gregory	'The Girlfriends of Dorian Gray'	#5
GAIMAN, NEIL	'The Price'	#3
	'The Wedding Present'	#4
GARRIS, Mick	'A Hollywood Ending'	#6
	'Starfucker'	#5

GARTON, Ray	'Pieces'	#3
GRAMLICH, Charles A.	'Splatter of Black'	#1
HIRSHBERG, Glen	'The Two Sams'	#6
HODGE, Brian	'Little Holocausts'	#3
	'Now Day Was Fled as the Worm Had Wished'	#5
HUNTER, C. Bruce	'Changes'	#5
	'The Travelling Salesman's Christmas Special'	#1
JONES, Gwyneth	'Destroyer of Worlds'	#5
KIDD, Chico	'Handwriting of the God'	#6
KIERNAN, Caitlín R.	'Estate'	#3
	'The Road of Pins'	#6
	'To This Water (Johnstown, Pennsylvania 1889)'	#2
	'Valentia'	#5
KILPATRICK, Nancy	'Necronomicos'	#5
	'Your Shadow Knows You Well'	#6
LAKE, Jay	'Eglantine's Time'	#6
LAMSLEY, Terry	'The Lost Boy Found'	#3
	'Screens'	#1
	'Suburban Blight'	#4
LANE, Joel	'The Bootleg Heart'	#5
	'The Country of Glass'	#4
	'The Receivers'	#6
LANNES, Roberta	'A Feast at Grief's Table'	#1
	'Mr Guidry's Head'	#4
	'Pearl'	#5
LEBBON, Tim	'Black'	#6
LEE, Samantha	'Aversion Therapy'	#6
LEE, Tanith	'The Abortionist's Horse (A Nightmare)'	#5
	'Midday People'	#6

LUMLEY, Brian	'A Really Game Boy'	#2
	'Uzzi'	#1
MASTERTON, Graham	'The Burgers of Calais'	#6
	'The Hungry Moon'	#1
	'Underbed'	#2
	'Witch-Compass'	#5
MATHESON, Richard Christian	'Barking Sands'	#5
	'Bleed'	#1
	'The Great Fall'	#4
	'Slaves of Nowhere'	#6
McAULEY, Paul J.	'Negative Equity'	#2
MILLER, James	'Absolute Zero'	#2
	'Weak End'	#4
MORRIS, Mark	'Eternity Ltd.'	#1
MORTON, Lisa	'The Death of Splatter'	#6
	'Love Eats'	#1
MURPHY, Joe	'Sweetness and Light'	#6
NAVARRO, Yvonne	'Mother, Personified'	#6
NEWMAN, Kim	'A Drug on the Market'	#6
	'Going to Series'	#5
	'Where the Bodies Are Buried 3: Black and White and Red All Over'	#1
	'Where the Bodies Are Buried 2020'	#2
NICHOLSON, Geoff	'Making Monsters'	#4
	'Moving History'	#6
PTACEK, Kathryn	'Skinned Angels'	#3
RATHBONE, Julian	'Fat Mary'	#3
RICHARDS, Tony	'The Cure'	#6
ROYLE, Nicholas	'The Comfort of Stranglers'	#2
	'Hide and Seek'	
	'The Lagoon'	#1
	'The Proposal'	#5

RUSSELL, Jay	'Lily's Whisper'	#2
	'Sous Rature'	#3
	'Sullivan's Travails'	#4
SCHOW, David J.	'The Incredible True Facts in the Case'	#4
	'(Melodrama)'	#2
	'Plot Twist'	#6
	'Why Rudy Can't Read'	#5
SIENKEWICZ, Bill	Cover	#5
SLATER, Mandy	'Food for Thought'	#1
SMITH, Michael Marshall	'The Handover'	#5
	'Hell Hath Enlarged Herself'	#2
	'A Long Walk, for the Last Time'	#6
	'More Tomorrow'	#1
	'A Place to Stay'	#4
	'Walking Wounded'	#3
STABLEFORD, Brian	'The Haunted Bookshop'	#5
STRAUB, Peter	'Fee'	#1
	'The Geezers'	#5
	'Hunger: An Introduction'	#2
TEM, Melanie	'Alicia'	#5
	'Aunt Libby's Grave'	#3
TEM, Steve Rasnic	'The Rains'	#2
	'Sampled'	#1
	'Sharp Edges'	#3
TESSIER, Thomas	'Curing Hitler'	#4
	'Ghost Music: *A Memoir by George Beaune*'	#2
TIMLIN, Mark	'Everybody Needs Somebody to Love'	#3
TROTTER, William R.	'Honeysuckle'	#5
TUMASONIS, Don	'The Prospect Cards'	#6
TURZILLO, Mary A.	'Bottle Babies'	#5
TUTTLE, Lisa	'Haunts'	#5
	'My Pathology'	#4
VANDERMEER, Jeff	'At the Crossroads, Burying the Dog'	#1
	'In the Hours After Death'	#6

VAN PELT, James	'The Boy Behind the Gate'	#6
	'Savannah is Six'	#5
WAGNER, Charles	'All My Friends Are Here'	#1
WAGNER, Karl Edward	'I've Come to Talk With You Again'	#1
WILDER, Cherry	'Saturday'	#5
WILLIAMS, Conrad	'Haifisch'	#6
	'Something For Free'	#2
	'The Suicide Pit'	#4
	'The Windmill'	#3
WILSON, Gahan	'Final Departure'	#5

II: Index by Title

ABORTIONIST'S HORSE (A NIGHTMARE), THE	Tanith Lee	#5
ABSOLUTE ZERO	James Miller	#2
ALICIA	Melanie Tem	#5
ALL MY FRIENDS ARE HERE	Charles Wagner	#1
ANIMAL LIFE	Clive Barker	#2
AT HOME IN THE PUBS OF OLD LONDON	Christopher Fowler	#5
AT THE CROSSROADS, BURYING THE DOG	Jeff VanderMeer	#1
AUNT LIBBY'S GRAVE	Melanie Tem	#3
AVERSION THERAPY	Samantha Lee	#6
BARKING SANDS	Richard Christian Matheson	#5
BEAUREGARD	Eric Brown	#5
BLACK	Tim Lebbon	#6
BLEED	Richard Christian Matheson	#1
BOOTLEG HEART, THE	Joel Lane	#5
BOTTLE BABIES	Mary A. Turzillo	#5
BOY BEHIND THE GATE, THE	James Van Pelt	#6
BURGERS OF CALAIS, THE	Graham Masterton	#6

CHANGES	C. Bruce Hunter	#5
COMFORT OF STRANGLERS, THE	Nicholas Royle	#2
COUNTRY OF GLASS, THE	Joel Lane	#4
COVER	Bob Eggleton	#1
COVER	Bob Eggleton	#2
COVER	Bob Eggleton	#3
COVER	Les Edwards	#4
COVER	Bill Sienkewicz	#5
COVER	Gary Blythe	#6
CURE, THE	Tony Richards	#6
CURING HITLER	Thomas Tessier	#4
DEAD COP, THE	Dennis Etchison	#2
DEAD SNOW	Trey Barker	#6
DEATH OF SPLATTER, THE	Lisa Morton	#6
DESTROYER OF WORLDS	Gwyneth Jones	#5
DINOSAUR HUNTER, THE	Stephen Baxter	#6
DRUG ON THE MARKET, A	Kim Newman	#6
EGLANTINE'S TIME	Jay Lake	#6
ENTERTAINING MR ORTON	Poppy Z. Brite	#4
ESTATE	Caitlín R. Kiernan	#3
ETERNITY LTD.	Mark Morris	#1
EVERYBODY NEEDS SOMEBODY TO LOVE	Mark Timlin	#3
EVERYTHING, IN ALL THE WRONG ORDER	Chaz Brenchley	#5
FAMILY HISTORY	Stephen Baxter	#4
FAT MARY	Julian Rathbone	#3
FEAST AT GRIEF'S TALE, A	Roberta Lannes	#1
FEE	Peter Straub	#1
FINAL DEPARTURE	Gahan Wilson	#5
FOOD FOR THOUGHT	Mandy Slater	#1
FREE DIRT	Ray Bradbury	#3

GEEZERS, THE	Peter Straub	#5
GHOST MUSIC: *A MEMOIR BY GEORGE BEAUNE*	Thomas Tessier	#2
GIRLFRIENDS OF DORIAN GRAY, THE	Gregory Frost	#5
GOING TO SERIES	Kim Newman	#5
GREAT FALL, THE	Richard Christian Matheson	#4
HABIT OF HATING, A	John Burke	#6
HAIFISCH	Conrad Williams	#6
HANDOVER, THE	Michael Marshall Smith	#5
HANDWRITING OF THE GOD	Chico Kidd	#6
HAUNTED BOOKSHOP, THE	Brian Stableford	#5
HAUNTS	Lisa Tuttle	#5
HELL HATH ENLARGED HERSELF	Michael Marshall Smith	#2
HIDE AND SEEK	Nicholas Royle	#6
HOLLYWOOD ENDING, A	Mick Garris	#6
HONEYSUCKLE	William A. Trotter	#5
HORROR UNDER WARRENDOWN, THE	Ramsey Campbell	#3
HUNGER: AN INTRODUCTION	Peter Straub	#2
HUNGRY MOON, THE	Graham Masterton	#1
INCREDIBLE TRUE FACTS IN THE CASE, THE	David J. Schow	#4
INSIDE THE CACKLE FACTORY	Dennis Etchison	#4
IN THE HOURS AFTER DARK	Jeff VanderMeer	#6
INTRODUCTION	The Editors	#2
INTRODUCTION	The Editors	#3
INTRODUCTION	The Editors	#4
INTRODUCTION	The Editors	#5
INTRODUCTION	The Editors	#6
I'VE COME TO TALK WITH YOU AGAIN	Karl Edward Wagner	#1
JOB	Gemma Files	#6

LAGOON, THE	Nicholas Royle	#1
LAST REEL, THE	Dennis Etchison	#3
LAUNDRY IMP, THE	Christopher Fowler	#1
LILY'S WHISPER	Christopher Fowler	#2
LITTLE HOLOCAUSTS	Brian Hodge	#3
LONG WALK, FOR THE LAST TIME, A	Michael Marshall Smith	#6
LOST BOY FOUND, THE	Terry Lamsley	#3
LOVE EATS	Lisa Morton	#1
MAKING MONSTERS	Geoff Nicholson	#4
(MELODRAMA)	David J. Schow	#2
MIDDAY PEOPLE	Tanith Lee	#6
MORE TOMORROW	Michael Marshall Smith	#1
MOTHER, PERSONIFIED	Yvonne Navarro	#6
MOVING HISTORY	Geoff Nicholson	#6
MR GUIDRY'S HEAD	Roberta Lannes	#4
MUSEUM ON CYCLOPS AVENUE, THE	Harlan Ellison®	#2
MY PATHOLOGY	Lisa Tuttle	#4
MY PRESENT WIFE	Dennis Etchison	#5
NECRONOMICOS	Nancy Kilpatrick	#5
NEGATIVE EQUITY	Paul J. McAuley	#2
NEVER TO BE HEARD	Ramsey Campbell	#4
NORMAL LIFE	Christopher Fowler	#4
NO STORY IN IT	Ramsey Campbell	#5
NOW DAY WAS FLED AS THE WORM HAD WISHED	Brian Hodge	#5
OUT OF THE WOODS	Ramsey Campbell	#2
PEARL	Roberta Lannes	#5
PELICAN CAY	David Case	#5
PIECES	Ray Garton	#3
PLACE TO STAY, A	Michael Marshall Smith	#4

PLOT TWIST	David J. Schow	#6
PRICE, THE	Neil Gaiman	#3
PROPOSAL, THE	Nicholas Royle	#5
PROSPECT CARDS, THE	Don Tumasonis	#6
PUPPETS, THE	Ramsey Campbell	#1
RAINS, THE	Steve Rasnic Tem	#2
REALLY GAME BOY, A	Brian Lumley	#2
RECEIVERS, THE	Joel Lane	#6
RETROSPECTIVE, THE	Ramsey Campbell	#6
ROAD OF PINS, THE	Caitlín R. Kiernan	#6
SAMPLED	Steve Rasnic Tem	#1
SATURDAY	Cherry Wilder	#5
SAVANNAH IS SIX	James Van Pelt	#5
SCREENS	Terry Lamsley	#1
SELF-MADE MAN	Poppy Z. Brite	#3
SHARP EDGES	Steve Rasnic Tem	#3
SKINNED ANGELS	Kathryn Ptacek	#3
SLAVES OF NOWHERE	Richard Christian Matheson	#6
SOMETHING FOR FREE	Conrad Williams	#2
SOUS RATURE	Jay Russell	#3
SPANKY'S BACK IN TOWN	Christopher Fowler	#3
SPLATTER OF BLACK	Charles A. Gramlich	#1
STARFUCKER	Mick Garris	#5
SUBURBAN BLIGHT	Terry Lamsley	#4
SUCH A NICE GIRL	Storm Constantine	#3
SUICIDE PIT, THE	Conrad Williams	#4
SULLIVAN'S TRAVAILS	Jay Russell	#4
SWEETNESS AND LIGHT	Joe Murphy	#6
THERE LIES THE DANGER…	Basil Copper	#6
THIS IS YOUR LIFE (REPRESSED MEMORY REMIX)	Pat Cadigan	#3
TO THIS WATER (JOHNSTOWN, PENNSYLVANIA 1889)	Caitlín R. Kiernan	#2

TRAVELLING SALESMAN'S CHRISTMAS SPECIAL, THE	C. Bruce Hunter	#1
TWO SAMS, THE	Glen Hirshberg	#6
TUMBLEWEEDS	Donald R. Burleson	#4
UNDERBED	Graham Masterton	#2
UNDER MY SKIN	Les Daniels	#6
UZZI	Brian Lumley	#1
VALENTIA	Caitlín R. Kiernan	#5
WALKING WOUNDED	Michael Marshall Smith	#3
WEAK END	James Miller	#4
WEDDING PRESENT, THE	Neil Gaiman	#4
WE'RE GOING WHERE THE SUN SHINES BRIGHTLY	Christopher Fowler	#6
WHERE THE BODIES ARE BURIED 3: BLACK AND WHITE AND RED ALL OVER	Kim Newman	#1
WHERE THE BODIES ARE BURIED 2020	Kim Newman	#2
WHY RUDY CAN'T READ	David J. Schow	#5
WINDMILL, THE	Conrad Williams	#3
WITCH-COMPASS	Graham Masterton	#5
YOUR SHADOW KNOWS YOU WELL	Nancy Kilpatrick	#6

ABOUT THE EDITORS

STEPHEN JONES is the winner of four World Fantasy Awards, five Horror Writers Association Bram Stoker Awards and three International Horror Guild Awards, as well as being a multiple recipient of the British Fantasy Award and a Hugo Award nominee. A former television producer/director and genre movie publicist and consultant (the first three *Hellraiser* movies, *Nightbreed, Split Second,* etc.), he has written and edited more than 155 books, including the *The Art of Pulp Horror, Fearie Tales: Stories of the Grimm and Gruesome, A Book of Horrors, Curious Warnings: The Great Ghost Stories of M.R. James, The Mammoth Book of Folk Horror* and the *Best New Horror, Zombie Apocalypse!* and *Lovecraft Squad* series. You can visit his website at www.stephenjoneseditor.com

DAVID A. SUTTON is the recipient of the World Fantasy Award, the International Horror Guild Award and twelve British Fantasy Awards for editing magazines and anthologies (*Fantasy Tales, Dark Terrors*). More recently he has edited *Phantoms of Venice, Houses on the Borderland* and *Horror on the High Seas.* He has also been a genre fiction writer since the 1960s with stories appearing widely in magazines and anthologies, including *Phantasmagoria, Gruesome Grotesques, The Ghosts & Scholars Book of Shadows* and *The Ghosts & Scholars Book of Folk Horror.* Collections of his stories are *Clinically Dead & Other Tales of the Supernatural* and *Dead Water and Other Weird Tales.* In addition, he is the proprietor of Shadow Publishing, a small press specialising in collections and anthologies.

COPYRIGHT INFORMATION